Other books by Henry Denker

I'll Be Right Home, Ma
My Son the Lawyer
Salome: Princess of Galilee
The First Easter
The Director
The Kingmaker
A Place for the Mighty
The Physicians
The Experiment

Plays by Henry Denker

The Headhunters
Time Limit!
A Far Country
A Case of Libel
Venus at Large
What Did We Do Wrong?
Something Old, Something New

THE
STAR

Henry Denker

MAKER

SIMON AND SCHUSTER
NEW YORK

01

C/C

Designed by Elizabeth Woll
Manufactured in the United States of America

1   2   3   4   5   6   7   8   9   10

Library of Congress Cataloging in Publication Data
Denker, Henry.
The starmaker.
I. Title.
PZ3.D4175St   [PS3507.E5475]   813'.5'4   76–55323
ISBN 0–671–22431–X

TO EDITH,
my wife

Prologue

Hollywood, 1953

"The reason so many of them came," the old producer said, "was to make sure he's dead."

"The only way to make sure that bastard is dead," the director replied, his words slightly colored by a Viennese accent, "is to drive a stake through his heart."

After that brief exchange, both men started up the steps of Sinai Temple on Wilshire Boulevard. At the entrance, the rabbi waited to greet them, like the host at a Beverly Hills cocktail party.

At the curb, cars continued to arrive: long black Cadillacs, silver Rolls-Royces, Mercedeses, Ferraris, Jaguars—the high-powered symbols of Hollywood success. Uniformed guards from Magna Studios helped the Los Angeles police keep the stream of cars moving efficiently.

Reporters, photographers and newsreel cameramen covered the event with all the attention and excitement of a gala film premiere.

One two-time Academy Award winner, a short, stocky actor with an honest face, looked around as he stepped out of his car and remarked, "They should have held this at night. So they

9

could use big arcs to sweep the sky. But maybe they'll interview the mourners in the lobby."

His companion, a tall, attractive woman, was too discreet to smile openly. But she whispered, "After all, this *is* a premiere. It's the first time the sonofabitch has died."

"If it's a hit, he'll probably follow it with a sequel." He took her arm and escorted her up the steps.

Celebrities from all over the world continued to arrive. Producers and directors whose names were internationally known. Writers, some of whom were as famous as the stars for whom they wrote. Executives from other studios. Labor leaders. Politicians. It was the largest Hollywood turnout ever to assemble for a daytime event. Every studio in town had shut down for the day in deference to the funeral of H. P. Koenig.

Finally the stream of cars slowed and one long black Cadillac pulled up alone. As if by prearrangement, the photographers, newsmen and newswomen pressed close around it.

A young but distinguished-looking man stepped out. Lean, tall, his dark hair already showing the first touches of gray, he was grim and silent. He turned to assist an aging woman from the car. Although she did not weep, and she carried herself proudly for so small a woman, she had the undeniable look of a widow about her. She was followed by two young women, obviously her daughters. The widow and one of her daughters started up the steps together. The other held the arm of the young man, who now had to deal with the press.

"Do you have any statement to make, Mr. Cole?"

"Any comment, Mr. Cole? You knew him well," one newswoman asked, probing the recent strained relationship between H. P. Koenig and David Cole.

"Whatever I have to say I'll be saying in there," Dave Cole replied.

He took his companion's hand and led her to the steps, where he paused to stare up disapprovingly at the rabbi, who continued to serve as a welcoming committee of one. In a community where everyone else strove to become a celebrity, the rabbi himself had striven and succeeded. Counselor and spiritual adviser to the motion-picture mighty, he had achieved a national reputation of his own. This day was an event of surpassing importance for him. So ignoring Cole's look, the rabbi took him by the arm, then leaned over to bestow a kiss of consolation on the young woman's cheek. Thus, close and confidential, he was able to ask, "David, how would you like me to introduce you?"

Cole was tempted to say, "List my last four pictures and their grosses." Instead he said simply, "Just my name."

"Nothing about being head of the studio?" the rabbi asked, disappointed.

"Just my name," David Cole insisted, then guided H. P. Koenig's daughter into the sanctuary.

The rabbi took his place in the pulpit. The undercurrent of malicious whispers died out slowly. Having achieved a respectful silence, he announced a bit regretfully, "In accord with the family's wishes there will be no special service. The eulogy will be delivered by David Cole."

David came forward and stared out at the huge crowd that filled every seat in the great temple. There were even several rows of standees. It would have gratified H.P. to know that his final production had filled the house, even though admission was free.

They were waiting patiently to hear what David Cole would say about H. P. Koenig. But the whole world had always waited on H.P. It was his proudest boast—the most important men and women in the world of entertainment waited endlessly for the privilege of seeing him even for a few moments.

David Cole could still remember the first time he had been left fretting in Koenig's legendary waiting room. It was the day that had determined his destiny, public and private, though he had not realized that at the time.

He had been conscious only of how long he had waited, and how young and impatient he had been.

1

Hollywood, 1947

David Cole impatiently glanced at his watch for the twenty-third time. He made the gesture broad and obvious, hoping to evoke some response from the receptionist. But she was too immersed in *The Holywood Reporter* even to be aware of it. Dave Cole had never been in Hollywood before, so he didn't know what etiquette or local custom demanded of him at this point.

One thing he did know. He had been waiting two hours and fifty-three minutes for his nine-thirty appointment with Harry P. Koenig, president of Magna Pictures, head of the studio, and universally acknowledged to be the single most important man in the entire motion-picture industry.

Dave had heard stories about H.P., but he had assumed that like all other legends, they were vastly inflated by the biting wit of such men as George Kaufman, Charlie MacArthur and Groucho Marx.

Koenig had been dubbed The Weeper. And Harry the Hun. Even Attila the Jew. But only Jewish writers and producers dared call him that, since they could not be accused of anti-Semitism.

Cole's agent in New York had assured him that if at times H.P.

seemed a monster, he was at heart a decent man, with the soul of an artist and the acumen of a brilliant merchant. It was just that weighed down by the burdens of running the world's largest studio, H.P. was terribly and perpetually busy, so that what appeared to be rudeness was in reality only a reflection of the pressures that plagued him.

H.P.'s time was considered so precious that not only barbers and masseurs but even his doctors were forced to wait on him at the studio. If David Cole had cause to doubt that, it vanished when an old man entered the waiting room, small black bag in hand. He carried himself with the air of one who did not expect to be kept waiting. Nor was he. At the sight of him, the receptionist immediately put aside her *Hollywood Reporter*. "Good morning, Dr. Prinz."

"Good morning, Dorothy."

No further word was necessary. The receptionist turned to her battery of phones, pressed a button, reported the doctor's presence. She smiled, nodded and gave the doctor immediate access to the royal suite. She was about to hang up when the voice on the other end asked a question to which she responded, "Oh, yes, Mr. Cole's still waiting."

She paused a moment; then, slightly embarrassed, she explained, "David Cole. The new director. No, sir. I'll ask." She stared across the wide expanse of the waiting room. "Mr. Cole, you from Broadway?"

"Yes," David said furiously. "And if I'm kept waiting any longer, I'll be *back* on Broadway Monday morning!"

His answer lost something in the translation, as the receptionist simply reported, "Yes, sir, he's the one." Then she hung up and said, "You may go right in, Mr. Cole."

That's better, Dave thought. But he cursed his agent who had assured him that H.P. admired his work and had insisted on having him at Magna. David approached the door in a belligerent mood, but before he could reach it, it swung open and three people emerged.

One was a woman dressed in a severely tailored black wool suit. She was short, slight, with hair blatantly blond. The second person to emerge was a slender man with watery eyes who reminded David of a philosophy professor he had had in college. The third was a very young man with the alert, darting eyes of

14

a fox on the prowl. Each carried a thick file of notes. The blonde addressed the receptionist in a voice as hoarse and brusque as a man's. "We didn't finish. H.P. wants us back after lunch."

They were gone. Now David Cole entered a room that he'd heard damned by hundreds of actors, directors and writers who had made the pilgrimage West only to return to Broadway, claiming to have turned down H.P.'s notoriously dramatic bland-ishments and bribes in order to retain their artistic souls. To put it more simply, they had failed. They knew it. David Cole knew it.

Now David was about to confront H. P. Koenig and was deter-mined not to fail. But the room was empty. The huge desk of highly polished rosewood was deserted. The fan chair, an antique of expensive red leather which had been bastardized by being mounted on a swivel, was turned at such an angle as to indicate that its occupant had left it hastily only moments before.

A series of huge oil paintings hung high on the paneled oak walls. Each was a full-length idealized portrait of a Magna star who had won an Academy Award. One portrait pinned David Cole. He stood before it, stared up at it. It was Imogene Hopkins. She looked down at him, smiling. He noted that all the portraits seemed to be looking down and smiling. Her eyes were more serene and misty than he remembered them. The portrait in-dicated only the slightest bit of cleavage, modest, almost girlish, leading one to assume that her breasts were delicate and small. He knew otherwise. She was a woman, full-breasted and with hungers to match.

Suddenly a voice shouted, "Cole, where the hell are you?"

Following the direction from which the voice had come, Dave crossed the long office, entered a carpeted corridor. At the end of it was an open door, and Dave found himself staring into a fully equipped doctor's examining room.

Glass-enclosed cabinets containing a variety of medical instru-ments and appurtenances lined one wall. In one corner was a dental chair with all the equipment necessary for drilling, filling and X-raying.

In the center of the room, H.P., fabled Little Giant of Holly-wood, stood stripped to the waist before Dr. Prinz. H.P. com-manded Dave to enter with a single gesture of his imperious forefinger.

Resentful, Dave entered nevertheless. He stopped just inside the door, trying not to stare at the half-naked little man. A roll of flesh bulged over the top of H.P.'s expensively tailored trousers. But the upper part of his torso still showed clear evidence of the muscled chest, shoulders and biceps he'd possessed as a young man. Dave remembered once hearing that H.P. had assaulted a well-known he-man star during a contract dispute and beaten him badly. He could believe it now.

"Okay?" H.P. asked as the physician folded his stethoscope. "Done?"

"Specimen, H.P.," Prinz reminded.

As the doctor crossed to the medical cabinet to find a clean glass beaker, H.P. turned to stare at David Cole. "Aha," he said, "another director from New York! Another genius!" Then, as if etiquette demanded it, he asked, "Would you like to have your urine tested?"

"No, thanks."

By that time H.P. had the beaker. He unbuttoned his fly and commenced to urinate as he commanded, "Tell me about yourself!"

Dave stared at H.P., the man whose photo he had seen taken with cardinals, governors and at least two Presidents of the United States. He did not answer H.P.'s question.

Without interrupting his slow and stubborn bladder, the little man looked across at Dave and demanded, "Well? Tell me! Brag a little!"

"I took it for granted you knew," Dave responded. "My agent said—"

"Agents!" H.P. scoffed, handing the beaker to Prinz and carefully tucking his penis back into his neatly tailored trousers.

"Look, kid, do me a favor. And yourself, too. Go out to the commissary and get yourself some lunch. Then come back ready to tell me what you've done. Okay?" Before Dave could agree, H.P. repeated his own "Okay" and turned back to Prinz.

"Why you arrogant, crude, tasteless sonofabitch!" David Cole exploded. He turned and left the examining room, charged through the office and into the waiting room and slammed the door so hard that the receptionist put down her copy of *Daily Variety* to glare at him.

When the elevator finally appeared and the door opened, he

burst in, colliding with a tall, handsome, mustached man, obviously an actor, obviously a star.

The actor smiled. "Sorry, kid."

Dave apologized angrily, "Sorry! My fault!"

"Been to see H.P.?" the star guessed, still smiling. Cole nodded. The star held the door open long enough to say, "Don't let it get you. He's the best. So you can imagine what the rest are like."

As the door closed, Dave suddenly realized that in his anger he had failed to recognize Magna's greatest star, Clark Gable.

Dave felt embarrassed, but not so much that it diminished his anger. He had refused to be humiliated, even by H.P. He had made his heroic declaration and stormed out. He would keep going till he got back to Broadway and Sardi's. There he could regale his colleagues by adding still another chapter to the legend of H. P. Koenig, the Monster of Magna. As time went by, he would enlarge on his story and add all the brilliant and cutting remarks he should have made to H.P. but couldn't think of moments ago.

Still, it was a long way back to New York, and he had no play waiting for him. He would have been on salary here at Magna. A damn good salary. And if he had had the chance to direct an important film . . . but that was all past now.

In the lobby a uniformed guard stopped him.

"Mr. Cole?"

Dave nodded.

"Mr. Koenig said to sign his name on your lunch check. And be back at two-fifteen."

"I don't think I'm staying for lunch," Dave said crisply.

The guard smiled, shoved his peaked cap back on his head, shook his head. "I've got orders not to let you off the lot. Sorry."

"Is this a concentration camp or a picture studio?"

"All I know, we got orders not to let your car leave the lot," the guard said. "I think you better get yourself some lunch. We got the best commissary in Hollywood here at Magna."

Dave hesitated, finally nodded. The guard looked relieved. "The commissary is on your right, after you pass through the main gate."

"Thank you."

David Cole came out of the executive building onto the broad steps. He stopped to look at the silver plaque that dedicated the

17

building to Marvin Kronheim, the creative head of Magna who had died in his early thirties. Kronheim had been a genius whose outstanding ability was his recognition, understanding and appreciation of artistic talent. If Kronheim were alive today, no successful Broadway director would have been treated as Dave Cole had just been.

Dave reached the main gate, where two uniformed security police stood guard. He expected to be challenged and was ready to identify himself. Instead, one of the guards raised a hand to his cap and said, "Go right in, Mr. Cole."

He followed the signs to the commissary, where he stood near the cashier's desk seeking some familiar face from New York. He saw none. Instead, the tables were filled with actors and actresses dressed in full costume. Indians eating with cowboys. Bengal Lancers with girls in swimsuits.

"Waiting for someone?" asked a smiling hostess. She was tall and attractive and for an instant reminded David of Esther Williams. On second glance he saw that her jawline was just a bit too wide—probably the single feature that kept her out of pictures. Still, she carried herself as if she were just waiting to be discovered.

Dave was finding out that Hollywood was full of beautiful women who wasted their youth trying to be noticed, approved, discovered, made famous. But who, in the end, would fail for one reason or another and would never understand why. Yet they would continue to make up, dress, dye their hair, badger directors, go to bed with assistant directors and young men in Casting. Till finally they married some technician or became middle-aged waitresses with sagging breasts and arches.

"Are you waiting for someone or do you want a table for one?" the hostess asked again.

"I was looking . . . I thought I'd find—" he started to say.

"Old friends from New York?" she guessed. Because she was right, he found himself smiling back. "Follow me." She led him down the aisle to another room.

"The Green Room," she announced. "You'll find all the New Yorkers here."

She lingered at his side as he surveyed the Green Room. Here

18

all tables were limited to four persons. And at every table he saw at least one well-known star.

At the far end of the room he saw a face that stirred a hot surge in his groin. It was Imogene Hopkins. Even in profile her face was unforgettable. She was smiling, talking animatedly to a handsome man whom Dave recognized as the brilliant English star Laurence Olivier, whose performance in *Hamlet* had helped William Shakespeare win his first Academy Award.

As Dave approached the table Olivier, assuming that Dave was expected, rose politely to greet him. But Imogene only turned, resentful at having been interrupted, and asked, imperiously and coolly, "Yes?"

"Don't you remember . . ." David Cole started to say, but stopped himself. Of course she remembered. It was simply that she chose not to acknowledge him. "Sorry," he said, "I thought I knew you. My mistake."

No one would ever guess that only three nights ago she had fucked him and sucked him in her berth aboard the overnight TWA flight from New York.

He had first noticed her at midnight when the plane landed in Chicago to refuel. Passengers were asked to deplane during the stopover, and as Dave started to comply with the request he saw her, sitting in the small first-class lounge, nursing a drink. She was already dressed in a negligee, and he realized that she was one of the fortunate eight persons aboard who had secured berths on the overnight flight. She had noticed him, too, and her look was one of open invitation.

Dave responded as would any healthy young man of twenty-eight. He felt a surge of desire in his crotch and a tightening of anticipation in the pit of his stomach. He sank down in the seat opposite her. The tall young blond stewardess approached him. "Sir, you'll have to leave the aircraft during refueling. Airline policy."

"If you don't mind, I'd rather not." Then he improvised, "Doctor's orders."

"Oh," the stewardess replied apologetically, as if she'd committed some unforgivable social blunder. "Well, in that case you can remain aboard. Would a drink help?"

19

"It certainly would. Scotch and soda," he said as he continued to stare at Imogene Hopkins.

Her face was as finely planed as it appeared on the screen, but her features seemed softer—weaker, actually, made so perhaps by more than a few drinks. Her glistening black hair was simply done; her neck was long and graceful. And whether by design or accident, her negligee was so loosely arranged that her breasts were partly exposed and swelled invitingly above crimson lace edging.

She continued to stare at him. Unembarrassed when he caught her at it, she simply smiled.

When his drink came she held up her glass and said, "I hate to drink alone." He indulged her by touching glasses. They drank, looking at each other over the rims of their frosty glasses. Her blue eyes were curious and provocative.

Because he could think of nothing else to say, he announced, "Cole. David Cole." His name obviously meant nothing to her.

"Imogene Hopkins," she replied, smiling. No one in the civilized world had to be told her name.

Going along with her joke, he asked, "And what do you do, Miss Hopkins?"

Without changing her expression or her small virginal smile she said, "I fuck. Unless you have something more interesting in mind."

It was not the first time he had had a pass made at him by a woman. But never by a woman so famous or attractive. And never so directly. It took a moment for him to adjust.

A voice on the far-off airport intercom was summoning the passengers for Flight 819 to reboard. Still smiling Imogene Hopkins leaned close to Dave—so close he could stare right down her negligee at two full, round and famous breasts.

"Berth A, lower. And do be discreet about it." She disappeared into it, pulling the curtains closed behind her.

He waited in his lounge seat till all the passengers were safely aboard, seated, belted and settled down for the overnight leg of the flight to California. Then he went over and parted the curtains of Berth A and slipped inside.

He pulled the curtains shut and turned to Imogene. She had already turned back the blanket and was covered only by a sheet which was wrapped so close about her body that he could tell she was naked. He started to undo his tie, but she gently brushed his hands aside and whispered, "Let Mama." Slowly, she undressed him. Though she barely touched his body, it was one of the most sensual experiences of his life. By the time she was through he was erect and hard and ready. But she held him off, setting her own pace, as though it were the prerogative of stars.

He was tense, tingling, so hard that it hurt. Still she put him off. She held him close, let him slip between her soft smooth thighs. But she would not admit him.

He could feel the plane begin to vibrate now as the engines started to warm up. It was as if he were living two moments at once. He was conscious of her, of her soft body, and at the same time he was keenly alert to every tremor of the aircraft.

It was only when the plane pulled up to the takeoff runway that she drew him atop herself and permitted him full entry. She enfolded him with strong arms and long, strong legs, imprisoning him so completely that she, not he, set their rhythm. Her rhythm seemed paced to the acceleration of the aircraft as it finally began its long, determined thrust down the runway. At the very instant the craft finally overcame gravity and lifted itself off the earth she rose up under him with one great surge as she came. Then she relaxed and he stayed within her, soft now but content. They lay that way feeling the craft strain and climb.

In a little while she whispered, "It always feels like taking off. So the first time, I always try to make it happen that way. Someday I'm going to have my own plane and my own pilot and just do takeoffs and landings."

Lying there, pressed against possibly the most famous breasts in the world, David Cole didn't know whether she was serious or joking. When she felt him growing hard within her again she whispered urgently, "Go on, go on, go on!" She kept whispering to him, urging, inviting, pleading, demanding. Her voice made her seem like a voyeur at her own seduction. But the rest of her was an accomplice, a willing and hungry accomplice.

He exploded in her so hard and furiously that the pain that had accumulated within him seemed to pass into her. He lay back, breathing hard, damp with perspiration. In a while she pushed back the window curtains to see the night sky. They were flying above a solid layer of clouds that were lit by a brilliant three-quarter moon.

"Can you feel it too?" she asked. He was puzzled. "Sometimes, lying here like this, I think I can actually feel the moonlight. Do you think that's possible?"

"I never think about things like that."

"What *do* you think about?" she asked.

"Right now?" he asked, drawing closer to her.

She could feel him growing against her. She kicked back the sheet that covered them. "Let me see you in the moonlight," she said. He lay there outstretched and completely naked, his desire no secret. She kissed him. On the ear, the cheek, the lips, in the mouth, on the neck and down the chest. She was upon him, seizing him, devouring him till he writhed and rose up and finally burst forth. She rested her face against his thigh as satisfied as if he had had sex within her.

His arms around her, he fell asleep, remembering that first moment of climax when they were airborne in fact and in her sexual fantasy.

He knew that that was one moment he would never forget.

"Good morning, ladies and gentlemen," the pilot woke them on the intercom. "It is six A.M. Rocky Mountain Time. In about ten minutes we will be passing over the Grand Canyon. Since we're a little ahead of schedule, we will circle the canyon. If you've never seen it at sunrise, you will enjoy one of the most awesome and memorable experiences of your life along with your breakfast. The stewardesses will start serving shortly."

Dave lay pinned by Imogene Hopkins, who was still sleeping, pressed into his shoulder. Dave was wondering how to disentangle himself, how to slip from the berth without attracting attention. There was a discreet tug at the curtains as the blond stewardess slipped her face between them.

If she made any judgment, she masked it well behind her smiling, friendly "Breakfast? We have orange juice, scrambled eggs, sausages. French toast. Rolls. And coffee."

He hesitated, wondering if she was reading him the entire menu only to have the chance to keep staring at them.

"Eggs. Sausages. And coffee. Black," he said.

Before the stewardess could turn away, Imogene said quietly, "I'll have my usual."

Dave was surprised. Obviously the stewardess was not. The curtains closed. They were alone again.

"Ever see the Grand Canyon?" Imogene asked.

"No," he murmured, still irritated by the bland smile of the blond stewardess.

"Then you better get over on this side."

They started the difficult maneuver of moving so that he would be at the window. While they were thus engaged, the curtains fluttered again. Poised over Imogene, as if caught in the act of intercourse, Dave found himself staring into the pretty face of the stewardess, who smiled impishly and announced, "Breakfast!"

He sat up in the berth, the breakfast tray resting on his knees. He stared down at the Grand Canyon as the huge plane made a slow, easy, graceful bank over that spectacular natural wonder in all its beauty at sunrise.

"Fantastic!" he said. "Don't you want to see it?"

"Christ, I've seen it a hundred times," Imogene said, sipping her usual breakfast, black coffee. Then, "You're from New York. And this is your first time out here," she deduced.

"Uh-huh," he managed between chewing and staring.

"Going to be out here long?"

"I hope so."

The way he said it seemed to alarm her. "You're not an actor, are you?"

"No, why?"

"You might be. You're good-looking enough. And dark. The best leading men are dark. Kronheim always used to say that."

She had mentioned the magic name. She had actually known Kronheim. Had heard him express his wisdom about pictures. If David Cole were not so sensitive about appearing an awestruck movie fan, he would have asked her to tell him more about Marvin Kronheim, the late young genius of Magna films. But one day soon he would. One day when Imogene and he were intimate and relaxed, when he was acclimatized to Hollywood and felt more sure of himself.

She glanced at her elegant gold watch on the window ledge and said, "Hell, I've got to get dressed. There'll be photographers at the airport."

She pulled her negligee around her, took some things from her makeup kit in the luggage hammock and slipped out of the berth.

"You'd better get dressed." It was the blond stewardess. "We're landing soon." When her warning didn't seem to have the desired effect, she explained, "Everybody has to deplane before she does, so they can take pictures of her. That takes a good half hour."

Later, at the airport, he waited while the other passengers scurried about collecting their luggage. He stood just inside the terminal building watching as Imogene Hopkins posed at the top of the hatchway stairs. When all the posing was done, she came down the steps for the last time and disappeared into the big black studio limousine that waited out on the field for her.

There were no studio limousines for directors. At least not for young directors fresh from New York. Dave Cole took a cab to the hotel where his agent had made a reservation for him.

Now, in the Green Room of the Magna commissary for the first time in his life, David Cole stood staring at Imogene Hopkins for a brief moment before he turned away. This was the second time today that he had realized the truth of the Hollywood saying that L.A. was a place where you were more careful whom you welcomed to your table than whom you admitted to your bed.

His thoughts were interrupted by a familiar voice. It was a character actor he had directed two seasons ago. Their conversation was standard.

"Hey, what are you doing here?" the actor asked.

"Just been signed by H.P."

"Long term?"

"Two years. Thirteen-week options, of course."

"Oh." A noticeable letdown in the actor's voice. "The most important thing, kid: get a good assignment the first time around. In fact . . . wait . . . who's your agent?"

Much as he resented being called "kid," he knew it was a term of affection.

"Gloria Simms and Betty Ronson made the deal for me."

"They're very good back East," said the actor. "But out here—especially at Magna—only one man. Vic Martoni."

"Martoni?" It was a new name to Dave.

"He's got a pipeline directly to H.P. He can do miracles. Of course, if you were a girl he'd be able to do a lot more for you." The actor smiled as he said that. "But Martoni's your man. He's an agent's agent."

"What about Gloria and Betty?" Dave asked. "They made the deal."

"Believe me, they'll be willing to split commission with Martoni."

Dave didn't answer. But in his mind he resolved that he couldn't do that to two women as devoted to his career as Gloria and Betty had been. The waitress arrived, proffering a menu. It was so familiar he might as well have been back at the Stage Delicatessen a block from Broadway. Corned beef, pastrami, kosher-style frankfurters, matzoh brei. But boxed and starred was H.P.'S MATZOH-BALL SOUP.

"I didn't know he cooked, too," Dave said.

"Legend says it's made exactly like his mother used to make it. He's a very sentimental man, H.P. Or likes to pretend he is. If you want to make a good impression, be *sure* to order matzoh-ball soup. And mention it to him the first chance you get, if you ever get one."

"I've got to meet him in an hour," Dave informed.

"Really?" For the first time the old actor seemed genuinely impressed. Somehow an appointment with H.P. had placed a barrier between them. That damned Hollywood caste system again.

2

This time when Dave entered H.P.'s huge waiting room the receptionist showed him right in.

H.P. was sitting in his chair enveloped in antiqued red leather. He did not greet David Cole. His eyes were filled with tears, as if he had just received news of some deep personal tragedy. Dave felt he was intruding, except that the same three people who had left the office just before lunch were seated about the desk. Wiping the tears from his eyes, H.P. finally said, "Once more."

The blond woman said, "Then Randy gets down on his knees beside his bed and prays to God to save his mother."

"Prays to God," H.P. repeated. "For his mother, yet." He began to weep again. "Touching . . . very touching." He wiped away more tears and asked suddenly, "So what does he say?"

"The dialogue for the prayer hasn't been written yet. It's just in treatment form," she replied in her brassy voice.

"Not written yet?" H.P. reacted. "Well, when it is, I want to see it! I want it brought to my personal attention, Lillian!"

"Of course, H.P."

"Okay," he said, indicating he was ready to hear the rest of the story line. When she was done, H.P. turned to Dave and asked:

"How did you like it?"

"I . . . I didn't hear it all," Dave said, caught off guard by the suddenness of H.P.'s question.

"What you *did* hear, how did you like it?" H.P. demanded.

"It sounded . . . fine . . . very good," Dave said.

" 'Fine'?" H.P. scoffed angrily. " 'Very good'? It's fantastic! It's a two-handkerchief picture! Women will sit there and cry. Even men. It's the best Randy Bentley film we've ever made! That kid down on his knees. Praying to God, Save my mother! Who could resist it? Unless a person hates his own mother!"

Suddenly it seemed an accusation. Dave found himself saying, "My mother is a very fine woman. Poor. But the things she did for her kids, you don't find women like that anymore." He hated himself for feeling the need to defend himself or prove his respect and love for his mother. That was his own private world and H.P. had no right to invade it. Yet he had. And he had evoked from Dave the precise sentiment he sought. Dave wondered if his response had anything to do with the warning the old character actor had given him in the commissary. Get a good first assignment. Or was it the fabled effect of H.P.? By fear, enticement or otherwise, H. P. Koenig had a genius for enforcing his will.

Having paid his dues by expressing loyalty to his mother, Dave seemed to have earned himself a seat, for H.P. gestured him to a large, deep leather-covered armchair. "I once fired the best director in Hollywood for making nasty remarks about women," H.P. remarked. "Can you imagine a man saying, 'All women are whores'? Can you imagine that?"

Before Dave could answer, H.P. continued, "Threw the sonofabitch out of this very office! Myself!"

H.P. turned back to his committee of three.

"Okay. The other stories."

Each in turn, The Professor, The Ferret and Miss Brass Voice dramatically recited several projected stories for future Magna films. Turned away from them, H.P. sat silently and listened. The storyteller would continue until H.P. said, "Enough," which meant he was turning down the story. Once he listened through to the finish, weeping. That meant he approved the story.

"Put what's-his-name on the script. You know, that one who won the Pulitzer Prize."

The three storytellers competed with one another to be first to identify the writer H.P. had in mind. What impressed Dave was that among them they rattled off the names of six recent Pulitzer Prize authors and playwrights, all presently under contract to Magna. H.P. was a miser who hoarded talent.

H.P. turned back to his three story editors and dismissed them, adding to the man Dave had dubbed The Professor, "Don't forget tonight, Albert." The Professor smiled and was gone.

H. P. Koenig didn't move. He sat dwarfed in his huge chair, turned away from Dave. Then, as if thinking aloud, he said, "It's a big responsibility. It shouldn't be the job of any one man. You have the nation, the world in your hands. Because what people see up on that silver screen makes their lives! It can uplift them! Or it can destroy them. You got to give them values! God! Motherhood! Patriotism!"

Dave didn't know whether H.P.'s declaration called for an answer. He remained silent. The older man swiveled to face him. "What did you say your name was?"

Dave's earlier resentment was returning, but patiently he answered, "Cole. David Cole. The director. From Broadway."

"Oh, yes. So many things on my mind. . . ." It was as near to an apology as he had heard H.P. utter. Suddenly he spoke again, demanding, "Cole? What did you change it from? Cohen?"

"No, it's just Cole."

"You're sure?" H.P. persisted.

"It's what it says on my birth certificate," Cole assured him.

"Good," H.P. said. "Stars is one thing. But writers and directors, I don't like it if they change their names. A man should be proud of his name, his origin. The lower it was, the more proud he should be. It shows he came a long way. Like me. My name . . . Koenig . . . people used to say to me, Change it. Anglicize it. Koenig means king. It's the right name for a man like you. But I say, I was born a Koenig and I will die a Koenig. Out of respect for my father and mother!"

His declaration was followed by a command: "So never change your name!"

Then H.P. focused on him accusingly. "All right, what did they tell you about me?"

He had caught Dave unaware again. The man had a habit of asking sudden, disconnected, unnerving questions.

28

"You've heard a lot of talk about me. In New York. Out here. From your friends. Your agent. What did they say about me?" he demanded.

Dave hesitated for a moment, wondering—was the man seeking flattery? Or the truth? If the former, Dave didn't feel able to comply. If the latter, he had no intention of answering and thus terminating his contract in the first thirteen weeks. It turned out no response was called for.

"I'm glad you didn't give me any crap. Or try to flatter me," H.P. declared. "Oh, I like flattery. And when I want it, you'll know. But I like the truth sometimes too. And this is one of those times. Today"—he turned to confront Cole—"today is an anniversary. A very sad anniversary."

He turned to a portrait that stood apart on the wall. It was an idealized version of a delicate, handsome young man, with deep and sensitive eyes—Marvin Kronheim. He did not look out of place in that gallery of the world's most beautiful women and handsome men.

"Marvin," H.P. said with profound sadness. "He was like a son. To a man who needed a son. Daughters. That's all my wife ever gave me. Daughters!" He made it sound as if he had spent a lifetime drilling for oil and had come up with sand. "A man loves his daughters. But they are not sons." Then he caught himself and exclaimed, "She's a fine woman, my wife. A good, decent Jewish wife. But still, only daughters. Maybe God meant it to be that way. So when Marvin Kronheim came along my heart would be open to him."

H.P. hesitated, as if weighing the wisdom of confiding a highly personal secret.

"Nights, even now, I talk to him. When I'm alone and have a difficult problem, I talk it over with him. He was a genius. Stories! Casting! A genius!"

He turned to Dave. "These days, every young man I meet, I look into his eyes. I search there for the same depth, understanding and brilliance that Marvin Kronheim possessed. Because when I find him I will make him crown prince of Hollywood! Every king should have a crown prince!"

H.P. got up and walked over to David, but handed down no verdict. All Dave knew was that the man had made Dave feel a

29

sudden desire to become another Marvin Kronheim. He disliked himself for it. In the short space of a few hours he was becoming the kind of Hollywood sycophant he had frowned on during his years in the theater.

Whether H.P. had read Dave's mind or was pursuing a strategy of his own, the little man's look changed from one of penetrating search to a softness that seemed to entreat sympathy.

"Nobody understands. Nobody cares," he lamented suddenly. "Do you realize the responsibility? While the rest of the world is sleeping, I am awake, thinking, planning, scheming, putting together ideas and talent to make this a better world for millions of people."

H.P. sighed as if his troubles were too heavy to bear. "Do you realize that more people go to the movies every week in this country than go to church?"

Before Dave could attempt to answer, the phone chimed. With a gesture that begged Dave's indulgence, the little man lifted the receiver, saying, "They never interrupt me unless it's a matter of life and death." He listened, then finally uttered a reproving, "I see. Uh-huh. I'm glad you told me."

He hung up. "Children!" he exploded. "They're all children!" He made a sweeping gesture encompassing his entire gallery of stars. "You can't trust them. You have to watch over them day and night."

He paced back and forth, making an obvious display of the fact that he was wrestling with an enormous problem. After a few moments he returned to the phone. "Sarah, go over to Stage Six and get Wendy Morse and bring her here! I don't care if it means holding up production for a few hours. I want her here! That's right!"

He hung up. "Bitch! Goddamn bitch! I got a fortune tied up in that little girl and she gets herself into a situation like this!"

He drummed his meticulously manicured fingers on the arm of his chair. "Of course, a girl doesn't get into a situation like this all by herself." He turned suddenly to Dave. "Cole! The French . . . got a saying: *cherchez* something."

"*Cherchez la femme*—look for the woman," Dave supplied.

"Yeah! Well, in this case, *cherchez* the goddamn man!" H.P. exploded. "Taking advantage of a child like that." By way of

30

sudden explanation and apology he said, "I never finished high school. But if I had, I'd be working for someone like me. Instead of *being* me."

The man had areas of self-doubt, even though he tried to conceal them. He was human after all.

"The Junk Man," H.P. said, "That's what they call me. And when they're not calling me that they say I was a tailor. They say the same about Goldwyn. And Cohn. And Laemmle. We were all supposed to be tailors. So where's the shame? It's honest work!

"And when you think about it, how different is tailoring from making pictures? The fabric is the story. The writer and the director cut the pattern. The actors sew it. If it's too long we cut a little here. If it's too short we add a little there. The important thing is the garment should fit! Fit the customer! And when you got a hundred million customers a week, you better fit them good. Real good!"

H.P. sat in silence until Sarah announced Wendy Morse. Then he turned to Dave and said, "If you want to be a second Marvin Kronheim, just watch. And learn."

The door opened. A short, homely middle-aged woman, with the reproving eye of a house detective, waited in the doorway till a young girl entered. Dave Cole knew her instantly. At a time when Shirley Temple was beginning to be forgotten, this girl, barely sixteen, had just risen to starring prominence.

H.P. adopted the attitudes of a gentle but reproaching father.

"Wendy . . . darling . . . come here."

Her eyes sparkling with unshed tears, the young girl stared at the studio head but did not move.

"Come, darling. Sit on Uncle Harry's lap. He wants to talk to you."

The girl started forward. The little man took her hand and drew her close to him. Then he set her carefully on his knee.

"Now, your director tells me the scenes haven't been going well the last two days. Neither the acting nor the singing. Something is bothering you. What?"

Wendy Morse didn't respond. H.P. coaxed, "Don't you want to tell Uncle Harry? Uncle Harry who promised to make you a star. And who did. Is this the way you repay him when he asks you a simple question?"

31

The girl's eyes brimmed over; tears started down her cheeks. H.P. dabbed at her wet cheeks with his pocket handkerchief.

"All right. Don't tell me. Maybe I can guess. You're worried. You're very worried. Because you missed your last two periods."

The girl broke down and sobbed.

"Did you tell anyone?"

Her face hidden in H.P.'s handkerchief, she shook her head.

"Good!" H.P. said. "Now, I want you not to worry. Especially not to tell anyone else. Not even your mother. I will take care of everything. Of course, we'll have to do it over a weekend. Otherwise, if we close down production for a few days it will make all the columns. So just don't tell anyone anything. And don't worry."

The girl seemed reassured and about to rise, but H.P.'s strong hand kept a firm hold on her.

"There is one thing you *will* tell. And you'll tell it to *me*. *Who is he?*"

The weeping girl shook her head.

"I'll find out anyhow. So you might as well tell me!" H.P.'s voice was assuming a threatening tone.

She shook her head. "I can't."

"Is it Julian? Julian Sakowitz?"

Dave was stunned. Sakowitz was one of the most talented directors on the Magna roster, a man easily into his late forties. The girl's attempted denial only confirmed H.P.'s accusation.

"All right," he said, "you don't have to say anything. Keep your secret. Now go back to work. And don't worry. Everything will be taken care of."

He kissed her on the cheek and let her slip from his lap. As she went to the door, Dave noticed her long legs and pert breasts. Suddenly, the idea of a man approaching fifty seducing her didn't seem so farfetched.

H.P. was silent. Then he looked at his watch and said, "The day's shooting is practically over. Come with me!"

Dave found himself jumping to his feet and again warned himself not to obey the man so quickly. Control. That was the key word in dealing with this powerful little man.

Instead of going out the door, H.P. led Dave farther into the suite. There, at the press of a button, a door opened, and they entered H.P.'s private elevator. As the car started down, H.P.

muttered, "You work, you plan, you scheme, and then some prick like Sakowitz destroys it all! I'll kill him! I'll kill him!"

When they stepped out of the car and into the fading sunlight of late afternoon, H.P. seemed no longer as furious as he had been. They walked through the main gate and along the studio street.

"You see all this?" he remarked as he pointed out to Dave the street, which seemed endless and was flanked on both sides by huge windowless concrete stages. "A city! A whole city—a world unto itself."

They arrived at an iron gate so wide the largest trucks could pass through it unhindered. It was guarded by two men in Magna Studio uniforms. Both men saluted H.P. with the reverence and respect army men accord a general. H.P. responded with a single brisk nod of his head. Without a command, the guards went out into the broad street and stopped all traffic in both directions.

Majestically and slowly, H. P. Koenig and David Cole strode across the wide boulevard. Only when they were safely across was traffic permitted to resume.

"Here's a whole world," H.P. said pridefully. "The biggest and best back lot in all of Hollywood!"

They walked past streets—whole towns—that had been used in famous Magna productions. All seemed perfectly complete and intact, except that the structures were only flats, with no depth—mere fronts of buildings, offices, homes on quiet streets and thoroughfares that could be decorated to become Broadway or Fifth Avenue. They passed beyond the modern streets to period streets.

Dave recognized the Parisian set in which Marie Antoinette was beheaded. On his left were the enormously wide, high steps that had served as temple settings for half a dozen biblical epics Magna had made.

Awed and engrossed by what he was seeing, Dave heard H.P. say, "Wherever you want to be, in whatever period of history, I can put you there. One thing I insist on, authentic!"

They were approaching one location where a huge production was in process. As they drew closer, the costumes identified it as an eighteenth-century film based on a recent best seller, a novel dealing with a miraculous event. The issues it raised were

33

still being debated. But the book had entranced hundreds of thousands of readers, and so it was being made into a Magna film.

The shot being photographed involved a high angle of an entire ancient French village. The camera was mounted on an enormous crane and stood a good sixty feet above them. Dave and H.P. drew close to the foot of the crane as the voice of the assistant director came through a megaphone.

"All right, now! All extras! This is a walk-through for Mr. Sakowitz! Ready! Action!"

The costumed extras moved through the ancient cobbled streets. Since they had been carefully rehearsed, they moved with confidence as they gathered at the town well.

At the top of the crane, Julian Sakowitz stared through the camera lens. When they had walked the scene, he called out, "Let's go for a take!"

During the actual take, H.P. stood by patiently. Dave watched intently. They all awaited the verdict from on high.

"Print it!" the assistant ordered, indicating that Sakowitz approved.

"Set up for the scene at the town well!" the assistant commanded the crew. The extras began to relax, most of them reaching into their costumes to bring out packs of cigarettes.

By that time, word that H.P. was on the set filtered up the crane. At once Julian Sakowitz climbed down, smiling and gracious. "Well, H.P.," he said, "did you like it?"

"Can I have a word with you, Julian?" H.P. said.

"Of course," Sakowitz said, this time no smile. Soberly he led the way to his mobile dressing room.

Not sure whether he was wanted or not, Dave trailed along at a slight distance; but H.P. ignored him, following Sakowitz up the steps and slamming the door.

In a moment Dave discovered that it was not necessary to attend the meeting to be privy to it. H.P.'s voice could be clearly heard within twenty feet of the dressing room:

"You sonofabitch!" he began. "You miserable, perverted sonofabitch! Fucking a kid like that! Sixteen years old. Do you realize that I could turn you over to the District Attorney? You'd get ten years for statutory rape! Why, you've got a daughter who's older than that little kid. What the hell came over you?"

34

"I don't expect you'll believe it, but I am in love with that girl. I don't know how to explain it any other way."

"Does your wife know about this too?" H.P. demanded.

"She knows there's someone else. But she doesn't know who. Don't you understand, H.P.? I want to marry that girl."

"You're out of your mind!" the little man shouted.

"Maybe. But I can't help it. I especially want to marry her now."

"Then you know?" H.P. demanded.

"Yes. Yes, I know. That's why I want to do this quickly."

"Oh, so you want to do this quickly," H.P. repeated. "You never gave a thought to what this could do to her career, did you?"

"She doesn't need a career," Sakowitz said simply. "She doesn't want one. She's frightened. All the time. Terribly frightened. That's how it started."

"Tell me!" H.P. commanded.

"When we were shooting *Puppy Love*. She was so tense, so awkward I felt sorry for her. One day I took her into a corner of the set to talk to her and I put my hand on her arm. At my touch she began to cry. She's frightened all the time she's acting. Frightened of the actors, the cameras, the crew. That little quiver of her chin that's so touching? The reason it's touching is that it's real. She is terrified. And the audience, in its dumb beastly way, unconsciously realizes that and feels sorry for her. That's part of her appeal. No girl should have to live a life of fear. She would be much better off if she gave up acting altogether."

"And have you told her that?" the little man demanded.

"I've been . . . very truthful with her," Sakowitz admitted.

"*While* you were fucking her?" H.P. screamed. "Or did you have the courtesy to wait till you were done?"

"I don't wish to discuss that with you," Sakowitz said.

"Well, you listen to me, you very considerate cocksman. I don't want *you* or *anyone* telling any of *my* stars what to do! Especially about their careers. I don't care how you feel about that girl, her career is in *my* hands. The investment I have in that girl—"

"Don't tell me, I know!" Sakowitz said angrily.

"You shut up and listen! This is my studio. And she is my property! And I will decide when she acts and when she doesn't!"

"She's a minor, and you can't hold her contract over her head like you've done with the others."

"*I* am not going to tell her. And I'm not going to wave any contract over her head. Or threaten her. *You* will!"

"Oh, no."

"You will see that girl this afternoon. And you will tell her that this thing between the two of you is over. That the real thing you love about her is her talent. And in fairness to her talent she is to forget you and go on with her career. *That's* what you'll tell her," H.P. ordered.

"It'll destroy her!"

"If you're so fucking interested in that girl, how come you let her become pregnant?" H.P. demanded. "Now she'll have to go through the trauma of an abortion. Well, you will do what I said, and you will do it this afternoon."

"Oh, no—"

"You said yourself she's a minor. By your admission and hers, you are guilty of rape. Even she can't protect you from prosecution. I don't have to tell you how many judges there are in Los Angeles County who owe me favors!"

Dave heard no more till Sakowitz made one final plea: "I don't give a damn what you do to me, but don't destroy that girl!"

"Okay, *don't* tell her. Just keep walking. Off this lot! And out of Hollywood! You won't get another job in any other studio in this town. And you know I can do that!"

"Yes," Sakowitz admitted, "I know."

The dressing-room door opened. Dave watched as, pale and defeated, Julian Sakowitz came down the steps and walked toward the main gate of Magna Studios. H.P. stood in the doorway of the trailer and watched as the director left the lot on which he had shot some of the best films ever made in Hollywood.

Suddenly the man turned to Dave and said, "I hope you learned something from this! I take care of my children like a real father. But when they misbehave I have to punish them, like a father."

He started back toward the studio. Dave caught up with him and together they walked silently back to the Kronheim Building, where they ascended to H.P.'s office in his private elevator.

In a while, H.P. pressed down the button of his intercom and commanded, "Sarah, I don't want Wendy to leave the lot before I talk to her."

"Yes, sir, I'll see to it."

"And get Irving on the stage."

"Yes, sir!"

In a few moments his phone chimed softly. He lifted it and spoke before the director could identify himself. "Irving! I want you to work that little girl as hard as she can take. We've got to keep her occupied." There was a slight pause. "Don't worry about that. I'll see that she's in condition. That she sleeps when she should and that her energy level is up when she needs it."

He added a bit more softly, "This weekend she has to have off. But starting Monday I want nine- and ten-hour shooting days. . . . Fuck the overtime for the crew! I want that girl working! . . . Right!"

He hung up. Now that his anger had been appeased, he seemed to shrink in size—a harmless little man. He began to weep, not making any effort to wipe away the tears.

"That sonofabitch! He was a friend of mine. And such a fine director! Why did he have to do that to me? Why did he force me to fire him?"

Dave tried to think of some graceful way to excuse himself, but none occurred to him. None that would satisfy this monster given to alternate seizures of rage and tears.

H.P. lifted his private phone, dialed a number. When there was an answer, he spoke in a different tone than Cole had heard him use before.

"Hello, Doctor? . . . Yes, yes, it's me again. I will have need of your services over the weekend. Friday evening. . . . Yes. Just tell me what time you want her there. . . . Nine? Good. The usual preparations? . . . A sedative? That's all? . . . And be very, very careful this time. There can't be any slipups. She must be ready to go back to work Monday morning! . . . Good! . . . Yes, I know, in cash."

He hung up.

"Children! They're all children. You have to wipe their noses. Arrange their abortions. Cure their dripping cocks. There's a reason why I'm the most highly paid man in the country! The

37

President of the United States doesn't earn one tenth what I make in a year!"

Dave was learning that no matter what the little man did, he always managed to end up justifying, ennobling and pitying himself.

Dusk had begun to settle on the room, but H.P. made no effort to turn on the lights. Refracted into a rosy glow by the high clouds, the setting sun created a warm, soft mood that conspired to allow the little man to reveal confidences he might not otherwise have cared to disclose.

"I could have saved her life," he said suddenly and with bewildering effect on Dave. "If I'd known how sick she was, I would have brought in the best doctors in California, in New York!"

He swung his chair around so he could stare at the portrait of Caryl Standish, Hollywood's leading blond sex symbol till her sudden and untimely death.

"I took better care of her than her own mother. That's what killed her, that crazy mother of hers. Christian Science! If I'd only known! I could have saved her. But no. Secrets! They all try to keep secrets from me! Result? She dies. And right in the middle of a picture!"

It was difficult for Dave to determine: Was her sin in dying or in dying when she did?

The phone chimed again. This time the receptionist announced that Wendy Morse had arrived and was waiting to see him. H.P. put his hand over the mouthpiece. "Cole, you better leave now. I'll see you sometime in the next couple of days."

"I hope we can talk about my first assignment."

"Oh, sure," H.P. said, all too swiftly.

Dave Cole left.

When he was gone, H.P. pressed down on his intercom button. "Sarah! Get Sonny Brown over here right away!" He released the key and went to open the door for Wendy. She sat down stiffly, picking at the cuticles around her fingers.

"Darling, I want you to relax," H.P. began. "In fact . . ." He went to his desk, opened a drawer, took out a vial of pills. "Here," he said, "take one of these. It'll make you feel better." He

38

poured some water for her. "Go on, go on! Take it! You won't feel so tense and nervous."

Wendy managed to swallow the pill, though it went down feeling like a rough pebble in her tight throat. H.P. took her hand so she would stop picking at it.

"It's going to be all right," he crooned. "Uncle Harry has arranged everything. By Sunday night it will all be over with. By Monday you'll be back at work and nobody will know. Not even your mother."

The girl seemed relieved.

"Now, there's one other thing. This afternoon Julian came to see me."

The girl stared at him, questioningly.

"He came of his own accord. And he confessed to me. He said he was sorry for what he had done. And that the only way he could make up for it was to leave Magna. Leave Hollywood, in fact. So he wouldn't endanger your career. That's how much he loves you."

The girl's eyes filled with tears.

"He wants you to devote yourself to your career. He wants you to become the biggest star in Hollywood! What a magnificent sacrifice for a man to make! Of course, you can't let his sacrifice go unrewarded. That's going to take lots of hard work. And I will personally select every director and every property for you. Together we'll see that Julian's ambition for you is fulfilled! Right?"

"You mean I won't see Julian again?"

"I told you, he decided to bow out of your life. Forever. He sat right there, in the same chair you're sitting in now. Cried like a little boy and said that's all he wants. For you to be happy. My heart was breaking for him. It was the finest demonstration of nobility I've ever seen."

He patted her hand, leaning close to her, aware of her youth, her lovely profile, her sensuality.

They were interrupted by the receptionist. H.P. asked Sonny to wait. Then he resumed consoling and instructing Wendy.

"Darling, take the rest of this bottle of pills with you. If you feel nervous tonight or tomorrow, take one. Friday afternoon take two. And wait in your dressing room after the shooting. Sonny Brown will pick you up. Everything will be taken care

39

of. By Monday this whole thing will be forgotten. If you're feeling tired on Monday, I have other pills to pick you up. Just don't worry."

As she reached the door, he called out to her, "Remember! Not a word to anyone. Especially your mother!"

As soon as she was gone, Sonny Brown entered. His official title was Director of Public Relations of Magna Studios, but his real job was to fix any and all problems that might annoy H.P. Actually, he had started out as a police reporter, so young that he had earned the nickname Sonny from the other men who covered headquarters. A tall man, and handsome, with an appearance that fostered confidence, Sonny Brown was at home anywhere and everywhere.

When Magna entertained members of royalty, it was Sonny who arranged their hotels, meals, teas in the stars' dressing rooms. When a Magna star was caught in a raid on a whorehouse Sonny was there within hours, paying off the police, dealing secretly with the judge and seeing to it that the entire matter was ignored by the press.

When Marvin Kronheim was caught by the Bureau of Internal Revenue in a major tax fraud it was Sonny's idea for H.P. to go personally to the White House and see the President. The President did intercede, and Marvin Kronheim's tax defalcation was treated as an honest error and forgiven.

By Sonny's creed there was nothing in this world that could not be fixed; no story that couldn't be puffed up or hushed up, depending on the desired result. In his little book he had the names of judges and call girls, criminal lawyers and abortionists, in all parts of the world. There was no big-city political boss Sonny couldn't call by first name. And whatever the sexual perversion of any visiting celebrity, Sonny Brown had a number in his book that would gratify it.

It could honestly be said of Sonny Brown, all secrets were safe with him. His loyalty to the studio and to H. P. Koenig was beyond question.

"Sonny . . ." H.P. began, "we have trouble."

"I know," Brown said. "Sarah briefed me."

"Good. Friday night."

"Dr. Sarafian?"

"Right. Pick the girl up here at the studio. She'll already have taken her sedatives."

"Okay, H.P."

"Keep me advised every moment."

"Of course," Sonny swiftly reassured him.

"About her mother—"

"I'll call and tell her we had an emergency in Chicago. Wendy's last picture is slumping and we needed some live promotion."

"Good!"

"And I've got those photos from her last personal appearance in Chicago in case anyone wants to see some evidence."

"Perfect!" H.P. said. "I don't sleep much, but what sleep I do get I owe to you, Sonny. And I won't ever forget it."

"It's my job," Sonny Brown said, not troubling to mention that it was a job that paid him seventy-five thousand dollars a year with an unlimited expense account.

"Oh, by the way," H.P. said, "we'll need some kind of release to the trades about Julian Sakowitz."

"I've already got one set up and awaiting your approval."

"What does it say?"

"Because of the strain involved in working on a difficult production like *Miracle Song*, he suffered nervous exhaustion and asked to be replaced."

"Good enough." Since the final major problem of the day had been solved, H.P. could sit back and relax. "Ah, Sonny, Sonny. I take care of the studio. And you take care of me. You're the only one. The rest are ingrates! You know that, Sonny. Don't you?"

"Of course, H.P."

In addition to judges, clergymen, doctors and lawyers, Sonny Brown knew how to handle studio heads as well.

3

Dave Cole returned to the Château Marmont, where most of the
New York actors, directors and writers stayed. The evening was
warm and he decided he could stand a refreshing swim. He
slipped into a pair of trunks, grabbed his robe and towel and
went down to the pool.

He dived into the pool expecting an invigorating swim, but it
was even warmer than the air. He had just discovered that in
Southern California, even in the warmest weather, all pools were
heated.

Nevertheless, he did his promised laps. It reminded him of the
summers he had spent as a lifeguard at Rockaway Beach.

He had never known when he applied for that job that it
would lead to a whole new career.

New York, 1940

It had been the end of summer. He was already a mahogany
brown, his tan accented by the faded red swimsuit across which
was sewn in worn felt letters, LIFEGUARD. The suit was flatter-
ingly tight, since an entire summer of swimming had given him
a deeper chest expansion and thicker biceps. Having shrunk, the

suit was tight around the crotch, too, making him seem a bigger jock than he actually was. Though he had never received any complaints. He was conscious and unashamed of the fact that he strutted a little. Hell, he would never be younger, never more sexually capable. Might as well make the most of it.

Summer had been interesting. He had by actual count had twenty-three one-night stands, eight of them right under the boardwalk. He had had four different affairs with young married women whose husbands commuted to the city every day. They were the best, the married ones. They knew more, desired more, were less inhibited than the single girls. And there was no danger of being confronted by a weeping, terrified girl with a late period.

It was in the last weeks of August that he met Betty Ronson. He discovered later her name was really Bessie Aronson. She was a small dark girl, who wore glasses all the time except when she went into the water. He first noticed Betty when she crossed the sand and stood at the water's edge, allowing the rising tide to play at her toes. She had a neat, compact figure. Nothing spectacular, no enormous boobs for sure, but a nice rounded behind held neatly in place by her swimsuit. She seemed not much different from the other girls who came out for the weekend.

She went into the water almost waist deep, then dived through a wave and started swimming straight out. She swam strongly, but he knew that unless she was acquainted with the undertow she might be swimming straight into trouble.

He tossed aside his battered white sailor hat with the faded Red Cross insignia on it, climbed down from his perch and swam out after her. He overtook her, dived under and came up in her path, smiling.

"It gets dangerous out there," he said. "The undertow, especially this time of the month."

"I know," she said, smiling. "I live on the next beach."

They were both treading water and facing each other. The sun glinting on her water-speckled face made her seem more attractive suddenly. Though she was not a particularly good-looking girl, there was something provocative about her.

"If it bothers you, I'll go back," she said.

43

"It would be safer," he suggested.

"Okay," she said, turning toward shore and starting back in easy strokes.

He accompanied her to where she'd left her beach towel. She ripped off her cap, revealing glossy black hair. She was drying it when, without any prologue, she asked, "Ever think of becoming an actor?"

He stared at her, sure she was kidding him.

"*Have* you?" she persisted, quite seriously.

"Not since I was a kid and my mother used to take me to the Yiddish theater. Why?"

"Think about it."

"Right now?" he asked, bewildered.

"Right now. And later. Sometime before Labor Day." She gathered up her towel and swim cap. She took a cigarette, and he picked up her matches to offer her a light. She leaned over his cupped hands, her eyes amused at his obvious skepticism.

"People ever tell you you're good-looking?" she asked. "Particularly women?"

He flushed slightly.

"I've been hearing about you all summer. So I decided to come over and have a look for myself," she said. "I'm glad I did."

He knew he was called on to say something, but he didn't quite know what.

"Well?" she asked. "Are you going to think about acting?"

"I'll think about it," he promised.

"Tell you what: we'll meet up there, under that light on the boardwalk." She turned to point. "After supper. Say about eight-thirty. Okay?"

"Okay," he said, then remembered that he had a date for tonight with one of his steady lays. He'd find some way out of that.

She was already waiting when he approached the light at eight-twenty. They had both obviously looked forward to the meeting. She was dressed in a sleeveless print and had a light sweater thrown over her shoulders. He wore white sailor pants and a lifeguard's red sweat shirt.

44

"Hi," he greeted, appraising her at the same time. Her black hair was neatly arranged and she looked even better than she had when she emerged from the water. He realized it was due to the fact that she was wearing her glasses now. They were neat and unobtrusive. They seemed to accent and frame her features. She also looked more businesslike and, in an odd way, innocent.

"Walk or sit?" he asked, indicating one of the benches that lined the boardwalk rail.

"Let's walk," she said.

"Sure." He gestured her to the wide, weathered wooden stairs that led down to the beach. They crossed the loose sand till they reached the smooth hard surface left by the retreating tide.

"I never told you my name," she began. "Betty. Betty Ronson. And I work in an agent's office. A theatrical agent. I'm her assistant."

"I see."

"We're always looking for new talent. Especially men. Good-looking young men with sex appeal."

"You think I'm the type?" he asked, not quite sure she wasn't giving him a line.

"Yes, I think you're the type," she said frankly. "It can't all be your suntan." She looked up at him, the moonlight on her face. It refracted off her glasses, obscuring her eyes for the instant. He reached out and took the glasses off, to stare into her eyes.

"*Now* say it," he demanded.

"*I* think you're the type," she repeated quite firmly.

"Okay," he said, taking her suggestion seriously for the first time. "What do we do about it?"

"You're free after Labor Day, aren't you? I'll make an appointment for you and you'll come meet Gloria Simms, my boss. You'll like her. She's a very honest, straightforward person. Quite different from most agents."

He stared down into her moonlit face, aware he was still holding her glasses.

"I don't know if you look prettier with these on or off," he said.

"You don't have to say that. I know I'm plain. And I don't mind. In my business it's an asset in a way. You're not competing with your clients."

45

"I wasn't saying it to be polite."

"No, you're saying it to pay me off. Because you think I can be of use to you," she said frankly. "You don't have to."

"No, honestly," he said. He reached out to embrace her. At first she seemed unmoved, but gradually she moved toward him.

"You don't have to," she said.

"What if I want to?" She didn't answer. He whispered, "I want to. Feel me and you'll know I want to. Or are you one of those Jewish broads who have to hear 'I love you' before you let a guy put his hand up your dress?" he asked.

"I'm not that kind of broad. Or any kind of broad," she said. "And I don't want to hear 'I love you,' especially from a man who doesn't know me well enough to love me or hate me. I just want it done with a little dignity," she said simply but firmly.

"You're not a virgin, are you?"

Nice girls didn't answer questions like that honestly. Finally she admitted, "No."

She was looking away from him, the moon outlining her delicate profile. He took her hand and led her to his lifeguard's station. They sat down, leaning against the legs of the tall stand. He had learned from experience that the stand would shield them from any moon watchers on the boardwalk. He slipped his arm around her, his fingers reaching around just enough to touch her small breasts. She wriggled slightly, freeing herself.

"Don't rush me." But it was a plea, not a command. In a while he drew her closer, and this time she did not resist.

He slipped off his sweat shirt and spread it out to protect her from the sand. With a little help from her, he undressed her. He found her small body to be well formed and pressed his face against her breasts. Her fingers moved across his chest, toying with his hair. She was ready soon enough. He was in her and found her warm and eager and intense.

When it was over they lay side by side, staring up at the dark sky, listening to the sound of the rushing water. Soon he was ready again.

It was long past midnight. She had dressed and needed her sweater to keep her warm against the night breeze. The moon was gone and a mist was beginning to move in over the water.

"We better go," she said. They rose, dusted off the sand and started back toward the boardwalk. As they walked they talked about David's possibilities. It still seemed unreal, and he wondered what his mother would say when he told her. But the idea was too fascinating to pass up. He took Betty's hand and said, "Make that date. I want to meet that lady Gloria Simms!"

Gloria Simms was precisely what Betty had promised. A small woman, she was open, direct, and stared at him quite penetratingly.

"What makes you think you can be an actor?" she asked.

"I didn't say I could be. I just came here to find out. What do *you* think?"

"You're not bad-looking. And you do have masculine appeal. Whether you can act is another question. Take this script and go sit out in the waiting room. Read over the first five pages a few times. When you're ready, let Betty know."

He sat out in the waiting room and read through the dialogue four times, giving his lines one reading one time, another reading another time. Finally he settled on his first reading and somewhat timidly announced to Betty that he was ready. Half an hour later Gloria was able to hear him. "Will you feel more comfortable sitting or standing?" she asked.

"Standing, I guess."

"Okay."

He read his lines, remembering to go slowly. Gloria let him read through the five pages and seemed surprised when it was over.

"You ever seen this play?"

"No."

"Not bad at all," she said. "Betty knows where to reach you, I assume."

"Yes, ma'am."

"If I could get you into an acting class, would you go?"

"Sure."

"I'll call you," Gloria said briskly. "You have instinct. I don't know if you'll be an actor, but you *do* have an instinct. What do you do otherwise?"

"I've been a lifeguard."

Gloria Simms smiled. "Yes, I know; Betty told me. What else do you do?"

"I'm at C.C.N.Y.," he said.

"What year?"

"Junior."

"Would you give it up if I got you a job?"

"Gee, I don't know," he confessed.

"We'll see," she said thoughtfully, bringing the interview to a close.

Weeks went by. He saw Betty frequently. Their relationship had blossomed into a steady affair. He didn't seek out other girls, and she kept him apprised of events in the office. Neither family had a car, so they made love at her place when her parents were out and at his place when his parents were away. When no apartment was available, he made love to her in Gloria Simms' office on Gloria's own couch.

One night Betty told him, "She's fixed it for you to get into acting class."

"Terrific," he said, and kissed her naked breast.

"And she's set up for you to read for an understudy part in the road company."

"Of what?"

"The play you read in her office."

"Great," he said, slipping between her thighs.

In a while he remembered to ask, "That reading—"

"Tomorrow at three," she said, as if it were a distant and unimportant event.

"I better pick out my scene and start studying."

"Gloria said not to. Otherwise, if the director asks you to try a different attack, you'll be too rigid."

"Okay," he agreed. Then he asked, "You all right?"

"Yes, I'm all right," she said softly, while he was still a prisoner in her.

He was not the only candidate for the understudy role. There were sixteen of them, all dressed in jeans, all wearing black leather jackets. They waited in the alley just outside the stage door. Some of the young men walked off to corners rehearsing their lines. Others kept staring nervously at their scripts. A few

48

tried to look bored. One by one, they were called in. Most remained inside from five to fifteen minutes and came out. When friends among them asked, "How'd it go?" they smiled, shrugged and said, "You know Jock."

It was part of the pretense that went with being in the theater. You always tried to give the impression that you were in, solid. You referred to Kazan as "Gadge" and Logan as "Josh" and the powers at the Theatre Guild as "Lawrence," "Terry" and "Armina." This though you had never met them and, most likely, never would.

Dave Cole's turn came eventually. Betty had prepared him for the procedure. He would be called in to the stage door. He must not expect to see anyone; the glare of the unshaded work light would be enough to read by but not enough to see the director, the producer or the author. A voice, most likely Jock Finley's, would call out, "Anytime you're ready."

It happened precisely the way Betty had said. Jock Finley called out the exact words: "Anytime you're ready."

Dave began to read the scene. The stage manager, a short, gray-haired man, delivered the woman's lines without expression. It was difficult to play against, but Dave had determined his own pace and it did not upset him too much. He read through the first four pages, noticing that the silence out front had increased. He began to lose confidence and stopped finally to stare out into the darkness.

"That enough?"

"Okay," Jock's voice came to him. It was followed by a whispered conference among his judges. Finally a different voice reached out to him from the darkness, "That'll be all. Thank you." No rejection. No verdict. Nothing.

Two days later Betty called, asking him to come right down to the office.

"Jock didn't think you were right for the part," Gloria said, and he felt the rejection in his stomach. "He *did* say you were an interesting type. He wanted you to come in and read for a play he'll be doing next season."

"Next season? Dave scoffed. "What am I supposed to do till then?"

"Continue your acting classes. Get a job. Support yourself."

"What kind of job lets you go to acting classes during the

afternoon and disappear whenever you're called for readings?" he demanded, no small degree of resentment in his voice.

Gloria Simms stared at him. "Tennessee Williams was washing dishes in the Automat when I read his first play."

"You want me to go to work as a dishwasher?" he asked.

"I want you to follow the first law of the theater. *Survive!* Do whatever you have to to stay alive and available."

Then Gloria looked up at him and said, "If Jock Finley wants you back, you must have something. I'd get that job and wait if I were you."

He found a job. At Nedick's on Times Square. He pumped orange drink. He served grilled frankfurters on rolls. Once he even served Jock Finley—who, fortunately, didn't recognize him.

In early summer, Dave went back to his job of lifeguard. He was assigned to a block not too far from where Betty lived, and they spent nights walking the beach, making love on the sand, talking about careers. Her ambition was to become as good and effective an agent as Gloria Simms. Then she would either become a partner in the firm with Gloria or go out on her own with young talent she had met during the past few years.

For David the big trick was to get that first part. He dreaded facing another year at Nedick's and began to think he should have listened to his mother. "Education," she kept saying, "education is the only way." He had lied to her at first. Saying that he was still going to C.C.N.Y., when he was actually going to acting school. Even when he brought home some of his Nedick's pay, she took it grudgingly and made him feel that he had betrayed her.

It had been a long and dreary summer. He was facing a difficult fall when Gloria's call came. Jock had sent for him, to see him for his new play. Gloria gave Dave a copy of the script a day before. He read it, wondered at its effectiveness. It must be an allegory because it didn't make sense on any other level. It was about a strange young man, with a fierce passion inside him, an animal-like passion. The play explored the origin of his strangeness and ended with his death. In the climactic scene, the young man was tricked into entering an animal cage. Then the door was slammed shut on him. When he realized he was a

50

prisoner, the beast within him exploded and he literally destroyed himself.

When Dave first read the scene he doubted it would play. But when he thought about it overnight, he knew that it would, and by the time he arrived backstage at the Golden he was convinced that he would get the part. It expressed his own fury with this world that frustrated and imprisoned him, that held out hope but denied him opportunity.

By now Dave was used to the routine. He looked over his competition in the alley. Most of them he had read against a number of times before. But there was one unfamiliar young actor who stayed off by himself at the iron gates of the alley. His eyes radiated an intensity that was almost fanatic. His lips twitched, and he clenched and unclenched his fists like a boxer trying to strengthen them. His face was lean, the features precise. He had a stubble of beard and wore tattered jeans. His name, Dave discovered later, was Christopher Swift.

Dave's turn finally came. When he finished his audition, he knew he had done the scene well.

"That's good! Very good! Can you wait?" Jock asked.

Can I wait, David Cole raged silently. What the hell do you think I've been doing for most of two years?

The next candidate, Christopher Swift, took the stage with a confidence Dave was forced to envy. When the stage manager took up his place to read against him, the young man said, "I'll do this alone." He looked around, found a chair and placed it center stage. He found a second chair, which he placed in such a way that standing between the two created a sense of confinement. He looked at the script in his hand and flung it toward the wings, paused for a long time, until the silence became oppressive.

Then he exploded suddenly, right into the middle of the climactic scene. Some of his words were indistinguishable, but his passion was unmistakable. His torment was so real that the theater was electrified. This was no reading, no rehearsal, not even a performance. It was life itself.

Even Dave Cole, intent and anxious as he was to have the role, had to accept the fact that he was in the presence of genius. Or madness. But he knew it was the kind of madness to which Jock Finley was susceptible. Before the director said a word,

51

Dave knew that he had lost the part. He handed his script to the stage doorman and left. It was the biggest chance he'd ever had, the best reading he'd ever given, but it was not good enough.

He went back to Gloria's office to report another failure. But Betty was unusually warm in her greeting.

"Where have you been? They've been looking for you!"

"Who?"

"Jock! Go right in and see Gloria."

He opened Gloria's door, disbelieving. She was on the phone. When she hung up she turned to him, smiling. "I told you a year ago Jock liked you. Didn't I?"

"You mean I got that part?"

"Not exactly. He wants you for the understudy. And I say, take it. It's a good credit to have. To be able to say you worked with Jock Finley. And it pays pretty well."

"Okay, okay, I'll take it." At least it meant no more Nedick's, no more complaints from his mother, no more having Betty pay more than her share when they went out to a cheap dinner.

The day of the first reading, Dave Cole was the only understudy already signed and at work. The others would join them in a few weeks.

Through the first days of blocking out the physical movement of the play, Dave sat in a dark theater, noting the moves that Christopher Swift was being given by Finley. Dave was preparing to go on at a moment's notice, to know the principal's every line and every move so that substitution, if it became necessary, would be smooth, almost unnoticeable.

He was also taking advantage of the chance to observe Jock Finley at work. There was an art to the man's direction. Concepts that seemed obscure on paper became clear and specific as Finley instructed and moved his actors. Dave was awed by the control and the dominance that Finley exercised over actors and playwrights.

After the first four days, Finley brought in the only prop that would be used during rehearsal. It was the cage itself. Without it, Finley felt, Chris Swift would not be able to approach performance level. When the cast assembled for rehearsal that morning and first found the cage, Swift approached it grimly, suspicious and angry. To him, the cage was more than a set piece. It had some strange and special meaning. He studied it, shook the bars, inspected the door and the lock. Finley made no effort to hurry him. Instead, he whispered softly to Dave, "He's getting the feel of it. That's good. He hates it. That's even better." After watching Swift examine the cage, Finley added softly, "Yes, that's much better."

He called the actors to attention and started running them through the scene. Each time Swift reached the moment when he had to enter the cage, he brought the scene to an abrupt stop. There were moments when Dave thought, he won't make it, he can't bring himself to do it. They spent the entire morning on the scene. At the lunch break, Finley dismissed the cast without any comments except to remind them that the break was for precisely one hour and warning everyone not to be late.

Instead of going to lunch himself, Finley settled back in his seat, draping his legs over the seat in front of him. Dave started down the aisle to join the other cast members, but Finley interrupted him.

"Cole! Sit down." Dave took the seat behind Finley. He waited till Finley said, "I want you to do something for me."

"Yes?"

"Just before we resume rehearsal, I want you to go up there and examine that cage. Then I want you to go in and out of it a couple of times."

"That won't do Swift any good. He'll think I'm getting ready to replace him."

"You do it! I'll take care of Swift. I've got to find a way to use his fear of that cage in order to get a performance out of him."

"Okay, if you say so."

Finley dismissed him, but Dave noticed that instead of going to lunch himself, Finley went into conference with the stage manager.

Dave made sure to get back before the rest of the cast. Finley was sitting out front. Following orders, Dave practiced going into the cage, shaking it, then coming out again. When he noticed Swift, Dave became self-conscious. But he continued to carry on until Finley's voice came to them out of the darkness. "Okay. Let's get going. Top of the scene!"

Dave came down the temporary steps into the house. As he

53

passed Finley, the director slapped him approvingly on the behind.

The scene started. The moment came when Swift had to enter the cage. He approached it, opened the door, hesitated, then finally slipped in with somewhat less reluctance than before. Dave felt that Finley's strategy was working. The scene continued, but with not nearly the intensity and emotion that Swift had exhibited at his audition. Again and again Finley took him over that part of the scene wherein the cage door was locked and he was imprisoned. Still Swift could not mount the degree of dramatic intensity necessary to make the scene work. The more Finley labored the moment, the more obvious it became to Dave how much the success of an entire play could depend on a single climactic scene. Yet Swift could not respond to Finley's direction. The afternoon wore on.

Finally, just after six o'clock, Finley called the rehearsal to a halt and sent the cast home. But Swift, obviously troubled, remained. Finley walked up the aisle toward the lobby of the theater. Puzzled and intrigued, Dave followed. Finley slipped into the space behind the back row of seats, staring at Swift, who was still up on the stage.

In the wings, the stage manager appeared busy with some routine task. Swift studied the cage. It was a gaunt and menacing skeleton; its black bars cast long shadows on the stage floor. Swift swung the door open and closed. Thinking he was completely unobserved, he dared to enter it a bit more freely now.

Unaware of Dave's presence, Finley kept whispering to himself, "Get in there, you sonofabitch! And *stay* in there!" As if responding to Finley's unheard order, Swift entered the cage once more. This time he pulled the door closed behind him. He simulated an animal, suddenly caged and growing intensely angry. He shook the bars. Then he gripped them and held on. He thrust his face against them as if trying to slip between them and escape. He drew back, then came forward again. This time he gripped the bars and stared out as if at a hostile world. His face was a mixture of pain and hatred.

"*Now*, you bastard!" Finley said in a hushed whisper that only Dave could hear. As if on cue, the stage manager slipped out of the wings and swiftly locked the door of the cage. It took a moment for Swift to realize what had happened. When he did, he erupted in a fury of fear and betrayal. He started to scream, "Unlock this door! You goddamn sonofabitch! Somebody unlock this door!"

Instead of responding, the stage manager, still following orders, walked off the stage, out of the theater. Swift became more terrified than enraged. His hysterical voice shook the theater.

"That's it!" Finley said, in a whisper of triumphant accomplishment. "That's it!" He turned to go and found Dave behind him. "What the hell are you doing here?" he shouted over Swift's tortured pleading.

"You're not going to leave him in there," Dave said.

He started for the stage, but Finley reached out and seized him by his jacket. "Stay here!" he ordered. "He's not the kind of actor who survives on technique. He's got to *feel* it, *be* it."

"You could drive him insane!"

"That's the kind of actor he is. So sensitive that insanity is part of his art. Maybe it *is* his art," Finley said coldly. "I'll see that he gets out when the time is right."

He did not release his hold on Dave until they were out in the lobby, with Swift's cries still in their ears. Dave broke loose finally, burst into the theater and raced down the aisle. He vaulted onto the stage, calling out, "Take it easy, Chris!" He struggled with the lock and finally opened the door. By that time Christopher Swift was lying on the bottom of the cage, weeping.

Dave sat down and took him in his arms. Swift was limp, whimpering like a child. Dave patted him gently, as one would soothe an infant. He could feel the desperate pumping of Swift's heart.

In a while, Swift whispered a hoarse "Thanks, Dave; thanks."

"Forget it, Chris. Come on, we'll go out and have a drink."

"I better not," Swift said. "Because if I do, I'll find that bastard Finley tonight and kill him!"

Dave knew he was capable of it.

The next morning at ten o'clock the entire cast had assembled except for Christopher Swift. At ten-fifteen Finley, outraged, called Swift's agent. He told him that unless Swift appeared for rehearsal by eleven o'clock, Finley would have him brought up on charges before Actors Equity and suspended indefinitely. By eleven o'clock when there was no answer from Swift's agent, Finley declared the entire production suspended.

The protests and pleas of the cast and the playwright could not move Finley. Meetings were held at the Dramatists Guild and Equity. Both organizations were powerless against the willful director.

At the end of two days he announced through a *Variety* reporter that he was ready to forget the outrageous and unprofessional conduct if Swift made a public apology, came back to work and promised not to skip a rehearsal again.

Swift's agent sent back word that there would be no apology. Finley remained adamant. Equity sent a delegation to Swift to plead with him on the ground that he was jeopardizing the jobs of fellow actors. Swift relented finally, but only on the condition that in the future he not be forced to be addressed by Finley directly. All communication between them was to pass through an intermediary—Dave Cole.

Though it was demeaning to Finley and he resented it bitterly, his lawyer prevailed on him to accept the situation. It was the first time Jock Finley was known to have compromised.

Rehearsals resumed. Though the air was tense, the work went much better. During working hours, Dave sat alongside Finley taking notes. Later he would pass along the directions to Swift. Outside of working hours, Swift and Dave were inseparable. Dave gave Swift his notes while they ate and drank, or in the mornings while Swift was getting dressed and having coffee.

Dave came to know the brilliant but tormented young actor. And when he understood how delicate Swift's grasp on sanity really was, he began to despise Finley for risking driving the boy over the brink. True, it was the obligation of the director to use any device that wrested a performance out of the actor. But Dave felt there must be room for a little humanity as well.

One advantage for Dave was that sitting side by side with Finley, he was able to watch the director's mind at work, learn from him what made a scene go and what made a line work. How one made up for the deficiencies of the play by directorial sleight of hand or actor's tricks. Dave was determined to absorb all the tricks he could, along with a sound knowledge of the director's art.

Soon, along with Finley's notes, Dave was transmitting suggestions of his own. Eventually Swift came to realize that and to distinguish between the two. He preferred Dave's ideas to Finley's. Slowly and subtly Swift began to introduce them into his performance. Finley had no objection. Despite his hatred of Finley, or because of it, Swift was giving a performance that would make him a star.

By opening night, word had preceded the play. It was an opening night that was electric from the moment evening-clothed celebrities began to arrive.

Backstage, tensions had reached such heights that there was nervous laughter to cover the jitters, and numerous trips were made to the toilet.

In Christopher Swift's dressing room, the young actor sat before his mirror applying makeup. Dave sat alongside, wanting to encourage Swift, yet not knowing what to say.

"You think the sonofabitch will dare to come in here tonight?" Swift asked.

"It doesn't matter, Chris," Dave reassured him. "He can't help you or hurt you. Your performance is your own. And they'll know that before tonight is over."

Swift turned sharply. "Mine. And yours, Dave. I'll never forget it. If this works tonight, I'll never forget it." For the first time since they had met, Swift held out his hand and Dave shook it.

After the curtain went up Dave watched the first minutes, then, unable to bear the tension, left the theater. He started down the alley and almost bumped into Jock Finley.

"Once the curtain goes up, there's nothing more useless than a director or a playwright," Jock said, flipping his cigarette into the street. Suddenly he said, "You think I'm a prick, don't you? A cruel and vicious prick! Well, tomorrow, when that crazy, arrogant young psychopath is a star, just remember who got the performance out of him!"

Dave nodded. If the director was already a troubled man, Dave could see no value in adding to his self-reproach.

"By the way, kid, did you ever think of directing?"

"Sometimes," Dave conceded, concealing the fact that he had been directing Christopher Swift for several weeks now.

"It's great work," Finley said, "provided you're tough enough.

Opening night is always the last thirty seconds of the football game. And you're always behind. You've got to be tough if you want them to score in the last thirty seconds. Like tonight. We have a hit. And he'll be a star. And after that I don't give a fuck what happens to him!"

Finley started out of the alley.

"Aren't you going to wait around for the final curtain and the party?" Dave asked.

"Opening night parties are shit!" Finley said. "I'm going to get myself laid."

Dave returned to the theater shortly before the end of the first act. Then, during the break, he moved slowly through the lobby and out onto the street where groups of the audience gathered to smoke and discuss the play.

The critics stood off by themselves, unapproachable, treated with the same reverence as the Supreme Court. Dave tried to read their faces. Brooks Atkinson seemed kindly disposed. Howard Barnes, being younger and representing a weaker paper than the *Times,* lent great gravity to his role by seeming deeply immersed in his thoughts about the play. The critic from the *Mirror* was drunk and in no condition to review any play.

Dave decided not to go back in. But by the middle of the third act he couldn't resist, for Swift's big scene in the cage was coming up. As he slipped into the theater, the silence told him that the audience had become involved and rapt in the play. There were not even the usual nervous coughs.

Chris was approaching the cage now. For an instant, when he hesitated, Dave felt a sudden grip of nerves. For a long moment the house was hushed, the audience seeming to hesitate with Swift, feel his dilemma, his torture, and then move with him when he finally entered the cage. Dave realized Chris had used that moment with overwhelming effectiveness. Now Swift was in the cage, and his antagonist in the play cruelly locked the door. There was a gasp of anger and shock from the audience.

Then began Swift's tortured outcry and his struggle for freedom. It mounted to a frenzy. It shook the theater until one woman in the audience cried out, "Let him free!" It did not interrupt or disturb young Swift. It was seven minutes of the most chilling acting Dave Cole had ever seen.

When Swift finally sank into defeat, the only sound was the whisk of the curtain coming down. Then the audience burst into an explosion of applause and cheers, rising to their feet to cry out their bravos. Even the most cynical of them—agents, competing producers, jealous directors—were standing and cheering.

Dave hurried backstage to Swift's dressing room. The producer and cast members were waiting there, as well as a host of celebrities. But Swift was hiding behind his locked door. Dave took over, urged them to stand back and knocked.

"Chris, it's me."

"Dave?"

"Yeah. Can I come in?"

"Okay. Just you, though."

The door was unlocked. Dave felt the crowd of enthusiastic well-wishers surge behind him. He slipped inside and Swift locked the door. He had not removed his makeup. He stood there trembling with the tension and excitement that he had generated in the last half hour.

"Jesus, Dave, hold me!" he pleaded.

Dave Cole put his arms around the terrified actor. "You did it, Chris," he said. "It's one of those magic nights they talk about. Even that dirty bastard Finley would have been proud of you tonight."

Swift didn't answer.

"If you don't believe me, wait for the notices," Dave said. Outside the door there was knocking and clamoring. "Do you want to see anybody?"

Swift shook his head violently.

Eventually Dave said, "I think you ought to go over to Sardi's. If only to be polite. You've got a lot of fans there tonight."

Swift seemed to consider it. Then he said strangely, "I'll hate to come back here."

Dave smiled. "I'll bet you remember this dressing room for the rest of your life."

"If I live that long," Swift said. His eyes grew moist. Whether it was out of sentimentality or fear Dave would never know, but Swift said, "You're not an actor, Dave. What you are is a director. You can *see* it, *feel* it, but never *do* it. Don't you realize that the worst thing that can happen to me is what's going to hap-

59

pen?" Swift asked. "Sure, they're going to love me. I knew that two weeks ago in Boston. I was saving most of that tension for tonight."

There was an animal shrewdness in the way he talked, a cunning that Dave had never suspected before.

"But in the end," Swift continued, "who did I screw? The critics? The audience? No. Myself. Because from now on every time I step out on a stage, they're going to expect—demand—what I did tonight. And I don't know if I can do it."

The party at Sardi's was all that it promised to be. The reviews started coming in just after midnight. They were all raves: Broadway had discovered a great new talent. When Christopher Swift saw those reviews, he left Sardi's in a hurry.

The next day Christopher Swift told *The New York Times* that Jock Finley had had nothing to do with his performance. He gave all the credit to a young man named David Cole, who, he said, had been his coach and personal director during the out-of-town tryout.

Finley made loud and bitter complaints about the ingratitude of actors. What irked him most was that in the interview Christopher Swift had called David Cole "the brightest young director in an American theater that needs young directors more than it needs sadistic hacks like Jock Finley."

Within two weeks, David Cole was called in to take over the direction of a play that was on the road and "in trouble."

4

Dave Cole rescued the play. In the course of his work, he learned one more valuable lesson about directing. Jock Finley had taught him that if you wanted to get the best out of an actor you challenged him, making impossible demands on him. But Dave learned if you wanted the best out of an actress, there was a different and more compelling technique.

You made love to her. This was especially true on the road.

There was one serious and unfortunate personal consequence. It occurred two seasons later, on his third play. Dave was up in Boston with the pre-Broadway tour of *Contretemps,* starring Elena Holt. Reports had filtered back to New York that the play was going to be a hit. Betty became excited enough to prevail upon Gloria to pay her way up as a business expense. Gloria was delighted, for Dave had become a profitable client.

Betty arrived at the elegant Ritz, overlooking Boston Common, and checked in, securing a room on the same floor as Dave's. It was late, and the performance was over, so she knew he would be back soon. She bathed, perfumed herself and put on the new negligee she had bought especially for the occasion.

After an hour she called Dave's room, but didn't leave her name. She wanted to surprise him. He did not answer. She assumed there was a postperformance meeting. In an hour she called again. By two-thirty in the morning, after having called, by her own count, eight times, Betty decided to slip a note under Dave's door.

Call Room 612 as soon as you come in!

She underlined each word, but she didn't sign it; she wanted to preserve her surprise. Wrapped in her new negligee, she went down the silent carpeted hallway to Room 623 and slid the envelope under Dave's door, leaving just a bit of it showing so that he would be sure to notice it when he came in. On her way back to her room she was suddenly confronted by the door to Suite 619–20, which opened for a serving cart to be shoved out.

It was also open long enough for Betty to hear Elena Holt call out, "Darling, why must you always be so damned neat? Come back to bed!"

"It's my Jewish mother," she heard Dave answer, laughing. "We were brought up to believe you don't make love till the dishes are done."

"Your poor old man," Elena said. The sound of her laughter was cut off when Dave shut the door and locked it.

Betty was stunned. She went back to Dave's room and managed to withdraw her note from under his door. Then she returned to her own room, too shocked to cry.

Instead, she sat before her mirror and stared at herself. She knew that if somehow she did manage to marry Dave Cole, for the rest of her life she would be competing with other Elena Holts, younger and younger, while she herself grew older. If she couldn't measure up now, how could she hope to compete when she was forty?

In the morning, without ever making her presence known to Dave, she left Boston. The entire episode would have remained her own private tragedy if Gloria Simms had not had a need to call her that day. Informed that Miss Ronson had checked out of her room, Gloria happily assumed she had moved in with Dave. Her call caught him as he was coming out of the shower.

"Dave? Gloria. Terribly sorry to interrupt the honeymoon, but I've got to talk to Betty. One of our writers just got out to the Coast last night and—"

He interrupted her brusquely. "Betty? What do you mean, *Betty?*"

"Well, she's up there, isn't she? And she checked out of her room this morning, so I figured naturally she moved into your . . ." Gloria didn't complete the thought.

"I haven't even seen her. When did she come up?"

"Last night. Didn't she call you when she arrived?"

"I . . . I never got back to my room till half an hour ago."

"Oh. I see," Gloria said, trying to suspend all judgment. "Sorry, Dave. Sorry."

"If you see Betty . . ." And this time it was Dave who couldn't complete the thought. "Hell! I guess there isn't much I can say, is there?"

"No, Dave, I guess there isn't," Gloria said softly.

The first opportunity Dave had to speak to Betty was after the opening party for *Contretemps* in New York. He tried to explain the exigencies of his profession. She listened stolidly. When he professed his love for her, she interrupted.

"No, Dave. Not love. Gratitude, possibly. I got you started, helped you get where you are now, and soon, I guess, you'll be going on to pictures. So you appreciate all that and you're grateful. Because, basically, you are a nice person. But let's not call it love.

"And don't try to inveigle me into a lifelong competition with all the beautiful stars you'll meet and make love to in the years to come. I couldn't run that kind of race. So it's better for both of us if we recognize that now, instead of fifteen years and three kids from now. If you want, I'll continue as your agent. But that's all, Dave. That's all."

If she had been emotional, Dave might have been able to change her mind. But she was firm, direct and quite businesslike. Whatever tears she had had were shed and done with.

He accepted her terms for their future relationship.

Once Dave and Betty parted, there were many actresses, stars, younger, older, more beautiful, famous—none of them offered him the solid basis of continuity that he had had with Betty. Fortunately, his career was so constructively hectic that he had no time to brood over it. As it was, his agency–client relationship with Betty and Gloria proceeded without any friction or recriminations.

New York, 1946

David Cole was casting his sixth Broadway play. The three stars had been set. He had now to select the supporting players. Alone in the theater, he was pondering the last minor role he had to fill when he glanced up toward the dimly lit stage to see a young girl enter. She was slender, which made her seem taller than she actually was, and carried herself well. Probably a young actress who either was late or had wandered in on her own without a scheduled reading, banking on the possibility that a director would at least let her read out of compassion if not courtesy.

Tired and having already made his decision about the part, he still hadn't the heart to turn her away.

"Can I help you?"

"I'm looking for David Cole," the girl answered timidly.

"Is it about *The Sanctuary*?"

"Yes, it is."

"Okay. You'll find a script on the chair in the wings. It's the part of Eloise. Pages two-nineteen to two-twenty-three. A short scene, but very effective. Take a minute to look it over."

The girl hesitated, seemed about to say something, but at the last moment turned and went toward the wings. She's so timid and sensitive, Dave remarked to himself, she's either a great actress or a total disaster. More likely the latter.

She took an unusually long time to familiarize herself with the scene. When she reappeared, she had taken off her trench coat and was dressed in a simple well-tailored skirt and a silk blouse that revealed a pleasing figure, with young, shapely, if not large, breasts.

"Shall I . . . ?" she asked tentatively.

"Whenever you're ready."

She began the scene as timidly as she had first ventured onto the stage. Then her hands began to tremble. Eventually she stopped reading of her own accord, lowered the script and stared out into the darkness.

"That's pretty terrible, isn't it?" she asked.

"Have you ever acted before?" Dave asked gently.

"Twice," she said, then admitted, "in college."

"Uh-huh," Dave commented. He considered the situation for a moment. "Got time for a cup of coffee?"

"Yes. If you do."

He took her to the coffee shop across from the stage door. It was midafternoon so the place was empty and he could "do missionary work," as he liked to phrase it.

Once they were seated in the last booth and had ordered their coffee, he began at once, "Miss . . . I didn't get your name."

"Sally Ann Weston," she said glibly.

"Sally Ann Weston," he repeated, sure she had chosen that name because it sounded so stagy. But no matter. As he stared at her, he discovered what he had not been able to see in the glare from the work light.

She was an extremely pretty girl. No, he decided, her face transcended prettiness. She possessed a dark beauty and strong black eyes. If she could act, she would have been quite a discovery.

But Dave had no illusions about her talent. Nice, lovely, extremely attractive girl that she was, she was no actress.

"Honey, what I'm about to say will seem cruel. But believe me, in the long run it's the kindest thing I can do. Show business is a tough business. And Broadway is the toughest of all. It's tough enough if you have an agent. But you don't even have an agent, do you?"

"No," the girl admitted quickly.

"Nobody will take you on, is that it?" Dave asked, knowing the reluctance of agents to waste time with unpromising young talent.

"I don't know; I never tried," the girl admitted.

"Well, don't," Dave admonished. "Don't waste your time. Or theirs. Because frankly, and I know this is going to sound brutal, you could never make it as an actress. Not here. Maybe in pictures, where an attractive girl like you could get by on your face. But not on the stage. So I would go back to Westchester or

65

Chicago or Minneapolis or wherever you came from and forget about show business."

The girl did not respond. She stared down at her coffee and kept stirring it until Dave reached across and took the spoon out of her hand. She looked up.

Finally he said, "Well, go on!"

"Go on, what?" she asked.

"Usually when I tell that to an ambitious girl she starts to cry. And it gets to be quite a scene. Believe me, I don't do this because I enjoy it. But it's best in the long run."

He stared at her and saw a glow of mischievous amusement come into her dark eyes. He felt that he was the subject of her amusement.

"Where did you go to school?" he asked, to avoid her provocative eyes.

"Vassar."

"What did you major in?"

"French literature," she said, smiling. "Don't ask me why. There's hardly anything quite so useless."

"At least you didn't waste your time studying drama. You have no idea the untalented kids who show up at every casting call with degrees in Dramatic Arts. Hell, you can't teach acting in college. It must be learned. The hard way. Of course, some girls find it advantageous to be nice to directors. But that won't get you anywhere unless the talent is there. So to put it bluntly, don't waste your time. You haven't got it."

As he spoke, her smile became broader until he exploded, "Damn it, don't just sit there and smile. I don't have to do this, you know! I'm telling you this for *your* good!"

"I didn't come here today asking to read. If you recall, this was *your* idea," she said.

Dave bristled. "What do you mean, my idea? You walked in, after the others had gone, and you—"

"I what?" she interrupted. "I said I was looking for David Cole. And you asked was it about *The Sanctuary*. And I said it was and you told me to find a script and read."

"If you didn't want to read for the part, what *did* you want?"

"A job as production secretary," she said. "I like the theater. I know I don't have acting talent. I know that better than you do. So I thought that as a production secretary—"

66

"Oh, I see," Dave said. "And you let me go through all that."

She smiled, and eventually he smiled.

"You're a very pretty kid, though," he said finally. "I wish you did have the talent."

"What about production secretary?" she persisted.

"I'm afraid that job's filled. We've got a girl who will double as production secretary and understudy for one of the small parts. Saves expenses on the road."

"What if it didn't involve any expense? If I offered to pay my own way and not take any salary. Just to get the experience."

"I'd like to say yes, but the job's filled. Sorry," Dave said. "But if I hear of anything, where can I get hold of you?"

She shook her head. She had obviously heard that line many times before.

"I'm not making a play for you," Dave protested. "I really mean it; if I hear of any opening I'll let you know."

He studied her face, especially her dark eyes. He had found something there he didn't want to lose. Yet he was sure that if he let her go out the door he would never see her again. To keep her from leaving, he asked, "You're not from Westchester *or* Chicago, are you?"

"No," she admitted.

"You don't have any regional speech. In fact, you don't have any distinguishable accent at all. And there's only one place in this country where there is no local accent. The final melting pot. California. Right?"

"Does it matter? Besides, I'm late for an appointment." She had risen from her seat in the booth.

He rose with her. Their eyes met, stared into each other's, until she turned to get her coat.

"Sally Ann Weston!" he commanded.

She turned to face him.

"That isn't really your name, is it?"

"Of course not," she said, smiling, and started out quickly.

He was tempted to pursue her. He paid the check and stepped out into the evening air. He saw her far down the street just as she rounded the corner.

The last glimpse he had of her was a slender girl who moved with grace and ease. But it was her dark, challenging eyes he remembered most.

5

Hollywood, 1947

It was now three days after Dave Cole's first meeting with H. P. Koenig. Dave came up out of the warm water of the Château Marmont pool to hear his name paged over the speaker. He swam to the side, leaped up onto the sunbaked concrete and took the call. It was Betty Ronson from New York. She was pleasant, but as brisk as her attitude had been since Boston.

"Dave, hi. How's it going?"

"Oh, fine. Picking oranges and lemons right outside my window and swinging from tree to tree like Tarzan."

"Seen H.P. yet?"

"Spent one most enlightening and delightful afternoon with him."

"Did you discuss an assignment?" Betty asked.

"Not yet. Why?"

"Anybody mention the name Vic Martoni to you?"

Martoni . . . Martoni . . . Yes, come to think of it, a New York character actor had implied all sorts of sinister things about him.

"Yes; an actor I know—"

"Okay," Betty said, relieved that she didn't have to explain too much. "Well, Gloria and I entered an arrangement with him.

Since we don't have Coast representation, we've appointed him to handle you at Magna. So we want you to call and see him soon as you can."

"What happens? I mean, how does it work for you and Gloria?"

"We split commissions."

"Betty?" he asked, demanding an explanation.

She finally admitted, "If you want the right assignment, the right treatment at Magna, it's better to be represented by Martoni. He pimps for H.P. When a man puts on a holier-than-thou attitude in public like H.P. does, he needs a little assistance in private. That's it, in a nutshell."

Dave thought back to H.P.'s self-righteous attack on Julian Sakowitz. So the old bastard liked his regular piece of tail. Only he made sure to be more careful and circumspect than Sakowitz. He had an agent named Martoni to pimp for him. More important, H.P. didn't work for a tyrant named H. P. Koenig.

As soon as Betty hung up, Dave jiggled the phone, asked the operator to get him the phone number of Vic Martoni. She already knew it and asked, "Shall I put you through?"

"Yes, please."

In a moment a warm, confident voice was asking, "Cole? David Cole?"

"Yes. Mr. Martoni?"

"Vic. Dave, I'd like to meet you. How about lunch tomorrow?"

"Okay. Where and when?" Dave asked.

"The commissary. Magna. Let's say twelve-thirty?"

"Okay, let's say," Dave agreed.

Dave drove onto the lot, was directed to a parking space. He was surprised to find a sign which designated that this seven-by-fourteen-foot piece of California real estate was, temporarily at least, the sole property of DAVID COLE. It gave him a sense of importance.

He made his way through the commissary into the Green Room. The hostess greeted him by name and led him to the farthest corner table to a handsome man in his mid-fifties, with black hair so shiny and with such a precise wave it seemed to have been set by the studio hairdresser. When the man rose to shake hands, David saw he was not nearly so tall as he seemed sitting down. He wore an exquisitely tailored gray tweed suit, with a figured gold-and-maroon tie.

Throughout lunch they were interrupted frequently by Magna's biggest stars and most important directors coming over to the table to pay court to Martoni. Dave began to feel important just being in Martoni's company.

"Look, sweetie," the agent said, "let me tell you how it works. You stick to what you do best, directing. Let me handle the studio politics. Of course, that doesn't mean you won't have to be careful. You have to learn the likes and dislikes of H.P. And it won't do any harm to be on the right side of Sonny Brown. He's very quiet, but he's got a lot of muscle. As for the rest, let me do all thinking, planning and especially talking. Right now, I am looking for the best opportunity for you on your first picture. We got to find a good property. One that cost the studio so much money to acquire that they'll give it top-drawer casting and a good fat budget to protect.

"One thing more, baby: This is a funny town. There are more beautiful women in this town than the rest of the world combined. And the most beautiful are right here in this studio. There's hardly a secretary on this lot who couldn't be a beauty-contest winner somewhere else. That's not your problem.

"Your problem is don't get into bed with any of them without checking with me first. You may not know who you're screwing. Who she belongs to. And what lifetime enemies you're going to make for one good fuck. So keep your nose clean and your pants buttoned. Until you check with me. In the meantime, if you want a piece of something, I got a string of starlets who'd be only too happy to oblige. Nobody fucks with the enthusiasm of an ambitious starlet.

"Got it?" Martoni asked. But there was a strong hint of command in his affable advice.

Dave just stared.

"Remember one thing! There is no man in the world who has the power of life and death over anyone in show business except H.P. And he doesn't hesitate to use it. If you doubt me, see if Julian Sakowitz ever works again. Unless he finally takes a job over on Poverty Row for some wildcat producer.

"So watch your step and let me do the rest. I like you. I've heard nice things about you. You can go far. But never cross me. And don't screw anything till I say okay."

Dave didn't nod, but he didn't disagree either. Martoni had all the insidious power of a Mafia chieftain.

If any proof was needed, two days later Dave was summoned to a meeting in H.P.'s office. When he arrived, a conference was under way. H.P., his committee of three storytellers and a producer were deep in discussion of a play that Magna had bought though it was still on the road.

H.P. waved Dave into the room and started to introduce him but had obviously forgotten his name.

"Cole," Dave had to supply; "David Cole."

"Of course. Come on, Cole, sit down. And listen." H.P. gestured to one of his storytellers, who proceeded to relate the plot of the play. Then H.P. sat back beaming at Dave. "Well?"

"Mr. Koenig, I know that play. In fact, it was offered to me to direct for Broadway. I turned it down."

H.P.'s expression changed from beaming expectation to personal affront. "What do you mean, *you* turned it down? When they told me the story I cried like a baby!"

"There's a defect in the story. An incurable defect," said Dave, remembering at the same time Martoni's warnings about crossing H.P.

"An incurable defect!" H.P. mocked. "We paid out a hundred thousand dollars for the property and *you* found an incurable defect!"

He made Dave's declaration sound like treason. The three storytellers glared at Dave with the impatience of hanging judges.

"It's not just my opinion," Dave continued with a bit less conviction than before. "I have two friends in the cast. And they tell me the author's rewritten the third act four times and it still doesn't work."

"What was wrong with the original third act?" H.P. demanded, as if personally attacked.

"It just didn't work in front of an audience," Dave explained.

"I cried like a baby," H.P. reminded Dave. Dave was not moved.

The blonded brass-voiced woman spoke up, a bit vehemently

71

and defensively. "There are no difficulties that can't be straightened out in a good screenplay!"

"And think of the production values we'll add," The Professor joined in.

"And the casting! H.P. thinks it's a perfect vehicle for Gable and Garson!" the third storyteller added, and H.P. nodded his confirmation.

Dave was not moved to change his mind, but one thing he did realize. This was one of those studio political situations about which he'd been warned by Martoni. If it was, he could play the game. Any Broadway director knew one basic fact of life. When in doubt, flatter the star. There was no doubt who the star was here.

"If I may be permitted to explain?" Dave asked. H.P. made a small, impatient gesture with his hand. "There's a reason why the story works in this room. A reason why you hear it and cry. The same reason why this is the greatest studio in the picture business. *Sensitivity. Your* sensitivity. Sure, if the audience out there was as sensitive as *you* are, as quick to grasp the deeper meanings of human relationships, they would sit out there and cry too! But the fact is they are not. And *they* don't cry. And that's not the way I would like audiences across this country to feel about a Magna picture. I certainly wouldn't risk Gable and Garson in a story like that."

H.P. sat back in his oversized desk chair.

"The young man has something," H.P. finally declared. "This may well be too deep for an audience. Tell you what. Put Wildberg on the script. If anybody can cure this, he can. If he can't, we'll put it on the shelf and take our loss. Better to lose a hundred thousand than two million."

The Professor said, "I'll talk to Wildberg after lunch."

"Good!" H.P. had disposed of the meeting with one word. As they started toward the door, H.P. called, "Cole! Wait a minute!"

The other three left. H.P. did not invite Dave to sit down.

"I like you, kid. You did exactly what Marvin Kronheim would have done. You held your ground. And you protected the studio, even at risk to yourself. I like that kind of loyalty. It takes guts!"

72

Thereupon H.P. dismissed him with a wave of the hand that reminded Dave of a papal gesture.

Whatever Dave's reaction to H.P.'s pretenses, one thing the old man had made quite clear. He was still searching for a successor to Marvin Kronheim. Dave now considered himself to have become a possible candidate.

When he returned to his office, his secretary held out a message from the man Dave had dubbed The Professor. The message asked only that Dave call back upon his return to the office.

"Lochinvar?" the scholarly man's voice asked gently. "Lochinvar come out of the East, that is. Dave Cole?"

"Yes."

"Are you by chance free for lunch today?" the man asked.

Dave hesitated; then, "Yes, I'm free."

"Good. Say about one o'clock?"

"Okay."

"I think it would be better if we went off the lot. People have a tendency to gossip whenever I'm seen lunching with anyone. What kind of food do you like?" he asked pleasantly. "Mexican? Italian? French? Jewish? I have secret little hideaways to fit any and all ethnic desires. How long has it been since you've had a good kosher corned-beef sandwich?"

"The day before I came out."

"Oh." The Professor seemed disappointed. He had wanted to brag about a little Jewish delicatessen that had authentic New York corned beef. Instead he offered, "There's a little Italian place . . ." He gave Dave the directions. It was clear The Professor did not want them to be seen leaving the lot together.

They arrived at the restaurant within minutes of each other. The proprietor knew The Professor well and led them to a small, secluded booth in the back. He knew the kind of wine The Professor drank and brought it immediately.

Throughout the meal, the older man inquired about Dave, his background and certain of his specific experiences in the theater. The man had obviously taken considerable interest in researching Dave's career.

Yet the man was disarming. He was slight, well into middle age, with wispy hair that gave him the appearance of an absent-minded academic. It was only when they were having their bitter Italian espresso that he came to the real business of the meeting.

"So tell me, how did you make out with Vic Martoni?"

"We got along pretty well," Dave said, deliberately not making the statement too strong.

"That's important," The Professor said.

"So I understand."

"It is also important that you get along with The Three Witches." When Dave appeared puzzled, The Professor smiled. "The three of us. H.P.'s storytellers. We have the ear of the king. We are the Inner Circle. We see him every day. A privilege no one else has. If there is anything you want transmitted to him, let me know. We can do it, something no one else can. Except Vic Martoni. And the trouble with Martoni is that he'll only transmit what he wants to. Not necessarily what *you* want him to. After all, he represents most of the talent on the lot. So when your interests clash with some other director who is getting more money, naturally he is going to protect that director and sacrifice you.

"This is a very pragmatic town. Professional life and death is decided in moments. Everything is a weapon. Money. Sex. Greed. Vanity. Perversion. Half the trick in this town is finding out what the other fellow's weakness is. Girls. Boys. Gambling. Masochism. Sadism. Each of us is vulnerable under the right conditions."

Dave wondered why the older man was telling him all this. But The Professor just smiled and said, "Go on, ask."

Dave was embassassed.

"You think of me as The Professor. Don't deny it, because everyone does. And why? Because that's what I was once. Professor of English Literature. At a girls' college in the East. Then why am I no longer there? Because I too have a weakness. Young ladies. Very young ladies. Given a choice I always preferred freshmen to seniors. There is something about a young, innocent girl that I still cannot resist. When my weakness was discovered, I was released—an end to my teaching career.

"I turned my abilities to writing. And I discovered that while

74

I don't do that well, I do have a sense about stories. I met H.P., strangely enough, when we both screwed the same young actress. He was furious, of course. But then we got to know each other. When I brought him a few ideas for pictures he came to respect me. Eventually, when he took over Magna, he hired me. That was twenty-two years ago."

He interrupted only long enough to signal for fresh espresso.

"Now, you are saying to yourself, why am I telling you all this? A good question. I owe you nothing. In fact, after today I ought to look upon you as an enemy. You broke one of the cardinal rules. Never, never disagree with The Witches! Anyone in the studio could have told you that. Why, that cold-assed bitch with the brass voice and balls to match, she's already planning to cut your heart out. And the small ferret? He won't rest till he's a producer himself. He'll undermine you every chance he gets.

"So why should you trust *me*? Don't I have ambitions? Of course. But mine are easily gratified. I like the work I do. I am most respectful of the huge and undeserved salary I receive. And for a man with my particular weakness, to be allowed to work in a studio like Magna is like a dope addict working in a heroin factory. I look out from my office window and see all the young cunt that passes through those gates and I am in heaven. Because if it is there, I get my share. Young girls like me. I am pleasant, mild, and my sexual habits are not particularly distasteful to them. When I whisper the magic words, 'I can get you into pictures,' legs open wide with amazing alacrity!

"Then what is my need for you? I have taken a fancy to you, Lochinvar. Very few people would have stood up to H.P. today. That *is* a lousy play. And it *does* have a fatal defect. But we never recommended it to H.P. in the first place, even though he would have you believe we did."

"Then who did buy it?" Dave asked, puzzled.

"Vic Martoni. He represents the playwright on a split-commission deal with his New York agent. Just as he represents you. Vic sold it directly to H.P. during an evening they spent together at Marge's."

"Marge's?" Dave asked.

"A whorehouse. From time to time H.P. goes there and buys out the whole place. One night at Marge's, Vic told him about that play. H.P. agreed to buy it. Probably while one of the girls was going down on him and he wasn't even listening. In any event, the deal was made and we were stuck with it. From that time on we had to keep selling H.P. a story he bought without ever consulting us. When you came in, you made our little game too transparent. So you made two enemies today. And one friend. I am not so corrupt that I can't appreciate a little honesty."

The Professor smiled. "Listen," he said suddenly. "Everyone calls me The Professor. I would appreciate it if you called me by name. Albert."

"Okay, Albert. . . ."

"Now, I will confess to two things that puzzle me. Why did H.P. choose you to bring in this morning? Why not half a dozen other directors on the lot who are free right now?"

"Maybe Martoni insisted."

"Don't kid yourself, Lochinvar. You're not that valuable to him yet."

"Then why?" Dave asked, becoming concerned now himself.

"I don't know," The Professor confessed.

"What was the other thing that puzzled you?"

"In the face of what you said, why does H.P. still want a screenplay?"

"Maybe it's as simple as he said—to see if it can be made to work," Dave suggested.

"Hell, no. We've got a hundred stories in better shape that are still lying on the shelf. Why this one?"

He reached for the check, saying, "We'll see. Sooner or later, we'll see." He was totaling up the figures when he stopped, glanced at Dave and asked, "Did he ever say anything to you about Marvin Kronheim?"

"Yes. Why?"

"That he's still looking for another young man to take Marvin Kronheim's place?"

"Yes," Dave said, feeling a warm glow.

"Well, don't believe a word of it," The Professor said abruptly. Dave glanced at him dubiously. The older man continued. "He loves to talk that way. Because everyone else in Hollywood regards Marvin Kronheim as the only authentic genius this town ever produced. But the truth is, H.P. considers *himself* that genius. The night Marvin Kronheim died, while the rest of

Hollywood cried, the old man went out whoring. If there's one thing he's *not* looking for, it's another Marvin Kronheim.

"He only uses the idea to seduce young men like you. But if ever you show any signs of really succeeding Kronheim, you're dead. Remember that!"

They were out in the sunlight again. The Professor touched Dave's arm as he started for his car. "Look, Dave, I've entrusted you with a lot of myself today. Don't betray me. You'll not only destroy my illusions, you'll make yourself another enemy. And out here no one needs any more enemies than he already has."

He smiled, went off to his car and drove out of the parking lot.

For the next three weeks, Dave Cole found little to do at Magna. Whenever he called to make an appointment to see H.P. about an assignment, he was advised to busy himself observing things on the lot. Meanwhile, his thirteen weeks were running out and his option could be dropped. He phoned Gloria. She obviously phoned Vic Martoni. The next day Martoni dropped by his office.

"What's the trouble, kid?"

"I'd like to go to work."

"Look, when the time comes, H.P. will have an assignment for you. Meantime, get around. Learn picture making. Go onto the stages where other directors are shooting. Go into editing rooms and watch those guys at work. *They* really make the pictures. Talk to makeup men, designers, costumers. It's a whole different world here. Get the feel of it."

"My thirteen weeks are running out," Dave reminded him.

"Don't worry. I'll have you renewed. Maybe with an increase," Martoni assured him confidently.

"I haven't done a day's work since I got here. How the hell does anyone know if I'm worth an increase?"

"*I* know," Martoni said, smiling. "That's all it takes."

On the basis of what The Professor had told him, that should be enough, Dave consoled himself.

"I still don't like the idea of getting paid for doing nothing."

"Look, kid, getting paid for doing nothing is part of the game. If you're bored, find yourself a piece of cunt and amuse yourself. Only check her out with me first. And if you're too bashful, let me know and I'll send a few girls around. But whatever you do, just wait, patiently. Till I give the word."

Martoni started to depart, turned back to say, "And stop calling New York! Out here when you get into trouble or you want anything, call *me*! Got it?"

"Got it," Dave agreed, realizing how powerless a principled lady like Gloria Simms would be out here.

It was almost two weeks later. Dave was returning to his office after lunch with some New York actors out on a one-picture deal. They had made the usual jokes about Hollywood. About buying Coco-Colas one bottle at a time instead of in six-packs because they didn't know how long they were going to stay. About how limited and crude the arts were out here. About the Rolls-Royces that had begun to appear in supermarket parking lots since the war.

It had been good fun, but now the actors had returned to their set and Dave was on his way back to his empty, and thus far useless, office. When he entered, his secretary nervously held out the phone to him. "H.P.'s office!"

Dave took the phone. In a moment Sarah Immerman was on the line. "Mr. Koenig would like to see you at three o'clock." Then she asked the most rhetorical of questions: "Are you free?"

When he was ushered into the office he found The Three Witches there. H.P. was deep in thought while his storytellers waited.

"Cole! We have it finally. Wildberg's shooting script. We think he's licked the story. Beat it into shape."

Dave made no comment about the parlance of an art form in which every script was looked upon as a wild beast that had to be beaten into submission.

"Well, that's good," Dave said, still puzzled as to the reason for his presence.

"What we'd like is for you to read it. And be ready to discuss it in the morning," H.P. ordered.

"Sure," Dave agreed, stealing a glance at The Professor, who seemed to deliberately ignore him.

"Sarah will see you get a copy before you leave the studio tonight."

78

He left, wondering what special significance there was to the meeting. The same piece of news could have been passed on by a phone call from H.P. or even from Sarah. He found the script on his desk. Was tempted to read it then and there, but decided to go back to the Marmont and spend the evening on it.

It started well enough. The establishing scenes were done in action, with good suggested use of the camera for setting locale, main characters and their station and function in life. But once past the first dozen pages, the script settled down to almost the identical dialogue Dave remembered from the stage version he had read and rejected for Broadway.

Whatever talent H.P. thought that Wildberg possessed, all the writer had done was a cut-and-paste job on the original play. It should have taken three days, not almost a month, and Wildberg was reputed to be getting four thousand a week.

The question now was one of tactics. To go back to H.P. and tell him the truth would only anger the old tyrant. But to direct this script as his first picture would undoubtedly do his career enormous, possibly even fatal, damage. Dave decided to call Vic Martoni. He couldn't reach him. And it was too late to call Gloria or Betty in New York. He was contemplating where to have dinner when he remembered that little Italian place The Professor had taken him to and decided he might be just the man to talk to now. Fortunately Albert Grobe was listed in the Beverly Hills phone book.

Albert seemed sympathetic. He listened to Dave's heated criticism with little interjections of "Uh-huh . . . uh-huh . . . uh-huh." He seemed to be agreeing all the way. Then Dave asked, "Now, you tell me. What I do?"

"What you do," the older man said in a kindly voice, "is shoot the picture."

"How can I, feeling the way I do? Even worse, how can I put Gable and Garson through something like this? It would ruin me. No star would want to work with me again!"

"Wait, Dave." The Professor tried to calm him. "Look, I have a . . . a date this evening . . . with a young lady. She's due here at eight-thirty. If you came right over, I could spend an hour with you. But after that, well, you understand—"

"Of course," said Dave, grateful for the hour.

The Professor's house on Rodeo Drive was one of those imposing structures that imitated a Southern mansion. Next to it stood an imitation Norman château—testimony to the fact that Southern California had no identity of its own. Dave was admitted to the house by a tall, very proper black butler. He was shown into a library which looked out on a lanai and swimming pool.

In a moment Albert Grobe appeared, dressed in black silk slacks and a brocade smoking jacket with a crimson scarf around his neck. "Ah, Dave, my boy!" he greeted, moving to the bar, and asked, "What'll it be?"

"Scotch. Water."

Grobe prepared a drink for Dave but none for himself. "Now, then, your trouble?"

"That script! It stinks!"

"My boy, my boy, let's not become emotional. We are dealing here with a situation that demands the utmost diplomacy. You would like to reject the script, but obviously H.P. wants you to do it. So you can't refuse it."

"But I will!" Dave insisted.

"Oh, no," Grobe said. "Because if you do, then H.P. will fire you. And worse, he will spread some terrible story about why he fired you so that no studio in this town will hire you. We are living in a feudal state here in this kingdom of palm trees and free cunt. And sitting on the throne is H. P. Koenig."

Grobe hesitated, then finally came to a decision. He went to the phone and dialed a number.

"Look, baby, instead of eight-thirty, nine-thirty? Hmm? Something came up.... No, no, something else.... Liebchen, I wouldn't lie to you. There's no other girl. And you *will* get your screen test. See you at nine-thirty. Adam will pick you up.... Right. Good girl."

He blew her a kiss through the phone, then hung up and buzzed. The black man appeared in the doorway. "Adam, the young lady—pick her up at nine-fifteen insead of eight-fifteen."

"Yes, Mr. Grobe."

"And did Mattie get everything else ready? Dinner? And something for later?"

"Yes, sir."

"Then when you deliver the young lady, you can go to bed." The butler turned and left the room.

When they were alone, Grobe sat down opposite Dave.

"Lochinvar, you're a little too young and too idealistic to understand now. But if you stay around this town long enough you will. Let me say only that H.P. is a terrible person. And a marvelous man. He is a man of high moral standards. And a degenerate. He is a man of tremendous ability. And no talent. He is a man of great power. And of equally great conflicts and indecisions.

"What I am saying is that H.P. is a giant; his defects are as great as his assets." Grobe got up and began to pace. "This thing about the girls..." He was obviously referring to his phone call. "That's only one of the perquisites of the job. It's the job itself that keeps me here. That's what makes me put up with H.P.'s rages and excesses." He paused and turned directly to Dave.

"If I didn't sense something in you, I wouldn't bother to talk to you like this. To understand this town, first you have to understand H. P. Koenig. You have to know where he came from and what he is. A young boy of eight comes to America from a small town in Lithuania and can't speak a word of English. He goes to live in a tenement in the slums, and his mother and father both have to work to keep the family alive. At the age of ten he promises his mother that he'll make money for her, more money than the President of the United States!"

Grobe smiled. "Which mother hasn't heard some such boast from her son? But which son winds up making ten times what the President makes? You want to know what determination is, Dave? At the age of fourteen he owned his own junkyard, his own horse and wagon. At the age of seventeen he owned three junkyards. Now, you want to know what gambler's courage is? At the age of nineteen he sells it all to open a little movie theater on the East Side of New York. And of course he succeeds. But in him success only feeds ambition.

"At the age of twenty-seven he leaves his wife and two young children and goes West to make his own pictures. Once he gets here, he discovers this is the place he's searched for all his life.

"The first picture he ever made, he wrote the script himself. And being what he is, the first star he ever hired he screwed. From the beginning he was possessed by this need to dominate people, to own them, to force them to his will. You can hate him

81

for it, or admire him, or envy him. You can fight him or submit to him. But the one thing you can't do is deny that he built the studio that entertains more people the world over than any man in history!"

Albert Grobe dropped into a chair. "I think of him as an institution. A phenomenon. Whatever it's done to him, to his wife, to his daughters, he has built himself a kingdom. He is an emperor who controls the finest actors, the greatest writers, the most talented directors and musicians. They stand all kinds of abuse from him. But in the end, even those who hate him respect him.

"How do you contend with a man like that? You accept him. That tough little junk dealer rules the world we live in, Dave. Accept it. And do the best you can at the same time. Because he'll recognize it. One thing that man knows, Dave: quality. Give it to him and you'll get along with him."

They were interrupted by the arrival of Grobe's date. A cast-off of H.P.'s, she was still a sensuous young girl with a splendid physique, which was her only passport to a career. Grobe asked her to wait one moment more.

"Dave, about that script? I agree with you. It's bad. But do it."

"And ruin myself?"

"That's where Vic Martoni comes in. Call him. Make him tell H.P. that you won't do the picture without a two-year, no-option extension of your contract."

"I still can't believe H.P. wants to put Gable and Garson in a picture like that," Dave argued.

"Did he say he was going to put Gable and Garson in this picture?"

"He certainly did that first time," Dave reminded.

"That was the first time. This is *this* time," Grobe corrected gently.

"Look, what the hell is going on?" Dave demanded.

"Dave, please, the girl is waiting. And I've been thinking about her all day. Cheap little floozie. But did you see those breasts? Monumental. Almost as pretentious as her ambitions."

6

Dave Cole turned his car off Sunset Boulevard onto North Roxbury. It was a cool morning. Years later when Hollywood and Beverly Hills were slowly choking to death in smog, Dave would look back longingly to such clear cool days.

Beside him lay a revised script. He had talked to Martoni. Martoni had talked to H.P. H.P. had agreed to his terms. He had even agreed to have Wildberg's script rewritten to comply with Dave's suggestions. Now Dave was on his way to have his first meeting with Lora Lindsay, whom H.P. had chosen to star in Dave's first film.

Lora Lindsay had long been one of Magna's most valuable properties. She was no great actress but she projected an air of fine breeding. Her posture was admirable, if a little stiff. She spoke with clean and precise diction. Dave had always felt that her acting was the same; clean, precise and far from moving. But like all ambitious young directors, he had persuaded himself that the latent talent was there and he would be the one to get a performance out of her.

His male star would be Geoffrey Horn, a well-regarded though not top-drawer piece of Magna talent. He was reliable, dark, handsome. Usually he played the second lead, who loses the girl at the finale. Or he was the man with whom the heroine was

83

tempted to commit an indiscretion but didn't, returning to her husband still unsullied.

Dave found Lora Lindsay's house and pulled into the driveway behind a maroon Rolls-Royce. He rang the doorbell and waited. When there was no response after a reasonable time, he rang again. Finally the door swept open. Lora Lindsay stood before him. She was dressed in a negligee of pale blue topped with fragile lace to match. "David?" she said with the same open smile she used in her films.

To himself Dave thought, The phony bitch! Imagine, staging a simple thing like opening her own front door.

He looked at her closely. Her eyes were too close together to make her a true beauty. Her other features were fairly regular, though her nose was a bit wider than he had expected. Dave realized suddenly why most of her stills were in profile.

She swept him through the lavish house and out to the pool in back.

A maid appeared with a huge tray of coffee and delicate pastries. Lora served, always smiling. "Do have one of these pastries. Delicious. Chasen's makes them specially for me."

When he was burdened with coffee and pastry, neither of which he wanted, Lora Lindsay began to talk.

"I'll want Walter Flannery for my cameraman, of course. And Edie to do my wardrobe. But I must see and approve all her sketches first. Only Bill Thornhill can touch my hair. And I want the same makeup man I had on *Heaven Bound*."

She stopped suddenly. Something in Dave's eyes betrayed his disapproval.

"I only say these things up front so we don't get bogged down haggling later," she explained, still using the famous Lindsay smile.

"Of course," Dave agreed with little enthusiasm. "Did you read the script?"

"Oh, the script. Yes. I read it."

"What did you think of it?"

"It's a change. A refreshing change," she said. "That's the trouble with being owned by an octupus like Magna. You do what you're told or else they put you on suspension. You know what Cohn is doing to Jean Arthur at Columbia, don't you?"

Dave nodded. Everyone had heard that Jean Arthur was on

suspension for more than a year now, forbidden to work anywhere for anyone, in pictures or on the stage, until she fulfilled her commitment to Cohn.

"Well," Lora Lindsay was saying, "I'll show H.P. When I first got this script I said, 'It's not me, not me at all.' But when I read it over, I decided, I'll do it *because* it's different. I'll show him a Lora Lindsay he's never seen before. I have been in every damn costume epic Magna ever made. Disraeli's wife. Marie Antoinette. Lady Hamilton. Always the same. Well, for once I want to be a real woman."

Dave felt better, much better; she had arrived at the same conclusion he had. If there was any hope for this script it lay in doing something startling with Lora Lindsay.

Throughout their conversation, Dave had been aware of the sound of tennis balls being hit with proficient regularity. Now two men came from the tennis court that was beyond the pool house. They were both middle-aged, dressed in whites. As they drew close Lora called out, "Darling, come meet Mr. Cole!"

The taller of the two players approached and held out a hand. As they shook, Dave recognized him as one of those actors whose name you never remember, but whose face you know at sight. He was handsome, rugged, well muscled and undoubtedly attractive to women, though not so attractive as to become a star in his own right. He seemed delighted to meet Dave and even went so far as to say, "Oh, yes, the brilliant young director from New York." He smiled at Dave, his white, regular teeth gleaming.

"Did you win, darling?"

"Six-two, six-four."

"Great!" she said. She kissed him carefully on the cheek so as not to touch his sweaty body. The smell of him made her suggest, "Go take a swim." He obeyed, disappearing into the pool house to change.

Dave noted as he left that she seemed to own him in the same way that Magna owned her. Everyone in this town seemed to live by the sufferance and indulgence of someone else.

Dave drove to the studio feeling much better. At least she was open-minded about the role, determined not to give another routine performance. She would be amenable to direction and willing to work. Things were not so bad as they had seemed.

When he had lunch with Albert Grobe that afternoon, Dave sounded very optimistic.

They had been shooting on Stage Eleven for four days. Lora Lindsay was ecstatic. She had unbounded confidence in her young director and praised him to everyone who would listen. She even went to the commissary for her meals, something she was known not to do while shooting.

Overall, it was a happy company. The cast liked and respected their director. The crew liked Dave's sensitive approach to their various crafts. Everyone seemed to enjoy working on the picture. Except Dave Cole.

As he stood behind the cameraman watching each take, he had a strange and empty sense that something was missing. He watched as Lora did her lines with great security, made her every move exactly as he had blocked it. But there was no electricity. She was cold. The first few days he reassured himself that it was his lack of familiarity with motion-picture technique. In the theater he was used to viewing the total scene. It came to a climax and you knew it. Here, working in short takes, in bits and pieces, it was hard to tell. He had to believe when they were edited together they would work.

In the office of H. P. Koenig, recessed into the lower right-hand desk drawer, there was hidden an electronic panel with as many switches as there were stages on the Magna lot. With the flick of his finger H.P. could listen in on every performance, every conversation. It was the way he could secretly find out who worked efficiently and who did not. And also what people said about him. Many a career had been blunted without anyone's ever knowing why H.P. had suddenly gone sour on some director or star whom he had formerly looked on with favor.

He was listening in on Stage Eleven. He had heard all the noises that accompanied the change in setup, heard the chief grip notify Dave Cole that they were ready. He heard Dave give last-minute instructions to Lora and Geoffrey Horn about how he wanted the scene played. Then H.P. heard the call for silence, heard the slight hum of the arc lights during the silence and finally the word "Speed!" indicating that sound and camera were rolling. At last he heard Dave's command, "Action!"

H.P. leaned back in his huge swivel chair and listened. As he did, The Professor entered the room. H.P. held up a well-manicured hand. Albert sat down without saying a word and listened to the entire scene. When Dave called out, "Cut!" H.P. flipped off his electronic eavesdropper.

He smiled at Grobe and said, "God, isn't she terrible!"

Dave Cole was in the cutting room staring into the Moviola at the rough cut of his first ten days of shooting. What he saw not only reinforced his earlier fears, it magnified them. There was no performance on that film. He tried to account for it by the fact that so many of Lora's shots were in profile. He would discuss that with Walter Flannery. Surely there were other angles that could be used to heighten her performance and give it more impact.

He went to the set and approached Flannery at once. The cameraman had been with Magna since H.P.'s earliest days. He was not particularly outgoing, but he had a reputation for being one of the best women's cameramen in the industry.

"Can't we do anything to give her some variety?" Dave asked.

"You don't like her profile shots?"

"No, I don't."

"Well . . ." Flannery began slowly, "we really don't have much choice. She is a difficult face. You can sometimes shoot down at her full face, or at a sharp angle looking up. But head-on, it's suicide. It's her eyes."

Dave nodded grimly.

"Why do you think she insists on me?" Flannery asked. "Who else can shoot her and make her look beautiful?"

"Then how the hell did she become such a big star?" Dave demanded impatiently.

Flannery didn't answer.

Dave put in a call to Albert Grobe. Yes, Grobe would have lunch, but not in the commissary or on the lot. They met at a little French place The Professor suggested.

Albert Grobe was unusually silent. He listened sympathetically, while eating without particular gusto. When Dave had unburdened himself of his complaints about Lora Lindsay and the film, Grobe leaned forward, ready to talk.

"He's a strange man, Dave. He is a powerful friend but a terrible enemy."

Dave glanced up, puzzled, but The Professor ignored the look. "What he saw in her from the outset I don't know. But then who ever does? A certain face appeals to one man. A pair of breasts to another. I have seen young, pert, shapely behinds that have haunted me for days. Lora Lindsay . . . whose name, by the way, is really Pauline Fritsen . . . she appealed to H.P. in some way.

"She was just an extra when he first saw her. How she made him notice her I don't know, but she did. She made love to him, flattered him, lived for him. More important, she made him *think* she did. But always she played the great lady, very superior, very *Gentile*. He saw her only in that light, that's why she was always cast in that role. The best acting she ever did was in her bedroom. She allowed herself to be made love to by a man who always felt inferior to her. She was the most important conquest he ever made. She granted him favors as if she were a queen. So he made her a star.

"Then, two years ago, with so much success behind her, she became smug. She must have thought she didn't need him anymore. Or else she fell in love, really in love, with that ham. He never could act, so he plays tennis. She fell in love and she married him. The irony of it is that while she was smart enough to play that game with H.P., she doesn't know that her tennis player is playing exactly the same game with her.

"When she's not working, he plays tennis. But when she *is* working, he is screwing everything in town."

Grobe leaned back from the table. "So how does it all add up? H.P. never forgave her. She disgraced him before the whole movie industry. She had been his, as a star and as a bed partner. When she decided to get married, she didn't even ask his permission. A terrible blunder."

"You can understand why she would be reluctant to ask," said Dave.

"She never should have married at all," Grobe said. "Now, why are *you* being asked to direct a script that you, I and H.P. know is no good?"

88

Dave flushed at this last bit of news.

"Yes, of course H.P. knows it's no good. Whatever else you may think of him—tyrant, bastard, prick—he knows what's good and what's bad. He wants this picture to fail so badly that Lora Lindsay's career is totally destroyed."

Dave felt a heavy, sick feeling in the pit of his stomach. He was the smallest pawn in the perverted game of the little demon. Of the almost one hundred pictures that Magna would make and release this year, one very bad one would make little difference to the studio. But this was the only film that David Cole would direct for twelve months. To know it would be a disaster even before it was completed enraged him.

"What I would do," said Grobe, "is forget about her. Direct the picture as a picture. Make the best use of the camera and movement so it is quite clear that David Cole is a very good director saddled with a very bad actress. Convince the critics of that. They're ready to clobber her anyhow. She's been lording it over Hollywood too long now. Let her get all the blame. You become the victim. The critics'll fall all over themselves trying to be nice to you."

Lunch was over. Dave felt no better. As they started across the parking lot, he asked, "What's going to happen to her?"

"That's the most devilish part," Grobe said, truly saddened. "H.P. has a way of getting stars to live beyond their income. He never likes to do business with anyone who is secure. This will leave her not only destroyed, but broke. She won't be able to afford her tennis player anymore. That's really what H.P.'s waiting for. For her to come begging. And when she does, he'll take her in, screw her good and then turn her out. One never, never crosses H.P."

For the remaining five weeks of shooting, Dave followed Grobe's advice. He placed his emphasis on the directorial touches in the film. After one particular day's shooting, Walter Flannery rewarded him by saying, "Wyler couldn't have done that scene better." But each morning's dailies revealed relentless proof that Lora was becoming worse. Dave worked with her. Some nights he took her out to dinner so that under the guise of social conversation he could prepare her for the next day's shooting. He kept up an unflagging flow of praise for her work, feeding her desire to be told that she was emerging as a fine actress, not a costume designer's dummy. He tried to convince her that those full-face shots she so feared did much to create a bond between her and her audience.

Toward the beginning of what was scheduled to be the last two weeks of shooting, H.P. showed up on Stage Eleven, elaborately friendly and charming. He kissed Lora and whispered to her, "I haven't had time to see the rushes, but the things I hear! Wonderful!"

To Dave Cole he whispered only, "Don't waste any time. Bring it in on schedule."

In the last dozen days the pressure began to tell on Lora. Dave remembered that Jock Finley had once said to him, "The worst trouble with a miscast actor is not that he doesn't get better. It's that the longer he continues in the role the worse he becomes. Surgery is the only treatment. Get rid of him!"

What Finley had never told Dave was what one did when the miscast performer was the star of the production and there was no possible way to replace her.

Dave detected the first signs of Lora's collapse when she went dry in a short sequence with Geoffrey Horn. It was a simple scene, demanding no great depth of emotion.

Lora simply could not remember her lines. After the fourteenth take, she finally took Dave aside and said, "It's the fucking lines! Wildberg is nothing but a hack! I want the scene rewritten!"

Though he tried to reassure her, Dave knew it was fruitless. Once an actress lost confidence, nothing but a new scene would do. At the lunch break, instead of going to the commissary, he sat down in his office and rewrote the scene himself. He dictated the new version, had it typed and mimeographed.

When Lora returned to the stage, Dave took her hand and found it cold. He couldn't let her fall apart. That would interrupt shooting, put the picture over budget. Most important, it would keep him from a new film H.P. had promised. Whatever else Dave had to do, he had to keep Lora on her feet and working before the camera. He led her to her dressing room, sat her down and improvised enthusiastically, "We're lucky! Very lucky!" She seemed to brighten with curiosity if not enthusiasm. "As I was walking toward the commissary, I ran into Leonard Greene." When she didn't react, he repeated with significance, "Leonard Greene. From Broadway. He has two plays running now. Both hits!" That impressed her. "I was responsible for the Theatre Guild doing his first play. So I insisted that he return the favor. We sat down together in my office. I told him the story, described the scene, and he went to work right then and there, and here it is!"

He presented the new pages. Lora read them intently. He had simplified her dialogue as much as he could, throwing all mandatory exposition to Geoffrey Horn. She read the pages a second time. Then she looked across at Dave and smiled. "Well, that's much better. It makes sense now."

Dave patted her hand and said, "Okay, then, let's do it." He lifted her to her feet, kissed her on the cheek and said, "Get into your costume. I'll have makeup in here in a moment."

The crew had returned and was relighting the setup. Walter Flannery asked if there were any changes Dave had in mind for camera angles, but Dave said no. Just soft lighting that would be kind to Lora. He had noticed in the rushes that dark shadows were beginning to appear beneath her eyes.

Lora played the scene, but her general nervous state heightened, made worse by the fact that H.P. had started to show up on the set every day. Though outwardly pleased, he could not conceal from Dave the deep satisfaction he was deriving from his carefully planned vengeance. Finally one day Lora became so distraught that Dave knew it was H.P.'s presence that was upsetting her. He drew H.P. aside and insisted as politely as he could, "Please, Mr. Koenig! Get off the set!"

H.P. glared. No one in the entire history of Magna had ever asked him to leave one of his own stages.

"Please?" Dave repeated. "If not for her sake, then for mine." When H.P. did not budge, Dave said, "You're not revenging yourself on me for any reason, are you?"

The little man's smooth-shaven, perfumed cheeks grew red with anger. Slowly he turned and started across the stage toward the heavy door that was topped by a large red EXIT light. Whatever secret vow he was making to repay Dave for this bit of insubordination might have dissipated had it not been for a chance

91

remark from one of the grips. Just as H.P. passed the last flat of the set, he came upon two men talking. "The old bastard!" one man muttered. "What he can't own he destroys."

H.P. did not hesitate for an instant. He seized the grip, spun him around and hit him so hard that he had to hold the man up. Then he hit him once more, splitting his lips and breaking two of his teeth. Only then did H.P. let him slip from his grasp and walk off the stage.

It happened so swiftly and so quietly that no one noticed until a second grip called after H.P.: "You dirty whoremaster! You'll pay for this!"

Dave raced to the area behind the set to find the bleeding stagehand. "Call First Aid. Get the doctor!"

The doctor had the man removed on a stretcher, since he might have suffered a concussion. That done, Dave apologized to the cast and persuaded them to go on with the rehearsal so they could get the troublesome sequence in the can before they quit for the day. Finally Dave was ready to resume his rehearsal.

But then, one by one, the huge arc lights were turned off.

"Lights!" Dave commanded.

No lights went on. Instead, the chief grip came forward and confronted Dave.

"No lights! This stage is struck! In fact, this whole fucking studio is struck!"

"What do you mean, struck?" Dave demanded.

"I just called union headquarters and told them what happened. They're pulling every man in this whole goddamn studio! Come on, boys!" They all walked out of Stage Eleven, leaving Dave, his two stars, his cast and Walter Flannery, his cameraman.

By the time Dave reached H.P.'s office, he found he was only one of more than thirty directors trying to see the old man.

Almost half an hour passed before H.P.'s door opened and Albert Grobe came out. "Gentlemen, Mr. Koenig is too busy to see each of you individually. The studio will be open in the morning at seven. The crews will be here, ready to go to work. You have his word on that. Just write off this afternoon, and we will take it into account in the event you run over schedule."

Slowly the directors began to clear the waiting room. Dave started to go with them, until Albert Grobe said to him, quietly,

"You better wait. He wants to see you." When the others were gone, Grobe showed him into the huge office. The great man was nowhere in evidence. Dave heard him call from another room. "Cole? Come in here!"

Dave started down the corridor. In the examining room he found H.P. lying face down on the massage table, covered only by a blue Turkish towel. A black masseur worked on him. Dave noticed that H.P.'s right hand, which hung over the side of the table, had a bandage on it. While the masseur worked, H.P. talked, his speech unnaturally accented by the digs and pounds of the powerful black man.

"It was your fault, the whole thing," H.P. accused.

"What whole thing?" Dave asked resentfully.

"If you hadn't ordered me off the set it would never have happened! Now I'll have to go to a lot of trouble to straighten it out."

The masseur was done. He patted H.P. on the shoulder and left the room. H.P. lay there staring up at the ceiling. In a while he said, "That cunt! What I did for that girl! Who else in the world could have made her a star? With that face? That skimpy little talent?"

He fell silent, but only for a brief time. "I loved that girl. If I wasn't a decent family man I would have divorced my wife and married her. And how did she repay me? She married that lousy tennis player!"

Dave listened, realizing that the only way the man could justify himself was to become the victim. His psychotic need to destroy Lora Lindsay was her fault. His brutally attacking the grip was Dave's fault. H.P. himself was always an innocent victim.

"Well," H.P. said, getting off the table, "we'll have to put things together again."

"Is it true, what Albert said, that we'll be back to work tomorrow?" Dave asked.

"Yes, it's true." H.P. knotted the towel around his bare middle and started toward a closet where fresh clothes were waiting for him. As he stepped into his pants he asked, "You think you'll get her through it?"

"I hope so. But the way things stand, I make no promises."

"Do it! Fast as you can. I don't want her to break down before it's done." H.P. noticed Dave glaring at him in the mirror.

93

"Twice before. Sleeping pills. I saved her both times. This time she's on her own."

Ten minutes later, H.P. was alone with Vic Martoni. "For Christ's sake, H.P., what the hell did you do this time?"

Vic Martoni was the only man in Hollywood who could talk to H. P. Koenig in that tone. H.P. sat back in his huge chair and let Martoni finish his tirade.

"Christ! This time it's out of hand! I couldn't do a thing here. I had to call national headquarters! The big man had already heard. Nobody in the unions breathes without a word from him. You know that."

"How much does he want?" H.P. asked, unruffled.

Martoni did not answer directly. "How could you hit a poor sonofabitch like that? What for?"

"He made a remark I didn't like."

Martoni continued his lament: "Two broken teeth. A broken jaw. Bad cuts inside the mouth."

"How much does he want this time?" H.P. repeated. "Fifty grand? Seventy-five?"

"We'll find out," Martoni said as he dialed the operator on H.P.'s private line. His contact in Chicago was obviously waiting for the call.

"Fats?" Martoni asked. "Vic. He's ready to deal. How much?" Martoni was not satisfied with the answer. "What do you mean? Talk to *me*! *I* handle these things!"

Fats was implacable.

H.P. finally took the phone. "Yes?" he said cautiously.

"Mr. Koenig, this is Zingone. You heard of me?" Zingone was one of the most notorious labor racketeers in the country.

"Yes, I heard of you."

"That was a very nasty thing you did, hitting a workingman who was only doing his job. I mean, the people we represent, they are good, honest, hard-working Americans. An honest day's work for an honest day's pay. That is our motto. And this man was doing that when you attacked him and best the shit out of him. In fact, I think what you done was a violation of the Wagner Labor Relations Act."

"Look, how much?" H.P. demanded.

94

"I'm trying to explain," Fats Zingone replied with meticulous patience. "You have crapped all over yourself and I am trying to figure out how to clean you up. But it is not so easy as you think. I mean, you seem to need the help of our advisory service. If you had our advice, you'd never get into this mess in the first place."

"What do you mean?" H.P. asked cautiously.

"Well, first we got the matter of the man's medical bills—"

"We'll pay them," H.P. interrupted.

"And also there is the permanent damages he suffered. Two teeth, a broken jaw—"

"Okay," H.P. agreed.

"Now, to get to the heart of the matter. If you want your studio to reopen tomorrow morning or any morning, you better agree now to retain our advisory service on an annual basis."

"How much does your 'service' cost?"

"For a studio your size, and with your enormous labor problems, say two hundred and fifty thousand," Zingone suggested, then added, "a year."

"A year!" said H.P., furious.

"We got a minimum ten-year contract," Zingone explained.

"I don't know how my stockholders would take that."

"You'd lose more than that in a single month if you had a strike," Zingone warned.

"There's all kinds of problems," H.P. countered. "I mean, we'd have to account for the money, to lawyers, accountants, stockholders."

"Oh, we have a regular form contract for situations like this," Zingone said. "I'll have our lawyers get in touch once I know we have a deal."

"Okay. We have a deal," H.P. finally agreed.

"Good. I look forward to working with you for a long, long time," Zingone said. It seemed to be his final statement until he added, "Oh, by the way, send the poor prick some flowers. It'll help to get the boys back to work tomorrow. Say something nice on them, like 'Sorry.' "

H.P. heard the phone go dead on the other end. He hung up, turned his swivel chair so he could look up at Martoni and accuse him. "You sonofabitch! You took advantage! You Wops all stick together!"

Martoni smiled. "H.P., they were looking to hit you soon any-

95

how. They got the same deal at half the studios in town. You just brought it on yourself a little bit sooner by what you did today."

Before H.P.'s resentment against him could harden, Martoni asked, "You busy tonight?"

H.P. knew what that meant. "I could be free. Why?"

"I'm having a little party. Two girls who've just come to town. One is a small blonde, looks about fifteen—"

"Jailbait!" H.P. drew back.

Martoni laughed. "I said she *looks* fifteen. Got the face of a baby and the tits of a woman. And she knows her way around. She does a blow job like you never had before."

"What time?"

"Dinner if you want."

"You know I always have dinner at home," H.P. said righteously. "Say about nine?"

"Nine," Martoni agreed. As he started out the door, H.P. spun him around. "Vic, if I find out you're getting a cut of that labor contract, I'll kill you."

Once Martoni had gone, H.P. explained the arrangement to Rob Rosenfeld, a Magna vice-president and house counsel and a protégé of his.

"Christ, H.P.," the lawyer exploded, "that's a payoff! A transparent bribe! If the stockholders ever get wind of this—"

"Rob!" H.P. interrupted. "It's your job to see that they *don't* get wind of it. Sign that contract, then bury it. If worse comes to worst, I can always say we did it for the benefit of the company. We did it to keep production going."

"H.P., *we* didn't do anything," Rosenfeld dared to correct.

"Oh, your ethics again," H.P. said, smiling but noticeably irritated.

"It's one thing for you to explain it away like that. But I'm an attorney. I could be disbarred if this ever came to light."

"Then make sure it doesn't come to light" was all the solace H.P. would give him. "Now, get it done!"

Sullenly but submissively, Rosenfeld started for the door, but H.P. stopped him, "Think of it this way, Rob. With all the Magna stock bonuses I've given you, disbarment might be a blessing. It would be like early retirement."

H.P. laughed at his own joke. Rob Rosenfeld smiled, but only faintly, a bit sick in his stomach.

The next morning, work resumed on all the stages of Magna Studios. On Stage Eleven, Lora Lindsay appeared on time but with an unusual request. She wanted to see the dailies from now till the end of shooting, a procedure she had assiduously avoided in the past.

At the lunch break Dave cornered Walter Flannery, who said, "She sees herself in this stuff she'll never finish the picture. The bastard!" It went without saying that when someone at Magna used that expression he was talking about H.P.

Dave refused to permit Lora to see the dailies, creating the first real break between them. She turned on him, abusing him in language that made some of the grips disappear behind the set. Dave knew she was nearing the breaking point. It was a race against time, and so he revised his schedule so that all her scenes were moved up and shot back to back. It added to the budget of the film, but it was the only way to get her through the ordeal.

Finally her scenes were finished. Dave consulted with his editors, who assured him that they had all the footage of her they needed to cut the final film. He released her, asking that she stand by at home, in case any retakes were necessary. He did that only to give her something to sustain her.

Two weeks later when the rough cut was finished, Dave arranged a secret screening for himself, Walter Flannery and the head cutter. They sat through one hundred and nineteen minutes of a disaster.

"Maybe when H.P. sees it, he won't release it," Flannery said hopefully.

Dave knew otherwise. He turned back to the projection booth. "Okay, guys, you can go to lunch!" Once the projectionists had left, Dave asked, "Can we talk here?"

Knowing H.P.'s propensity for listening devices, Flannery said, "Sorry, but I have a lunch date," meantime scribbling a note to Dave saying, *Meet me at the diner down on Washington Boule-*

vard. Dave nodded, handed the note to the cutter, who also nodded. Within ten minutes the three were sitting in the cramped booth safely surrounded by truck drivers, salesmen and policemen.

Dave wanted advice, all the advice he could get, from two older, more experienced men who had been brought up in films. The cutter felt that if they called Lora back and reshot three crucial scenes they might have a fighting chance. But Flannery vetoed that. He had been through many films with Lora, seen her in periods of high expectation and low despair. But he had never seen her like this. Whatever they could do would have to be done without her. The most the cutter felt he could do was eliminate her more embarrassing bits of performance.

Dave's determination was slowly being eroded. To make him feel better, Flannery said, "*You* don't have to worry. No director in Hollywood can fault you for what's on film. It shows imagination and some very good instincts. At least when Lora isn't on."

When Dave returned to his office, he found a message from H.P. Dave called back.

"I hear you've got a rough cut."

"Very rough; it needs more work," Dave evaded. "We're re-cutting right now."

"I want to preview that film in Anaheim as soon as possible," H.P. said.

"We may have to reshoot two scenes."

"We can't afford it," H.P. ordered. "We'll go with what we have. When can I have a print?"

"In a few weeks, when the editing and sound mix are done. I haven't even heard the score yet," Dave said, fighting for time.

"I'm penciling in a preview date three weeks from Friday." H.P. hung up without waiting for a reply.

Dave held the dead phone for a moment before slamming it down. The sonofabitch was implacable. He not only wanted her blood, he wanted it delivered on schedule. Dave drummed his fingers on the phone; then, not trusting his own secretary, he placed a long-distance call himself to Gloria Simms. Gloria was down in Washington seeing a new play one of her clients had written. Betty took his call. Dave insisted on contacting the author of the play on which the film was based. While Dave held on, Betty reached the author's agent on the phone, secured his number up in Connecticut.

"Ogden? Dave Cole."

"Oh," the playwright said, not particularly pleased, since he still remembered that Dave had originally refused to direct his play.

"Og, you know I'm doing the picture."

"Yes! With that 'brilliant' American actress Lora Lindsay."

Instead of arguing, Dave said, "Okay, okay, so she's terrible." Dave always used that technique with recalcitrant stars and authors. Find something to agree on, then proceed to the real issue.

"Og, bear one thing in mind. Lousy as she is, when your next play comes up and your agent is looking for a preproduction deal, what will the studios say? 'Hell, look at his last play. Magna did it as a film and it turned out to be a disaster.' So it isn't a matter of what happens to her. Or even to me. It's what the film will do to *your* reputation."

Silence from the other end told Dave that Spencer was well aware of the backlash.

"Now, Og, I want to know one thing. In any previous draft of the play did you have anything that could make it the man's story rather than the woman's?"

Dave waited tensely.

"Well, matter of fact, in the first draft I had a prologue and an epilogue. The man came out and did it in one."

"By himself?" Dave asked, encouraged for the first time. "Could it work on film?"

"If you took him back to the scene at the fountain. Where their last farewell takes place."

"The fountain," Dave said. That set was still standing, thank God. "Okay, Og, listen to me. Send me a copy of your version with the prologue and epilogue!" When Spencer hesitated, Dave pressed. "It's a matter of life and death! Send it airmail special!"

Monday night the script was delivered to Dave Cole at the Château Marmont. He spent the night on it. By morning he had rewritten the material to fit the screenplay. He called Vic Martoni and asked him to use his muscle in getting H.P. to permit him to reshoot two scenes. Martoni called him within fifteen minutes.

"Does the reshooting involve Lora Lindsay?" the agent asked.

"No. Only Geoffrey Horn."

"If it's not Lora, H.P. said okay. Only don't take more than two days. And no overtime."

"Okay! Okay, Vic; thanks a million."

Within hours Dave had arranged the shooting schedule. One day on the prologue, one day on the epilogue. Geoffrey Horn was called back. Dave told Thornhill to make up Horn so that it would be clear that the prologue took place years after the rest of the film. He asked Walter Flannery to light the set as if the action were taking place on a winter evening. With process shots as background they could re-create the New York scene.

He took Horn aside before the shooting and worked with him on his lines, impressing on him that his chance to salvage his role in the film lay in the prologue and epilogue.

Dave took one more precaution. He called the chief grip aside and asked him to foul up the microphone so that H.P. could not listen in on Stage Eleven. When the man demurred, Dave reminded, "He's the bastard who put one of your crew in the hospital."

With the head cutter at his side, with Walter Flannery on the camera, Dave ran Geoffrey Horn through the prologue. Then the three conspirators huddled in a corner.

"Will it cut?"

"It'll cut."

"Will it give us a strange eerie feeling that will overhang the whole film?" Dave asked Flannery.

"I'll add a little out-of-focus feeling," Flannery volunteered.

"Great. Let's do it."

They shot the prologue in seven hours. The next day they came back and shot the epilogue. There was no flak from the front office, no word from H.P. The old man wanted to know only one thing. Would an edited film be ready to preview in two weeks? Dave's answer was yes.

After they had watched the dailies Dave insisted on viewing the entire rough cut, first without the prologue and epilogue and then with the prologue and epilogue cut in. There was a tremendous difference. It made the film Geoffrey Horn's picture. It enabled them to cut Lora even more. At midnight, when Dave was done, he had a much stronger film than anyone would have expected.

Like all capitals, Hollywood runs on guts, nerve and gossip. Before seven the next morning Lora Lindsay was on the phone. During the incoherent tirade that followed, Dave realized that she had heard about the additional shooting.

"You're trying to ruin me! I never should have let any young bastard from New York direct me! Lora Lindsay deserves the best. You are an untalented, deceitful shit! . . ."

Suddenly her voice faded. Her husband must have wrested the phone from her hand, for Dave was cut off.

When Lora's agent asked that she be allowed to go to Anaheim for the preview, permission was refused. When H.P. saw her husband trying to slip into the theater, he ordered, "Get that fucking tennis player out of here!" The man was removed before the film was allowed to begin.

Too nervous to sit, Dave paced in the back of the house. The opening titles rolled by, the prologue was on. Backed by appropriately haunting music, it was an impressive piece of film and set the mood for the rest of the picture. Since Lora's scenes had been edited, the focus and the sympathy had subtly shifted to Geoffrey Horn. By the time the film was over and Walter Flannery was starting up the aisle, the preview audience was applauding. Walter seized Dave's hand and said, "Thanks. For everybody."

"Will it do it for *her*?" Dave asked.

"It won't hurt her," Flannery said, "and that's a miracle."

H.P. strode up the aisle, a portrait of angry frustration. He didn't stop to talk to Dave but gave an order to Sonny Brown: "I want to see those audience-reaction cards!"

In the manager's office, H.P., Sonny Brown and Dave Cole culled the cards, calling out any comment of significance.

"Here's one likes it very much."

"This one likes Geoffrey Horn."

"This one even likes Lora Lindsay."

" 'Loved the picture, loved Geoffrey Horn!' How do you like that?"

The cards were being placed in two piles, favorable and unfavorable. The favorables were outrunning the unfavorables by three to one. H.P. grew more and more grim with frustration.

They had almost finished when the phone rang. Sonny answered, then swiftly handed the phone to H.P.

"We have to get back to L.A.!" H.P. ordered. "Right away!"

"What happened?"

"She slashed her wrists," H.P. said. He tossed his stack of cards on the desk and walked out.

They drove back to Los Angeles in silence—H.P., Sonny Brown and Dave Cole. As they drew near the city, Brown instructed the chauffeur to drive to Cedars of Lebanon. But H.P. countermanded the order. They were going to Lora's home first. Brown was puzzled, but he never questioned any order of H.P.'s.

They were greeted by several weeping maids. H.P. ordered them to their quarters. He went directly into the living room. Without any preamble or explanation, he picked up a heavy onyx ashtray and hurled it through the lanai door.

Dave attributed the vindictive action to H.P.'s fury and asked no questions as they reboarded the limousine and sped off to the hospital.

By four o'clock in the morning, infusions of blood having failed to help, Lora Lindsay died. In addition to her husband, Dave Cole, Sonny Brown and H. P. Koenig were in the waiting room when the word came down. H.P. gestured to Brown. They moved to a corner for some whispered conversation. Brown took Lora's dazed husband by the arm and led him from the waiting room.

As Dave walked down the long, silent corridor, he saw Brown in heated conversation with the tennis player. Something changed hands. Brown started back to the waiting room. When Dave reached the front door of the private pavilion, the police were holding back an army of photographers and reporters. Fortunately, Dave was unknown to them and was allowed to pass unchallenged.

In minutes, H.P., Sonny and Lora's husband appeared. H.P. seemed distraught. Tears flowed freely from his eyes and he

102

ignored the insistent demands of the reporters and photographers. Brown raised his hands to restore quiet. Carefully and precisely, as if he were reading from a press release, Sonny said:

"Lora Lindsay is dead, from wounds that occurred when she accidentally walked through a glass lanai door of her home. It's an enormous shock to Magna Studio and to her fans. Sharing her husband's grief is H. P. Koenig, who brought her up from a bit player to become one of Magna's most talented and illustrious stars. All of Hollywood mourns her loss. Now, if you don't mind, no more questions."

Brown made way for H.P. to move through the crowd. They entered H.P.'s limousine, and as the car started away, Brown handed a note to H.P. Even in the dim glow of the car light he could read the bitter words:

Good-bye to all of Hollywood, my friends and my enemies. Especially to those who conspired to destroy me. But above all to that monster H. P. Koenig. He used me and when I didn't want to be used anymore he tried to destroy me. The world should be warned against bastards like him. I hate him and I want the world to know that those were Lora Lindsay's last words. I hate him!

H.P. crumpled the letter in anger.
"The police or anyone else see it?"
"He said no."
"Good." In a moment, H.P. asked, "What does he want?"
"A contract."
"To do what, play tennis?" H.P. asked bitterly.
"A lifetime contract to act."
"Act?" H.P. pondered a moment. "Okay. Start negotiations. String them out long enough for this to die down. *But never make the deal.*"

Two days later, Lora Lindsay was buried in Forest Lawn amid a crowd of vulturously curious fans. H.P., David Cole, Geoffrey Horn, and Walter Flannery served as honorary pallbearers. H.P. cried all the way from his limousine to her grave and at the last moment threw a single red rose into the grave.

They were driven back to the studio together—H.P., Dave Cole and Sonny Brown.

"You did a hell of a job on the picture, Cole," H.P. said. "I think you're ready for bigger and better scripts."

Dave didn't answer, not even to say thank you. Was it praise he was being fed, or a bribe? In a while H.P. spoke again.

"I guess she realized age was catching up with her. That's the trouble with stars. They can never retire gracefully."

No one in the car contradicted him.

The picture opened six weeks later. The reviews were not raves, but Dave was lauded as a promising young director who had brought a touch of the theater's realism to Hollywood. Two important critics mourned the fact that Lora Lindsay died at a time when she was just beginning to reveal an unsuspected depth and maturity. Though Dave knew that that promise would never have been realized, he derived some satisfaction from knowing that in the end he had ensured a decent epitaph for the unfortunate woman.

7

After the tragic experience with Lora Lindsay, Dave decided that he would make one more film to solidify his position in the picture business, then go back East and devote himself to Broadway. He had alerted Gloria and Betty to notify him when they came across a promising new playscript.

This evening he returned to his office, tired from a day on the set, and found a message from Betty. He called the office, then realized it was already past nine o'clock in the evening in New York. He tried her at home.

"Betty?"

"Dave, we found it! A new script by Ogden Spencer. Very exciting. They want to go into rehearsal right after Christmas.

"Fine! I'll be done in plenty of time. Airmail it to me."

"He hopes you'll do it. Especially since you were thoughtful enough to call him on his other play and ask about that prologue and epilogue."

"If I like it, I'll do it," Dave promised.

Night after next, the script was waiting at his hotel. He took a swim, had just one drink and settled down to read. He liked the situation but found some points of disagreement with the plot development. He left an early-morning call so he could phone East before going off to the studio. He reached Ogden Spencer, discussed his suggestions. When Spencer agreed they were feasible, Dave said, "Okay, Og! I'll finish up here and come

East. Meantime, go to work on the revisions and send me pages!"

Dave went off to the studio feeling more invigorated than he had in some weeks.

He finished shooting his next film, meticulously superintended the editing, viewed the rough cut and sat in on the recording of the music track and then the final mix. The film was done! Those who saw it agreed it was good. Even Albert Grobe, who was always friendly but never gave up his right to be a forthright critic, liked it. A date was set down to preview the picture out of town. Riverside, this time.

Dave was invited to ride in H.P.'s limousine. Along with them was Albert Grobe. The three of them sat in back, while Sonny Brown rode up front with the chauffeur. Behind H.P.'s limousine followed a procession of studio cars bearing publicity men and advisers whom H.P. trusted in determining whether or not to make further revisions in the film.

Each car was provisioned with food and drink for the long trip, so that no time was lost stopping along the way.

As Albert Grobe doled out the Scotch, H.P. remarked a bit sadly, "Oh, how Marvin Kronheim used to love these outings! Of course, he always insisted on using the private car."

"Private car?" Dave asked.

"In those days we had a private railroad car, outfitted like a club with a buffet table, a bar, card tables. A man could really enjoy the trip. But once Marvin was gone, somehow all the fun went out of it. Oh, how I miss that boy."

Albert tried to avoid Dave's eyes. They both remembered Albert's description of what really happened the night Marvin Kronheim died and H.P. became sole and undisputed head of the studio.

Dave's picture was good. The reaction cards were favorable. There were always a few carpers, but most of the audience liked the story, liked the stars, enjoyed the picture, would even pay to see it again.

On the way back, H.P. reached over several times to punctuate his remarks by patting Dave on the thigh.

"You know, kid, I didn't think you'd reach this point as a director in just two films. I thought you'd louse up four or five pictures before you learned how to use a camera right."

H.P. was quiet for a moment. Then he said, "You know, Larry Holtzman came up to me after the preview and asked if I would assign you to the film he's getting ready for production."

Larry Holtzman was a name Dave had heard for years, a name highly respected in the picture industry. Holtzman's request was a compliment of no small importance. But it was a problem, too. Dave had already worked out in his mind the way in which he was going to notify H.P. that he was going back East to do a play. Now he would have to face the problem head on.

"H.P.," Dave began, "actually what I was planning on doing next was going back East."

"Back East," H.P. repeated as if he were mouthing the foulest of obscenities.

"To direct a play," Dave hastened to explain. "Ogden Spencer's new play."

"Spencer . . ." H.P. tried to recall. "Spencer? Didn't he write that piece of shit that Lora was in just before she died? That's probably what killed her. Spencer!" He turned to Albert Grobe. "Remind me never to buy anything that sonofabitch writes!"

"Of course, H.P.," Grobe said perfunctorily.

"This is a good play," Dave said. "It could make a terrific film for Tracy and Hepburn."

"I don't want to hear about it!" H.P. glowered and remained silent for the rest of the trip.

The limousine dropped off H.P. first, then Dave. As he got out of the huge car, Albert Grobe said, "Dave, anytime you have something like that to say, let Martoni do it. And never say anything that spoils a night of triumph like this one."

When Dave arrived at his office the next morning there was a command waiting. H.P. wanted to see him. He took the elevator two stories up to the executive floor. When he entered the office, he found H.P.'s huge chair swung around so that only its back greeted him.

"Gratitude!" said the little man without turning around. "Not many men in this business, in this world, would give a kid like you such a chance. And don't tell me what you did on Broadway. You think that's a big deal, to take seven or eight people and a script and spend four weeks rehearsing it and turn out a play? You like to tell each other that it's art. But I say it's shit! Pictures! That's the art of the twentieth century! I have had a greater effect on the human race than any man who has lived till now. What I decide at this desk affects people all over the world. Magna films are an international language! All this I offer you and you want to go back and do plays!"

"H.P.—"

"From now on, you will call me Mr. Koenig!"

"Okay," Dave said, and added earnestly, "Mr. Koenig, nothing in my decision to go back was a reflection on you. I am a director. My profession is to direct plays as well as pictures. I've done two pictures. I'd like to go back and do a play as a change of pace; that's all there is to it."

"So that's all there is to it?" H.P. demanded, slowly swinging his chair around to face Dave Cole for the first time. "Did you really think you could fool me?"

"I didn't intend to fool anyone. I'm being as open and honest as I can."

"It's obvious you don't care about gratitude. And you don't give a damn about me. Or what I've tried to do for you. Well, at least think of yourself! Your own career! Everybody knows a man doesn't leave Hollywood unless he's failed! If you go back now it means that I canceled your contract."

"All I want is three months to cast and rehearse a play."

"All *I* want is that in three months you should be in production with Larry Holtzman's picture!" H.P. declared. "If you leave here now I will consider it a breach of your contract."

"I never intended to breach my contract. I thought we would discuss it and you would agree to a leave of absence."

"Young man, you may not consider *my* interests, but I'm not built like that. I feel it is my duty to warn you what a breach of contract means in this town."

H.P. got up, started to pace and talk.

"You won't be the first one who's had to have a little education in the sanctity of contracts."

He turned to his gallery of portraits.

"Look up there! See him? And her? And her? The biggest stars in Magna Studios. They too wanted to go do a play. Or take time off to go on vacation. Or get fucked. Or any other goddamned thing that came into their crazy minds. I put them on suspension! Couldn't work. Couldn't earn a dime! I pay out bigger money than anyone in the world. All I ask in return is a little consideration. But it seems that's too much to ask."

Slowly the man trudged back to his desk, slumped into his huge chair, covered his face with his hands. Soon Dave heard little gasps and he realized H.P. was weeping. Dave knew that H.P. could cry on cue. But before long Dave felt truly compassionate and apologetic for having reduced the man to this state.

He waited guiltily until the old man wiped his eyes and looked up at him.

"I thought, I found him at last. My new Marvin Kronheim. Then you go and do something like this," H.P. said. "It will take a long time to restore my faith in human nature. A long time."

"It's only three months I want—" Dave tried to say.

"It isn't the three months! It's the deception! Last night driving out to Riverside, I felt I was with a friend, a son. And you sat there like a viper hiding such a secret from me. On the way back you let me go on and on about how much I loved your picture. It didn't matter to you that back in New York your agent, that shmuck playwright Spencer, his agent, your producer, they were all laughing at H. P. Koenig. They had snatched you away from me. With your connivance! Why is it that people always pick on me? Because I've succeeded? Because they're jealous of me? Why?"

He rose from his chair, held out his hand. "I want you to know that I hold no grudges. I wish you luck. But I want to warn you now that if you're banking on the success of your new film to bring you back here in triumph, you're going to be sadly mistaken.

"Because I will bury that film! There will be no budget for advertising or publicity. It may go down on the books as an artistic triumph, but it will be a box-office disaster. A year from now you won't be able to get yourself arrested in this town! Now go, and good luck!"

They shook hands—H.P. not exerting any pressure, merely allowing his hand to be shaken.

"If you had come to me like an honest man," H.P. said suddenly, "and said what was really on your mind, I would have respected you. But no, you chose to do it this underhanded way."

Dave looked down at the man, totally baffled.

"Admit it! After last night's success you want a new contract, don't you?"

"No, I give you my word," Dave protested.

"You would have done better to be honest about it."

When Dave returned to his office, he realized he had a visitor. He knew it even before he entered the room. The fragrance of Martoni's cologne hung in the air.

"Close the door, kid," the agent ordered. Dave bristled. Without raising his voice Martoni repeated, "I said, close the door."

Dave closed the door and dropped into his desk chair.

"Look, we were all young once. H.P. Me. All of us." Martoni spoke softly, but there was the clear undertone of a threat inherent in his words. "What is it, kid? What's back there? A piece of cunt? Tell H.P. He'll bring her out here. Even give her a contract. The old man only wants to make you happy."

"I only want to go back and direct a play." Dave tried to make himself understood.

"An ambitious man like you doesn't destroy his whole career in pictures just to direct a play."

"Christ!" Dave exploded. "I'm not plotting to commit a murder! I'm just trying to take three months to direct a play that I happen to believe in."

"There's some cunt in the play," yelled Martoni.

"The play isn't even cast yet!" Dave shouted back.

"A young buck your age can't see past his own prick if it's stiff!"

"Look, I don't think this discussion is going to get anywhere," Dave said, starting for the door.

Martoni didn't budge. "How did it end up between you and the old man?"

"We shook hands and he said I could go."

"Shook hands?" Martoni asked, attaching unusual significance to that action.

"Yes," Dave said.

"Too bad," Martoni concluded sadly.

"Why?"

"You heard about the kiss of death?"

"The Mafia signal?"

"Right. When the old man shakes hands under such circumstances, it can mean only one thing. He thinks you double-crossed him. You're going on the Hollywood blacklist." Martoni got up, indicating he had washed his hands of Dave.

"Call Gloria," he said. "She'll wrap this up."

Within the hour Dave Cole received a call from Betty Ronson.

"Dave, I got a call from Vic Martoni—"

"I know," Dave said grimly.

"So I talked to Og Spencer. He won't hold you to a deal that would mean jeopardizing your career. If you want out, he'll understand."

"I think it's gone too far for that."

"Maybe not," Betty said hopefully.

"What do you mean?"

"Og's agent got a call from Walter Fleishmann, head of Magna's Story Department here in New York. They want to make a preproduction deal for the play."

"What?" Dave said incredulously. "H.P. said he would never buy a Spencer property again!"

"It has nothing to do with the play. It has only to do with you."

"He wants me to do the play first and then the picture?" Dave asked, relieved.

"You'll never get to do the play. That's why H.P. is buying it. The one thing he can't stand is losing. The second thing he can't stand is to have anyone walk away from him. *He's* got to do the walking away. This'll give him the last word," Betty explained. "So what I advise you to do is apologize. Else you'll be black-listed out there and have no play to come back to here."

If there was one thing Dave Cole was determined not to do, it was apologize to H. P. Koenig. "If this is the reward for making a good picture, I wonder what would have happened if I'd made a bad one!"

"Absolutely nothing. This is H.P.'s highest form of praise. He wants you enough to destroy you."

"Yeah," Dave said, not too happy about being wanted in quite that way.

"Look, Dave. You apologize to H.P. I'll talk to Martoni about getting you a new contract on better terms."

"You think you can?" Dave asked.

"H.P. wants possession. Let's make him pay for it."

111

Later that afternoon, Betty Ronson called Vic to tell him that Dave Cole could be persuaded to remain at Magna, provided his contract was renegotiated so that it would reflect the success of his latest film.

Martoni was profuse in his praise.

"Girlie, I've never seen you, but you must really be something. That's a terrific idea you came up with—to get H.P. to buy Spencer's new play and shut Cole out of it! It's the kind of thing I should have thought of!" He laughed in open appreciation of her stroke of strategy.

Much as she appreciated his praise, she did not permit herself to be diverted.

"Don't forget the deal I want for Cole."

"It's do-able. I'll get it," Martoni assured her. Then he added, "What's a bright girl like you doing wasting her time in New York? Get smart. Come out here. I'll show you where the gold really is."

"Let's talk about it sometime." It was what Betty had had in mind all along.

She hung up quickly before Martoni could pursue the subject. Just as H.P. desperately wanted what he could not have, so Martoni would want her more if he felt she was not anxious to make a deal with him.

As for Dave, whatever career risk she had exposed him to, she was able to justify it on the ground that he had deceived her in the past.

Besides, it had worked. And that was all the justification necessary.

It took Dave Cole two whole days before he could force himself to call Sarah Immerman and request a meeting with H.P. The meeting was not arranged until four days later.

The afternoon of his appointment arrived. Dave showed up in the waiting room on time and knew just how long he would be forced to wait.

Two hours later, the receptionist said, "Mr. Koenig will see you now, Mr. Cole."

He entered the huge office and found H.P. standing at the window that faced out toward the entire Magna lot. His hands were clasped behind his back and his feet spread apart.

Dave suddenly realized the old bastard was doing an imitation of Charles Laughton in *Mutiny on the Bounty.* Dave had heard that H.P. had a penchant for imitating some gesture or pose that a star of his had made famous.

"You wanted to see me?" H.P. asked without turning to face Dave.

"Yes."

"Well?" H.P. asked, pained, as if the breach between them were beyond healing.

"Mr. Koenig," Dave said, "I wanted to say I'm sorry about the past unpleasantness. I guess working in the theater, where a director's with a production for ten or fifteen weeks, I didn't realize the sanctity of long-term contracts. If I had, I would never have agreed to go back without first coming to you and discussing it."

Dave required a moment of hesitation before he could bring himself to add, "And of course, abiding by your decision."

There was silence, a discreet but uncertain silence. The little man used the moment to build suspense. Dave remembered that when he was a small boy his father used to do the same. The punishment was not in the whipping but in the uncertainty that preceded it.

Dave had never liked the word "deign." It was archaic, stilted and foreign to his vocabulary. In the Bronx no one "deigned." The principal at Morris High School did not "deign." At City College, not even the august Dean of Students "deigned." But for H. P. Koenig, the only word Dave could think of was that the old bastard finally "deigned" to turn and face him. As if turning God's shining and forgiving countenance upon him.

"My boy," H.P. said, "I can understand that someone like you, young, impetuous, might think that it is a small thing to decide to go back East for a few months. I want you to know that I like to see a young man throw himself into something like that, with all the *risks* it entails. I mean, if you went back and the play failed, your agent would have had to throw you on the block."

H.P. reached up and put his hand on Dave's shoulder.

"I was only protecting you from what could have been a very

dangerous mistake. It may not have seemed that way to you. I know how my actions are interpreted by others. People seize on every opportunity to slander me. In the last twenty years we have been through the worst depression and the worst war in our history. People look to Magna and to me for a little sunshine, a little cheer. To make sure they get it, I have to appear to be a tyrant sometimes. I have to make men like you stick to the business of making pictures instead of deserting the country for a handful of admirers back in New York. The critics may be in New York. But the audience is west of the Hudson," H.P. proclaimed as if he were setting foot on the soil of the New World for the first time.

"I thought . . ." H.P. modulated his voice as if giving vent to an intimate personal revelation. "I thought for a time that we understood each other. That you sensed these things about me. I was wrong. But I go on hoping that one day you will. So . . ." H.P. paused as if he were reaching a previously undetermined decision. "I have decided that we should start off on a new foot. With a new contract."

Dave realized that Betty Ronson and Vic Martoni had gone to work swiftly.

"Yes, a new start deserves a new contract. Your salary will go from a thousand a week to fifteen hundred. With increases every thirteen weeks till it reaches four thousand."

"Thank you."

"Now I'll tell you what I want *you* to do. As a token of good faith. Move out of that hotel you're staying at. The Marmont is a place where all you New York refugees gather so you can make jokes at our expense. Think of yourself as one of us. Get a house. Say to yourself, From now on I belong here. This is my home. Hollywood, U.S.A.!"

"I'll think about it."

"While you're thinking, remember it doesn't do any harm to live like a man earning a lot of money. To show you what I mean, I would like you to come to a little dinner at my home Friday night. I'm screening a new film. It'll do you a lot of good to be seen there. Lolly will be there. She'll be sure to note the appearance of a new face at my table."

There was no need to explain who Lolly was. Louella. Though her writing talent was meager, her employer's many newspapers had endowed her column with great power. She held sway as the most important syndicated gossip columnist in the nation by virtue of printing only praise about the actress of modest abilities who was her employer's mistress.

Dave did not minimize the opportunity that H.P. was according him, even though he resented it. But curiosity prompted him to accept the invitation. When he did, H.P. patted him gently on the cheek. All had been forgiven. But only because in the end H.P. had had his way.

That evening a call came in to Betty Ronson, who was working late at the office. It was from Vic Martoni.

"Baby, it worked. Like a charm. Congratulations!"

"Dave went to him and apologized?"

"He did."

"Good!" Betty said, then asked. "You're sure Dave doesn't suspect anything?"

"Not a thing. He's delighted with his new contract. And H.P.'s delighted with his new property. Perfect all around."

"Okay," Betty said thoughtfully.

"Did you give any thought to my suggestion?" Martoni asked. "It could mean an interest in the agency out here."

"I'll think on it," she said, even though she had made up her mind once he had offered a cut of the business. "And I'll let you know."

"Terrific!"

Betty waited several weeks before she gave Martoni her answer. The time lapse not only would give her leverage with him, but would enable her to make a better deal with Gloria Simms for her half of the New York agency.

She called and gave Martoni her word that she would join his agency, provided that all the clients she brought with her were to be considered signed by her personally and to remain her properties if she were ever to leave the Martoni agency.

For a young woman of only twenty-six she had made herself quite a deal.

When Dave Cole approached the spacious Koenig estate on the quiet street off Sunset Boulevard, he thought there had been a recent crime. Four uniformed Beverly Hills policemen guarded the entrance. Dave drove up to the circular driveway, where he was forced to identify himself. Once he was checked out on the guest list, he was instructed to leave his car. One of the policemen drove it away and parked it out of sight.

The huge house was a replica of a French château. It looked so unreal and overpowering Dave felt sure that once the door opened he would discover it was only an enormous scenic flat. A tall butler answered his ring and led Dave across a long black-and-white marble foyer to the living room. Most of the guests had already arrived. Though he knew none of them personally, he recognized Lolly, a United States Senator, the head of a large Wall Street banking house, Gable, Astaire and a well-known Catholic Monsignor whose parish was the world of the wealthy and famous.

As soon as H.P. saw Dave, he led him about the room introducing him. Enough rich hors d'oeuvres were served to make dinner unnecessary, but in half an hour Dave found himself in a dining room that he decided would make an ideal setting for an English baronial film. The long table accommodated thirty-six. Dave sat near the foot of the table close by Mrs. Koenig, a small woman, running to fleshiness. She spoke meticulously, as though still trying to overcome a Lower East Side accent. Across the table from him sat a slender dark-haired girl with deep, piercing black eyes who looked strangely familiar. He could not place her, though she continued to stare at him with undisguised interest. Each time he caught her glance she gave him a small, provocative smile.

After dinner the guests moved into the library for coffee. Dave studied several unattached female stars whom he had not met on the lot. In particular one blonde whose reputation made her especially intriguing. Dave was engaged in taking this sexual inventory when a voice behind him said, "Not her."

He turned swiftly to face the girl with the mischievous eyes who had sat opposite him at dinner.

"I hear she's a terrible lay. She'll talk you to death. Before, during and after. At least, that's what all the men say."

She smiled. Dave finally smiled too.

"Hi, I'm David Cole."

"Sally Ann Weston," she replied.

"Sally Ann..." he started to repeat, then stopped, remembering where he had met her. "You said that wasn't your real name."

"It isn't."

"Then what is?"

"Sybil," she said, with a finality that indicated she expected he should now recognize her. When he didn't, she laughed. "God, don't tell me no one warned you."

"Warned me about what?"

"Who I am. And why you're here," she said, enjoying his discomfort.

"H.P. said I'm here to meet people. The 'right' people," he added sarcastically.

"The only 'right' people you're here to meet is *me*. I'm Sybil Koenig."

"Oh," said David.

"That's not what you're expected to say. You're expected to be impressed. And entranced. I'm supposed to be a dark and fascinating beauty. But I can see neither of us are what we're supposed to be."

The butler arrived at that moment to announce that the movie was ready. H.P. shepherded his guests toward his miniature theater, with its richly upholstered easy chairs. He glanced toward Dave and Sybil.

"Play it smart," Sybil whispered, taking his sleeve. "Don't go."

"He's waiting." Dave returned her conspiratorial tone.

"He *wants* to wait. Just stay right here!"

Dave called out to H.P., "Be there in a moment."

Instead of appearing annoyed, H.P. smiled approvingly and joined his guests.

Dave and Sybil were alone now except for the butler, who was gathering up glasses and emptying ashtrays.

"Let's get out of here," she said as she took Dave's hand and led him onto the patio and into a garden that was meticulously cultivated. It had been lit by the head of Magna's highly expert Lighting Department. Being only a recent resident of this magical city, Dave was still not used to the idea that plants and trees, magnificent in themselves, needed to be colored with subtly placed red, green, amber and blue lights. The effect was

117

as synthetic as Hollywood itself.

She led him past the lighted trees—tall palms that inclined tiredly, elephantine tamarisks, magnolias heavy with fragrance. They went up a slight incline to a huge lighted swimming pool.

"Sit," Sybil said, pushing him toward one of the pool chairs. Then she dropped to the close-cropped lawn, tucked her long skirt under her legs, kicked off her slippers and teased the cool grass with her toes. Dave noticed she had delicate feet, slender as she herself was and as nicely shaped.

"You're Jewish, aren't you?" she said.

He nodded.

"Good. That'll make this easier. You know what a *shadchen* is."

"A matchmaker," Dave answered.

"We don't talk Yiddish around here. But my grandmother, when she was alive, used to tell me about the old days." Sybil laughed. "Well, we're back to the old days."

She had a warm laugh. Her dark eyes were saucy and had a way of making her points for her. "Only instead of calling in a matchmaker, Papa does it himself. He doesn't trust anyone else to find the right man for his daughter, who is becoming a problem of sorts."

"What's the problem?" Dave asked, able to relax with her now.

"Me. Twenty-four and an old maid," she said, still smiling. "So he picked you. He always fixes on some young man he thinks might make a good husband for his daughter and a good father for his grandsons. It's a wonder he didn't run a semen test on you to discover your breeding possibilities."

He laughed. At least she had a sense of humor about the situation.

"Then he sets up a trial run to see if you've got the guts to stand up to him. That whole brouhaha about your going East was a test to see if you'd buck him. And if you did, whether in the end you'd finally bend to his wishes. That's most important. He doesn't respect an abject man. But neither will he tolerate anyone who'll fight him to a finish.

"You passed both tests with flying colors. Not many candidates get to one of his Friday-night screenings. By Monday morning you'll be famous."

She cocked her head to look up at him. "I'll say one thing for

118

you; you're the best candidate yet. You're talented too."

"A little."

"More than a little. I heard what you did to save poor Lora's reputation. Though in the end it didn't help, did it?"

"No, it didn't," he admitted sadly.

"At least she went out with a few good reviews."

Sybil dug her toes into the grass. "He thinks you have tremendous potential," she said finally. "That's one reason he wants you to marry me. He wants to keep Magna in the family."

The import of her statement stunned Dave. Was this another of her jokes?

"I'm serious," she said. "And the only reason I'm talking to you so frankly is that your problem is mine too. One thing I have promised myself: He is not going to run me. He is not going to decide when and with whom I conceive and give birth. I want my sons to be my sons, not his grandsons."

She frowned as if she'd revealed too much.

Out of respect for her confidence, Dave was silent for a minute. Then he asked, "Is that why you came to New York? To escape?"

"Uh-huh. I wanted to make my own way in a branch of show business where I wouldn't be dependent on him or dominated by him."

"Where you could just be 'Sally Ann Weston'?"

"God, that was a terrible name to pick, wasn't it?"

"Sally Ann Westons should be blond, with turned-up noses. You're not a cliché."

"I guess you can't be the daughter of an original like H. P. Koenig and be a cliché," she said. "I didn't make it in New York, anyway."

"Couldn't even work for free?" he asked.

"I did get a job with one producer. And I was damned good until Josh Logan recognized me at an out-of-town tryout. After that, it started. The producer wanted me to get Magna to make a preproduction deal; the male star wanted me to put in a good word for him for a part in a new Magna film; the playwright, a nice young man with whom I'd got to be rather close, wanted me to get him a deal out here. Everybody wanted something. I was H.P.'s daughter all over again. That's when I realized there was no escaping it. That's my fate."

"Did you know I was coming to dinner tonight?"

"Yes," she admitted.

Then another and more disturbing thought occurred to him. "Did you have anything to do with my being signed by Magna?" he asked.

"No!" she replied firmly. Then she smiled. "You see why it's no fun being H.P.'s daughter. It poisons everything. You're imagining all sorts of devious plots already. No, Mr. Cole, I did not have anything to do with your being brought out here!"

She turned away, her dark eyes sad now. It gave her added beauty.

"I wish we'd met again under other circumstances," he said.

"Don't say anything just to be polite or considerate. It isn't called for. And it can only get you into trouble."

"Why?"

"Because this won't come to anything. The nicest thing I can do for you is tell my father that I didn't care for you. That'll let you off the hook."

"And if you told him you *did* care?"

"Then he'd insist you marry me. And you'd have to. He can make anyone in this town do anything he wants."

She turned to face him. "Davie, go home. Before you get hurt."

"I can take care of myself."

"Sure. The same way you arranged to return to New York and direct that play."

He didn't reply, but reached over, drew her close and kissed her. When he released her she remained motionless except for a slight tremor that ran through her body.

"Now you *better* get out of town," she whispered. "Because I *do* like you. And that'll be bad for both of us in the end."

"Does it have to be?"

"That's the sad part. It doesn't have to be. It just always is," she said. "We'd better go in. The screening will be over soon."

They started for the house. He reached for her hand, but she pulled away and walked ahead of him with a natural grace. She was one of the most honest women he had ever met. She was also the only woman who had ever refused him. It was both frustrating and refreshing.

8

Sybil had been right about one thing. Once Dave Cole was invited to the Koenig home, his social status soared.

Agents schemed to have young actresses meet him. Word spread that if Dave Cole whispered your name into H.P.'s ear, your fortune in Hollywood was made. Actually, once Sybil informed her father that the young director did not particularly appeal to her, H.P.'s enthusiasm for Dave Cole cooled somewhat.

Dave saw Sybil only twice in the next few weeks, each time when some foreign dignitary came to make the grand tour of the Magna lot. H.P. insisted that Sybil attend such receptions, although her mother always contrived to avoid them.

On both occasions when Dave and Sybil met, she seemed polite and superficially cordial. The second time, he lingered at her side during cocktails.

"I'd like to see you. May I call?"

"No."

"Why not?"

"Because I happen to be deep in an affair with our Japanese gardener."

Before Dave could say anything more, she was halfway across the room to greet one of Magna's stars.

Dave Cole's days were filled with work. Shooting a film was exhausting physically, emotionally. The interminable waits between setups were different from the constant drive during the production of a play. The impetus of theater rehearsals was like the sex act. Feeding on itself, demanding more and more till the inevitable climax of opening night. By contrast, the daily tempo of filming was like interrupted sex play that only created frustration. Dave's impatience was so pronounced that his cinematographer urged him, "Take it easy, relax. Spend a little more time in your dressing room. Or someone else's dressing room."

It was no secret whom the cameraman meant. Lush blond Christine Donlan was notorious for having affairs with either her leading man or her director.

Just then Dave's assistant came up and interrupted him. Dave could tell by the look on the young man's face that there was trouble.

"What now?"

"She's unhappy."

"What is it this time?"

"Her last line in the scene. She'd like to change it for the close-ups."

"I'll discuss it with her when we get into the scene. Meantime get hold of the writer and ask him to hurry down."

"Dave, unless you want to have a scene before you do the scene, take my advice, see her now," the assistant suggested gingerly. "She's threatening not to come out of her dressing room."

"Okay," Dave said wearily.

For directors, life was an endless series of confrontations with stars. Dave had discovered that you could beguile a male star with challenges, or divert him by seeming to join in a conspiracy against the author and the producer.

Actresses were a different problem. They were more emotional. They had the advantage of tears. And there was always the imminent threat of a nervous breakdown.

Grimly Dave headed for Christine Donlan's dressing room. As he climbed the steps, he heard her order her dresser, "And then you get the hell out of here!"

Dora, a heavyset, middle-aged woman, stalked out. Christine was sitting in the glaring lights of her dressing table staring at herself. Her eyes flicked upward to make contact with Dave's in the mirror.

"Darling, what's wrong?" he asked, making every pretense of sympathy.

Christine's chin quivered, a sure sign she was close to tears. Inwardly Dave was unmoved. He'd seen her use that same technique before. But he knew that if he allowed her to cry it would mean a time-wasting repair job by the makeup man. So he placed his hands gently on her shoulders and let her press her cheek against his hand, as if needing his reassurance.

"Darling, what is it? Nerves? Well, you're doing beautifully. I wish you could see yourself in the dailies."

"You know I never watch my dailies," she pouted.

"Then take my word for it. You're fantastic," Dave told her in true Hollywood fashion.

No performance given west of the Rocky Mountains was ever less than fantastic.

"It's the scene we're doing now," Christine complained. She drew his hands down a bit so that they touched the tops of her swelling breasts. Dave leaned forward until their faces appeared side by side in the mirror. She turned to him and closed her eyes. Dave knew he had to kiss her. As he did, she raised her arms and let her robe slip loose, pressing her naked body against him. When she felt him rise, she reached for him. Soon they were both naked against each other.

She pushed him slightly so that he fell back onto the studio couch. Then she was atop him, kissing him feverishly. He seized her, held her off and said gruffly, "Let's not forget who's the man around here." He slid from under her, suspended himself above her for a moment; then as her arms went around him he eased himself into her. Her experience and technique matched her desire, and she proved a most enjoyable partner. He spent himself in her with no reservations. It was no longer a duty; it had become an adventure, with a skilled and desirable partner.

She lay beneath him, whispering how wonderful he was. She let her tongue play inside his ear in such a way that without withdrawing he had become hard again. This time she so locked him in her arms and legs that toward her climactic moments it

123

was painful for him to breathe. It was a relief when it was over.

"Skyrockets," she whispered. "It was like skyrockets going off. You do it to me; you do it."

She slid gently from under him. When he turned on his back, she crouched above him, letting her full round breasts hang over him. Slowly she began to move above him, letting her nipples play lightly across his lips. Suddenly there was a knock on the door.

"Mr. Cole, they're ready with the setup."

Back on the set, her pouting and need for a change in her lines were forgotten. The author of the script stood by waiting eagerly to supply four new versions of Christine Donlan's final line. But she went through the original scene seven times without making a single protest. When the final take had been approved, the author beckoned Dave to a corner.

"Her line worked fine. What was all the bitching about?"

"It was just a matter of convincing her that the scene was right," Dave explained. "So I convinced her. Now go back to your office. You know how nervous actors become when the author hangs around the stage."

Dave had no more trouble with Christine Donlan after that. The picture slowly rounded into shape. There were only the exteriors left to shoot. They worked on the back lot using the New York street, the small-town street and some of the country locales. H.P. had been right when he said, "Whatever part of the world you want, we can do it better right here."

At the huge tank on the back lot, they were finishing the close exteriors of a sea saga which starred Spencer Tracy. The scene involved Tracy and a young cabin boy adrift in a dory after their whaler had been caught in a storm and gone down. Tracy and the young actor had to work out in the glaring California sun, day after day. It was very thirsty weather.

Whenever Dave had a break in his own shooting schedule he would slip over to the tank set. The veteran director welcomed him, flattered that one of H.P.'s bright young men sought the chance to watch him work. Several times, after Tracy had done what Dave considered a superb take, the director would whisper

"He's so drunk, if he bends over he's going to fall out of that dory."

But it never showed in the rushes. Sober or drunk, Tracy was the consummate film actor, aware of what the slightest movement of his eyes, his lips or his smile would accomplish when projected on a screen forty feet wide. Dave promised himself that one day he must make a film with Tracy.

Dave's film and Tracy's film wound up shooting the same week. Since a Spencer Tracy film was always an event, H.P. decided to give a huge end-of-shooting house party at his estate down in Palm Springs. He selected as the theme for the party the New England locale of Tracy's sea epic. The Koenig Palm Springs estate was decorated to simulate a New England seaport, with ropes, huge anchors, harpoons and nets. His numerous staff was outfitted with studio-designed costumes to look like sailors and tavern maids. And the guests were all instructed to prepare to appear in costumes as well.

The guest list included the most important of Magna stars. Tracy. And his friend. Gable and any blond young woman he cared to escort. Three Barrymores had been invited. Only one accepted; he was drunk at the time he said yes. Magna's most important producers and directors rounded out the list.

When Dave got his invitation, Christine Donlan insisted that he be her escort. They came down in her Rolls—Dave driving, Christine beside him, her elaborate nineteenth-century costume for the party stretched out over the back seat.

They passed sprawling farms and small villages and were approaching the desert when Dave saw a town nestled below him. This must be the fabled resort. Dave leaned forward to take his first good look.

Christine said, "It's fascinating. You'll love it. Let's stop."

"Why? We're so close."

"Let's stop," she insisted.

He braked the car to a stop off the road. She seized his hands and pressed them against her breasts. When he made no further advances, she tore open the string of her expensive silk peasant blouse and thrust her breasts at him. While he kissed her nipples, she stroked his hair and made small sounds of delight. In a while she had invaded his pants, playing with him until he pulled her out of the car and took her on the hard, stony desert mountainside. When he was done, she said softly, "That's better. Now the weekend won't be such a bore. Once we get there, we probably won't have a moment to ourselves."

Palm Canyon, the main street, was a broad avenue lined with tall palm trees. When they reached the center of town Christine directed Dave to turn right. The Rolls climbed an inclined street until they rode parallel to a high adobe wall which extended for several blocks.

Finally he asked, "Where is it?"

"This *is* it," Christine said. "A small kingdom walled off from the outside world. If the peasants ever rise up, we'll be well dug in. Every time I come here I feel like Marie Antoinette ready to fight off the rabble. Or throw them some cake."

All the history Christine Donlan knew she had learned from Magna's costume epics. To her, Ronald Colman was the most important man in Europe.

Finally they reached the ornate ironwork gates. Two costumed servants waited to direct their car to the parking area and to unload their luggage. Dave and Christine were directed to the pool.

Most of the other guests had already arrived and were eating from the buffet at the far end of the patio. To indicate her dominance over him, now that they were no longer alone, Christine said grandly, "Darling, do get me a drink." Then she began talking with a group of actors close by.

Dave resented her attitude. But rather than make a scene he started the length of the pool to the bar. He ordered a Scotch and soda for himself, and while he sipped it, he ordered for her. Double gin. On ice. He knew her formula well by now.

As he stood facing the bar, a familiar voice mimicked, "Darling, do get me a drink!" He flushed and turned. Sybil Koenig wore her small, impish smile. He wasn't sure whether she was mocking him or Christine until she said, "Davie, errand boy for an alcoholic. What would your mother say about you now?"

"I want to see you. Alone," he said urgently.

"Nobody sees anybody alone at one of these."

"Sometime over the weekend we can find time," he persisted.

"I'll try."

But he knew she was not making any promises, only putting him off.

The next night was the costume party, and by the time Christine was ready she was well on her way to getting drunk. The alcohol worsened her bad humor, and Dave was wary as he escorted her to meet the other guests for cocktails. They had just arrived when H.P. announced his surprise for the evening. They were all going up to Whitewater for dinner! Most of the guests, knowing Whitewater, pretended to be delighted by the idea, but Dave was completely mystified.

A caravan of limousines and station wagons was waiting. The guests piled into the limousines; the station wagons were reserved for staff. To escape being confined in the same car with Christine, Dave subtly edged back, allowing everyone else to precede him. He did this under the guise of politeness, but his strategy was betrayed when he heard Sybil say, "Move back one more step and you'll wind up in Beverly Hills."

Her dark eyes were mischievous but not hostile.

"I don't blame you. She's a man-eater," Sybil added. "Let's go in my car." When Dave brightened considerably she warned, "Don't misinterpret. I'm only doing this to save a human life. Yours."

He followed her to an open Cadillac convertible, cherry red to contrast with her black hair and eyes. She waited till the caravan had pulled out of the compound. Twelve long black limousines followed by six station wagons. Sixty guests followed by thirty-six in help.

"Looks like a well-attended funeral," Dave said.

"Or a picnic dreamed up by Louis the Fourteenth."

"Your father do this often?"

"Too often."

"What the hell *is* Whitewater?"

"You'll see," Sybil said, amused.

They were gradually climbing up from the desert floor. To their left the sun was just going down behind Mount San Jacinto. To their right the pale moon was already shining.

After an uncomfortable silence Dave asked, "You play tennis?"

127

"I play everything," Sybil said. "I was brought up to."

"Could we manage to get in some tennis tomorrow?"

"Why ask me?" she countered. "Ask Christine."

"You have to understand about that."

"What makes you think I don't?"

"It has to do with the picture. That's the way it started."

"With her that's the way it always starts," Sybil said. "Is she that good? What is it she has that makes her so irresistible? Granted, she's got those impressive breasts. What do you men do, buy by the pound?"

"I wish you'd try to understand."

"I want to understand," she countered sharply. "That's why I'm asking. Just what is it about her? Vanity? The thrill you men get from screwing a woman that famous? Do you really enjoy it more with her than with other women? Tell me."

He was unable to answer.

"Of course, you're a gentleman. You don't screw and tell."

They were silent the rest of the way.

"What is this place?" Dave asked as they pulled in past a sign saying WHITEWATER.

"A fish hatchery."

"A *what*?" he asked, sure she was joking.

"That's right. You'll see."

They pulled into the parking lot, and as they got out of the car he said, "Remember, I want to go back with you."

"If you get permission from your mother," Sybil said. "Come on!"

As they passed through an opening in the high green hedge, Dave first thought he was seeing another huge Hollywood pool. But when he glanced to his left he saw that a thick, heavy jet of water gushed into the pool. A closer look revealed that it carried hundreds of fish. Trout. Bass. Perch. Not fingerlings as he expected in a hatchery, but fish of eating size.

Surrounding the pool were H.P.'s guests. Each in full costume. Each with a drink in one hand and a fishing rod in the other. H.P.'s servants moved among the guests handing them fresh drinks or baiting their hooks with pieces of raw liver. The guests had only to drop their lines into the pool. Squeals of delight erupted frequently as someone caught a fish.

David found himself standing alone. A servant shoved a rod

into his hand and baited the hook. Another handed him a Scotch and soda. He stood at the end of the pool feeling revolted. Finally he tossed aside his rod and drew back, almost stepping on Sybil's foot.

"What's the matter, sport—don't you like fishing?"

"Chalk it up to being Jewish. We never hunt or kill anything unless it's intended to be eaten."

"Oh, they're going to be eaten. That's your dinner swimming around there. Come on, I'll show you."

She took his hand and led him away from the pool to an area where a dozen rustic cabins stood. Billows of smoke curled up from the chimney of one of them. Just outside the door, two station wagons were lined up side by side, their tailgates opened flat to serve as bars.

Sybil led Dave into the cabin where part of H.P.'s staff was already at work cleaning fish and dredging them in flour for two blacks in high white chef's hats to fry. Great kettles of corn were boiling. Two enormous bowls of salad stood mixed and ready.

When enough fish had been caught, H.P. herded his guests into the cabin. They lined up and were handed plates heaped with crispy fried fish, hot steaming ears of corn, salad, slices of crusty sourdough bread and huge pats of butter.

The heat and smell of frying fish killed Dave's appetite, and when he had received his plate he was happy to go outside, find an empty table and sit down.

The other guests, some drunk, a few still sober, were eating dutifully. Dave stared with amazement at several of the most famous celebrities in the world, stuffing themselves with food they would have disdained anywhere else. All to please their lord and master.

H.P. himself did not eat. With a huge Baccarat crystal wine goblet in his hand, he passed among his guests like a beneficent father, seeing to it that all were satisfied and eating well. As he worked his way over, Dave knew that soon he would have to eat or face H.P.'s disapproval. When H.P. provided fish, everyone ate fish.

H.P. had already noticed him and called out, "Dave!" Dave was aware that Sybil was watching too. She stood back from the table, plate in hand, her dark eyes darting from her father, who was already a little tipsy, to Dave, who had not touched his food.

"Dave," H.P. shouted. "What's the matter? You don't like my fish?"

"If I'd known, I'd have told you," Dave said. "Allergic."

"Allergic?"

"To fish. It's really very common," Dave explained. "I get a reaction. My throat swells up. I can't breathe."

H.P. turned sympathetic immediately. "My boy, why didn't you tell me? I'd have brought some steaks for you."

"No. It's okay. I had a big lunch. Your buffet was fantastic."

H.P. snapped his fingers for a servant, who appeared instantly. "Find something for Mr. Cole to eat! As long as it's not fish! And take this away!"

The plate was whisked away. Soon it was replaced by one that offered only corn, salad and chunks of bread. Dave didn't eat that either. But his crime passed unnoticed, since the strolling Mexican musical combo H.P. had ordered began to play. Under H.P.'s domineering direction, all the guests joined in a drunken version of the Mexican hat dance. When they had exhausted themselves, someone in the crowd shouted for H.P. to dance. He pretended to reluctant shyness. But when Anita Albright, Magna's dancing star, took his hand and pulled him to the center of the earth floor, he seemed happy. Anita Albright, almost a head taller than H. P. Koenig, allowed herself to be led by him. He proved most adroit and skillfull, moving with an ease that belied his short, stocky physique.

As he watched, Dave remembered hearing that Anita was one of the most frequent passengers in the private elevator that led directly into H.P.'s suite. Rumor said she had extracted her first contract from him by going down on him. So it was her mouth, not her feet, that had actually brought her to stardom. Afterward, when directors had trouble getting her to enunciate dialogue clearly, people would whisper, "How can she, with that in her mouth?"

By now most of the guests were exhausted. Several of them had disappeared into the woods and secretly vomited up their excesses. Others wandered off to dark corners and were involved in sexual activity of one kind or another. The party had ended.

Despite his efforts to keep track of Sybil Koenig, Dave couldn't find her. Instead he located the convertible, slipped into the passenger seat and slumped down low to elude Christine. He waited. Finally he heard steps approach on the gravel walk. As Sybil reached for the door, she became aware of him.

"She was looking for you. They had trouble getting her into the car."

"She drinks a lot of gin."

"Straight," Sybil said pointedly.

"That's only because she doesn't give the ice a chance to melt," he pretended to explain.

"Were you planning on going back with me?"

"The other cars are gone," he said. "You have to take me home."

"Next, you'll plead you're an orphan."

"I would have if I'd thought of it first." As she was getting into the car, he volunteered, "I could drive."

"Okay," she said, handing him the key. As he pulled away, Sybil sighed, as if in relief.

"Glad it's over?" he asked.

"These damn things are always such a bore. The guests really don't want to be here. They come out of fear of offending him. And to get their names in the trades on Monday morning."

"Your mother?" he asked cautiously.

"She never comes down when he's here."

"Why not?"

"I'd think the answer to that would be obvious," Sybil said, making no secret of her disapproval of her father's promiscuous conduct.

"How does she take it? What does she do with her life?"

"Charity. The betrayed wife's excuse for being useless," Sybil said.

"Someone has to do it."

"It would be better done if it weren't so necessary. For her, I mean. She's a very nice lady."

"I know. And she raises very nice daughters."

They drove through the night.

After a while she asked, "*Are* you an orphan?"

"Only half. My father died in 1945. I was due to be drafted. But he died suddenly. Heart attack. I got a compassionate deferment. Then the war was over and they didn't need me anymore.

I tell myself he did it for me," Dave said. "If he had to, he would have. I know that."

"Yes," Sybil said, as if she understood and was envious.

"But it was because of my mother that I met you," Dave said suddenly.

"Hmm?"

"She gave me my taste for show business," he said.

"Was she in it?"

"No. But she went to everything. Vaudeville. Yiddish theater. Movies. She laughed at every joke. Cried with every victim. Because my father was always busy, she used to take me with her.

"But the strange thing was, when the time came my mother didn't want me to go into show business. She had it all laid out for me. College, then whatever professional school we could afford. With Jews, lawyers, doctors and dentists are interchangeable. You simply choose the one you can afford."

He interrupted himself suddenly. "Why am I telling you about Jews as if you were an outsider?"

"Go on, about your mother."

"I never figured I'd get into the business as an actor."

"Oh?" she said, surprised.

"An agent saw me on the beach when I was a lifeguard and suggested it." He sounded a bit apologetic.

"So you were a stallion even then?" Sybil remarked icily.

Angry, he slammed on the brakes. The car skidded across the sand-covered road.

"What is it you resent about me?"

"Do you really want to know?"

"I damn well do!"

"I detect in you the same things I distrust about my father," she said simply.

"Me? Like *him*?" Dave laughed. "That'll be the day!"

"Won't it, though," she said coolly.

He turned to stare into her face. In the pale light of the moon only her dark eyes stood out, bright and accusing.

"Do you get some kind of kick out of putting me down?" he demanded.

"No."

"Or do you hate me because your father happens to like me for the moment?" he asked. "You know him well enough to know that that will change."

"It will."

"Then what is it?"

"Davie, you're a very bright boy. But about some things you are totally blind."

Frustrated, he put the car into low gear and slowly climbed out of the sand and back onto the road.

"If you want to see the desert away from the lights," she said, "take the next right. But be careful. It's not paved."

He slowed down, found the dark trail. Several times small animals sped across the road, barely avoiding the fat balloon tires. Once, a jackrabbit, stunned by the headlights, remained fixed in their path until Dave was forced to stop. Then the animal scampered away into the darkness. Dave followed the trail to a high plateau, where he brought the car to a stop.

Sybil drew her legs up under her and sat kneeling so that she could face back.

"Turn off the lights," she said.

He did and turned around too.

"Down there," she pointed, "that's the town. Those lit-up, blue areas, they're swimming pools. More swimming pools per capita in this town than anywhere else in the whole world. Did you know that?"

"No," he said, turning slightly to stare at her lovely profile.

"Back there, if you look away from the town, is the desert. Raw and untouched until some land developer discovers how to destroy it. That's the real desert. And the mountains beyond. Dark. Severe sometimes. Brooding other times. Depends on how you feel."

"How do *you* feel? Tonight?"

In the distance a coyote howled. Sybil was silent.

"You didn't answer me," he said. "How do *you* feel tonight?"

"Sad."

"Is that all?" he asked.

She reached for the ignition key to start the car, but he caught her hand and held it.

"Please, don't spoil it."

"Spoil what?" he demanded. "You've done nothing but put me down all evening!"

133

"You are stupid!" she exploded impatiently. "If I didn't give a damn about you would I have wasted my time?"

"Sybil . . . ?"

"Don't try to take advantage of what I said. Don't think that just because I . . . I'm fond of you . . . I'm going to roll over on my back and let you screw me. Because that's what it would be. You know how to screw. But you don't know the first thing about making love. Well, no man is going to *screw* me. You're not going to come to me still wet from Christine Donlan. Or any other star you happen to be laying. Got it?"

"Yes, sure, 'got it,' " he said angrily.

He started the car and began the slow descent toward the desert floor.

"What makes you think I'm not capable of love?"

"You're no different from anyone else in that town. You want to make the best film. Direct the biggest box-office grosser. Get the highest award. Own the biggest house, provided, of course, it's not bigger than H.P.'s. That would be an unpardonable sin.

"On the surface it all seems greedy and selfish. In the end it won't be. Because you'll only destroy yourself."

She paused, then added, "I don't want to have to watch it when it happens to you."

He brought the car to a stop. He turned to her, took her in his arms. She didn't give herself willingly. He kissed her, found her lips warm, but no more encouraging than that. He sought her eyes in the darkness. They were misted over.

"What if I wanted to do it your way?" he asked. "Could I see you then?"

"I'll think about it. But don't call me. I don't want my father to get any wrong impressions. Else before you know it he'll have Adrian designing my wedding gown."

"Soon?" Dave persisted.

"Soon," she said, but with not too much conviction.

For three weeks Dave waited for a call from Sybil. Then he tried to call her at home. She was never there. He left messages. She never returned his calls.

In the meantime Dave considered H.P.'s advice to buy a house. He looked at a dozen places before deciding that he was not a

134

house person. All his life he had lived in small apartments. The thought of a house seemed too much of a responsibility.

So he compromised. He moved into one of the luxurious bungalows at the Marmont. It also relieved him of the imperative Hollywood custom of having "a couple." A well-run Hollywood house was always staffed by a couple.

9

Dave Cole's fifth film grew out of a famous dinner with C. S. Begelman, a quixotic and amusing satirist whose favorite pastime when he visited Hollywood was improvising tongue-in-cheek gibes at studio tyrants such as H. P. Koenig.

Albert Grobe, a great admirer of Begelman's work in *The New Yorker*, arranged a dinner party in his honor. Never suspecting that Begelman might insult any of his guests, Grobe had invited H. P. Koenig, his wife, Sybil and a small group of writers and directors who would enjoy Begelman's sophisticated wit. Hoping to further the relationship between Dave and Sybil, Grobe had also invited Dave. As usual, Mrs. Koenig found a good reason not to attend.

After dinner, warmed and encouraged by considerable brandy, Begelman moved into high gear. He started by giving an imitation of a Hollywood story conference. Since two of the most successful recent pictures were Bing Crosby and Ingrid Bergman in *The Bells of St. Mary's* and Howard Hughes's braless epic *The Outlaw* starring Jane Russell, Begelman concocted an outlandish scenario combining the most exotic features of both films. His improvisation concerned a clergyman in the Old West who became involved with a woman whose morals and bodice were equally overburdened, with similarly elastic results.

The guests were greatly amused, which served to spur Begel-

136

man on. Gradually he began to play to H.P., whose vanity never let him suspect he could be the victim of this entire charade. Begelman accomplished that in a way so sly and subtle that no one realized until too late that he was poking fun at Magna's reigning monarch. When everyone suddenly did, there was silence. H.P. gave no outward sign of displeasure. But slowly the smile vanished from his face. Drunk as he was, Begelman was unaware that everyone had ceased to laugh. When he finished, collapsing into a chair, H.P. rose, politely thanked Albert Grobe for his hospitality and started to leave. Only at the door did he remember and turn back to address Sybil, demandingly.

"Coming, my dear?"

Everyone remained silent, not daring to offer to drive her home for fear of further offending her already irate father. But she surprised them all by saying, "I'll be along soon. Dave Cole's offered to drop me."

Without another glance, H.P. swept out the door and was gone. Even before his limousine was out of the circular driveway, a number of guests turned on Begelman, accusing him not only of insulting H. P. Koenig, but of endangering all of them by forcing them to be witnesses and thus, in Koenig's eyes, participants in his humiliation. Grobe and Begelman's long-suffering wife managed to get the writer into his car. When Grobe returned, he observed grimly to Dave and Sybil, "We'll all pay for this. Somehow."

On the drive home, Sybil felt compelled to apologize.

"I'm sorry."

"About what?" he asked.

"Uncle Albert was right," she said. "They'll all pay for it somehow. I shouldn't have endangered you even more by saying you'd drive me home."

"I don't mind. I've been trying to speak to you for weeks now. You never take my calls."

"I'm out a lot," she explained weakly.

"You never call back."

"After tonight, do you wonder why?"

"You kept refusing my calls before tonight," he reminded.

"It's all part of the same thing. No matter what we start out

137

talking about, we always end up discussing *him*," she pointed out. "We're here together now because of *him*. You're taking a risk driving me home now, because of *him*. You're going to have to answer for it tomorrow, to *him*. Don't you see, nothing that happens to us has to do with *us*. It only has to do with *him*."

"It doesn't have to."

"If you want to work in his town, you have to live by his rules," she said.

"You said yourself he approves of me," said Dave.

"Which is exactly why *I* don't," she said angrily. "Maybe that's why I made you drive me home. Maybe from now on he won't approve of you so wholeheartedly."

They were silent until they reached her house.

As she slid out of the car and stood facing him, her eyes misted over with tears.

"It isn't you, Davie. It's him. I have to settle with him first. Try to understand?"

He nodded.

She kissed him quickly, but before he could embrace her she was gone, whispering, "I'll try to make it up to you for tonight."

The next day, when Dave arrived at his office, his secretary nervously demanded, "Where have you been? I called all over town! You were due in H.P.'s office five minutes ago!"

"I was at Linny's having breakfast. If you have to report to Sarah, tell her it was scrambled eggs and coffee. Black!"

"I called the Marmont. I even called *her* home," his secretary dared to say.

"Her" could refer only to Christine Donlan.

"And she told you I wasn't there?"

"Yes. But she has a vocabulary like a stagehand!" his secretary said primly.

"Why not?" said Dave. "She was probably in bed with one when you called."

"You better get up to H.P.'s office," his secretary said, closing the discussion.

Despite the fact that more than a dozen other people were waiting, Dave was immediately admitted to H.P.'s private office.

As he opened the door, the first person he saw was The Professor. Grobe gave a slight head gesture warning Dave not to make a sound.

H.P. was lost in his huge desk chair, facing away from his visitors. Next to Grobe Dave recognized Larry Holtzman, the producer, and a playwright from New York who had had two hits in three seasons and was now being paid five thousand dollars a week at Magna, though he had yet to write a single line for the studio.

Standing before H.P.'s desk and addressing the back of his red leather chair was the now sober satirist C. S. Begelman, retelling the story he had told at Grobe's party the night before. Begelman perspired as he tried to recall some of the more colorful bits of invention he had dreamed up in his alcoholic haze. When he hesitated, H.P. called out an impatient correction without looking at him. When he finished, there was a long silence.

Finally, the red leather throne swung about. H.P.'s face was thoughtful. Without looking at Begelman, he said, "They tell me you write very funny things. I never read. But if I did, I wouldn't read any of your shit!"

Begelman's face reddened, but he dared not leave H.P.'s presence without permission. One never knew by what devious means H.P. could influence a creative man's career, no matter the medium he worked in.

"Your trouble," continued H.P., "your trouble is, life is one big joke to you. Well, not to me. And not to *my people*."

To H.P. all audiences were "my people."

"What's funny about a holy man, a man of God, being sucked in by a tramp? If people can't believe in a minister or a priest, who can they believe in? It is sacrilegious!" shouted H.P., who never attended any house of worship except for a funeral.

"Well, you smart bastard, I am going to teach you a lesson. I am going to buy that story! Tell your agent to get in touch with me right after lunch. Then you get your ass out of this town."

A darling of book critics, a famed wit of the Algonquin Round Table, Begelman flushed and started for the door. There he stopped.

"The story is not for sale!"

"Everything you smart bastards write is for sale!" said H.P. "Else you wouldn't write it! Tell your agent to call me!"

When Begelman was gone, H.P. said, "I want a script. I want a good, strong, serious script on that story."

He glanced at the playwright. "You start working on it! Today! Holtzman, you work with him. And Dave, you are also assigned to the project. I want this picture to be a hit."

Only Dave dared to speak. "H.P., do you realize that if you do that story straight you're going to wind up with Somerset Maugham's *Rain*? It's Sadie Thompson and the Reverend Davidson all over again."

"Of course! And that was a big hit. So what have we got to lose? All right, boys, get going!"

They started out with a noticeable lack of enthusiasm, H.P. calling after them, "And it wouldn't do any harm she should wind up a nun at the end!"

"Like Mary Magdalene?" the playwright suggested sarcastically.

"Exactly!" H.P. said seriously. "You're on the right track already!"

Dave tried to call Sybil and tell her of the aftermath of the evening, but she was not at home. Well, she would learn the news from the *Reporter* when it was announced that Magna Studios had just bought a new original screen story from C. S. Begelman, the first serious story of his career.

It was eleven weeks before the writers had a script suitable to be read to H.P. Protocol presented a problem. Should the story go through The Three Witches? Or should Dave, as the director, present it himself?

Taking along Grobe and Holtzman for support, Dave decided to tell the story to H.P. himself. When he was done, H.P. sat in his large chair weeping happily.

"Fantastic! Fantastic!" he kept repeating. "You caught it exactly. It's what I always saw in the story. And those scenes in the desert, that sandstorm, that's what I call a moving picture. The camera tells the whole story. The storm is the wrath of God. And the two of them out there risking their lives! They come out of it clean again and forgiven. It's Yom Kippur in the desert. Great!"

Dave, Larry Holtzman and Albert Grobe remained silent. H.P. swung around and picked up his phone. "Sarah, get me Ted Bassett in Casting! I want production to start at once. I'll show that smart-ass bastard Begelman!"

Holtzman nodded vigorously, as was expected of him.

By the time the day was over, H. P. Koenig had cast blond sex bomb Gladys Holmes as the prostitute and Will Carlin as the young, handsome minister. Carlin was only a second-string star, since the picture would belong to Gladys. It would be her first part to combine sex and serious acting.

Production had proceeded on schedule, and now Dave was several weeks into shooting the picture, which had been titled *Redemption*. He woke as early as six to prepare himself emotionally for the scenes he would attempt to shoot that day. Of course, there was no telling what might intervene and upset his planned schedule. Carlin might have had a bad night and come in with a hangover and look like hell. Or Gladys Holmes might have begun her period and be out of sorts. In that mood she always refused to play a love scene. In all, it was a difficult film, and Dave was prepared for further problems the moment Gladys' agent called him on the set.

"Dave? Vic Martoni. Listen, kid, I don't know what you did to Gladys, but you upset her very much."

"I upset her? How?"

"Do I know?" Vic pleaded. "You know these cunts. Who can make sense out of them? I'm only calling to say, shoot around her for a few days."

"Shoot around her? We're in the closing scenes! She's in every shot! Hell, the rest of the schedule is eighty percent her and Carlin!" Dave exploded.

"Oh, I'm sorry to hear that," Martoni said, giving a fairly convincing performance. "Listen, I'll tell you what. You talk to H.P. and I'll talk to Gladys. And we'll see if we can't work this out."

"Okay. And whatever it is that I'm supposed to have done to her, tell her I'm sorry."

"I'll do my best," Martoni promised.

141

They waited around on the set all morning. Dave attempted to shoot bits and pieces of the scene until the editor came down from the cutting room to tell Dave it was a waste of film.

They broke for lunch. They continued their vigil till four o'clock in the afternoon, when Dave received a phone call from H.P.

"Dave! Wrap for the day," H.P. said grimly. "And come up here to my office."

When he arrived, Martoni was there. The agent's complaint was that when Gladys Holmes had called Dave the previous night to ask a question about today's shooting he did not volunteer to go over to her house and discuss it with her. Instead he handled the whole thing by phone.

Martoni turned to Dave. "When a sensitive actress like Gladys Holmes calls her director at night and wants to talk to him, that's a signal that she needs something she's not getting on the set. They are lonely women, these stars. Would it have been asking so much if you had gone over to see her? Or even given her a little screw? It would have shown that you cared about her, about her performance. That's all she wanted."

Dave was silent, waiting to hear what H.P. would say.

"*Did* she call you, Dave?"

"Yes, she called. And I spent an hour on the phone trying to work out her problem."

"An hour on the phone?" H.P. lamented. "Half an hour in bed with her would have done better. Dave, never say no to a star when she's offering herself to you. Especially Gladys. She's a very good fuck."

Having dispensed that paternal advice, H.P. turned to Martoni. "Vic, what can we do to get production started up again? We're losing twenty thousand dollars a day."

"Well," said Martoni, indicating that he had no swift solution, "flowers aren't going to do it. Or apologies."

"What if I called her myself?" H.P. offered.

"No, H.P. I don't think so. That girl needs some tangible proof that she's appreciated."

Dave could see the flush of anger begin to rise in H.P.'s face. "Such as?"

"You know what I think would be a nice gesture, H.P.?"

"No. What?" H.P. asked, forcing himself to remain civil.

142

"It would be a nice gesture if you were to tear up her contract and offer her a new one. Say ten thousand a week instead of seven-five like she's getting now."

H.P.'s face grew crimson, but he kept his shrewd mind under control. An extra twenty-five hundred a week salary for one hundred and four weeks came to two hundred and sixty thousand dollars. To scrap the film already shot and start over would cost far more. The answer, distasteful as it might be, was obvious. H.P. nodded, a barely perceptible nod. It was all the assent Martoni needed.

"You won't regret it, H.P. You'll see, it'll turn out to be a smart move in the end."

"Sure," H.P. agreed with no enthusiasm. He knew when he had been screwed by an expert.

"Then call her. Tell her yourself. I'm sure she'll be ready to come back to work in a day or two," Martoni said, holding out his hand to seal the deal.

"Vic, one day I'll cut your heart out," H.P. warned.

Martoni left and H.P. turned to Dave. "You see what you cost me by not going over to screw that bitch last night? A director is like a doctor. He has to make house calls. You failed me, Dave. One of the few times you have."

The only satisfaction Dave derived from the entire distasteful episode came two days later when it was learned that Gladys Holmes had actually been unable to appear on the set because she had been forced to undergo an abortion that could not wait till shooting was over. The Martoni Agency had opportunistically seized on that emergency to force H.P. into a new contract.

The author of that shrewd bit of blackmail turned out to be Betty Ronson, which was when one writer dubbed her The Black Widow, hinting at some tragedy in her past that made her so rapacious in her business dealings. No one suspected her past affair with Dave Cole.

Once the truth of Gladys Holmes's absence came to light Dave called her.

"Damn it, Betty, you could have wrecked my picture and hurt my career. No matter what we were in the past, you're my agent now! If anything like that happens again, I'll have to get myself new representation!"

She listened without protest. When he was done, she said simply, "I'm Gladys Holmes's agent too. We had to look out for her interests, *Davie*."

This last gentle diminutive was her way of letting Dave know that she had learned of his relationship with Sybil Koenig. It added to his suspicion that Betty's unethical manipulation of the Gladys Holmes situation bore a bit of malice toward him as well.

Dave slammed down the phone—a gesture that gave Betty great satisfaction.

10

Shooting on *Redemption* had been completed. Dave supervised the editing of the film. When he had it in its final form it was run for H.P. and Sarah Immerman, H.P.'s authority on female taste. Sarah approved, particularly Dave's direction of Gladys Holmes. Women would like the star in this new, serious role.

During the drive back after the preview, H.P. was smug.

"That smart bastard Begelman! That film will make three million dollars. And I bought his idea for a lousy twenty-five thousand. And that bastard Martoni thought he was screwing me. A two-year deal for more money. After what I saw tonight, she's worth ten times what she's getting. Star quality. That girl really has star quality now.

"Dave, you accomplished a miracle with that girl. You turned her from a blond sex bomb into an actress. A real actress. She's got a whole new career ahead of her.

"Talent, Dave, talent is the key to everything! Whatever you do, find the talent and control it. Sometimes you have to use insults or threats. Sometimes you have to kiss its ass. But the main thing, hold on to it. When you learn how to do that, you'll be ready to be head of a studio like Magna."

Dave couldn't decide whether the man was making a promise or just dangling another carrot.

"Yes, Dave, one day you may be facing responsibilities like this."

Dave glanced sideways. H.P. looked older tonight. When he leaned over and patted Dave's arm, the promise suddenly seemed almost a reality.

Suddenly H.P. asked, "You ever been married?"

"No."

"Good." After a long silence, "Dave, one thing: when you do get married, make sure she's a woman you can love and respect. Otherwise it's a lonely life.

"The stars and the starlets, it's fun. I've had almost every woman star in the business. And when it's over it all feels the same. Might as well be any little tramp you pick up on the street. Then why do I do it? Because if I stop, it'll mean I'm getting old. Well, I'm resigned to dying, but not to getting old. There's a difference."

The old man was in a mood for intimacies tonight, for suddenly he said, "They're scheming, always scheming. Back there in the New York office. They want my head. Jealous. Because I earn more than the whole executive staff in New York put together. So they hate me. Everybody hates me. Even the women who make love to me hate me. I can feel it."

He said no more till they reached Beverly Hills. As he was about to get out of the car, he said, "Dave, you did yourself and Magna a world of good tonight. You found me a new dramatic star. Tomorrow I will give the order. The entire advertising campaign is to be built around the *new* Gladys Holmes!"

Three days later, Dave was summoned to H.P.'s furious presence.

"Is something wrong?"

H.P. did not respond.

"I've been going over the outtakes. I cut a few scenes where I thought Gladys looked a little too mature, but with that performance I don't think we have to worry about her age. And from now on we don't need to have her dresses designed to shove her breasts up so far that a baby could nurse on them. And the designers don't have to put tucks in the back of her dresses to

146

make her behind wiggle every time she walks. She is now an actress."

H.P. said only two words, but they held incredible contempt. *"Gladys Holmes."*

Dave did not know how to reply.

"Dave," H.P. said sadly. "Dave, during the shooting, those two days that she missed?"

"She had an abortion. Martoni and Betty Ronson used that to get her a new contract. So?"

"Last night Sonny Brown called Dr. Kroger to do a curette job on one of the starlets. Guess what Kroger told him!"

"The man who brought Gladys to Kroger's was... Are you ready, Dave? Teddy Fletcher!"

"The singer?" Dave asked, amazed.

"The sonofabitch bastard spade singer! In your wildest dreams would you ever imagine that a girl like Gladys Holmes would fuck Teddy Fletcher?" H.P. shouted. "She could have any white man in this town. Why did she have to pick on a schvartzer?"

"How do you know it's true?"

"We give Kroger too much business for him to lie. What's even worse, this morning I got a call from *Hollywood Confidential*."

"And they're going to print it?" Dave asked in amazement.

"Print it? They are going to do a whole series on it!"

"Christ!" Dave said, knowing what such a story, true or not, could do to his film.

"So," H.P. said realistically, "it doesn't matter how well the preview went. Once this gets out, you can kiss your picture good-bye."

"You're going to shelve it?" Dave asked.

"What else can I do? If this gets out, the exhibitors'll kill us!" H.P. warned.

"Isn't there anything we can do?"

"We can try."

H.P. had barely got out the words when his phone chimed. He listened a moment and said, "Send them in!"

Fragrant, dapper as usual, Vic Martoni entered accompanied by Betty Ronson. For a moment David remembered the Betty Ronson he had once loved, that shy girl who had had all the ambition but none of the guile.

147

As soon as the door closed, H.P. unleashed all the fury he had stored up from his previous encounter over Gladys Holmes. Martoni and Betty listened patiently.

"And another thing. There's been a breach of ethics. A very serious breach! You two had a duty to be honest with me about that abortion. It was an outrageous breach of professional ethics to let us go on and make an expensive picture with that cunt without telling us the truth!"

H.P. indicated Dave. "You have endangered this man's career by letting him make a picture that we don't dare release. You could at least have told *him* the truth!"

H.P. had exhausted himself for a moment.

"H.P.," said Betty finally, "if I told you we didn't know about it, you wouldn't believe me."

"After the way you two screwed me on that renegotiation I'd never believe you! Only this time I would have made an exception."

"Well, we didn't know," Martoni intervened, truly troubled by the situation.

H.P. added to his concern by reminding, "Fucking a schvartzer to whom she is not even married, getting pregnant and having an illegal abortion is not exactly moral conduct. She's got a morals clause in her contract. And don't you forget it!"

Betty and Martoni were fully aware of that. They had one primary concern: how to handle the problem. It was especially thorny since Betty also handled Teddy Fletcher, a client she had picked up when she was still in New York. In fact, Gladys Holmes had originally met Teddy Fletcher at a welcoming party in Betty's house.

"It's a tricky problem," Martoni confessed. "I mean, Fletcher is pretty high-strung."

Betty agreed: "The old yessir, nosir, nigger entertainer is on the way out." Dave glanced at her. She would never have used that expression in the old days. She pretended to be unaware of his rebuke. "It started a long time ago, with Benny Goodman putting white and black musicians on the same bandstand. It's a new world now. Fletcher won't like the idea of my trying to run his private life."

"Don't I know," H.P. commiserated. "I want to do a nice thing. So I bring Lena Horne out here. I'm taking a big step forward, putting a black scene in a picture. Giving them something to come to the picture houses for. I was very sweet to her. I explain nicely how she would have to have all her meals in her dressing room. So there wouldn't be any trouble. And I didn't even try to lay a hand on her. And how does she show her gratitude? She marries a white man! To make matters worse, a Magna white man! She didn't give me any choice. I had to cancel her contract. So don't tell me about that kind of trouble. The question now is, what can we do to save Dave's picture?"

Dave understood the significance of the question. When a picture was a hit it was a Magna picture. If it seemed doomed it became the producer's picture, or the director's picture. H.P. had just disowned all responsibility for *Redemption*.

"Look," said Betty, "we have a great deal at stake, too. If Gladys doesn't care about her career, we do. And we have Dave to protect."

"You could explain all that to Teddy," H.P. suggested futilely.

"*Talking* to him won't do any good," Betty said.

"Then what will?" H.P. demanded.

Martoni consulted his watch. "Ten-thirty here, twelve-thirty in Chicago."

He moved to H.P.'s desk, picked up the private phone. "If the right people talk to him, that's another matter."

He spoke into the receiver and waited. Then:

"Rocco? Vic. Yeah. Fine. Except one thing. Look, we got a problem. What would it do to your schedule at the club if I canceled out Teddy Fletcher? He plays the last three weeks in March. No, no, it's not something that I'm pulling. I swear we don't have a better offer for those weeks."

Martoni looked at H.P. questioningly. H.P. nodded. Martoni proceeded to inform Rocco of the entire situation. He ended by saying, "I thought if we canceled him out of all his bookings it might convince him. You know, Rock?"

Martoni felt he had laid sufficient groundwork. As Rocco talked he assumed an expression of surprise. "You have another solution?" He proceeded to listen, interrupting only to say, "Uh-huh, I see," and when Rocco finished, Martoni said, "Then I'll depend on you. He's out here now at Ciro's." Martoni hung up. "It's settled. Fletcher won't be seeing Gladys Holmes again."

"Rocco Mascarella?" H.P. asked.

"Right," Martoni said. "And you can credit the little lady. It was her idea."

H.P. beamed at Betty, then asked Vic, "How long will it take?"

"Not long," Martoni said. He glanced at Dave. "Kid, your picture is safe."

The meeting was evidently over, and Dave followed Betty, catching up with her at the elevator.

"So you talked it over. You and Martoni knew exactly what he was going to do before you ever walked into that room."

"You'll be better off in the long run," she said.

"Teddy Fletcher too?"

"Teddy Fletcher. Gladys Holmes. And you," she answered smugly.

"Suppose I don't want to be better off, if it has to be handled that way?" Dave demanded.

"I'm afraid you don't have any choice. An agent is like a surgeon. If something is wrong, it's his duty to remove it. I've just saved your picture. You could at least be gracious about it."

"Christ, Betty, what's happened to you?"

"It's a little late to wonder. And I would think you'd be the last one entitled to ask," she shot back viciously.

Before he could answer, the elevator door opened and she stepped inside, making no secret of the fact that she preferred to occupy it alone. For himself, he had no desire to talk further.

Teddy Fletcher had finished his second show at Ciro's. After four encores he stepped into his tiny dressing room, his black face gleaming with sweat. He dropped into the chair before his dressing-room mirror. His dresser stripped him of his tuxedo and his limp dress shirt. He wiped the exhausted singer dry with a rough Turkish towel. He massaged the tense knots in his shoulders, then doused him with witch hazel. The black dresser had once been a handler of boxing champions.

He dried him off again, kneading his tight muscles at the same time. Then he splashed him with a strong male cologne. Teddy Fletcher was ready to slip into fresh shorts, shirts, slacks and sport coat. He peered out of his dressing-room door to make sure he would not be besieged by fans. Several young girls were waiting. He got rid of them by signing a few autographs and was free to leave at last.

He slipped out of the employees' door. The night was misty. The lights wore eerie haloes. In the parking lot he spotted the white Cadillac. Gladys was waiting. He felt better at once, a little less tired, eager to see her, to hold her, even though he might be too tired to make love tonight. People never realized that a singer sang with all of himself, not merely his voice and his throat.

But she was here, so the night would be better now. He slipped into the white convertible. They kissed. A long, intense kiss. She knew his moods well enough to release him and let him lean back and relax.

"We're going home," she said. "I've had Edna fix a little supper for us. And some champagne."

"Good," he said, grateful.

She pulled out of the parking lot. They were oblivious of another car that pulled out of the lot right behind them. She turned left onto Sunset, heading west. The boulevard was deserted. Hollywood was really not a night town. When they crossed into Beverly Hills there were still no other cars except for the car behind them. At North Maple she turned right and stopped in her driveway. The other car pulled up at the curb. It was only when Fletcher got out that he spotted the tail.

Years of playing nightclubs had given him a sixth sense about unexpected trouble. "Get into the house!" he said to Gladys. "Lock the door!"

"Why? What's wrong?"

"Get into the house!" he ordered so fiercely that she moved up the path.

"I'll call the police."

"Don't call anybody!" he warned. "Just get inside!"

Fletcher waited in the dark driveway. Two men got out of the car and started toward him. Fletcher held his ground. He thought he recognized one of them from tonight's audience.

"Fletcher?"

"Yes."

"Rocco asked us to look in on you. He said there was some kind of trouble."

"There's no trouble," Fletcher said. "I'll be in Chicago to play

151

my three weeks. My voice was never better. Tell Rocco there's nothing to worry about."

"But he *is* worried. He figures if you keep screwing around with Gladys you are liable to get beat up. Or even killed. And that would upset Rocco's whole schedule. So he thinks it might be a good idea if you didn't see this broad no more. Y'know?"

"Tell Rocco I'll be there. On schedule. I'll do my three weeks."

The second man moved suddenly, seizing Fletcher by the arm. He spun him around and slipped his free arm around the singer's throat. If he exerted even a small part of his strength he could have crushed Fletcher's larynx.

"What good would it do if you showed up in Chicago and couldn't sing? Couldn't sing no more nowhere? What would you do, shine shoes? You got a good thing. Don't fuck it up by screwing white girls. Got it?"

If Fletcher hadn't heard enough, the crushing pressure on his larynx would have convinced him.

"Okay," he said hoarsely. "I'll tell her."

"You ain't going to tell her. You ain't going to see her again. You ain't going to talk to her again. You are going to come with us. We will drop you at your hotel. And if you try to get in touch with her, we'll do what we said. Understand?"

Fletcher nodded. The muscle man jacked Fletcher's arm up behind his back and shoved him down the driveway to their car.

Gladys Holmes watched it all from a window of her dark house. When they started shoving Fletcher toward their car, she raced to the phone to call for the police. Then, realizing what she would have to tell them, she left the receiver down.

The next morning H.P. received a call from Martoni.

"It's okay. You can forget all about Teddy Fletcher."

"Good. Thanks, Vic. Next time, I'll return the favor."

152

11

The success of *Redemption* in a few small-town previews was encouraging but not conclusive. H. P. Koenig decided on a star-studded premiere in the East. With a big send-off from the New York critics, the rest of the country would be hungry for the film.

H.P. had his private motives as well. He was always conscious of Sybil's resistance to any suggestion of his. She was like her mother, silent, but persistent in her refusal to be dominated. Perhaps that was why she avoided Dave so assiduously. But a New York premiere would be an event she was not likely to refuse.

But she did refuse.

Furious, H.P. had no alternative but to proceed with the premiere. To cancel it might indicate to the critics and the exhibitors that he had lost confidence in the film. At the airport in New York, H.P. chose Dave to ride into the city with him, using the opportunity to instruct him in the politics of Magna Pictures' New York office.

"Jealousy!" H.P. declared. "The place is rife with jealousy. If they didn't depend on my studio they'd devour me like vultures. They live off me. Still they hate me."

H.P. was silent for a time. Suddenly he said, "Sullavan! The man to watch out for is Dan Sullavan."

He said no more until they crossed the bridge into Manhattan. As he looked out at the active busy streets, he lamented, "If only

153

Sybil had come along. I wonder why she didn't. Did she happen to say anything to you?"

"We haven't talked. Not for quite a while."

"Still?" H.P. asked sadly. "She worries me, that girl. Sometimes ... " H.P. hesitated, for he never liked to admit the possibility of his own mortality. "Sometimes, I say to myself, if I could see her married to the right man, I'd die happy. She has everything a man could want. Looks. Good figure. Brains. And she's very well fixed for life. What's wrong, Dave?"

Knowing that the truth would enrage H.P., Dave said, "Some girls take longer to accept the idea of marriage than others. Better than a quick marriage and a quick divorce."

They reached the top floor of the Magna Building on Broadway and Forty-fifth. Waiting for them was a tall lean man with ruddy hollow cheeks and watery blue eyes: Dan Sullavan. Sullavan greeted Dave warmly, showed them into his office, offered them drinks. There was some pretense at friendly conversation. But the friction between the two older men would have been apparent to Dave even if H.P. had said nothing. One day, Dave promised himself, he would discover the reason for it.

Most of the conversation revolved around Dave's film. Sullavan liked it. The entire New York staff was high on it. They expected great things. But of course, tomorrow's reviews would tell the story. They had arranged a number of promotional interviews on the radio for Dave. But those would follow the premiere.

So until this evening's opening at the Capitol, Dave was a free man. He decided not to go to the hotel directly. Instead, he walked east along Forty-eighth street. He arrived at 30 Rockefeller Plaza, consulted the board for Gloria Simms' new offices. Gloria threw her arms around him and kissed him—not a casual, barely making contact show-business kiss, but one of genuine affection.

"We had two people in your cast. They came back raving about the picture. And they loved working for you," she said. "I'm very proud of that, Dave. I feel we trained you, brought you up."

The unfortunate pronoun introduced the subject of Betty. Gloria had to ask now.

"How is Betty?"

"Fine! She seems to love it out there."

To change the subject, Gloria said, "You know, Dave, I've got this most terrific young girl coming along. I think she's ready for pictures. In the right part she could be fantastic."

"They're always fantastic, till you get them on the screen," he said.

"No, she really is. A tremendous talent. Almost too big for the screen. How long are you going to be in town?"

"Three days. Do some radio interviews."

"Then I'll arrange for you to see her," Gloria insisted.

"Sure," Dave agreed. "Have her call me. I'm staying at the Plaza."

He was inserting the gold studs into his dress shirt when the phone rang.

"Mr. Cole? I'm supposed to call you. They say you're a big Hollywood director. And you will make me a star. If I had a dollar for every time I've been told that, I wouldn't have to act at all."

The girl spoke in a burst of words punctuated only with an infectious laugh that let him know she was joking.

"Who is this?" he asked—not impatiently, because he liked the sound of her.

"Ethel Barrymore," she quipped, adopting a deep and vibrant voice.

"Did Gloria tell you to call?"

"Yes," the girl said. "Now, let's be honest about it. I had to call because Gloria said so. And you had to be polite because you owe her a favor. But you really don't want to see me."

"She says you're a very good actress."

"There isn't anyone better. Not in the whole goddamn theater. But I'm not your kind of actress."

"Don't you think I should be the judge of that?" Dave asked. "When are you free? I'd like to get a look at you."

"I know that line. You Hollywood directors are all the same. You'd like to get me into bed. I don't blame you. I'm sensational n bed," she mocked.

"I'm serious. Can we get together? For a drink? *Not* in my uite."

155

"Suite?" she echoed, sarcasm in her voice. "They must have a lot of confidence in your new film."

"Would you like to see my opening tonight?"

The girl hesitated. Then, with the air of taking a dare, she said, "Okay."

"Then I'll see you there?" he suggested.

"I'll be the one with the gardenia in my teeth," she said, laughing.

"I'll look for you," he joked back. "The ticket will be at the box office. Whose name shall I leave it in?"

"Lawrence. Kit Lawrence," she said.

As soon as he hung up, the operator rang. "Your limousine is waiting, Mr. Cole."

He rode alone in the limousine, unaware of the fact that when H.P. had originally arranged for the premiere it had been his plan to have Dave escort Sybil. When they stepped from the car, the interviewer was to announce to the crowd and the radio audience, "And now, the talented young director of *Redemption*, David Cole, accompanied by Sybil Koenig, the charming and beautiful daughter of H. P. Koenig." H.P. had written that himself, and he had passed it along to Sonny Brown with a bold handwritten warning: *Must use!* But in the end, Sybil's intransigence had thwarted the old man.

As Dave's limousine pulled up at the Capitol Theatre, a voice on a loudspeaker announced him. He stepped into the glare of the powerful lights and was escorted to the platform on which a master of ceremonies waited at a microphone to greet him.

All during the interview Dave kept concentrating on a young tawny-haired girl who stood just outside the lobby. Her smile and her sparkling eyes seemed to be passing judgment on him. She was impish and womanly at the same time. Just as Dave finished, she drew a white gardenia out of a paper cone and slipped it between her teeth. When he gaped, she laughed.

"Kit Lawrence?" he asked. She smiled, admitting it. "You did come with a gardenia."

"I always do what I say I'm going to do."

"Do you want to come to the opening-night party?" he asked

pulsively. "I don't have a date." She hesitated. "Please?"

"I'm not dressed for it," she said.

True, she was dressed in a velvet suit that had seen better days. There were places along the collar that had frayed and worn through to the backing. She wore a white silk blouse simple, frank, and so open that it revealed the tops of her young breasts in a way that stirred him. She was so fresh and bright, so young.

"You come with me anyhow," he insisted. "Meet me right out here after the picture. Promise?"

She eyed him, speculating, then smiled and said, "Okay. After the picture."

The film was over. The applause was enthusiastic. H.P. embraced Dave and kissed him on the cheek. Dan Sullavan shook his hand, pounded him on the back.

Gradually the theater emptied out. Most of the important guests had been swept off to "21." Dave searched for Kit Lawrence and found her in a corner of the deserted lobby. Her gardenia was now weary and drooping. He took it from her hand and examined it.

"I guess I twisted it too hard during the picture," she apologized.

"Was it that bad?"

"It was that good," she insisted seriously. "I just hope *they* know it."

"Everybody seemed to like it," Dave replied modestly.

"I mean the critics. When you live in the theater, 'they' or 'them' always means the critics."

"I was in the theater once myself," he reminded, chiding her.

"I know. It shows in your work. You get good performances out of people. Even movie stars like Gladys Holmes."

"You're too young to be so cynical," Dave said. "How old are you?"

"Old enough to be cynical. Young enough to wish I weren't."

"Let's go to the party. Maybe we can change your mood." He took her arm to lead her to his limousine.

"Can't we walk?" she asked. "It's only a few blocks."

"Okay." He guided her across Broadway and east on Fifty-

157

second Street. "Don't you like limousines?"

"I don't want to acquire the taste before I earn the right," sh
explained. "But one day I will."

"Gloria says you're going to be a star."

"Lots of people do. But most of all I'd like to be a great actres
Once before I die, I'd like to find the ideal part in the ideal pla
and do it to the full."

"Twenty and you talk about dying?" Dave asked.

"Twenty-two," she corrected, as if it gave her the right to b
fatalistic.

"Twenty-two," Dave repeated. "I'd like to be twenty-tw
again."

"Why? To go back and relive all the terrible days? To kno
what you have inside you and walk around wondering why th
whole world doesn't recognize it? You must know the feelin
You want to run down Broadway and cry out, 'Damn it, look a
me, know me! Appreciate me! I have talent!' Didn't you ever fe
that way?"

"Yes," Dave admitted. "But not that intensely. You'll be
star," he promised as they reached "21."

In the private dining room reserved for the Magna part
liveried waiters served champagne, Scotch, vodka, brandy. Thre
men in high white toques presided over a luxurious hot and co
buffet. All the guests interrupted eating and drinking to co
gratulate Dave all over again.

Eventually most of the guests departed. Dave felt he coul
finally stop smiling, being polite to strangers and saying, "Than
you." He looked around for Kit. He didn't see her. For a mome
he feared that she had slipped out, deserting him. But while h
was having his last words with H.P., who by now was quite me
low on brandy, Kit reappeared. She had obviously been to th
ladies' room to tidy up her face. Dave freed himself to join he

H.P. took serious note of the fact that she was an extreme
attractive girl. Not the usual starlet type, but a girl of som
quality. He wondered how deeply Dave was interested in he
He must make a point of finding out. She was obviously an ac
ress. Well, if Dave ever suggested giving her a screen test, H.P.
answer would be no. Now he regretted even more strongly Sybi
obstinate refusal to come to New York.

"Ready to go?" Dave asked.

"Ready," Kit said, smiling up at him. "Can we walk?"

"Sure. Where do you live?"

"I meant up to the Plaza," she said simply.

"You don't have to."

"If I felt I had to, I wouldn't."

He unlocked the high mahogany door of his suite. There was a cooler of champagne waiting, a note tied to its neck: *A great night deserves a great nightcap.* It was signed *Dan Sullavan.*

They drank toasts. She to him. And his successful night. He to her. And her own success that was sure to come. She slipped out of her velvet jacket. Dave realized that the promise of her breasts was more than fulfilled. Her nipples were prominent and proud against her silk blouse. Dave's desire replaced his anticipation. He took her in his arms. She reached for his hands and drew into her bodice, pressing it against one of her breasts. She could feel what it did to him. As she sighed, he realized that it gave her great pleasure as well. He unbuttoned her blouse, pulling it down over her shoulders to bare her breasts completely.

As he stared, she asked, almost shyly, "Do you like them?"

"Yes, I like them. Very much."

"Good. Because they're never going to be better than they are now," she said strangely.

They undressed and he led her to his bed. She embraced him and drew him into herself with an artfulness that belied her twenty-two years.

The overpowering feeling of ecstasy had ended. They were both quiet and serene.

"I wanted to know how it felt," she said softly. "Success, I mean. Most times when I have a man in bed it's to console him. Just for once I wanted to know how it feels to make love to a successful man at the very moment of his success. This is better, believe me."

"You could know how it is," he said, "if you didn't have this damned attitude about yourself and dying. You've got the talent."

She didn't respond.

"Look, I'll see that you get a screen test. Better than that, I'll

159

have you flown out to the Coast specially to test for a part in my picture."

"You're the one man I won't work for," she said. "Else this night will turn into a cliché. I'll be just another girl who got into bed with you for some ulterior purpose."

"Let *me* decide that."

"Oh, no. It's what I'd think of myself that counts. So don't try to seduce me with offers. Just make love to me. That'll be enough."

She drew his face between her breasts and enveloped him.

Twice during the night he woke to find her staring down at him. Her disheveled tawny hair added a natural wildness to her soft face and her searching eyes. He pulled her close and kissed her. She embraced him fiercely and she made love to him. For a girl so young, she had all the instincts of a good mistress and a comforting mother. She was a rare girl. Yet there was something ominous about her that troubled him. He felt instinctively that he must look after her. Just before dawn they fell asleep in each other's arms. They were still embraced when the phone rang.

"Dave?" He had trouble identifying the voice. "Dan Sullavan. I wake you?"

"No." His gravelly voice belied the word.

"It's worth it. I got the first newspaper reviews. Sensational! Congratulations! And we've got the tear sheets on *Look* and *Life*. Both terrific. Kid, you're a smash!"

"Thanks," Dave mumbled.

"Just thought I'd let you know," Sullavan said. He tried to seem very casual and offhand as he added, "By the way, if you have a little time today, drop by the office. Love to get to know you better."

"Sure. If I can," Dave agreed, never intending to.

He hung up.

"Something wrong?" Kit asked.

"When strangers are too nice too suddenly, there's bound to be something wrong sooner or later."

"Trouble can always wait. Big trouble can wait a long time. But moments like this are gone before you know it," she said desolately. "Kiss me?"

He kissed her, and while they made love all else was forgotten.

160

At the end she embraced him fiercely, holding him within her as if reluctant to let him go, ever.

They had breakfast at the window overlooking Central Park. She wore his robe and looked lovely in it. Her hair fell loosely over her shoulders. He stared at her more than he ate. She caught him staring.

"Worried about that call?"

"No. About you. Come to California! I'll fix it so the studio pays all your expenses. You can do whatever you choose once you're out there. Or I can get you that screen test. But I want you out there!" he insisted.

She laughed. "You're so young. So unrealistic."

"Goddammit, I'm thirty-one! And you're only twenty-two. Don't call *me* young!" he exploded.

She went to him, leaned against him, embracing him. Staring out at the park, she said, "What happened to us last night can never be repeated. We could meet again. Another time. Another thousand times. But it would never be the same. You may spend your life regretting that it's over, but to me, it'll be an experience I'll use again and again. Whenever I'm asked to play a scene in which I am deeply, truly in love, I'll think of you and last night and relive that feeling. The critics will say that it's magic. *Magic*. So this won't die. I'll keep it alive. In performance after performance."

He turned his face to nestle against her breasts. "Is that all you want out of life?"

"That's all," she said fervently.

"Nothing more permanent than that? No husband? No children?"

"I wouldn't be good for any husband. Any children."

He felt a moistness on his cheek. Her tears.

"Kit?" he asked softly.

"I can't explain it. Not even to my analyst. My trouble is that every man I meet wants me. But me, I can only live when I'm someone else, a character in a play. It's the only time I'm really alive. But even that palls after I've extracted everything from the role. It would be the same with marriage."

She rubbed her hand gently over his bristly face.

"Don't you see? At first I'd be the most wonderful and inven-

161

tive wife. But in a few months I'd become unhappy with the part. I wouldn't show up. I'd want my understudy to go on for me. It would be disastrous."

"How do you know? You've never tried. Try it with me!" he said, suddenly but seriously.

"Least of all with you," she said softly. "Because I could really love you. So I couldn't be that unfair or cruel to you. No, you better go back alone."

"I won't forget you."

"Very few men do," she said simply. There was no vanity in it, only sadness. As if she wanted to be forgotten.

It was an uneventful flight back for Dave. A limousine was waiting as he left the aircraft. He remembered how, when he had made his first trip West, he had envied Imogene Hopkins this luxury. Now that it was his, it didn't seem so special.

Kit Lawrence. Either he never should have met her or else he never should have let her go. He promised himself that the very first time he had the chance, he would test her for a part. But it had to be a good part and she had to be exactly right for it.

It sounded fine and idealistic when he first made that resolve. But by the time the car rolled onto the Magna lot he realized that, in his way, he was no longer so different from H. P. Koenig. Kit Lawrence would never have forgiven him for that.

Nor would Sybil Koenig.

12

H. P. Koenig and Albert Grobe were leaving Marge's place. Too elegant to be classed as a whorehouse, Marge's was always referred to by its patrons as The Club. On nights when he felt especially expansive, H.P. would buy out The Club, bringing with him only a favorite friend or two. Tonight it had been Albert Grobe. Though Albert preferred his own little games, he always accepted H.P.'s invitations.

On their way home H.P., who was slightly drunk, pretended to have a sudden inspiration. He patted Grobe on the thigh and said, "Al, you know what?"

"What?"

"It would be a very nice gesture."

"It would? What?"

"After all, he's a protégé of yours. You took him under your wing."

"Who?"

"Dave. Dave Cole."

"Oh, Lochinvar. Yes. Nice young man. He's got talent he hasn't even shown yet. *Redemption* is only the beginning."

"In release four weeks, and almost in the black," H.P. said proudly. "How do you think that shmuck Begelman feels now?"

"Nice gesture," Grobe reminded.

"What?" H.P. pretended to have lost track.

"You said something would be a very nice gesture. What?"

"Oh, yes. I thought, instead of my giving a party in Cole's honor, one of those big studio Publicity things, it would be nicer if you gave one small bash at your place. Your personal tribute to a young man whose career you sponsored."

"Good idea!" Grobe agreed. "After *Redemption* he's entitled to it."

"Of course, Magna will pick up the tab."

"Totally unnecessary," Grobe insisted.

"Please, Al. My idea, my tab. Okay?"

"Okay," Grobe agreed. It was fruitless to argue with H.P. at any time, but especially when he felt he was being magnanimous.

"Good!" H.P. slapped Grobe's thigh to bind the agreement.

Just as Grobe was leaving H.P.'s limousine, the old man seemed to have an afterthought. "You know, Al, what would also be nice?"

"Yes, H.P.?"

"Sybil."

"What about Sybil?"

"She doesn't like big parties. Behind that sharp tongue of hers she's really a very shy girl. But she might enjoy such an intimate party."

"I don't think she's very fond of Dave Cole," Grobe said. "He's tried to see her, you know."

"I told you, she's shy. Once she knows him better she'll like him. After all, what's not to like? If he didn't have brains he'd be good-looking enough to be a leading man. He's going far in the industry. So why shouldn't she like him?"

If the hour had been earlier and his energy level higher, Albert Grobe might have taken the trouble to explain. But once he realized what H.P. really had in mind, he simply said, "Okay. I'll give the party for Dave. And I'll invite Sybil. Only I can't guarantee that she'll come."

"Al, do it for me? Make sure that she comes." H.P. had phrased it as a request, but it was a command and neither man doubted its force.

Albert Grobe went to work on his assignment the next morning. He pinned down a date with Dave, though Dave bristled at the idea of being guest of honor, even at a small party. Grobe then selected twelve more guests and left himself free to con-

164

centrate on Sybil. He finally decided to call her direct.

"Sybil, darling, you have to help me."

"Of course, Uncle Albert. What's wrong?"

"Wrong? Nothing is wrong. That is, unless you refuse to come to a party at my house."

"Have I ever refused?"

"No."

"Then what could be wrong?"

"It's only fifteen people. A week from Tuesday. And I need a pretty, unattached young lady to round out my guest list."

"A week from Tuesday?" Sybil said. "I have a meeting that night. But for you, Albert, I'll cancel."

"Sybil, darling, you haven't heard it all yet."

"Oh?"

"The party is in honor of Dave Cole, for the terrific job he did on *Redemption*."

"Oh, I see. And I'm to be his dinner partner."

"That's the general idea, darling. Do it. For me. Please?"

"I do have my meeting. And besides, there's Gladys Holmes. And Christine Donlan. And Imogene." Sybil proceeded to name several other Magna stars and starlets with whom Dave was known to have had affairs.

"Darling, you don't understand. It isn't that kind of party. There'll only be one actress here and she's married to a very fine writer. It's an evening for nice, intelligent, civilized people, not a mating ceremony to see who winds up in whose bed for the night. You know I wouldn't invite you to anything like that."

Sybil was silent for a moment, though it seemed much longer to Albert Grobe. Finally she asked one question:

"Uncle Albert, be honest with me. If I don't come, is it going to get you into trouble with *him*?"

Him used in that context was a synonym for *bastard* and *sonofabitch* as used on the Magna lot. All referred exclusively to H. P. Koenig.

Grobe sighed, then answered truthfully, "Yes, my dear."

"In that case, I'll come."

"Thank you," Albert Grobe said, greatly relieved. "Week from Tuesday. Seven-thirty. I'll send Adam to pick you up."

"No need, Uncle Albert. I'll use my own car."

Some minutes later Sybil called back.

"I hope you haven't changed your mind, dear," Grobe said.

"No. Not about the party. But yes, send Adam to pick me up. It might be better that way."

There was a calculated note in her voice which made Grobe hesitate before calling Romanoff's and giving the Prince meticulous instructions about the menu for his party and the manner in which he wished each dish prepared. Albert Grobe was as sensual about food as he was about the young girls he seduced with such regularity.

Like a group of refugees, Albert Grobe's guests spent the evening enjoying his food and speaking of the old days in New York when they were struggling to find a place in the theater. He hadn't realized it at the time he compiled his guest list, but they all had come from New York.

For Dave Cole it was enough that Sybil was there. He was completely relaxed until one of the guests, a well-known playwright, brandy glass in hand, loudy declared, "They say this is lotus-land. That we make unreal pictures for an audience that swallows our garbage like pigs at a trough. Well, we are not in the business of entertaining, but of deceiving! And it is a cruel deception we practice. We sell contentment to people who have no right to be contented. We are apologists for a system that exploits human misery. We serve a cannibalistic system when we should be preparing the masses for a new freedom from economic exploitation. When the history of our time is written among the names to be despised and reviled along with Hitler and Mussolini will be men like the 'great' H. P. Koenig."

Even those in the group who bore no love for Koenig felt embarrassed. The playwright's wife, a small woman of tight athletic build from years of ballet training, flushed slightly and said, "The older the brandy the more Seymour exaggerates. It's really a compliment to the quality of your liquor, Albert."

She placed a subtle but restraining hand on her husband's arm but the playwright was too drunk to be stopped.

"How does it feel to have such a monster for a father?" he asked Sybil. "You seem like such a nice girl, one would never suspect."

Sybil's dark cheeks flushed slowly. Though she was one of he

166

father's chief critics, she couldn't bear to see him so viciously demeaned in public. After a moment's silence, she decided to brush off the attack with a joke.

"I don't know how you can make any comparison. After all, between them Hitler and Mussolini never made one good picture."

This allowed the other guests to laugh, and the incident passed without further crisis. But the evening had been ruined and the guests hastened to leave.

Only Dave and Sybil remained. Albert took Sybil's hand and said gently, "I'm sorry, my dear. I had planned it all so differently."

"It's not your fault, Uncle Albert. It's probably no different from what was said in a hundred other homes in Beverly Hills tonight."

"Let me take you home?" said Dave.

"Please." Sybil was relieved to have the evening over.

They were driving south on Rodeo toward Sunset when Dave finally said, "I suppose I could have defended him."

"Not without lying," Sybil said firmly.

"I know how you feel about him, but an attack like that was unjustified."

"If it was, why didn't anyone else say so? I'll tell you why. Because they were all afraid of being accused of being sycophants. In this town it's perfectly acceptable to *be* a sycophant. The crime is to be *caught* at it."

There was no good refutation, so Dave remained silent.

"I'd like to be able to defend him myself," Sybil said. "What daughter wouldn't? Only the man I know is even worse than the man you work for. Defend him? I should be the one to accuse him! This entire evening was his plan."

"It was?" Dave asked, suspecting that in her resentment she was accusing H.P. of crimes he had not committed.

"Oh, yes. Ask Uncle Albert. It was *his* idea that Albert give a party for you. *His* that I be invited. And if I refused to attend, Albert would have been in trouble. That's the only reason I agreed to come."

"I was hoping there might be another reason."

"That would have been the last reason," she said quietly.

"Why?" he demanded. "Because *he* wants it? Is that any reason for people to stay apart, simply because he wants them to be together?"

"That's it, you know. There's no way to rebel against him. He's like a stone wall. You can beat your fists against him till they're bloody. And it would never make any impression. All my days, all my nights are spent planning vengeance against him. But in the end it always fails. When I agreed to come tonight I felt that I was doing a favor for Albert. But the fact is, I was doing exactly what *he* wanted me to do. Because *he* had arranged it that way. Because *he* knew that I would never refuse Albert. So *he* had his way again, for the millionth time. How does one fight a man like him?"

"Why is it necessary to keep fighting?" Dave asked. "Live your own life."

"If it were only possible," she said vaguely.

It was the end of all conversation till they reached Sunset and Dave started to head west.

"No! Don't! Tonight I don't want to go home. I don't want him to feel he's won again."

Without pause, Dave turned the car and drove toward the Marmont. She made no effort to stop him.

A mist had settled over Beverly Hills. When they pulled into the grounds of the Marmont the lights wore halos. The ground was damp along the path to his bungalow. Dave unlocked his door. She hesitated a moment before entering.

The large living room was dimly lit; the maid who had tidied up had left it that way. At the far end, the huge fireplace was burning with a low blue flame. Simulated to resemble a wood-burning fireplace, it was actually composed of gas-fed synthetic logs. Annie, his regular maid, was a very caring old woman who treated Dave as her son. He could just hear the tiny, wiry Irishwoman saying to herself, The lad'll need a fire on a damp night like this.

When Sybil turned to him to remark on it, he said, "Annie. My mother away from home."

He took her hand and turned her about to face him. Realizing he was about to embrace her, she pleaded softly, "Dave, don't. Not tonight."

"Why?"

"Because tonight I wouldn't know—was it something I wanted or something I did to defy him?"

He held her closer. "Sybil... darling... we need each other. You want me as much as I want you. Only *his* wanting it stands in the way. Well, I won't let it. Not any longer."

She lowered her head, pressing it against his chest. He kissed her again. Slowly, all resistance went out of her, and he led her to the couch before the fire.

She had no will of her own; as he kissed her her body started to come alive. Gradually, her arms gained strength. She embraced him with a passion that testified to her long-suppressed desire.

Minutes later they were naked and lying before the fire. She had turned away her face as if not daring to look up at him. He found her as perfectly shaped as he had suspected that first day in New York. Her legs were long and graceful, yet strong from days of riding and playing tennis. Her belly curved delicately under his hand and trembled slightly under it as his fingers traced across it. Her breasts were not large, but they tilted proudly, presenting small erect nipples, rosy in a circle of light brown. Even in passion her face was strong, with well-angled planes. Her black hair, loose now, was a frame for her fine features.

When he kissed her her mouth opened wide and he invaded it with his tongue. She drew him to her with a fierceness that was part passion, part desperate need. Her long, graceful legs opened, needing to feel him large within her.

"Davie... Davie..." she whispered, her voice never rising but gaining in intensity until she rose up beneath him in one last climax of passion. Then she lay trembling under him, spent and weeping. "Darling," she kept repeating as she lay staring toward the blue flames in the fireplace. "Darling."

He kissed her wet cheeks and slender throat.

After a time, she joked softly, "Make me a star?"

"Never say that to me, even in fun!"

"Sorry," she said, "truly sorry. But Davie, what are we going to do?"

"What we should have done a long time ago. Get married," he said.

"If I asked you to, would you quit the picture business?" she challenged.

In the reflection from the flickering flames, her face was quite serious and searching.

"Would you?" she insisted.

"Why?" he asked.

"For one thing, then I'd know it's me you want and not Magna. More important, we'd get out of this town and away from *him*." She stared into the fire. "Whether he made it that way or whether it's all the money, there's something evil about this business. I want to escape before I catch it. Before the man I marry catches it."

"It doesn't have to be evil."

"Prove it!" she challenged. "Prove to me that if you ever became head of Magna, you wouldn't turn out to be exactly like him!"

"There's no way of proving that. You simply have to love me enough to believe."

"That's not easy, not for a little girl who believed in her father once. Or for a girl who saw what happened to her mother. I am never going to be like her! I am not going to settle for whatever portion of life my father decides to dole out to me. If I were she, I wouldn't sit by patiently and watch him screw every star who suits his fancy, while she has to pretend all the while that her marriage is a happy one.

"I am not going to bury myself in good causes because I find no good cause in myself. I am determined to survive. As a woman. As an individual."

"The way to do that is not by running away. But by rebelling. Declaring yourself to be free!"

She hesitated before admitting, "I've tried. Because of him I deliberately went out and lost my virginity. With a young actor who was under contract to Magna. I seduced him. Just so I could say to myself, I have defied my father, that sonofabitch. Of course, he found out. Else why did I do it?

"The truly terrible part was what he did to that young actor. He was ruined in this town. My father is a relentless man. Revenge is his greatest delight. His true form of orgasm. So that's what all my rebelling came to. I destroyed that young actor's career. Who knows? Maybe I'll destroy yours."

170

"That happened just before you came to New York," Dave concluded.

She nodded. "But I failed there too. And had to come back. Maybe it's not him I'm afraid of, but myself. Whatever it is, my answer is no."

He tried to persuade her in the only other way at his command. He took her in his arms again and kissed her. She surrendered herself willingly. This time with even more fervor than before. But when it was over, she whispered softly into his ear, "Don't use me, Davie. And don't try to exact promises from me. Not this way. I love you. I love the way you make love to me. But marriage has to be more than that. Much more."

The early mist still overhung Beverly Hills, making ghosts of the few cars that moved along Sunset, their eerie lights trying to grope their way. Dave's car moved cautiously along the winding street. When he reached for Sybil's hand, she pulled back slightly, but perceptibly.

"Sybil?"

She shook her head as if begging him not to talk.

"Are you afraid of what happened or afraid of him?"

"Just . . . just afraid."

He reached out, took her hand and drew her close to him.

"What we discovered tonight is ours. No one can take it from us. No one can spoil it. Unless we spoil it. And we won't. I promise you we won't."

She leaned against him, pressing her face into his shoulder.

As the car approached the corner of the Koenig estate, she said, "Pull up."

"Why?"

"Just let me out. I'll walk."

"Okay," he finally said. But before he would let her go he kissed her and held her a long time. Then he watched her move through the mist to her door. Once he knew she was safe, he headed back to the Marmont.

He knew that of all the nights he had spent with women, this one would be the most enduring. As for her fears, he was sure he could soon overcome them.

He would have felt less certain if he had known that H. P.

171

Koenig was sitting in his library at that moment, having his early-morning coffee. He had left the bed of a little Magna starlet at eleven the night before to return home so that he could greet his daughter and discover how his carefully planned evening had gone. As the night wore on and it became obvious that she would not return at what he deemed an acceptable hour, H.P. continued his vigil with growing fury.

By the time Sybil let herself in at the front door, it was five past six. H. P. Koenig was beyond fury now. He was already plotting his vengeance against David Cole.

No man used H. P. Koenig's daughter without paying a price. An extremely high price.

13

Albert Grobe was the first person admitted that morning to the presence of H. P. Koenig. H.P. pretended to be engrossed in box-office receipts. Knowing that one never intruded on H.P.'s concentration until he received permission, Grobe waited. Without looking up from the figures, H.P. asked with practiced casualness, "Nice party, Al?"

"Extremely. One loudmouth New York playwright. But everyone else had a good time."

"Sybil?"

"I think she did. At least, she said so. And she got off a good crack at that snide New York bastard."

"Yes?" H.P. asked, indicating his desire to know all about it.

Grobe realized he would have to repeat the playwright's line about Hitler and Mussolini. He phrased it a bit more delicately and then delivered Sybil's response.

H.P. smiled and nodded, pretending to appreciate his daughter's defense. "I'm glad it went off well. Did they seem to get along any better this time?"—obviously referring to his daughter and Dave.

"I think so," Grobe said.

"It was a late party, wasn't it, Al?"

"Late? I didn't keep check, but I think everyone left by midnight. Why?"

"Sybil too?"

"Yes," Grobe said, becoming wary now.

"Did Adam drive her home? The only reason I ask is I noticed her car in the garage."

"Adam picked her up."

"But he didn't drive her home, did he?"

"No. He didn't."

"Someone else dropped her off," H.P. said, as if drawing an unavoidable conclusion.

"Yes."

"Who?"

"Dave Cole, of course. Isn't that what you wanted?"

H.P. finally put aside the mass of grosses and turned to face Grobe. "Sit down, Al!" This time no smile, no affable invitation, but a command.

Alert for trouble, Al Grobe sat on the edge of a leather chair.

"Al, you are a man of the world, a man of much experience. Tell me, if a young lady leaves a party with a young man at midnight, and she does not return to her own home till after six in the morning, where would you say she'd been? Watching the tide come in at Malibu?"

"Who—who knows?" Grobe started to fumble. "They could go to Ciro's. Or the Mocambo. And then maybe to an all-night drive-in for breakfast."

"Al, there is only one place they go. And you know it. They go to his place. To his bed. And they fuck!"

H.P. rose from his red leather desk chair and began to pace. "Did you hear what I said? That sonofabitch, that prick, had the nerve to fuck my daughter! Do you understand what that means?" H.P.'s voice was so loud Grobe became concerned that those in the waiting room might overhear him.

"H.P., I have no idea where they went or what they did."

"*I* know! I was up all night. After all, I'm a father. I worry about that girl. That's the trouble these days—fathers don't keep tabs on their daughters. There's too much freedom, too much loose living! Well, someone has to set a moral tone."

The self-righteous statement made Al Grobe wonder, *How many daughters of how many fathers have you despoiled and degraded?*

Suddenly H.P. turned on Grobe and said, "And don't forget,

174

you're not blameless. It was *your* party. *You* invited that sonofa-bitch! *You* decided to make him the guest of honor. And they go right from *your* house to *his* bed!"

Grobe knew it would do no good to point out the truth. To H.P. there was only one view of anyone's conduct. His.

"I'm not saying it was your fault, Al. I'm only saying you had a hand in this. So we have to figure out some way to make that bastard pay!"

H.P. resumed pacing. "I can see what happened. He got her into his car. He used some kind of trick to get her to his place. And once he got her there, he forced her. That's right, forced her. She wouldn't do such a thing on her own. God knows what he made her do!

"But the real question is *Why*? Well, I'll tell you. He wanted to make a shmuck out of me! He wanted the whole town to know that he had the nerve to screw H.P.'s daughter! Well, I'll destroy the sonofabitch! I'll kill him!"

"H.P.," Grobe dared to say, "what makes you think it'll get around?"

"Why else did he do it? The prick had a bet with someone that he could get H.P.'s daughter into bed, fuck her and turn her out like a whore in the early morning! I'll have a contract put out on him. Vic'll know how to handle this. He knows about such things!"

Now that he felt H.P. was seriously considering such an act, Albert Grobe felt compelled to speak up, despite the risks.

"H.P., maybe there's something you've overlooked."

"What?" he demanded irascibly.

"Maybe two such young and attractive people are in love. I could sense something between them last night."

"In love?" H.P. demanded, enraged. "He's not in love with her!"

"How do you know?"

"Because a man who is in love with a girl does not fuck her! That's how I know."

Grobe knew it was fruitless to disagree or try to explain. To H. P. Koenig sex would always be an act of hostility and degrada-tion. Grobe had to find another argument, and quickly. He thought frantically.

"H.P., this has to be handled carefully," he warned.

175

"Of course. I won't touch it. I'll have Martoni handle it."

"So what will happen?" Grobe asked, devil's advocate now. "He'll put out a contract. Dave'll be beaten up. Or killed. Either way, it'll cause talk. Investigations."

"Sonny can handle the police and the D.A."

"Of course he can," Grobe agreed quickly. "But you know this town. Gossip will start. People will want to know *why*, and one way or another they'll find out. So instead of concealing this terrible insult you'll be the one responsible for making it public."

H.P. paced more slowly. There was logic in what Albert was saying. Grobe sensed that he had made headway and decided to continue.

"The last time this happened," Grobe ventured, "there was a reason. You wanted to warn every man in Hollywood that Sybil was out of bounds. But this time, what would you accomplish by having an open scandal? You have to find another way. A subtle way."

"Hmm!" H.P. grunted, beginning to accept Albert Grobe's concept.

"Besides, if the insult was directed at you, the revenge should come from you. Not from some two-bit hood. There is also the matter of waiting to see if this does become public. Maybe no one will ever know. Except you and me and, if something actually did happen, Sybil and Dave. But if you fire him it will only start the scandal."

"I wonder what he did to force her to do such a thing," said H.P., unable to conceive that it could have been an act born of love.

"My advice, H.P., would be to wait it out. Take your time. Plan your revenge. Till then I wouldn't even let him know you know."

H.P. was beginning to nod in agreement, and as he contemplated the various forms of revenge open to him, a small smile began to blossom on his face.

For the moment at least, Albert Grobe had saved Dave Cole from any drastic reprisals. Whether he would be able to forestall them in the future, he could only wait to see.

In the weeks that followed, H.P. kept close surveillance on Dave. He learned that Dave made frequent phone calls to the Koenig home. Most times Sybil refused to talk to him, which only served to confirm in H.P.'s mind who was the malefactor.

H.P. had no way of knowing that Sybil refused Dave for the very reason that she knew she was in love. And she did not want that love to degenerate into another Hollywood affair, of which she'd seen too many.

"Davie, if we have any chance at all, it's by not doing what everyone in this town does. What *he* does."

When Dave persisted, she put him off. When he promised to be content to see her only in circumstances under which they would not be alone, she tried to explain. "If I see you, we would end up alone. Not because you'd break your word. But I'd break mine. I love you, Davie. That's the trouble."

No amount of persuasion could change her mind. When they met at studio functions, she pretended only a casual interest in him. But her eyes soon gave her away. She could not deceive him.

He came away determined that her father's hold on her had to be exorcised.

H. P. Koenig sat in the projection room and stared at the screen, becoming more and more incensed by the footage he saw. On his right sat Marty Willmot, the producer; on his left, Elliot Wolfe, a Pulitzer Prize poet who had been brought in to polish the script in its last draft because the subject of the film demanded great sweep and beauty of language.

But what H.P. saw on the screen did not justify either his ambitions for the film or the amount of money he had already lavished on it. As he had often done in the past, he reminded himself never to make an important picture away from the studio. Only the temptation to advertise that *Via Dolorosa* had been shot, for authenticity, in the Holy Land and in Rome had overruled his earlier judgment. Now he was confronted with the dismal results.

The scenes were slow, turgid, wordy. Nothing seemed to move

except for the action shots of clashes between Roman armies and Jewish guerrillas and Roman soldiers pursuing early Christians through the catacombs.

But where the hell is the goddamn picture? H.P. kept asking himself.

Since the footage had been flown in at great cost by specially chartered plane, H.P. did not view it alone. Seated in the front row of the projection room were his trusted aides, The Three Witches, and Sarah Immerman, who he felt represented the average audience.

The footage was finally over. The hot white light reflected off the screen until the projectionist killed it. The room became dark. But there was no need to see any faces to sense the reaction. A heavy silence, with the poisonous consistency of polluting smoke, filled the room. Willmot tried to find some bright spots in the few merits the footage had revealed.

"The girl," Willmot enthused. "That's a new star! The way she's grown up. Who would have thought that from riding horses and playing little-girl parts she would develop into such a voluptuous young woman? As soon as the designer saw her figure he said, 'Marty, we got to show those tits. They are unbelievable!' H.P., wait till you see the costume he designed for her in the Emperor's-throne-room scene."

H.P. was unmoved. There was nothing new in what Willmot had said. H.P. had noticed that the girl was developing from the time she was only eleven. He had desired her from the day he first noticed that she had more than a supremely beautiful face and deep violet eyes. As her body matured and her breasts became almost irresistible to him, he had tried his best to seduce her—until the girl's mother had warned him of the consequences, since she was under age. Once he became aware that ambition would not subvert the girl or her mother, H.P. lusted for her from a distance, always regretting the fact that this one would prove to be a rare exception. So he did not have to be told of her sexual attractiveness.

What he would like to be told was what one did with a film already two million dollars over budget but with not enough footage to cut into a picture, and too much footage to abandon easily. H.P. knew he would have to act boldly. Surgery might

178

not cure the patient, but it gave everyone confidence that something was being done. Elliot Wolfe anticipated him.

"H.P., I'm about to make a drastic suggestion," the poet said dramatically.

"Yes?" H.P. asked impatiently.

"I would fire Christopher Swift!"

"Why?"

"He is very difficult," said Wolfe, "as anyone on Broadway could have told you. Half the production holdups are due to him. He's late on the set. He argues about every line and every word."

"You know," H.P. said, "I agree with you. It's time for a drastic change. But not the one you have in mind."

He turned to the producer. "Willmot, you are through! You will not go back to Rome. You will not stay on this lot. You will get out of town tonight!"

Willmot gasped. Wolfe tried to intercede, but H.P. cut him off. "As for you, Mr. Wolfe, you can take all your fucking poetry and your lousy dialogue and go back to wherever the hell you came from."

Willmot and Wolfe shuffled to the door of the projection room, where Willmot paused long enough to remark, "There's such a thing as a contract, you know!"

H.P. turned toward the half-open door and bellowed, "Sue me, you sonofabitch. I'll drag you through every court in this land. Before I'm done with you, not only won't you have a job, you won't have a cent to your name! The lawyers will be sucking on your bones!"

Willmot allowed the door to close softly, and H.P. turned to his four hanging judges.

"Well?"

No one was able to say anything encouraging, and if they had been, they knew it was fatal to disagree with H.P. when he was in a rage.

"The next time any poet comes on this lot I want him thrown the hell off!"

No one answered. No one had to.

"All right, what's the score?" H.P. asked, thinking aloud. "The action footage is okay. To reshoot that would cost too much. And Christopher Swift is in some of it. So we can't fire him.

179

Then there's the girl. With that face and those tits she is a star even if she doesn't open her mouth."

Finally he said, "And, of course, there is Markham."

Few stars in Hollywood were referred to by their last names alone. Among the men it was Gable, Tracy, Cagney, Muni. Only three women were accorded that distinction. Garbo, Dietrich and Markham, Aline Markham. She was a woman of impressive distinction, and, most unusual among female stars, she lacked what were considered stardom's three essential B's: two abundant breasts and one seductive behind. She was too slender and at times not even graceful. Yet she projected a vitality, charm and confidence that women admired and even men adored. She was as free and independent in her private life as she was in the roles she played. She had been living with a noted married star for several years. Though marriage was impossible for them, she persisted in devoting her life to him. In an age when such conduct was frowned upon for all other women, her fans accepted her because she breathed integrity both on the screen and off.

Before she would accept the role of Mary, the Mother of Jesus, in *Via Dolorosa*, Aline Markham insisted on meeting with the director in H.P.'s presence to make it clear that she did not intend to play the part like a blue-robed piece of statuary in a Catholic church. Either Mary was going to emerge as a real woman and a real mother or Markham would not take the part. If such an ultimatum had come from any other actress, H.P. would have put her on suspension. But he acceded to Markham's terms and she finally accepted the role.

From the footage he had just witnessed, she was giving the only effective performance in the film. Next to the young girl's tits, Markham was the best box-office insurance he had. As for the girl, she'd have to be treated very carefully, since H.P. had been banking on getting church support to promote the film. It had been his fond dream that *Via Dolorosa* would be mentioned and plugged from every pulpit in the country. So even for the role of Mary Magdalene, there was a limit to how sexy and whorish they could make the girl.

It all came down to Markham, the girl and a questionable performance by Christopher Swift. How to make a successful picture out of that was H.P.'s problem.

"What do you think of the direction?" he asked his four advisers.

"Could be better," the brass-balled witch said.

That was always a good opening gambit with H.P., for it invited his opinion, which one could then endorse.

"The direction stinks," H.P. said.

"Frankly, that's what I thought," the blond agreed. "I just didn't want to seem ruthless, that's all."

Albert Grobe said, "H.P., to my mind it is very doubtful this can be saved. Sometimes you just have to eat it."

"Two million over budget and you say eat it, Al?" H.P. asked gravely.

"Is a six-million-dollar disaster better than a four-million-dollar disaster?"

"Maybe there's a way," H.P. muttered suddenly. "Yes, there must be a way."

In his own shrewd and conniving mind, and long before anyone else, H.P. had come to the conclusion that it *was* hopeless. He was now considering how to slip out from under the responsibility. Some generals have built great reputations on their skillful retreats. It was just such a maneuver H.P. was searching for now.

"All right, everybody, go!" he ordered suddenly. "I want to see this again. All by myself."

When the room was cleared, he pressed down the intercom button and ordered, "Rerun it! From the top!"

14

An hour after he viewed the footage of *Via Dolorosa* for the second time, H. P. Koenig asked Sarah Immerman to get Dave Cole on the phone.

"Dave?"

"Yes, H.P.?"

"I know you're up to your ass in the script for your new film. But if you could spare a few minutes, come up and see me. I'd appreciate it."

It was the most affable invitation from H.P. that Dave Cole had ever received. Perhaps the old man had need to talk of some personal problem. He might even open the subject of Sybil, who had been adamant about not seeing Dave in recent weeks. Or perhaps the old man was just being the old man and humility was simply another of his ploys.

"Dave, I'm in trouble" was H.P.'s opening statement when they met. "Anytime you've got a four-million-dollar picture not even near completion and you're over budget, that's trouble. So I need your opinion. Because I don't trust any of the bastards around here. They all pray for my downfall. You're the only one I can trust anymore, Dave. The only one."

It was the King Lear approach again. But as a director, Dave felt that H.P. was overplaying it. Surely the old man had something of great consequence in mind if it called for a scene so elaborately tragic. Dave waited. He knew that soon the old man would get to his real purpose.

"Dave, I have to make a decision that will involve the careers of many people. Such a decision does not sit lightly on my head. 'Uneasy wears the head . . .' No, 'Uneasy lies the head that wears the crown.' I don't remember what picture that was from. But Ronald Colman said it. And he was right. It's terrible to have such decisions in your hands. One day, when all this is yours, you'll know."

Dave made a mental note: the King Lear syndrome was leading into the Marvin Kronheim bit, a very significant signal that this must be important.

"Dave, before I take action I want your advice. So do me a favor. See about forty minutes of footage, rough cut, and tell me what you think. But be honest. Above all else, I need an honest opinion!"

The footage of *Via Dolorosa* was kept in a special vault. H.P. had given strict orders that no one, absolutely no one, was to see it without his approval. He wanted no rumors circulating that would check his hand or keep him from making his own decision. Only one projectionist was allowed to handle it, so that if word got out, H.P. would know exactly whom to blame—a threat that ensured silence.

Dave arrived at Projection Room B, was admitted by Hyman Goldfarb, the projectionist, who locked the door behind him. Then Goldfarb retired to the booth and darkened the room. The footage, disconnected and only roughly edited, began to unfold. It was difficult to follow the story line, since the scenes were not connective. The action, while exciting and well staged, lacked impact because it was impossible to tell what its function was in the rest of the film. But certain elements did emerge. The three leading performances. Markham, as the Mother of Christ, was superb. Valerie Bristol as Mary Magdalene, with her spectacular cleavage and that face which was part angel and part whore, capped by those sensitive violet eyes which projected so magnificently in color, was certainly a strong plus.

Christopher Swift was a different matter. Playing the youthful and sensitive disciple John, he was half Christ himself in some scenes. Yet he was so completely out of it in other scenes that Dave was profoundly disturbed.

This was not the Chris Swift he had known in New York. The fire was gone, the intensity. The torment was still there, but far more subdued than it had been in New York nine years ago. True, after that one huge Broadway triumph, Swift had never had a second. He had earned a reputation for being difficult to work with.

Eventually Swift had come out to Hollywood, hoping for a fresh start. He hadn't made a great impression until two years ago when an agent named Edmund Pryce took him on. In only three pictures Pryce had elevated Swift to stardom. He was now considered one of the brightest young actors in the industry. In some way, his talent and sensitivity transmitted even better through the camera than directly to a live audience. Motion pictures held an added advantage for Christopher Swift. A director could edit out the scenes in which Swift either under- or overacted. With skillful cutting one could speed up his tempo. The word was around among directors that if you shot enough footage of Christopher Swift you could fashion a gripping performance.

Though Dave had not worked again with Christopher Swift he could never forget the talent that young man had displayed in the cage. Yet what he was seeing in this footage of *Via Dolorosa* did not reflect that talent at all. Dave was troubled, not only as a director, but as a friend.

The footage was over. Goldfarb asked on the intercom, "Anything you'd like to see over again, Mr. Cole?"

"No," Dave said. "No thanks, Hymie."

Dave didn't move. He sat in the dark wondering what it was that H.P. might ask him. Not to replace Markham, quite certainly. Or Valerie Bristol. Young, still a bit inexperienced, she would get by handily. It must be Swift. H.P. was going to ask Dave if he should replace Swift. Reluctant as he was to discuss that, Dave called Sarah Immerman to arrange an appointment. To his surprise, he was told that H.P. had left a message for him. Anytime he was ready, the old man would interrupt any other meeting to hear his opinion.

When Dave entered the office, H.P. sat staring into space. When he finally acknowledged Dave's presence, he sighed and said, "Well?"

"Interesting footage."

"That bad, huh?"

The word *interesting* had a connotation in Hollywood that could not be confirmed in Webster's or Roget's thesaurus. It was a polite euphemism for terrible, god-awful, hopeless.

"No," Dave said, "not a disaster. I mean it really is interesting."

"What are you saying, Dave? That I should advertise a multimillion-dollar production called *Via Dolorosa* and say in big headlines, 'H. P. Koenig and Magna Pictures want you to come and see an *interesting* picture? Is that what you're telling me, Dave?"

"Not at all."

"So what the hell good is 'interesting'? Don't you understand, Dave, I am facing a four-million-dollar disaster. How do I explain that to the New York office? Four million dollars down the drain, unless *we* do something about it, Dave."

For the first time the conspiratorial "we" had entered H.P.'s dialogue. Dave was acutely aware of that. H.P. wanted more than advice, it seemed.

"Tell me, Dave, what would you do? Fire Swift? Shut down the film? Keep shooting, hoping to avoid disaster? Tell me, Dave! Because for the first time in my career, I am stumped. What would you do, Dave? This is the most important decision of my career. I'll do anything you say!"

The old man started to weep. "For something like this to happen to me at this stage of my life, at the end of my career!"

He played heavily on that last phrase, since it contained within it the promise that he might retire soon and make Dave his successor.

Too bad, Dave observed silently, that on Oscar night there wasn't a category for Best Performance by a Studio Head. H.P. would win every year. Then Dave resumed his consideration of the picture. If it were shut down it would be the end of Christopher Swift's career. Yet the lines were partly at fault. Too wordy, too purple, too poetic for an actor to use convincingly. It

185

was one thing to challenge an actor, another to overwhelm him. Chris had doubtless been overwhelmed.

H.P. was waiting.

"There are several choices. One, of course, is to shut down the picture."

"Is that what you would do?"

Dave was encouraged. At least H.P.'s mind was open to alternatives. He did not suspect that the old man had now succeeded in drawing him into a well-calculated trap.

"The biggest trouble is Swift's dialogue. No actor can speak such a mouthful of pretentious words."

"They made me do it!" H.P. lamented, always the victim. "They told me the disciple John was young and poetic. Not like Peter, the big tough fisherman. They told me, 'If you can't show Jesus in the film, then show John.' That's what that shmuck Willmot kept saying. 'That way we'll get the impact and not run afoul of some religious groups that don't want any living actor to play Christ.' So we brought in a real live poet from the East to write the dialogue. And what does it turn out to be? Shit!'"

Having absolved himself of all guilt for the script, the old man was silent for only a moment. "Okay, we rewrite the script. Then what do we do?"

"Then *you* have to consider the direction," Dave said, restoring the pronouns to their proper perspective.

"It stinks, right?"

"It could be better."

"Dave, I can't just accept 'better.' I need the best! If Wyler was free I'd put him on it. The man who saves this picture will become a power to be reckoned with."

For the first time the old man's purpose became clear. He was trying to inveigle Dave into taking over the picture.

"Dave, the man who saves this picture will be the next head of this studio! I will see to it myself!"

When Dave refused to bite, H.P. leaned back in his huge red leather chair. "Dave, what do I have to do, draw you a map? Opportunity is not only knocking on your door, it is virtually trying to break it down."

"Okay, H.P. I'll think" was as far as Dave would commit himself. "Give me a few days."

Dave started for the door. H.P. made him turn back when he

186

intoned enticingly, "Dave..." Once Dave faced him, H.P. said, "While you're thinking, think what it would mean to be one of the few producer-directors in this town. You can accomplish it all in one picture. One big picture! That *is* something to think about!"

Once Dave left, H. P. Koenig sat back in his chair and smiled. Of course he knew Dave would say yes. No ambitious young man could say no, and once he agreed, H.P. would have him by the balls. Producer-director Dave Cole, not he, would become completely responsible for *Via Dolorosa*. The worst H. P. Koenig could be accused of was taking a chance on a promising young man who had already done several successful films.

More important, to H.P., the insult to his daughter would be avenged. Dave Cole would never survive this disaster.

The horoscope that appeared in the *Los Angeles Times* the next morning warned of dire consequences for Sagittarians who did not carefully consider their situations before taking action. Dave never read that section of the newspaper. Evidently someone with his interests at heart did. For that column, with advice to Sagittarians circled in red, reached his desk in an anonymous envelope along with the regular interoffice mail. Dave wondered who the anonymous correspondent was.

Was it someone who coveted the challenge H.P. had handed him? Not very likely. No director liked to take on a picture that was in trouble. No, there was only one person who was privy to H.P.'s plans yet concerned enough about Dave's welfare to take such action. The fact that the deed was done anonymously confirmed the fact that the person feared H.P.

Dave called Albert Grobe to arrange a luncheon meeting off the lot. Grobe, who had always been readily available, was suddenly booked for the rest of the week.

If Dave was going to get any information, he would have to get it on the phone.

"Albert, I got some interesting mail today."

"About what, Dave?"

"A horoscope."

"Horoscope?" Grobe pretended surprise.

"For Sagittarians."

"I'm not a Sagittarian."

"Neither am I," Dave said. "That's why I thought it was very significant that someone would send me that particular piece."

"Maybe it was intended for someone else. What did it say?"

"It advised caution before making any important decisions."

"What the hell," Grobe said. "That's always good advice."

"Is it, Albert?"

"*I* think so," Grobe said with special emphasis.

"Why, Albert?"

"Why does there have to be a why? Good advice is good advice."

Dave knew he would get no more from Albert Grobe. But he did know that some sort of trap was being laid for him and Albert was aware of it.

Grobe hung up the phone, feeling only a little less guilty than he had before.

By the end of the day Albert Grobe's concern for Dave Cole got the better of him. He called Sybil Koenig and invited her to dinner. To avoid giving the occasion any sinister or furtive overtones, he asked her to meet him at the Beverly Hills Hotel. It was only near the end of what seemed to be a pleasant meal that he broached the subject.

"My dear, what I tell you now must remain completely confidential. I don't know whom else to talk to, who has Dave's welfare so much at heart."

She glanced at him, her dark eyes probing to see how much he knew.

"What I know is not important. It's what your father knows."

"And what does he know?"

"Everything. He waited up for you the night of my party."

"Oh" was all she said, but she had admitted it all. "He feels his honor has been hurt. Is that it? My God, he's not going to do to Dave what he did to that young actor!"

"It'll be more subtle this time. But just as devastating."

"What can we do?"

"Not 'we,' my dear; my hands are tied. But you. You have to warn Dave. Tell him not to get involved in *Via Dolorosa*. H.P. is sure it's a disaster. He wants to lay it off on Dave to destroy him. I can't tell him. But you can."

Grobe reached out to cover Sybil's hand with his. "The way you feel about him, you have to."

188

She nodded.

"You love him, don't you?"

"Yes, Uncle Albert."

"Then what's standing in the way?"

"I have to be free of *him* before I can be any man's wife."

Albert patted her hand gently. In a way, he had the same dilemma. To be able to live the life he wanted and to be free of I. P. Koenig at the same time.

15

After weeks of refusing to see him, Sybil Koenig called Dave
Cole at the Marmont that night. He was not in. Too late for a
random date, she concluded; he must be sleeping with another
of his stars. She resented it because she was jealous. She resented it even more because she knew it was her own fault.
Actually, she was wrong. Dave had arranged to view the
footage of *Via Dolorosa* again and had become so intrigued
with it that he viewed it four times, until Hyman Goldfarb reminded him that as a union projectionist he was now not merely
on overtime but on golden time.

The next morning Dave's secretary announced a Miss Jones
was calling, but refused to state her business. He guessed who
it was and told his secretary to take the number. He called back
on his private line.

"Sybil?"

"Yes," she said softly. "I must see you."

"When?"

"Tonight."

"Where?"

She hesitated. "I'll come to your place. But I want two things
understood. I'll come in my own car, I'll leave in my own car.
And you must not try to make love to me. Promise me that?"

"Okay," he agreed reluctantly. "I promise."

Dave had had an early dinner and settled down to work on his script. He sat before the fireplace in the huge living room of Bungalow B of the Marmont. The gas logs blazed in a steady blue flame. Fake, but it kept the huge room warm on this raw night.

He tried to concentrate on his script, but it was no use. His mind was on Sybil.

She knocked on his door at ten past ten. He opened it, tried to kiss her on the lips, but she offered him only her cheek. She slipped out of her crimson cashmere greatcoat. As he took it he said, "You're late."

"I had to drive around for a while."

"To get up courage? Do I frighten you? Or does being in love frighten you?"

"To make sure I wasn't being followed."

"He'd do that?"

"He'd do anything."

"Does he suspect?"

She turned to face him. "He knows."

"What?"

"Everything."

"That night?"

"Yes—that night."

"He's never said a word to me, or given any hint."

"Of course not. That's why I'm here." She hesitated, then asked, "Give me a drink? I need it."

"Sure."

She went toward the fire, holding out her hands to warm them. He made her a light brandy and soda. She took a number of sips before she began to talk.

She told him everything Albert Grobe had told her about I.P.'s waiting up, knowing when she came home, assuming the rest. And determining that he must avenge his daughter's reputation.

"But now you're here again."

"Only to warn you not to touch that film. That's what Albert tried to tell you."

"The horoscope?"

191

"The picture is a disaster and you're the sacrificial lamb. He'll achieve two things that way. Escape from responsibility—"

"And revenge."

"Yes."

They were both silent for a moment.

"Sorry, Davie. It's my fault. That night it was my idea to come here. *I* seduced *you* to defy *him*. Now he's determined to have the last word, as he always does."

"What if I beat him at his own game?"

"Nobody ever has."

"Then I'll be the first!"

"Davie, Davie," she said sadly.

"I can do it!" he said, leaving her side and beginning to pace in his enthusiasm. "I've got it all figured out. I'll throw out that whole script. I'll keep the action footage. I'll not only keep Christopher Swift, I'll get a performance out of him! He's got the talent. I've seen it on stage where you can't fake it. He has it! And I can get it out of him. I can make this picture into a hit!"

She leaned back from the fire and stared up at him. "Good God, he's done it—given you dreams of glory that are going to destroy you."

"Maybe I have to do it. To prove that I can beat that bastard!"

"He'll destroy you."

"He won't," Dave said confidently. "I can make it work. I know exactly how."

"Every director knows 'exactly how.' Davie, no man starts out to make a bad picture. But this *is* wrong. At the start. He knows it. Albert knows it. And so do you."

"But I know how to fix it!"

Desperately she pleaded, "Isn't there anything I can do to change your mind?"

"Yes," Dave said suddenly. "Marry me! Now!"

She hesitated, then said resolutely, "I can't. Not until I've settled with him."

"I'll settle with him for you too. I'll make this picture into a winner. Then I'll be too big for his reprisals. We'll be free. Both of us."

"It won't be that easy," she pleaded. "He'll always find a way—always."

He went to her, lifted her up and held her in his arms.

"I'm asking you to leave his house and come live in mine," Dave said. "I'm asking you to give up being his daughter and become my wife. We need each other. I'm tired of being surrounded by people and being constantly lonely. I can see myself drifting into the same pattern as your father where I will have nothing but contempt for all women. He doesn't *dare* fall in love. I can't help myself. I *am* in love. Marry me, Sybil. Before it's too late."

"Would you be willing to leave here?" she asked.

"What would I do in New York?" he asked.

"What you did before you came out here."

"Direct plays?" Dave asked. "That's become a losing game. A crapshoot, with the odds against you. There's another reason, too. I have discovered that I *like* making pictures. It's exciting to have all those elements in the palm of your hand, to make them work the way you want them to work. To have limitless horizons. There's no period in time, no place on earth I can't make a film about. I can make people laugh or cry, be terrified or inspired. And I mean millions of people! I've discovered I can't give that up."

"*Neither can my father,*" Sybil said slowly.

"You think I *am* like him already?"

"Change a few words here and there and he could have made exactly the same speech."

He was on the verge of disputing her vehemently—until he recalled the day he had first met H. P. Koenig, who had said almost the same thing.

"Davie," she pleaded, "the only way for you to get free is to leave. Or fail. But if you fail big enough, no other studio will want you. That's what he's planning. And you're willing to walk right into it. He's making you do exactly what he wants. Well, I don't want to be owned by any man who is owned by him. We wouldn't have a chance, Davie—not a chance."

"You're wrong!" Dave said fiercely. "I'll beat him at his own game." He wanted her, but he remembered the promise he had made.

Until, fearful and needing him, she said. "Make love to me, Davie?"

193

H. P. Koenig arranged a huge studio cocktail party and press conference to announce the promotion of David Cole to the esteemed level of producer-director. It was attended by all press notables in the Hollywood area, including all the women who wrote for the fan magazines. The mandatory guest list included a number of Magna stars and also Albert Grobe. Betty Ronson who had negotiated Dave's new deal as producer-director, was much in evidence, accepting congratulations as if she were responsible for it all.

H.P. circulated among the guests, keeping Dave at his side every moment. The old man seemed to have a special eye for Albert Grobe, as if wishing to make sure The Professor was aware how well his strategy of vengeance was working.

Finally H.P. led Dave to the center of the room and announced, "Ladies and gentlemen! Please!" When he had achieved quiet, he displayed Dave and said, beaming, "If he hadn't decided to be a director, he could have been a star! Look at him!"

Then H.P. turned grave. "I want you all to know that for Mr. Cole's first assignment as producer-director, he is taking over the most important and expensive Magna film now in production, *Via Dolorosa*! A most important assignment for a man so young! But not since the days of Marvin Kronheim have I found a young man so brilliant and so full of promise! I have every confidence he will succeed."

The moment H.P. finished, Albert Grobe turned and walked out of the room. H.P. noticed. But instead of being offended, he was pleased. It confirmed that he had baited his trap for Dave with his usual deadly adroitness. When Dave failed, H.P. would remind the press of his high hopes and how dismally those hopes had been betrayed by David Cole. He would make that speech with tears in his eyes.

16

Dave couldn't leave without seeing Sybil, and he knew her habits well enough by now to know where to find her. He drove over to the Beverly Hills Hotel in time to meet her coming off the court after her tennis lesson.

"Drink?" she offered, taking an icy Coke from the cooler.

"Let's get out of here," he said suddenly. "I have to talk to you!"

They were driving up Coldwater Canyon, moving past trees that filtered the late-afternoon sun. He glanced at her from time to time and found it difficult to keep his eyes on the road. Her lovely face and dark, shining hair gained added luster and interest from the constantly surprising pattern of light and shadow.

"What's so important? You changed your mind. You're not going," she ventured hopefully.

"I *am* going. And I want you to come with me!" he said. "To Rome. You'll have a chance to live for yourself, think for yourself."

She didn't answer.

"Well?"

Still she was silent. In exasperation he exploded, "You know, life would be a hell of a lot easier if I was a poor struggling lawyer and you were a schoolteacher. And except for this crazy industry, that's exactly what we'd be. A lawyer. And a schoolteacher. And your old man would still be in the junk business.

"I would come to call on you, once a week, and take you to dinner and a movie. Downtown. We'd go by subway. Both ways. Then eventually your father would corner me one night and ask, 'So? What's going to be?' That would be my cue to tell him that I wanted to marry you. He would think it over and say to himself, 'Why not? A nice young man. Jewish. A professional man. So what if he's not doing so well right now? Things will improve. Besides, my Sybil has a steady teaching job. They'll get along.' It would be as simple and ordinary as that. By some people's standards, just plain dull. But it would be one hell of a lot better than what we have now!"

She didn't answer, only pulled her white tennis sweater closer around her.

"If it's too cold, I'll put the top up."

"Don't bother," she said, unnerved by his rebuke. "May *I* say something now?"

"Sure."

"You don't mind a little rewrite of your script, do you? You're a great director but a terrible judge of human nature.

"I'll tell you how it would *really* be. First, my father would not just be in the junk business. He would be the most successful junk dealer in the whole world. He could never, never be anything less than first.

"He would have sold scrap metal to the Japanese before the war. And to the Swedes *during* the war. So they could sell steel to the Nazis to make barbed wire for concentration camps. Then, by the time the war was over, he'd be worth millions of dollars as he is now. We would have a large triplex apartment on Fifth Avenue. And I would not be a schoolteacher. I would have gone to the best women's college in the country and be just as useless as I am now. After we met, I'd be attracted to you. Because you are good-looking and Jewish. We'd go out a few times. You'd come to our lavish apartment. You'd meet my father. By the third time you showed up he would talk to my mother. He would want to know what was going on. After all, by that time he'd have two mistresses. So he'd be very exacting when it came to his daughter. You've noticed, haven't you, that the most lecherous fathers are the most strict with their own daughters?

"So he'd have a talk with you. He'd want to know all about

196

who you were, what you did and what your prospects were. When he discovered you were a struggling young lawyer, he wouldn't say a word. But in a little while your practice would start to pick up. He'd throw you a company or two that he owned. Till gradually he drew you into his orbit. When he owned you, he would grant you the royal favor of giving you his daughter in marriage.

"Which is exactly what he wanted to do here. And the result would be exactly the same. I would say no!"

"Did it ever occur to you that you're punishing me to get even with your father?" he demanded angrily.

Very softly she answered, "Did it ever occur to you that I'm punishing myself too?"

He glanced at her. Her eyes were misting. He pulled up at the curb to park under a huge tamarisk tree, but she pleaded, "Don't stop. Keep driving."

They had reached the end of the winding road and arrived at the flatlands of the valley. They were both silent till they approached a roadside restaurant.

"Can we stop for a drink?" he asked.

"I'd rather not."

"Why?"

"Because it wouldn't end there. You'd want to make love to me. And I'd let you."

"What's wrong with that?"

"I don't want what we have between us to become a habit."

"You didn't feel that way the other night."

"That's when I discovered it could become a habit." She turned away, adding, "I wish I could be different. But I can't. It was watching what happened to my mother. At first when he left us in New York and came out here alone she put up with it. Thinking, Once he gets established, we'll resume being a family again. She used to tell me how he was off in a faraway place called Hollywood and when he was doing well enough to send for us we'd all be together again.

"The way she spoke of him was so real that I formed this great love for a father I had never really known. The two times he came back home he was loaded with gifts and promises about a new house with our own orange trees. Everything was so wonderful and exciting. Though at night I would hear my mother ask why he didn't take us back with him. It was not good for children to be without a father. Or a wife to be without her husband. He put her off each time, saying one more picture and if it was a big hit he could have enough money to buy his own little studio.

"The time finally came when he did send for us. He drove us to a house on a big wide street with tall palm trees along the curb. There really were orange trees in the backyard, and we picked them by the armload and let them spill all across the living room. My mother laughed, she was so happy. We all were. My father really was the hero she had promised us.

"Till that day.

"She'd driven off to the market to do some shopping. She came back too soon and empty-handed. She went straight to their room and closed the door. She was in there a long time. I went to the door and heard her crying.

"That night when he came home there was very little conversation at the table. He started to tell us stories of what had happened to him during the day. Mama didn't laugh. She didn't say a word. Soon he stopped talking. When dinner was over, she sent us off to bed at once.

"Emily was too young to know. She went fast asleep, but I slipped out of bed and heard. Mama had discovered all about the other side of his life. A woman she had met in the market blurted it out. He was more famous than he had ever let on. And more successful, too. He could have sent for us long before. But he didn't because of an actress who was his mistress. And when it was over with her there were other women. My mother wanted to know. Was it true?

"He was furious. He demanded to know who told such lies about him. He would find the gossip, find out who her husband was and destroy him. But the moment he made that threat his voice grew weaker and penitent. He knew he had betrayed his power and his wealth. So he began to weep. Soon they were both weeping. I don't know what it would do to you, but it's something a little girl never forgets, her father crying.

"He confessed everything. Of course, he never blamed himself. But the fact was, with every word he uttered he condemned himself. When he was done, Mama gave him no dispensations, no forgiveness. Finally, after her long silence, he asked her 'Please, don't do anything. How would it look for your family?

198

Or mine? We have to stay together. For the sake of the children.'

"Even then he needed a respectable facade. Perhaps he was aware of his sexually obscene tendencies and he needed to declare to the world that he was a decent family man.

"We know—all three of us: my mother, Emily and I—that most times after he's had dinner at home and goes out again he isn't going back to the studio. Or to see a preview. He's going to gratify his every lustful fantasy.

"I'm sure now that if it hadn't been for Emily and me, my mother would have left him that very night. There was never any love between them after that. She began to seek out things to do that would make her useful. Her charities began that way. That was the weapon she held over him, that she would leave him and shatter the illusion he had created. So he bought her off with money for her charities, and that's all the life she's had since that night. She carries on as if it were enough. But it can't be. It wouldn't be for me."

"What makes you think it would be like that with us?"

"How can I be sure it wouldn't?" she asked.

"What is there about me that makes you think I could turn out to be like him?"

"I don't know. It's like being a child and afraid. You can't explain why to anyone else. You just know you're afraid."

"I don't want you to be afraid," he said, taking her in his arms. "Come with me to Rome. I need you."

"I can't," she answered simply, "until I'm free of him. It wouldn't be fair to you."

"Then I'll free you. I'll beat that bastard at his own game. You'll see! You'll see!"

Albert Grobe insisted on driving Dave to the airport when he left Los Angeles for Rome. There was little conversation. Dave did not want to endanger Grobe, and Grobe had no need to warn Dave any longer.

As they started boarding at the gate, Grobe seized Dave's hand and clung to it. "Take care of yourself, Dave! If you feel the trap closing, get out before it's too late. Promise me!"

"Don't worry, Albert. I'll prove it to Sybil. And to this whole goddamn town!"

When his plane reached New York, he decided to spend the hour layover calling Sybil and revising the script. But his plan was upset when he heard himself being paged as he entered the terminal.

Tall, spare, gray-haired Dan Sullavan was waiting at the gate.

"I thought we could have a drink or a cup of coffee to make waiting less of a bore."

He led Dave to the closest bar. When they had settled down, it was clear that Sullavan's main purpose was to relieve not Dave's boredom but his own anxiety. As Sullavan asked more and more questions about *Via Dolorosa*, it became obvious that H.P. had concealed the disastrous footage from his own executive staff in New York. Dave was as noncommittal as he could be in the circumstances. Finally Sullavan asked bluntly, "How bad is it?"

When Dave hesitated, Sullavan said, "We have a right to know. We have to deal with the banks. After all, for the four million dollars they have a right to ask, and we have an obligation to answer."

"If I didn't think it could be saved, I wouldn't be here," Dave said.

"So it has to be 'saved,'" Sullavan remarked ruefully. "And you think you can do it."

"I think so."

Sullavan nodded. "What do I tell the banks? That there is a thirty-one-year-old kid who 'thinks' he can 'save' their investment? They'll love that."

Dave smiled and said, "Thirty-two-year-old kid, come next February."

But Sullavan did not seem to appreciate the joke.

"How much did H.P. tell you?"

"He didn't have to tell me much. I saw the footage. I read the script. I know the stars. I know what the trouble is. That's enough for me to go on."

"Uh-huh," Sullavan remarked glumly, causing Dave to wonder if there were further intrigues which had been withheld from him.

Dan Sullavan did not feel compelled to supply any additional information. He had sought out Dave Cole in hopes of extracting some fact he might use to undermine H.P. in the vicious intra corporate warfare that went on constantly. But obviously H.P. had this young director believing that he could make this film into a success. Then when disaster struck, H.P. would deftly slide out from under and this kid would take the rap. Sullavan reluctantly decided that the best he could do was limit the company's losses by insisting on strict economies for the rest of the shooting.

He still nourished one last hope that when Dave arrived in Rome and discovered the mess that awaited him, he would decide to abandon production, thereby saving the company several million dollars and placing the blame where it belonged, on H. P. Koenig.

They were announcing the Rome flight. Dave rose from his chair. Sullavan held out his hand. It was no longer warm and friendly. Dave released it as quickly as possible and started toward the departure gate.

Sullavan watched Dave go. With him went his last chance to avenge himself on H. P. Koenig—a desire that had burned in Dan Sullavan for years now.

Sullavan had a brother-in-law who had been a policeman on the New York City force. When Sullavan was elevated to the presidency of Magna Theatres, his brother-in-law suddenly retired from the force to enter the carpet business. Thereafter, all carpeting for all the Magna theaters was purchased from that company.

Eventually, H.P.'s accountants and private investigators diligently gathered figures to prove that between them, Dan Sullavan and his brother-in-law had profited to the extent of two million four hundred thousand dollars in the first five years of that arrangement.

H.P. also had his lawyers prepare a legal memorandum on fraud, conspiracy and similar commercial crimes in the Criminal Code of the State of New York.

One day, simply and undramatically, H.P. laid all that evidence before Dan Sullavan. Pretending great concern, H.P. could not forgo the opportunity of pointing out that it would not look good for Dan, his sister or her husband if the story ever became public. Especially since his sister had one son already ordained as a priest and another completing his studies at the seminary. And how would it look if Daniel Sullavan, Knight of Malta, the highest honor the Church could bestow on a layman, was unveiled as a common fraud?

There was no formal agreement, but from that time on it was understood that H.P. could run the studio any way he wanted and Dan Sullavan would support him in any showdown with the stockholders. H.P. had made for himself a powerful ally. And a bitter enemy.

Thereafter, to even the score, Dan Sullavan kept constantly probing for weaknesses in H.P.'s operations. He thought he had found it in *Via Dolorosa*. But again, H.P., wily jackal in the corporate jungle, had eluded him. Sullavan would have to wait for another day, another opportunity.

Sullavan watched from a distance as Dave passed into the waiting room for overseas passengers.

Nice kid, Sullavan reflected; too bad.

From the gossip that had reached him from Rome, no director was going to be able to get a performance out of Christopher Swift. If Swift failed, *Via Dolorosa* must fail.

And Dave Cole with it.

17

Three years before, when Christopher Swift had first arrived in Hollywood, he was already a gaunt-faced, troubled young man. His initial success on Broadway had been followed by so many difficulties that though there were other plays and other parts, professionals in the theater had begun to write him off as a one-time wonder.

He was able to secure only a small role in his first film, but he registered so well in his few scenes that he caught the attention of the famous agent Edmund Pryce.

Pryce was a tall, rotund man who carried himself with distinction and who had adopted a British accent to give him stature and cachet in a community where almost every other agent was Jewish. He dressed impeccably, never affecting sports clothes during business hours, and he carried a heavy gold-headed cane which he used as a prop. His hair was longer than was fashionable, but its silky, flowing whiteness was essential to his image.

Some people looked upon Edmund Pryce as an overage ham who hadn't made it as an actor. But no matter what they said about Pryce behind his back, every studio head, including H. P. Koenig, gave him ready audience. For Pryce had a unique talent for discovering young actors who eventually emerged as stars. He had an uncanny touch, especially in selecting new names for his clients. His formula was always the same. A one-syllable first name and a two-syllable last name. The first name was always crisp. Never more than three or four letters and always with a staccato masculine sound. The two-syllable second name was always apple-pie American. Pryce could be relied upon to produce one or two such gifted young actors in any given year, and though some fell by the wayside, enough of them endured to ensure him an income of several hundred thousand dollars a year.

This allowed Edmund Pryce to live in the style of English nobility which he affected. He occupied a large Tudor house high up in Beverly Hills. He had gardens that rivaled those of an English estate, and his house staff was British. His office secretary was a willowy blond young English widow who had lost her husband in the R.A.F. during the recent war and who had come to America to escape her memories. She was a discreet woman, who saw much, suspected more and said nothing. It was for precisely this reliable trait that Edmund Pryce retained her.

The morning after Edmund Pryce had seen a preview of Christopher Swift's first film, it was Mrs. Hilary who called him and arranged a teatime interview. Pryce served tea in his office every afternoon at four-thirty, as he had seen done in the offices of producers in the English theater. He bought only the most expensive British sweet biscuits and a special mixture of Chinese tea flown in from Fortnum and Mason.

When Swift was ushered into his office, Pryce was standing behind a large, graceful Chippendale desk, gold-headed cane in hand. He was smiling and fatherly.

He held the boy's hand a long time, made a careful appraisal of him. Swift was dressed in the kind of nondescript zipper jacket and jeans that Hollywood had come to expect from New York actors. At least, Pryce observed, the inevitable T-shirt was a clean one. It was the first habit he inculcated in his protégés: a respect for clean, fresh linen. Soon he would lure this young man away from that damned zipper jacket and jeans.

"Well, now, tell me about yourself," Pryce said, leaning back with his teacup in hand.

Christopher Swift related his experience in the theater and the manner in which his Broadway agent had secured his first film role. He had no agent in Hollywood, though he supposed he needed one.

"Good," Edmund Pryce said. "When I take on an actor, I want him free of all entanglements. Completely free. Are you married?"

"No."

"Involved?"

"No."

"Good." Suddenly Pryce asked, "Isn't your tea suitable?"

"Yes—yes, sir," Swift answered quickly, since he had been caught unaware.

"I noticed you hadn't been drinking it," Pryce said. "It's very important to cultivate civilized habits. Especially in this notoriously uncivilized town. You drink? Alcohol, I mean."

"Beer mainly."

"Well, we'll have to make a change in that."

Christopher Swift was beginning to feel a certain resentment at having his habits criticized, but he was well aware of Edmund Pryce's power so he kept his feelings in check.

"I saw your performance in *Shadows* last evening. A screening at Jack Warner's house. Very impressive. Shows great promise."

"Thank you."

"I must be frank to state it also reveals some weaknesses," Edmund Pryce said, with great calculation, his green eyes discerning just the right degree of self-doubt in the young man opposite him.

Pryce began to pace slowly, using his cane with practiced effect.

"May I be perfectly frank?"

"Yes, sure."

"I have done considerable research on you," Pryce said. Actually it had been limited to a single phone call to a producer in New York. "After your initial success your career seems to have gone steadily downhill. For a man with talent that is a significant fact. It's why I welcomed the chance to see the screening last night. Suddenly the whole problem became clear. What seems to be weakness, what stunted a promising career on Broadway, is lack of confidence. It was also apparent in your performance of last night.

"I propose to overcome that. In two ways. First, by *giving* you confidence. Second, and more important, by giving you the *ap-*

pearance of confidence. It will entail much sacrifice of money and effort on my part. But it will also entail great sacrifice on your part. Are you ready to make such a sacrifice?"

Christopher Swift nodded.

"Before you answer too quickly, listen to what I have to say," Pryce cautioned. "I am a most demanding man. I insist on monastic discipline from those few clients I take on. But I do make stars, as you know."

Swift nodded again.

"Every phase of your life will be under my control. The way you dress. The places you appear in public. The people with whom you associate. The roles you take. The directors you work with. Everything will be subject to my approval. Is that understood?"

"Yes . . . yes, sir."

"Good. Then we may proceed. I shall want you to cut off your association with your present agent in New York. We will have no further need for representation there. You will only go back to Broadway when I decide the time is right."

"I'm signed to a contract," Swift began to protest, "with an agent who's been very fair and honest."

"Fair and honest are good qualities in the average man. But not in an agent. An agent must be wily, rapacious and bloodthirsty on behalf of his clients. We will find some way to break your present contract. Now, stand up!" Pryce finished unexpectedly.

Swift rose from his chair.

"I said stand *up*," Pryce commanded, using his thick cane to straighten Swift's back.

Pryce circled him, scrutinizing him so meticulously that Swift began to shrink under his gaze.

"Have you ever seen the *David* in Florence? The original Michelangelo?"

"No, sir."

"So I thought. No young man who had ever seen that perfect work of art could carry himself the way you do. I must show you a copy. I have one in my home. Life-size. By Jove, that's it! You will come to my home this evening. Be there at eight for dinner. Mrs. Hilary will give you directions."

Christopher Swift realized that he had been dismissed.

The life-size copy of Michelangelo's *David* stood on a marble base that elevated it some two feet above floor level in Edmund Pryce's living room. When Christopher Swift was shown into the huge living room by Pryce's butler it was the first thing he saw and the only thing he was aware of. He knew little of sculpture, but could not ignore the reality of genius. He was behind it, staring up at the youthfully muscled back and the graceful buttocks, when he heard Edmund Pryce.

"Magnificent, is it not?"

"Yes, yes, it is." Swift spoke in a whisper, as if he were in a holy place.

"It is an image you must always bear in mind whenever you appear before a camera or on a stage. Elegance, grace, beauty. It will distinguish you from all the rest of the riffraff who call themselves actors in our time. Come! We'll have a drink."

There were drinks and hors d'oeuvre in the study, and later an elegantly prepared meal in the dining room. At no time did Pryce stop scrutinizing Christopher's smallest acts, making it impossible for the actor to eat or drink with ease.

Coffee was served in the living room. Pryce had some brandy, which Christopher refused. But he could not help admiring the practiced, graceful way Pryce rotated the brandy in his glass and sniffed it more often than he drank it. Throughout, Pryce kept talking about films, acting, stardom. But all the while he stared at the *David*, which was now highlighted even more since the room had been dimmed while the light on the *David* had been intensified.

"The training of an actor must be physical as well as mental. The Russians know that. And the British. The classical actor is disappearing in this country, lad. The hoodlum and the roughneck are taking over. A temporary fad foisted on us by Actors Studio. Whatever its emotional value, it will prove the ruination of the young actors in this country.

"I do not intend to let that happen to you. I want you to become another Ronald Colman, another Leslie Howard. A man of grace and elegance who can assume his place in any film of any time or locale.

"Imagine Brando in a costume role," Pryce said. "Ridiculous. I

207

demand grace from you, subtlety. And above all confidence.

"And let *that* be your model," Pryce said, pointing his gold-headed cane at the *David*.

As if seized by sudden inspiration, Pryce rose. "By God, we shall start there!"

Pryce used his cane to indicate that Swift take up a position beside the statue. Puzzled, the actor moved alongside the masterpiece.

"Stand erect! Proud! In your way you are as handsome as that piece of marble. *Feel* that you are! That's right. Let it come from within!"

Christopher Swift tried to project the image that Edmund Pryce was demanding.

"Better," Pryce encouraged. "Of course, burdened with those ridiculous clothes it isn't easy. You must never wear those rags again. I shall see that you are properly outfitted. Meanwhile, take off that jacket."

Christopher Swift slowly unzipped the offending item and let it fall to the floor. With a single disdainful flip of his cane, Edmund Pryce swept the garment into a corner of the room.

"Now that T-shirt! Mark Antony never appeared before the Roman mob wearing a T-shirt!"

Reluctantly, Swift pulled his shirt over his head and tossed it aside. Slowly but very determinedly Edmund Pryce forced the young man to strip until he was as naked as the David he stood beside.

"Now stand as *he* stands!" Pryce commanded.

Swift assumed the same pose, his hand reaching upward to hold the imaginary slingshot while Edmund Pryce walked around him inspecting him. Finally, his eyes wide with lust, he reached out to trace the boy's buttocks with his soft, well-manicured fingers. He felt the young man cringe, at first, then accept his touch.

For Pryce's purpose, the lad was a complete novice.

"Yes," Pryce said softly. "Without those ridiculous clothes you have the physique for it, and the carriage. I can make a star out of you. If you trust me. Do you trust me?"

Christopher Swift tried to nod, not aware of what would follow.

Pryce laid aside his cane and reached out to fondle the young

208

man's genitals. Swift drew back, but only for an instant. Edmund Pryce traced his scrotum with a delicate probing forefinger. He reached under it to allow it to rest in his hand as if it were some precious artifact. Then he slipped to his knees and kissed him. When Chris tried to turn away, Pryce pinned him with a tight grip on his thighs. Slowly the young man relented. Edmund Pryce took him in his mouth and with his agile practiced tongue he brought him to a full and large erection.

Christopher Swift had had that experience with women, but never before with a man. Yet the sensation was not so different. And he consoled himself with the thought that since he was not the aggressor, Pryce was the homosexual, not he. He allowed Pryce to have his way, his activity becoming fiercer until Swift had reached an orgasm, which seemed to release Pryce as well. He knelt there, pressing his face against the young man's thighs, embracing them, letting the ejaculate drip onto his face. Then Pryce kissed him there again and slipped to the floor, exhausted.

Pryce insisted he stay the night, and when he woke he saw the agent staring down at him like a satisfied woman. Chris decided that if the price of stardom was to allow himself to be used from time to time in this way, it wouldn't be forever. After his first starring role he would get rid of Edmund Pryce. No matter what any contract said. The old man might feel he had used him, but in his own way Christopher would use the old man.

So the arrangement began between Edmund Pryce and Christopher Swift. Within four months Pryce had secured him the lead in a low-budget film. It was well reviewed. In films, at least, Christopher Swift had moved from the class of "promising" to "rising young star."

Without relinquishing his hold on him, Pryce encouraged him to start being seen with young starlets, and even older female stars when it could be arranged. Always he demanded a strict accounting of every date and whether there had been sex or not. He did not object to an occasional affair, but Christopher must not become permanently entangled. It was good to have his name mentioned with those of prominent actresses, but not good to form serious relationships, Pryce warned.

The sexual relationship between Edmund Pryce and Christopher Swift continued and deepened.

Once Christopher had scored in his first leading role, Edmund

Pryce felt it was time to make his big move. He had Mrs. Hilary call and arrange an appointment with H. P. Koenig. Pryce appeared in H.P.'s waiting room in a proper British suit of clothes, an orchid in his lapel, a flowing bow tie, and carrying his ever-present gold-headed cane. He ignored the producers, stars and writers who were waiting, went directly to the receptionist's desk, pushed down her copy of *The Hollywood Reporter* with the tip of his cane and announced, "I am here. Tell Mr. Koenig!"

He didn't even take a seat, knowing that he would be admitted at once. For he had been the only agent ever to walk out on H.P. when he kept him waiting too long.

The negotiation was brisk and brief. Aware of the young man's magnificent performance in his first leading role, H.P. made a generous offer. Pryce promptly turned it down. H.P. raised his offer. Pryce remained adamant. H.P. doubled his original offer. Still Pryce refused. Until H.P. exploded, "Christ, what do you want? Blood?"

"We want, and we will only accept, a deal under which we have picture approval."

"Picture approval?" H.P. had bellowed. "I don't even give Gable and Tracy picture approval."

"No, but you will give it to this young man. Because his talent is both brilliant and fragile. He can be destroyed by one wrong role. Therefore we must have approval of which films he does."

By the next afternoon H.P. had acceded to Pryce's demand.

Within three pictures Christopher Swift had become a full-fledged star. Of all Pryce's discoveries Christopher became the most prominent and successful.

It was only in more recent months that Edmund Pryce had begun to detect a disturbing change in Christopher. Pryce never called him anything less than that. *Christopher.* For the name had a voluptuous feeling on his tongue. But in recent months there had been a subtle change between them.

At first Pryce suspected that Christopher was having an affair with the young actress who played opposite him in his current film. But his investigation proved that that was not true. Yet for some reason, Pryce had found it increasingly difficult to arouse the young man. He had never encountered this particular difficulty before. All his young men remained obedient lovers until he was through with them.

So he had him followed and discovered that Swift had begun to consult a psychoanalyst. Pryce looked on that with great resentment. He considered Christopher Swift his own *David*. He did not intend to have his creation destroyed, particularly by psychoanalysts, who were most hostile to homosexuality, treating it as if it were a disease, not the ultimate form of sexual expression.

Yet to forbid Christopher to go to an analyst might only bring on full-scale rebellion, for the young man was now at that stage of success where he might feel free to rebel.

It would take careful execution, this surgery by which Pryce would separate Christopher from his analyst. That became dramatically apparent to Edmund Pryce one night. For some time Christopher had been reluctant to come to dinner, knowing it meant he would have to stay the night. But Pryce insisted. Afterward, as was their habit, they retired to Pryce's bedroom. But there, Swift could not react. No matter what tricks and artifices Pryce resorted to, the young actor remained totally impotent. Finally Pryce turned away, partly in frustration, partly in fear.

Christopher Swift rolled over on his side. Soon his body was racked with sobs. Pryce reached out gently to comfort him. So it had come to this. Damn that psychoanalyst! He had brought this on. Now something *had* to be done!

What Edmund Pryce did not know was that Christopher's growing impotence was what had made him consult the analyst in the first place. When he felt it coming on he had tried having sex with young actresses. And with young boys as well. But he was impotent with both. He had had himself examined by medical doctors, who found no apparent physical cause. Analysis was his only hope.

Unaware of that, and reaching the only conclusion left open to him, Edmund Pryce assumed it was all the fault of the analyst. The meddler must be exiled from Christopher Swift's life by any means.

That means presented itself when the script of *Via Dolorosa* was submitted to Edmund Pryce for consideration as Swift's next film vehicle. He was about to reject it when he learned that authentic location shooting would be involved—the Holy Land for six weeks, then nine more weeks in Rome.

Four months at least—four months away from Beverly Hills,

away from that damned psychoanalyst. That should do it. Besides, Christopher was ready now for a classical role. And Pryce had always liked the character of the disciple John. In the Gospels, John was referred to as the disciple Jesus loved. It lent some credence to Edmund Pryce's favorite theory, that homosexuality was part of the relationship between Jesus and the original twelve. Had not some of them, like Peter, left their wives to follow Jesus? And had not Jesus said to the twelve, "Love one another"?

Yes, Edmund Pryce decided, the role of John in *Via Dolorosa* might well be suited to Christopher Swift and to Edmund Pryce's purposes as well. The next day he convinced Christopher that this was the role worthy of his talents. It was only after Christopher had agreed that Pryce told him the picture would be filmed abroad.

There followed forty-eight hours of terrible ordeal for Christopher Swift. He forced his analyst to cancel all his other patients and spend two whole days with him, discussing what it would mean to interrupt the analysis now.

Finally it was agreed that all through the time he was abroad the analyst would keep Christopher's hours open for him. Christopher would pay him his fee, and no one else would be allowed to have those hours. Christopher even tried to exact a promise that if he called the analyst would fly over to the Holy Land or Rome. But there the doctor drew the line. They could talk on the transoceanic phone for fifty minutes at a time if Christopher called at his usual treatment hour, Beverly Hills time.

Thus fortified, Christopher Swift had set out to star in *Via Dolorosa*.

18

None of this was known to H. P. Koenig when he cast Christopher Swift in the picture. Nor was it known to Dave Cole as he was on his way to Rome.

Dave was sure of only one thing. Christopher Swift was a gifted actor—eccentric and tormented, but nonetheless talented. Dave was positive he would extract that talent and make it work, as he had nine years ago.

He would not have been so sure if he had been aware of Swift's newest and worst affliction, superseding even his sexual impotence.

Not even Edmund Pryce had any suspicion of that.

Dave was met by Dino Cortese, Magna's representative in Italy. He was a younger man than Dave had anticipated. And infinitely more tense and damp than one would expect a young man to be on a cool day in the Eternal City. Cortese kept mopping his face with a large silk handkerchief, which he returned to his breast pocket and then withdrew to use again almost at once. He gave crisp orders in Italian to the chauffeur to secure Dave's luggage from Customs and saw to it that Dave was passed through Immigration with complete V.I.P. dispatch. Everything had been arranged and proceeded like clockwork. Still, Dino Cortese kept nervously mopping his face. Dave found it most unsettling.

Once they were safely in the back seat of the Magna limousine, Cortese gave an enormous sigh—not of relief, but of sheer exhaustion.

"I've been up all night," he said in fluent English. "I almost didn't get here to meet you at all!"

"Why? What happened?"

"Markham," Cortese said. "Markham was arrested."

"Aline Markham *arrested*? What for?"

Cortese shook his head in a gesture that indicated it was too painful to discuss. Dave seized him by the lapels. "What for?"

"What for? I'll tell you what for!" the distraught Italian exploded. "Dope!"

"What do you mean?"

"She was caught in the act of buying heroin!"

"I don't believe that!"

"*You* don't believe it! Imagine what it was like for *me* last night at eleven o'clock to be called by the Chief of Police. Fortunately, we have our deal with him so he let me know at once. I was able to keep it under wraps, as you say."

"Markham?" Dave considered. "Impossible."

"I saw the evidence. In fact, I bought it back—at a very fancy price," Cortese said. "If you have familiarity with these things, take a look."

He reached into his pocket and drew out four small, white paper packets, looking as innocent as Communion wafers. Dave reached for one, opened it and sniffed. It had an unfamiliar sweet smell.

"The real thing?"

"The real thing," Cortese confirmed, mopping his face again.

"Destroy it," Dave ordered.

"She asked me not to."

Dave stared at him, disbelieving. "Where is she now?"

"Her hotel. The Hassler. Right above the Spanish Steps."

"Let's go there."

"You're at the Excelsior. Don't you want to check in first? You've been on a plane for almost eighteen hours."

"Tell the driver to go directly to the Hassler!"

They arrived at the hotel in less than half an hour. Dave called from the lobby. Aline Markham invited him up to her suite. He asked Cortese to wait, but took the four packets with him.

Aline Markham was alone in her suite. She was not given to the effusive kisses and greetings that passed for etiquette in show business.

"Mr. Cole?" she asked, in a way that indicated that one would have to earn being on a first-name basis with her.

"Yes."

"Come in." Her blue eyes were clear and direct.

He went past her into a large sitting room that invited in the Italian sun and the hectic sounds from the Spanish Steps below.

"If you don't like noise, I can close the doors," she said. "I happen to like it. Noise means people, and I like people. The trouble with our damned industry is that it shuts itself away from the people it seeks to entertain. I like to hear children laughing. I like the vulgar sound of men whistling after women. I like this whole damn world. Except for a few little things in it. Now, you came here to talk about what happened last night. Talk!" she challenged.

Dave was not quite prepared for her. Much as he had heard about her famous frankness, Dave had not anticipated this.

"I've been on a plane for the last eighteen hours. Suppose you tell me what happened."

"Didn't Cortese tell you?"

"Yes."

"Well, it's true."

"That's all? No explanation?"

"I'd have to know you better to tell you the truth, Mr. Cole."

"Well, for starters, here." He reached into his pocket and brought out the four packets. "I understand you wanted them back."

She slipped them into the pocket of the tailored slacks she wore. "I'd have to know more, Mr. Cole."

"What can I tell you? I'm a director. And now a producer. And I'm here to save your picture if I can."

"Still not enough. Credentials, Mr. Cole!"

He started to list the plays and pictures he'd directed. But she cut him short. "Not *credits*, Mr. Cole. *Credentials*. Credentials for membership in the human race."

Dave had no idea how to respond.

"Mr. Cole, if you came here to save a picture, the first thing you are going to have to do is save a human life. For myself, if I

215

have to choose between saving another goddamn Magna epic and saving a friend, I am going to save my friend. If you want to help *me*, I'll help *you*. But first I have to know the kind of man you are. Can you tell me that?"

"Frankly, I don't know."

"Well, that's a start," she said. It was the first soft word she had spoken to him. "Why *are* you here? Didn't you know what you were walking into?"

"Most of it. But not all."

"And still you came?"

"Yes."

"Why?"

He stared at her. She had the most amazing ability to keep those blue eyes open and focused for long periods of time. She was thinner than he had expected, and less beautiful than she photographed, but far stronger than they had ever let her appear on the screen. He decided to tell her the truth about Sybil, about H.P. and about the warnings he had received not to take on *Via Dolorosa*. When he spoke about Sybil, Markham nodded with great understanding. When he spoke of his determination to overcome H.P., she smiled. When he finished, she said, "I know how it is to love someone in an impossible situation. And I can tell you it is better loving that way than settling for less."

She was silent for a moment, then added, "Well, now, Mr. Cole, I know what motivates you. And I like it. But you may not like what I'm going to have to tell you."

Suddenly she asked, "Would you care for some tea? A drink?"

"Only for whatever it is you're trying to avoid telling me," Dave said gently.

"Yes," she said, "I had better begin; and it all starts with Christopher Swift. He is a very strange young man."

"I know; I worked with him once," Dave said.

"I've seen him twice on the stage in New York. Both times good, but not spectacular."

"The one time I worked with him he *was* spectacular," Dave volunteered. "That's one reason I'm here."

Markham glanced at him, a look of reservation in her frank blue eyes. "As you know, in the script, by some ingenious exegesis, John becomes the brother of my son Jesus. Well, if he plays my son, I want to know him both as a character and as a human being. I always try to do that. It helps in my portrayal. But our Christopher turned out to be a difficult young man to penetrate."

"I know that," Dave said quickly.

"He was shy, secretive, never appearing on the set a moment earlier than called for, never lingering afterward. Valerie and I have dinner together often. Mainly she wants my protection from the young men who pursue her. If I had been as beautiful as she is at nineteen, I would have been impossible. Fortunately for me and the world, I'm rather homely. But I make up for it with spirit.

"But Valerie is probably the most beautiful young actress I have ever seen. What shows on the screen is nothing compared with what you'll see when you meet her. The violet of her eyes, the flawlessness of her complexion. I'm glad I'm old enough to be her mother. Else I'd be insanely jealous. As it is, all I am is proud of her. I almost think of her as our daughter."

It was an unconscious reference to the actor to whom she was so devoted and whom she could not marry. She was obviously unaware of the slip, for she went right on.

"But then, Valerie is not your problem. Christopher is. And the way it came to light startled us both. Eric . . ." She interrupted herself to explain that Eric Drews had till recently been the director of *Via Dolorosa*. "He gave us three days off so he could stage some of the outdoor shots while the weather was good. Quite innocently, I organized a little trip to Florence—Valerie, Christopher and myself—still in hopes of getting to know him better. We decided—no, I decided; I'm afraid I have a knack, or call it an overbearing need, to make decisions—I decided we would drive. Actually, that I would do the driving. Something about Christopher led me to believe that he really shouldn't be at the wheel of a car.

"We drove up to Florence, passing a lot of the debris of the war on the way. Since it was out of season, we had no trouble getting rooms at the Excelsior, overlooking the river. The first evening we had an early dinner and went right to sleep, for I had organized an early-morning sight-seeing tour.

"The next morning I was up at eight, breakfasted and dressed, waiting to go sight-seeing. Valerie joined me as planned. But not Christopher. We called. When he didn't answer, we went to

217

his room. He was awake, but said he was ill and not able to go out. We made the mistake of insisting, and in a while he came down, seeming better, though somewhat remote. We walked along the river to the Ponte Vecchio and then turned left. When we reached the Piazza della Signoria and saw that enormous copy of Michelangelo's *David*, Christopher began to react oddly. He looked up not with appreciation but with fear. He drew back from it, a bit at a time, until he was standing pressed against the far wall. At the time, I thought he was trying to get a different perspective.

"I went to him and said, 'If you really want to see it in its best light, we must go see the original.'

"'The original?' he asked strangely.

"'In the museum. The original made by Michelangelo himself. It's in a perfect setting.'

"It seemed to take a great deal of courage on his part, but he agreed. At the museum he didn't hang back but preceded us down the long corridor toward the original *David*. When he was in front of it, he began circling it. He reached out to touch the buttocks. When he came round to the front, I had the feeling that he would reach out for the genitals. But he didn't. He stood at the foot of the pedestal and stared up silently at the statue for several minutes. Then he suddenly screamed, turned and ran out, crying.

"We chased after him, but he was too fast for us. We went back to the hotel expecting to find him there, but didn't. Finally, long after dinner, he came back to the hotel, weary and red-eyed. When I asked him where he had been, he said only, 'Walking.' He was trembling, and I suggested some hot tea, but he said he had everything he needed.

"After that he refused to leave his room and spoke to no one. Except that I found out at the desk he had made a long-distance call to Beverly Hills, and spoken to someone there for fifty minutes at outrageous expense.

"I know that overseas calls came in for him. All of them from Edmund Pryce, his agent. But as far as I know, he took none of them. We were relieved to get back to Rome and go to work again."

She seemed to have finished, yet she had not said a single word about the four white packets he had given her.

"I suppose you have to ask. And I have to tell you," she said.

"I have to ask," Dave said gently. "Though maybe I can make it easier for you. This stuff is for Swift, isn't it?"

"Yes," Aline Markham said. "He doesn't seem able to get enough. Whoever sells it to him keeps cutting the strength and raising the price. He's so desperate now that he spends half his time looking for connections. The night he called me—he's staying here at the hotel—he was desperate. I went down to his suite and found him cold and trembling."

"Withdrawal?" Dave asked.

"Not voluntary. He'd run out, and his source refused to give him any more because he'd argued about the price. So I . . . I called Valerie . . . and together we went out and tried to find some for him. And we did. At the tables in front of Doney's you can secure almost anything you want—black-market currency, stolen jewelry and, of course, dope. All you need is dollars.

"And we have been buying for him ever since. It's the only way we can get him through the picture."

"So that's why he seems so out of every scene," said Dave. "You've seen the footage, I assume."

"Yes, I've seen it. And he *is* out of every scene. But it was either that or let word out and have him dropped. You know what that would mean."

"H.P. would want to recoup his lost production cost under the insurance policy, claiming that Swift is sick," Dave said.

"Then there'd be a long, protracted lawsuit as to whether dope addiction is an illness or not. Whatever the outcome, Christopher would become permanently unemployable."

"Is that what you meant by having to save a human life in order to save the picture?" Dave asked.

"That is precisely what I meant. If you'll help Christopher Swift, I'll help save the picture. If you won't help him, I won't lift a finger. Is that clear?"

"Clear," said Dave. "Do I get a few hours to think it over?"

He stood up and stared across at her. "And if we try to save him? And fail?"

"I'm not saying we can do it. I'm only saying we have to try. For all I know, he may be doomed. But I have no right to make that decision," Markham said.

"Do you have a right to go out and jeopardize yourself, as you did last night?"

"That isn't a right, Mr. Cole. That is a duty. And I intend to continue as long as I can. Valerie and I agreed."

"Those four little packets?" Dave asked.

"As soon as you leave, I'll go to his suite and give them to him. I wish there were some other way I could help him. But unfortunately, there isn't."

When Dave Cole arrived at the Excelsior, he found that Dino Cortese had had his things unpacked and was awaiting his instructions. But Dave had none. He dismissed Cortese, took a hot shower and lay down to think. Caution advised, Cut and run, but the more he realized that H.P. had lied, the more determined he became to succeed. Succeed and then take his victory home to Sybil.

Finally, the challenging image of Aline Markham decided for him. If that great lady could take the risk, so could he. He called her at once.

"Yes?" she answered crisply.

"We'll do it your way."

"Excellent!"

"Did you see him?"

"As soon as you left; I told you I would."

"Does he know about my being here?"

"Yes, and he was pleased. He told me what you did for him on Broadway. He trusts you."

"Good!" Dave said. "What do you suggest now?"

"That you call me Ali, and I call you Dave."

"That'll be an honor. A great honor. What about Christopher?"

"Come see me first, then have dinner with him."

"Will he?"

"I told you, he trusts you."

When Dave Cole arrived at Aline Markham's suite, Valerie Bristol was with her. Markham had been right. The girl was even more beautiful in person than on the screen. She had wide violet eyes, a heart-shaped face and vibrantly black hair. Th

220

footage that Dave had seen did not do her justice. It had only tried to exploit her figure, which was superb.

"I thought since we are all conspirators, we might as well meet as soon as possible," Markham said. "Valerie, Mr. Cole. Dave."

The girl seemed quite shy for someone so beautiful. Her acknowledgment of the introduction was almost inaudible.

"I told Christopher you wanted to have dinner with him. He'll be ready," Markham said. "In the meantime, Valerie can fill you in on a part of his problem."

The girl began hesitantly, as if it were her own secret she was about to reveal.

"You have to understand," she began, "I'm telling you this for Christopher's sake. He knows he's fighting for his life. And he knows we're all trying to help."

She paused before she spoke again.

"He's one of Edmund Pryce's boys. You know that."

"Yes, and his most successful," Dave said.

"You know what goes with that?"

"I know," Dave said. "That startled me. Chris wasn't like that back on Broadway."

"He wasn't?" Valerie asked, surprised.

"I'm sure he wasn't," Dave insisted.

"Strange," said Valerie. "That day in Florence, I know why he became so terrified. He told me. He tells me lots of things he won't tell anyone else." With some difficulty, she told Dave and Ali Markham Christopher's version of what had happened that first night at Pryce's home in Beverly Hills.

When Valerie was done, Markham spat out, "That bastard!"

Valerie had only one thing more to say: "Now, he has no feelings at all. None."

Dave looked at her quizzically.

"He can't respond. Not to anyone, man or woman."

"It could be the heroin," Dave said.

"The heroin only started afterwards. And that one long call was to his analyst. He had to tell him what happened at the museum," Valerie added.

"Does his analyst know about the heroin?"

"Chris is afraid to tell him. Analysts can't do much with addicts, and Chris is afraid he might kick him out."

"It doesn't get any better, does it?" Aline said to Dave. "You can still back out."

"I said I would meet him at seven-thirty. It's almost time."

"You didn't answer me."

"That *is* my answer. I'll meet him," Dave said.

The roof garden of the Hassler is one of the most delightful restaurants in Rome. Dave had tipped the maître d' heavily to ensure a private table.

For twenty minutes Dave looked out the window wondering if he should call down to Swift's suite. He decided to wait it out. Finally Christopher Swift arrived, gaunt and untidy. When Dave held out his hand to shake, Swift seemed to hesitate.

Dave said warmly, "Chris, hi! It's been a long time."

Swift avoided his eyes and said in a low voice, "Hi, Dave." Then he sat down and began to stare at the lighted city below.

"Drink?"

Swift ordered a Campari and soda, which he did not touch. His eyes were unfocused. He stared at the menu but didn't seem able to read it. Dave ordered for him, but the actor ate virtually nothing. It was only when coffee arrived that he seemed willing to speak.

"You want to talk to me, Dave? Okay, but not here. In my suite."

There was a DO NOT DISTURB sign on the door when they reached it. That intrigued Dave, since Swift had been out of the suite for almost an hour. But his curiosity was quickly satisfied once Swift unlocked the door and snapped on the lights. On the coffee table in the living room were an unused glass hypodermic barrel, a clean steel needle and a small white packet—one of those Dave had turned over to Aline Markham. Swift had laid them out deliberately. Before Dave could comment, Swift begged, "Replace me in the picture!"

"I can't."

"You have to. I'll never make it!" Swift was becoming panicky

"Look, we can close down the picture and take a loss, but the one thing I can't do is replace you. Sorry."

"But I'll never make it!"

"We'll work together, Chris. Like the first time."

"Dave, this isn't like the first time."

"You'll make it," Dave insisted, though he was unsure himself, since he had never dealt with an addict before.

"I can't face it," said Chris. "That thing keeps staring at me— and it knows, Dave; it knows."

"What knows?"

"The camera keeps staring." Chris began to tremble.

Dave reached out and gripped him by the arm.

"Now, sit down. And listen! First, I want to know, have you had a fix this evening?"

Swift glanced away and nodded.

"Okay. Then you have no reason to panic. And there isn't much I don't already know from Aline and Valerie. They're your friends. They told me in order to help you. Now, we've made a pact, the three of us. We need your help to make it work. We *are* going to finish this film! We *are* going to see you have what you need, when you need it. You're not to worry about that any-more. Understand?"

Swift nodded.

"We don't have to do this, any of us. If I closed this picture down tomorrow, Markham would be cast in a new film before the end of the week, Valerie would be back working at Magna. I'd be directing and producing somewhere. We're doing it for only one reason, Chris; because we respect your talent. And we're going to pull you through. *If you let us.*"

Chris Swift turned away. "I wish they wouldn't," he said. "I wish they wouldn't!"

"Wouldn't what?"

"Try to help me," he said. "I can't do it. I can't remember my lines. I can't face the camera. It knows. And if it knows, every-one in the world will know."

"Know what?"

"About me. About Pryce. I used to hate it. But I told myself it was necessary to please him. Then after a while I began to like it. I needed it. I wanted it. But then it started to go wrong. I couldn't respond. Not to him—not to anyone. I am nothing now. I went to an analyst; at least I could talk about it. When that didn't help, I tried dope. Because for hours at a time, it doesn't bother me anymore. I can feel young, I can feel strong, I can feel anything I want to feel. I can even delude myself into feeling potent, if I want to. But then I remember how much money this habit costs. What will I do? How will I get the stuff? Become a whore to some other Edmund Pryce?"

He turned away. As he did, Dave wondered if it was possible to save him, to complete the picture or to do anything but get up, walk out and take the next plane back to the States. It was only the determined image of Aline Markham that made him decide to try.

"Look at me," he said.

"I can't. You're like the camera now. You know!"

"Yes!" Dave said firmly. "But no one else does except Aline and Valerie."

"And Edmund Pryce!" Swift shouted.

"He's not here. He doesn't count," Dave said. "And we're going to find out what that camera really knows. If you're right, I'll let you quit. If I'm right you have to see it through. Agreed?"

Swift nodded—a single jerky nod.

"Now tell me a few things. First, how many hours a day can you work?"

"It's the lines. I can't remember the lines."

"I didn't ask about the lines! I want to know how many good hours you have a day—four, three, one? How many?"

"Three, four, maybe," Swift admitted.

"When? What time of day?" Dave demanded.

"Midmorning. I get up, I . . . I take my shot. . . . In a while I feel in control."

"Say from eleven to two?"

"I think I could make that," Swift said.

"Okay. Eleven to two," Dave said. "I'll set up a shooting schedule on that basis. And tomorrow we will do one scene. We'll see. Let the camera decide. But if it comes out my way you're going to see this picture through to the end! Understand?"

Aline Markham was on the phone when Dave knocked on her door. She called out, "Come in" and returned to her conversa-

224

ion. He could tell from what she said that she was talking to her lover in Hollywood. Hers were not the usual terms of endearment. But coming from her, the salty words took on another meaning.

She hung up and turned to Dave.

"I had to promise we'd do a test scene to prove he could still act," Dave said. "It was the only way."

"I understand."

"It'll have to be a scene you're in. He'll need all the support we can give him. And it can't be a scene that has many lines. In fact, if we continue, we'll have to trim his lines to the bone."

"We've been doing that," Markham warned.

"We'll do even more," Dave said. "Because sitting with him, watching him, he's got one thing going for him. His eyes. He's always had sensitive eyes. Now there's a difference."

"He's weaker," Markham said.

"He's vulnerable. We'll make that work for us," Dave said. "First we've got to find just the right scene for both of you. A scene he can do and be proud of, or at least happy with. I'll start looking as soon as I get back to my hotel."

"When was the last time you slept?" Markham asked.

"On the plane, I think—yesterday. I don't remember."

"Go to bed, get some sleep first. You need it, Davie."

He looked at her sharply.

"Something wrong?" she asked.

"Only one other woman in the world calls me that."

"And you miss her, don't you?"

"Always," he admitted; "always."

"I know how it is," she said. "I spoke to him not five minutes ago and I miss him already. Davie, it is good to be so committed to one person. It makes it all worthwhile. You'll find that out."

"Miss Markham," he asked, smiling gently, "may I have your autograph?"

She was so touched that she had to cover her moment of sentimentality by saying briskly, "Get the hell out of here and get some sleep! See you tomorrow."

He started for the door. She called out, "Davie." He turned back. "Come here. You're seven thousand miles from home, lonely and lovesick. I think you deserve a kiss." She kissed him

225

on the cheek. "Now go to bed like a good little boy. And if we're going to be working together, you'd better move over here to the Hassler."

The next morning Dave was wakened by the phone. It was Aline. "I found it."

"Found what?" Dave asked, still almost asleep.

"The scene. Page one forty-six of the script. Brief, powerful, not much dialogue. It could work," she said. "Sorry to wake you, but I wanted you to know."

She hung up and he groped for the script.

The scene was brief, one of the climactic passages of the film, coming just after the crucifixion of Jesus, involving only Mary and John. None of the other cast members would be present in the event Swift broke down, and Dave would close the set to all but the most essential crew members.

More important, it was a scene with tremendous emotional impact. Aline was right. If this scene went well, there was a chance they could pull it off.

"It's impossible!" Dino exploded when Dave told him that they would shoot from ten in the morning till three without a break.

"In this country and in France they work afternoons, nights. Never in the morning."

"Ten to three," Dave insisted.

"They have a union—a Communist union!"

"So tell the Communists you are dealing with a crazy American director who wants to work from ten to three. Tell them I am corrupt as all capitalists are and that I would even stoop to bribery. But have them ready to work tomorrow at ten."

"All right, all right," Dino said.

"Now get me the cameraman. And the makeup man. I want to talk to both of them at once. Then move all my stuff over to the Hassler!"

When he was done giving instructions, he went to discuss the crucial test scene with Aline Markham.

226

He picked up Chris in the car. When the actor was settled in the back, Dave said, "The first thing you have to do is re-create the mood of the events leading up to the scene. You have just deserted your brother Jesus. Turned and run like a coward."

"I can play cowards very well," Swift interrupted ironically.

"Shut up!" Dave said. "Today we are not dealing with the problems of Christopher Swift but with the problems of John, the disciple. Who has just seen Jesus arrested and hanging in agony on a cross.

"And now you have to go find your mother and tell her. Of *our* cowardice and *his* fate. Then you must take her to see for yourself, for it is her fate as well as his. And all the while there is the guilt tormenting you, because you blame yourself. This is a preordained event, yet you feel guilty.

"All those things must be in your mind when you begin your scene."

The limousine was pulling up at the huge Cathedral of St. Peter's, as close to the entrance as was permitted.

Christopher Swift stared at Dave Cole, questioning.

"There's something I want you to see."

They entered the cathedral, ignoring the crowds of tourists and pilgrims. Dave took Swift's arm and led him to a row of alcoves on the left, stopping before a white marble statue of a woman grieving over her dead son.

"Look at it, Chris," Dave said.

"The *Pietà*," said Christopher. "Michelangelo."

"Yes. *Michelangelo*," Dave repeated, emphatic where Swift had been tentative. "It's as close to perfection as it's possible to come. It even rivals his *David*."

Swift glanced hostilely at him, but Dave just said gently, "The same man who loved David created this. It is possible for a man to be what Michelangelo was and to create a piece as magnificent as this. Just as it is possible for an actor to be one thing in his private life and another on the screen. That's one reason I wanted you to see this.

"The other reason is that I wanted you to remember in the scene tomorrow that when you take your mother from her house

227

to Golgotha she is going to end up holding your dead brother in her arms like this. You have to think of that all through the scene."

Christopher Swift stared at the statue until it seemed to move before his eyes. When he turned away, his eyes were moist.

"There's still a lot of beauty in this world, Chris. Give it a chance."

"Too late . . . too late," Swift murmured, then pleaded, "Take me back to the hotel."

The next morning when Chris arrived on the set with Aline and Valerie, Dave was ready.

"The script? Where's the script?" Chris asked desperately. " told you I have trouble with lines."

"There are no lines," Dave said, as he had planned with Aline. "Just one word, 'Mother.' "

" 'Mother'?" Swift asked dubiously.

"That's all the dialogue there is. Now I'll explain the action to you while they're doing your makeup."

As they worked on Christopher's face, Dave talked to him.

"Remember what happened before the scene. You deserted Jesus as did all his disciples. But you feel your guilt more than the rest, and it is you who must tell your mother. You make your way through the storm-dark city to the house of friends where you know you'll find her. To the room where she i awaiting word of her other son.

"When you open her door you are so overwhelmed with guilt and fear you can't speak. If only she would accuse you—but she is silent. What can she say? She's *your* mother as much as she i *His*. She sees the guilt on your face and knows that you need not accusations but forgiveness. She holds out her arms to you. You cry, 'Mother,' and you rush to her and drop to your knees."

Dave paused, then said softly, "That's the scene, Chris. The rest is close-ups. We'll get those later. But I want the master scene in one take. No actor should be asked to do that kind o scene more than once. Okay?"

"Okay," Chris whispered. When Dave moved to leave, Swift reached out to grasp his hand. "Don't go, Dave. Wait with me."

228

It reminded Dave of the New York opening. In a while Chris was ready to face the camera.

Dave himself gave the orders.

"Everybody on this set. Quiet! I demand absolute silence for Mr. Swift."

When everything was ready, Dave nodded to Chris and said, "Action!"

Swift hesitated, trying to remember all the things Dave had told him standing before the *Pietà*. His tortured mind was struggling to put them all together, to build them into one overwhelming emotion. But he couldn't. Dave was becoming concerned now. Valerie Bristol moved closer to him, seized his hand. Her own was ice-cold. Dave wondered if he had put too much stress on Swift. Perhaps he should have picked a scene of simpler emotion.

It was too late for that now. This was the scene. This was the moment. The entire production of *Via Dolorosa* would live or die by this.

Sitting alone on her rough wood stool, Aline Markham shared all Dave's thoughts and fears. Unless Chris could be made to move, all hope for the picture was lost. Very soon the crew must become nervous too. Someone would whisper some impatient Italian expression that would shatter the moment and destroy everything. She had to do something.

Suddenly she pretended to hear a sound at the door. She raised her eyes, turned her head slightly and whispered, "My son?"

It was too low to be picked up by the microphone which was trained on Swift, but loud enough for the actor to hear. He started to respond, slowly at first, but with increasing feeling, so that when he flung open the door and cried, "Mother!" the scene had all the power and effect that Dave hoped for. Swift went to her, dropped at her side, buried his face in her lap and wept. Then, as Dave had directed, Chris raised his tearful face to her, trying to explain, trying to ask for forgiveness. At that point Ali Markham improvised a bit of action of her own. She gently placed her fingers over his lips, making it unnecessary for him to confess his guilt. Then she kissed him and took his hand, and together they left the room to go to stand at the foot of the cross.

229

After they left the set, there was a terrible silence. Then Dave whispered, "Cut." Then from up on the lighting grid a voice called out, "Bravo! Bravissimo!" and the entire crew burst into cheers.

They finished the close-ups, and Dave dismissed the crew. He went back to Markham's dressing room, where she was just ready to leave.

"I can't thank you enough," he said. "That opening move of yours, lifting your head, calling, 'My son?' That did it. Inspired!"

With a rare show of modesty she said, "The director sets the scene. The actors just do what comes naturally."

He kissed her on the cheek. "While they're developing the film can I take you to dinner? Then I have to go back and edit."

"Did you ever see an actress who wasn't hungry? Let's have dinner and then we'll both go edit."

When they had the piece of film in the form Dave wanted, he ran it through the Moviola twice. He and Ali Markham kept their heads pressed together so they could stare into the small screen at the same time.

The second time they viewed the scene, he couldn't resist whispering to her, "If I had the nerve, I'd ask you to marry me."

"If I were ten years younger, I'd say yes," she answered softly.

The next day Dave had Cortese arrange for a projection room to which only Markham, Valerie Bristol and Christopher Swift were admitted. The lights came down. The film began. It was brief. Only thirty-six seconds. When it was over, Dave ordered, "Run it again."

In moments there were sounds of sobbing. It was Chris. In the darkness, Markham reached out to press Dave's hand, a gesture of congratulations. Valerie turned to Chris and kissed him on the cheek. "You proved it. Just as Dave said, you proved you could do it."

Dave called for the lights. They came on. Valerie was wiping the tears from Christopher's eyes. Dave said to him, "We know what we have to do. And now we know we can do it. Four hours every day. But four great hours. Right?"

"Right," Christopher Swift agreed.

Later Dave took Cortese aside and gave him strict orders

Swift was to be supplied with four packets of heroin every day. Dave didn't care how Cortese got the stuff or what it cost.

That evening Dave found a message under his door: *Tonight it's my turn to buy dinner.* It was signed *A.M.*

She took him to a small restaurant that was not famous, just excellent. At ten o'clock, she said, "We have to go. I have to make a call."

She insisted he wait in her suite while she put the call through to California. Once she reached her man, she acted as if Dave weren't there at all. She carried on in their usual way, asking about his picture, how it was going, and was he staying sober enough to work. He said some intimate things which she avoided delicately. When it seemed she was ready to conclude the conversation she said, "Oh, by the way, you can spread the word around. We've got a blockbuster in the making here."

Dave made signs at her, but she ignored him. Her friend must have argued too, for she said, "No, I mean it. It's all due to this brilliant young director. He's done wonders. You tell them all. We're coming home with a hit!"

She hung up and smiled at Dave.

"We haven't even begun yet," he said.

"I know. But that's the least I can do for a very nice young man who's as kind as he is brilliant. Tomorrow everyone will be talking, and H. P. Koenig will be ready to bust a gut! For that alone it's worth it."

19

H.P. was enjoying his regular massage when Sarah Immerman decided it was time to tell him the word from Rome.

"There's a rumor going around Stage Seven..." she said standing tentatively at the door.

"There's always a rumor going around Stage Seven!" H.P. said. Then, because he savored rumors, he asked, "So?"

"They say *Via Dolorosa* is turning into a hit."

The masseur felt the muscles of H.P.'s body tense. "Relax, Mr Koenig," he urged.

H.P. did not relax, but he permitted the man to finish up then lay on the table contemplating the possible truth of Sarah's message. In the first place, it was too early to tell whether Dave Cole would be able to rescue the picture at all, let alone make it into a hit; but obviously something had happened, and if the rumor had emanated from Stage Seven it must come directly from Aline Markham's friend. If the picture had even a chance of success, H.P. would have to revise his aims. He could always settle with Dave Cole later. But he could vastly improve his position in New York by profiting from Dave's unexpected success.

The first thing to do was ascertain the facts. As soon as he was dressed, H.P. placed a call to Dino Cortese. At that time of the Roman night Cortese was sitting at a table outside Doney's waiting for his contact to show up. When he did, some large bank notes and some small white packets changed hands. Christopher Swift was safe for a few more days. When Cortese returned to his hotel and found the message, he immediately returned the transatlantic call.

"Mr. Koenig?" he began. "Dino Cortese."

"How's it going?" H.P. asked, not wishing to direct the conversation. He usually picked up more information that way.

"Well, it's . . . How do I say it? . . . It's like a miracle here."

"What kind of miracle?"

"Swift is working again. On a limited schedule—four hours a day. But Cole has shot more footage in the last three days than they did in the previous three weeks."

"Any good?"

"I haven't seen it all. But between Markham and Swift it's terrific."

"Good," H.P. murmured with no great enthusiasm. "And that's it?"

"Isn't that enough?"

"Three days of shooting doesn't make a hit, Dino. But keep me informed. Each day I want a report. How many feet, how many pages in the can. Understand?"

"Yes, of course."

"But don't say anything to anybody. I don't want to make them nervous."

"I understand," said Dino, hanging up.

H.P. leaned back in his chair and considered his tactics in the light of this changed situation. To start claiming credit for Dave's success too early might leave him out on a limb later. He must watch carefully and play his cards at the right moment.

That sonofabitch, he thought; that young sonofabitch who had screwed his daughter might get away with it after all. He had the one asset with which H.P. had never been able to contend easily—real talent.

That afternoon, Albert Grobe left the studio early. He knew that it was Sybil's habit to take her tennis lesson from the leathery pro at the Beverly Hills Hotel most Wednesday afternoons at four. He watched her for the last ten minutes and

233

saw that she was good. When she came off the court and saw Grobe for the first time, she came to him at once, asking anxiously, "Uncle Albert?"

"No, nothing wrong. He's okay."

She relaxed now and started to wipe her face with a towel.

Albert asked gently, "Which 'he' did you think I was talking about?"

She had to admit, "My father. I thought he might have had a heart attack. If they sent anyone to tell me, it would be you."

"No," Albert said. "No heart attack. Not even a nervous flutter. The man is made of cast iron. This is about the other he."

"Yes?" she said, blushing slightly.

"I thought you'd like to know. The first word back from Rome is good."

"I'm glad," she said, but without any obvious pleasure.

"If you don't mind taking a bit of advice from an old man, it wouldn't hurt if you sent him a note saying that you heard and you're glad."

"I'll think about it, Uncle Albert."

"Don't think! Do it! If not for your own sake, then for his. It would help him to know you're rooting for him."

"He's probably screwing every big-breasted Italian actress he can get his hands on," she said bitterly.

"You're not giving him any choice," Albert said softly.

She looked at him angrily, for a moment. Then she softened and said, "You're right, Uncle Albert. Right."

The next evening when Dave returned to his hotel he found a bottle of champagne waiting for him. He looked at the card that hung over the side of the cooler. It had been badly mangled in the transliteration, but the message was quite clear. Sybil was happy for him. He called Markham on the phone.

"I'm stuck with this bottle of Taittinger and I don't feel like celebrating alone. What do you say?"

"If we see any more of each other I'll have to adopt you. Bring it up."

He showered, changed, then lifted the entire ice-filled cooler in his arms and presented himself at Markham's door. She had ordered caviar.

234

"It's from her," Aline guessed.

"Yes," he admitted.

"She loves you."

"I hope so, but I don't know if it will do any good. A couple of times in the past I've found myself wanting to marry other women because I'm tired of waiting. Fortunately, each time they've been smart enough to say no. But one day there'll be one who'll say yes. I know the danger, but what do I do?"

"The same thing you're doing with Christopher Swift. Be considerate; work around her weakness. Her addiction is no less than his. She's hooked on her father, and she hates him. I can't think of anything worse for a girl."

Dave shook his head hopelessly.

"Patience, Davie, patience. Take it from someone who knows." She spoke sadly, but with a small smile.

The picture proceeded as Dave had planned. He extracted the best of Christopher Swift during the four hours they had agreed on, and shot around him in the afternoon. Both Markham and Valerie had to work under a handicap. But they forced themselves to adjust for Swift's sake and Dave's.

Dave had to keep several sets standing, so that he had the freedom to change scenes at will on those days when Swift had trouble making it. It added materially to the production cost, as Cortese pointed out, but Dave had no choice. It was either that or suffer the outrageous costs incurred by days of no shooting at all.

Each evening Cortese went back to his hotel and secretly phoned his report to H.P. Aside from costs, Dave was making the picture, and making it well.

"And Swift?" H.P. asked.

"He shows up every day. Most days he's very good. He's got something in his eyes that will make audiences feel that he is hearing the voice of God."

"The prick is high on dope. If he's hearing voices that's where they come from," said H.P.

"When you see him on film, you don't know that. It gives the picture an almost ethereal quality."

It was not like Cortese to enthuse, and H.P. began to believe the movie would be a hit. Perhaps it was time for him to go over and take a look for himself. If the footage was as good as Cortese said, it might just be time to begin to claim the credit. His line would be that H.P.'s brilliant young man had rescued a costly disaster.

H. P. Koenig was not the only one who was contemplating a trip abroad. Edmund Pryce had his own sources of information. They kept him informed of the progress of his young protégé. Christopher was working again. That was good. The footage was turning out well. That was excellent. It meant it might be time to begin hinting to H.P. about a new and much more rewarding contract. Always strike before the reviews was Pryce's tactic, while expectations were running high. Or while it was possible that a refusal to renegotiate the contract might affect a star's attitude and reflect on his performance before he completed the film.

There was yet another intriguing facet to the rumors, if they were true. If Christopher was working so well again, perhaps his sexual difficulty had cleared up. Curiosity and sexual avarice made Edmund Pryce consider a flight to Rome, though he justified it to himself as a shrewd business move. Yes, he decided, he would fly over and have a look for himself.

Since the air schedule to Rome was not so frequent then as it would be in later years, Edmund Pryce and H. P. Koenig were booked on the same flight out of New York. They were surprised and wary of each other when they met on the plane, though they pretended to be delighted.

"Ah, H.P.!" Pryce exclaimed, convinced now that the rumors must be true, else why would H.P. be making the trip to Rome himself?

"Edmund!" H.P. replied, his face lighting up in a smile, thinking: So the old fag with his gold-headed cane has heard the rumors and he's on his way over to make sure before he starts wangling a new contract. I'll cut his heart out before I give him a new contract.

They set side by side, drank together, ate two meals together and talked of the industry. They spoke of the series of Supreme Court decisions that could force Magna, as well as all other studios, to divorce its theater company from its production company.

They also talked of the Red scare that was sweeping Hollywood, and about the congressional and state committees' digging up all kinds of subversive scandal.

They talked of everything except *Via Dolorosa,* neither of them willing to risk betraying any information the other might not possess. Pryce drifted off to sleep, having been tucked in by a young dark-skinned Italian stewardess with unusually good breasts which H.P. had been able to glimpse when she leaned over to make Pryce comfortable. Though H.P. accepted a blanket from her, in a while, when Pryce was gently snoring, H.P. slipped across him and made his way to the galley. The young dark stewardess, who had been instructed that H. P. Koenig always received V.I.P. treatment on board, was quick to greet him and try to anticipate his wishes. More wine? Or perhaps something stronger? Or did he need an alkalizer after what had been an unusually rich and heavy meal?

He needed none of those. What he needed was to plunge his hands inside her uniform and fondle her breasts, which had excited him to a large and painful erection. Since most of the passengers had settled down to sleep on the long overseas leg of the flight, he was able to seduce her in the lavatory. It was one of the more exciting sexual events of his week, so he invited her to spend her two-day layover in Rome with him at his hotel suite. Because she had been told many times by male passengers that she ought to be in pictures, she agreed. H.P.'s sexual needs for the next few days were assured of gratification.

Dave had just completed shooting the scene in which the disciple John had come to Jerusalem to report on the raising of Lazarus. Ali Markham was in the scene. As was Valerie Bristol. The scene of her conversion from Magdalene the whore to Magdalene the saint would be shot later. Dave was concentrating on those scenes which involved Christopher Swift. With all of those in the can, he could settle down to shoot the rest of the picture.

The scene was laid in the same set in which Mary, the Mother, would receive from John the word about her Son's crucifixion.

237

They had just arrived in Jerusalem in advance of Jesus. For He had interrupted His journey to go to the tomb of Lazarus in answer to the pleas of his sisters Mary and Martha. Then Jesus had raised Lazarus, who had been dead four days. John had witnessed the miracle and raced on ahead to Jerusalem to spread the word.

The look of wonder in Christopher Swift's eyes, the ethereal stare that had been implanted there by the heroin he had taken at nine-thirty in the morning, made the scene work with unusual effect. Because it did, Dave dared to work tighter than usual on him. He took close-up after close-up. By two o'clock Dave was satisfied that he had had one of the best days of shooting since he had taken over the film. Cut together with the previous scene of the actual raising of Lazarus, it would be a moment of peak dramatic impact in the film.

Added to Swift's performance, the reactions of Ali and Valerie would make the scene even more powerful. But Dave would go for those reactions once Swift had left the studio. There were Markham's reaction shots, as the Mother who knew that such a public miracle must result in endangering her son Jesus. There was the devout reaction of Valerie Bristol, as the beautiful and now reformed Magdalene, to whom this miracle was confirmation of her belief that Jesus was truly Messiah and Son of God

Swift had been released for the day. The shots with Markham and Valerie Bristol were being made. There was a stir at the stage door of the closed set. With great irritation, Dave went to investigate the cause of the intruding noises that were upsetting his rehearsal with the camera crew.

H. P. Koenig and Edmund Pryce had arrived and insisted on being admitted. The Italian guard, who by now revered Dave, as did the rest of the crew, was not about to let any intruders enter, even if one of them loudly claimed to be head of Magna Studios. Dave permitted them to enter but made it quite clear that until he was done shooting, he wanted no interruptions, no conversation, no suggestions. This was one of the good days, when he was making up for the lost time that had put the picture so far over budget.

H.P. and Pryce were content to wait, silent and engrossed. Pryce kept looking around for some sign of Christopher. He would wait, sure that sooner or later his young lover must appear.

When Dave finished shooting, H.P. was convinced of one thing: this young, arrogant bastard of a director was good—goddamn good! He was excellent with actors, he knew what he wanted every moment of the time and he was able to get it on film. The rumors must be true.

There was one way to make sure. When they wrapped for the day, H.P. insisted that they be shown the rough-cut footage. Dave had no way of preventing that. H.P. and Edmund Pryce would be the first outsiders to see any of the new footage of *Via Dolorosa*. Aline Markham was notorious for not liking to see herself until there was a complete cut so that she could assess her total performance in the event retakes were called for. Today she insisted on viewing this incomplete cut with H.P. and Edmund Pryce. Dave knew she did that to protect him. If any weight was needed to counter H.P's criticisms, she would be there to supply it.

The screening room was darkened. The footage began. Dave did a running commentary, filling in the missing scenes which would be shot later. H.P. sat back in the huge soft lounge chair, his face grim in the changing light that reflected from the screen. Much as he hated to admit it, this was becoming the picture he had first envisioned when he decided to make *Via Dolorosa*. It had impact and reverence, yet it wasn't a stodgy costume epic. It was a dramatic film of great strength. He knew now he would have to forgo his vengeance for the credit involved in making a box-office smash. He would stop in New York on his way back and begin whipping up enthusiasm in the theater branch of Magna. Vaguely he remembered some warnings from his lawyers not to have too much direct contact with the theater operation and Dan Sullavan until the legal end of things was clarified.

But in his own mind H.P. had decided, Screw the Supreme Court! They couldn't be against a good religious picture. He would stop in New York.

The footage was over. H.P. insisted on seeing it all again. Despite the fact that Dave was tired and hungry, he acquiesced. He suggested that Markham leave, since it had been a most taxing day. She insisted on remaining. The footage ran again. In fifty-six minutes it was over. When the lights came up in the projection room, H.P. sat there, still staring and nodding his head. All he would grant was "Good. Good piece of film."

But Dave Cole and Aline Markham discovered something of vastly greater importance than H.P.'s reaction to the footage.

Edmund Pryce was no longer in the projection room. Sometime during the second running he had quietly slipped out. Both Dave and Ali had the same suspicion. They did not wait to exchange views with H.P. They raced down to the street where the studio limousine waited to take them back to the Hassler.

20

The gold-headed cane knocked commandingly on the door of Christopher's suite. When there was no answer, it beat against the door strongly enough to make notches in the hard old wood. Finally there came the sound of unlocking. The door opened slightly. Christopher Swift, eyes vague and staring, peered out. He tried to bring his eyes into focus when he realized who was there, tried to shut the door, but Edmund Pryce slipped his cane between the door and the jamb. Swift pushed against the door with all his strength.

"Open up, boy! Let me in!" Pryce commanded.

All resistance went out of Swift. He moved back. Pryce shoved the door open with his cane and entered. He locked the door behind him, throwing both bolts so that it could not be opened from the outside.

Swift had gone ahead of him into the living room which faced out over the Spanish Steps. He hurriedly tried to dispose of the evidence of his last shot. But Pryce brought his thick cane sharply across the young man's hands, causing him to drop the used hypo to the rug. Pryce coaxed it over to his feet with his cane. He looked down at it and then stared at the young man.

"Why, Christopher? Why?"

"Goddamn you, you know why!"

"All I know is what I did for you. I took an actor whose career was going nowhere and built him into one of the greatest young stars in this business!"

"That isn't all you did!"

"What else did I do? Love you? Yes, Christopher, I love you. The others, they were like whores to be used for my own pleasure and promoted for my own profit. But you—you I loved. And still love."

"For all the good it'll do either of us," Swift said bitterly.

"You mustn't worry about that! It's only a transitory phase. It happens, even to straight men. Or those who call themselves straight. It is nothing physical. It is only in your mind. And you can overcome it, Christopher, if only you will let yourself."

"I can't. I've tried!"

"What have you tried? *This?*" Pryce asked, flicking the used hypodermic across the room with a single contemptuous motion of his cane. "There is only one way, Christopher. Recognize what you are. Make peace with it."

"What I am? Or what you have made me?"

"What I never could have made you if you hadn't had the seeds of it to begin with. They say I subvert—pervert, if you like the word better—young, innocent men. With promises of success. Well, Christopher, I have news for you. They don't all acquiesce."

Christopher Swift stared at him in confusion.

"That's right, boy. I have been rejected. By more than a few. Only those who have it within them give in. As you gave in. I didn't *make* you do anything. I offered you the way and you took it. That's what you refuse to recognize now. And as long as you do, it will lead to more of this. And more, until the end. Which, I need not tell you, can be quite ugly."

He had disarmed the younger man, removed his one last defense.

"It's really useless to fight it. We are what we are. And we should not be ashamed of it. It's because of that that you are a star. People react to that part of you which is sensitive, tender and vulnerable. That's what they love about you. You are like them. For underneath, all men are sensitive, tender and vulnerable. But the world does not permit them to reveal it."

Pryce studied Christopher Swift's eyes. They were reacting to him, though the young, slender man stood unmoved. If Pryce was

242

to have his way, he knew it must be now. He came closer to Swift. He spoke more softly.

"Boy, come home. Come back to me. Give up the struggle. Make peace with yourself. Because I love you. Even if you never act again I will love you and take care of you for the rest of your life. I give you my word you're the only one I've really ever loved. The only one. Surely you must know that. Christopher?"

Christopher Swift turned away from Pryce. The older man reached out the gold head of his cane, pushed it firmly against his protégé's shoulder so that he turned him about until they faced each other. Pryce stared into Swift's glazed eyes.

"God, boy, what have you done to yourself?"

He embraced the young man, held him tenderly. Swift let himself be held. In a moment he was weeping.

"That's good, boy. Cry. It will help. When you're done crying, we will talk it all out. This isn't the end of anything, but the beginning. I have just come from the studio, where I saw the footage. You are magnificent. Every bit of tenderness comes through. Every sensitive line in your face, every look in your eyes is there on film, in color, and it is magnificent. This is only the beginning of your career. You'll win an Oscar for this performance, boy. The only problems you have are of your own making. We must get you through this film. We must get you off this deadly habit. And we must get you to accept who you are, what you are, and that we are bound together with a love stronger than exists between man and woman. There's nothing to be ashamed of, Christopher. Once you've accepted it, there is something magnificently peaceful about it."

Gently he lifted the young man's tearful face and kissed him on the lips. Swift did not resist him. He felt relieved and safe to be in the older man's arms. It seemed easier than fighting it. Or was it the heroin that made him so placid and pliable?

For the moment it did not matter to Edmund Pryce. He had been through this with other young male stars. But eventually he had brought them around. As he would bring Christopher Swift around.

Too bad the young man was under the influence of the drug. That would make it more difficult. Difficult or not, it had to begin now.

Slowly, and with the gentle care of a mother, Edmund Pryce

stripped Christopher Swift of his clothes until he stood naked among his discarded garments. Edmund Pryce stared at the young lean body, already showing the effects of the long periods of drugs, bad diet and lack of sleep. It would take considerable restoring to make him what he had been that first time. But Pryce was sure he could accomplish it.

"Stand up, boy," he coaxed, gently.

Swift made an effort to stand erect.

"Proud, boy! Stand proud!" He nudged him gently with his gold-headed cane. Swift came a bit more erect.

Pryce looked down at Swift's shrunken genitals, limp, defeated. He put aside his cane, slipped to his knees before him, seized him by the thighs and brought him so close that he could kiss him there. Swift did not attempt to free himself. He felt more secure in Pryce's strong arms than he had felt when he was free. He almost wished now that he could respond to the older man.

Pryce held him in his hand, tenderly, gently manipulating him, seeking to arouse some spark of response. For a brief moment they were both aware that there was the slightest pulsating that might lead to an erection.

At that moment there was a loud knock on the door.

"Don't answer!" Pryce commanded in a whisper. "Pretend we're not here."

"Chris!" Dave Cole called through the heavy bolted door. "Chris! Are you in there? Are you alone?"

The young man did not answer. Edmund Pryce rose quickly to his feet, gestured to Christopher to dress at once. Hastily he drew on his clothes. The knocking at the door resumed.

"Chris! Can you hear me?" Dave demanded.

Swift did not answer. Then he heard the voice of Aline Markham.

"Chris, it's me," she said as gently as she could and still be heard. "Open the door? Please?"

When there was no response, she reverted to the same tone she had used to force him into making his entrance in that crucial test scene in the film.

"Let me in, my son."

Christopher Swift could not resist her. He started toward the door. Edmund Pryce reached out with his cane to stop him, but

244

Swift brushed aside the cane and continued to the door and unlocked it. Dave and Markham burst into the room. Edmund Pryce stood tall and defiant, glaring at Dave.

"Get out of here!" Dave commanded.

"I don't think you're in a position to give me such an order," Pryce said confidently. "You may command your actors on the set. But there is only one person who can order me out of this room. Only one." He turned confidently to Christopher Swift. "Boy?"

Swift did not answer.

"Tell him!" Pryce commanded. When Swift remained silent, Pryce continued: "What he refuses to tell you is that he has made his peace with things finally. He is recovering from the difficulty which led him to this disastrous habit." He pointed his cane at the used hypodermic in the corner.

"Tell them. Or must I?" Pryce demanded.

"Chris?" Dave asked. He received no answer.

"We are even on the way to solving his other trouble, which I assume you know about. He is responding. In fact, if you hadn't burst in when you did . . . Tell them, boy!"

Instead of answering Edmund Pryce, Christopher Swift screamed. He screamed an unintelligible scream of agony and rushed from the room, down the long corridor. He did not pause at the elevator but made for the stairs and raced down. Dave started after him but could not catch him at the landing.

Left in the room with Edmund Pryce, Aline Markham turned on him and spoke without raising her voice. "Get out of this hotel. Out of this city. Out of this country. Tonight! If you're still here tomorrow, I will personally kill you!"

Edmund Pryce had no reason to doubt her word. He started for the open door, stopped and turned back to say to her, "I know how you feel about me. But I love that boy. I love him." It was a pathetic confession.

Christopher Swift eluded Dave Cole. He reached the lobby of the Hassler, ran through the front door, knocked the doorman to the ground in his flight and flew down the Spanish Steps. Dave Cole raced after him, calling. But by the time he reached the top of the steps he could find no sign of Swift. Dave had lost him. And with him, most likely, Dave had lost his film.

245

It was past two o'clock in the morning. In Dave's suite they awaited a phone call from Cortese, from the police, from anyone who might have news of Christopher Swift's whereabouts.

H.P. waited with them. He gave every evidence of great concern. But inwardly he felt some quivers of satisfaction. He would have the last word in his vendetta with Dave Cole after all.

Aline Markham turned on H.P. to accuse. "You never should have let Pryce come here!"

"How could I know?" he asked. "No one told me about any of this! I never knew about the drugs. You all kept it a secret from me."

Which was not true, for Cortese kept H.P. informed of such matters all the time. But for the moment, neither Dave nor Markham could dispute him.

"Where the hell is Cortese?" Dave demanded for the hundredth time. "There must be some word!"

But there wasn't, and Dave knew there wasn't. And if there were, if they did find Christopher Swift, in what condition would he be? Would they be able to resume shooting soon? Or ever? As he turned and saw H.P., Dave said to himself, *She's right. Sybil is right. Has been all along. A young man's life is at stake and I keep asking myself, Can I finish the film? The film! It's become more important than a human life to me now.* He despised H. P. Koenig for making him think such thoughts at a time like this. He despised himself even more for thinking them.

The phone rang. It was Valerie Bristol, and she was in tears. The police had wakened her and had been asking her questions. That was how she had discovered Chris was missing. She didn't want to be alone. Could she come up to Dave's suite and wait with them?

"Of course, dear. Come right up!"

Another hour had gone by. There were two calls from Dino Cortese, neither of them encouraging. They had checked the airports. Swift had not left the country. Dave knew that because he had searched and found Swift's passport, papers and money in a drawer in his dresser.

With no money, and with no heroin, time would become a factor soon. Dave turned to Markham and Valerie Bristol.

"When you used to make contacts for him, how did you know where to go?"

"He told us. Doney's. You sit there and wait at an outdoor table. Someone comes around the corner and gives you a sign. You follow him into an alley. You give him the money. He gives you the envelopes. He has to leave first. That's the rule. You stay in that alley till he's gone. That protects him."

"And if you don't?"

"He won't be there the next time. And no addict can risk that."

Dave thought for a moment. "Okay. Come with me."

"Where?"

"We're going to wait outside Doney's."

"It's closed at this hour," Valerie protested.

"We know only one thing for sure. He's on a string, an umbilical cord of heroin. He's got to go to one of two places. Here. Or Doney's. If he comes back here, the police will hold him. If he shows up there, he's going to need us."

Dave and Valerie started for the door. Aline Markham called out, "Wait for me!"

H. P. Koenig was left alone in the huge living room. He leaned back, content. Dave Cole was on a fool's errand. His picture was done for. Meanwhile, that Italian airline stewardess was in his own suite. That girl with the divine breasts. He shouldn't keep her waiting.

The Via Veneto was deserted and still. A random taxi went by, empty. The street lights were indistinct in the misty night. Chairs were piled on the tables outside Doney's, which was dark and closed. The night air was cold, and damp as well. At the one table which Dave had taken over, they sat. Dave Cole. Aline Markham. Valerie Bristol. Markham's face was lean and gaunt from their vigil. Valerie seemed no longer so young or so beautiful. Dave Cole stared into the night, searching every street that led into the Veneto, every storefront, every alleyway. With a probing eye like a camera's, he panned the dark, damp street endlessly. Twice police cars raced by, stopped to inspect them. When they realized none of them was the actor they sought, they picked up speed and went on.

It was hours since Christopher Swift had run off. He must be hurting badly by now. Unless he had done something drastic to himself. There was no accounting for a man as tormented as he had been in those last minutes when Dave saw him.

Suddenly there was a sound and a shadow in one of the alleys. All three of them came alert.

"Chris?" Dave called in a strong whisper.

The shadow withdrew into the alley. In a moment the man peered out again. Dave did not recognize him. Whoever it was, it was not Christopher Swift. The man made himself more prominent now. Dave thought he might have information. He started toward him. But the man forbade him, in a strong Italian accent.

"Not you. The girl!"

Dave considered that a moment, then gave Valerie a sign to go. She disappeared into the alley, but only for a brief time. When she returned she said, "He knows me. I made buys from him before. He thought we wanted to make a contact."

"Does he know anything about Chris?"

"He didn't even know he was missing."

They settled down to waiting again. Dave began to ponder; what if Chris had returned to the hotel, surrendered to the police? But there was no way to check. Another police car raced by. Evidently the search was still on.

They waited. Markham kept saying of Pryce, "The bastard, the bastard, the bastard."

Valerie trembled from the cold and began to sniffle. Dave put his arm around her to give her what warmth and comfort he could. She was hardly more than a child—a physically mature, voluptuous child. She pressed her face against his shoulder.

A horse-drawn wagon rumbled by, a strange phenomenon in this era of motorcars. The sound was distant, seemed unreal.

"Maybe he did go back to the hotel," Valerie said.

"If he did, he's safe," Markham said. "If he didn't, he might show up, and when he does he'll be desperate."

Valerie huddled closer to Dave. As she did so, she stopped suddenly, looking past him. Dave looked in the same direction. There was a figure there, in the misty darkness. Slender, bent, leaning against the wall that led to an alleyway. It could be Chris. Dave freed himself from Valerie and went toward the figure. But it turned and fled.

Dave raced into the alley without any thought that it might be a trap set by night thieves. He followed the figure down the long narrow lane till he cornered him at the dead end. The figure was cringing and trying to hide.

"Chris?"

The figure turned, raised his face and cried out, "Help me, Dave. For Christ's sake, help me!" He broke down and started to weep from pain. Dave took him in his arms and led him toward the street. All the way he whispered to him, "Don't worry, kid. You'll be okay. You'll be fine now."

"The pain, Dave. It's the pain."

He tore free for a moment and leaned against the wall to retch. Dave held him as he did, then wiped his lips when he was done.

"Come on, kid. The quicker we get back to the hotel the quicker we can do something about your pain."

Christopher Swift stared at Dave Cole in the dark and asked, "Is *he* there?"

"He's gone. Left the city."

That seemed answer enough for Swift. He went readily with Dave.

The four of them approached the Hassler on foot along the narrow, shop-lined street. Outside the hotel several police cars waited. Mingled with the police were newspapermen and photographers. The word was evidently out.

Dave stopped. "We can't expose him to anything like that. Not in his condition. We have to stave off that mob of vultures. Ali, honey, you're the only one important enough to take the heat off us."

"Don't worry, I'll handle them. Just sneak him in the back way and up to his suite."

Aline Markham picked up her pace till she was ahead of them. She marched straight toward the mob of photographers and newspapermen. When she came within the light shed by the hotel canopy, they recognized her. Flashbulbs began to explode. The questions started, in English and half a dozen other languages. The name "Swift" was in all of them.

She stopped, cocked her head in a puzzled, inquisitive way

and asked, "What *about* Christopher Swift?" as if she were totally unaware of his disappearance.

When it was explained to her, by half a dozen men, in four different languages all at once, she seemed to understand for the first time. She smiled sheepishly.

"Gentlemen, I'm afraid you've been misled by a very resourceful press agent. Christopher Swift wasn't missing. *I* was."

This brought forth a tidal wave of surprised reactions and new questions. Where had she gone? How long had she been missing? And why? She smiled primly.

"Do you want me to do your work for you?"

"Ah, a man!"

Markham didn't deny it.

"But what about—" one of the newsmen asked, referring, of course, to her friend in Hollywood.

"Now you can see why it was necessary for me to be 'missing.' Though I must confess I didn't expect this reception. Good God, what a way to carry on a little love affair! Might as well make love in the center aisle at St. Peter's."

"And the man?" one of the Italian newsmen asked directly.

"For the sake of your government I don't think it would be wise to mention any names," she said in perfect seriousness.

Instantly there was a fresh rumble of questions, as the newsmen sensed the possibility of a great story break.

"Now, really, I've said too much already," Aline Markham protested, bringing the unscheduled press conference to a close. She started to move toward the hotel entrance, but several newsmen blocked her way. She stared at them as only Aline Markham could stare. They parted and gave way like the waters of the Red Sea. She strode into the hotel lobby, past the astonished doorman, the porter and the night clerks. She marched right to the elevator and pressed the button for Christopher Swift's floor.

Dave and Valerie had sneaked Chris in the back way, past the kitchen help who were setting up the early breakfast trays. Dave commandeered the service car to get them up to his floor. Valerie went ahead to make sure there was no one in his rooms. Dave half-led, half-carried the pain-racked young actor to safety and seclusion. Once inside, Christopher gave Dave instructions in quick, jerky, breathy words while Valerie held on to him. Dave

250

carried out Chris's orders and for the first time in his life gave someone an injection.

Within minutes Swift's pain eased. His lips stopped trembling. He seemed to relax. Valerie continued to hold him till he was quiet and at peace.

By that time Aline Markham had made her way through the crowd of newsmen and up to Swift's suite. She surveyed the situation and took charge at once. She called Room Service. Told it was too early, she bellowed out orders that brought immediate action. Within fifteen minutes a good hot breakfast was delivered. Eggs and ham and fresh rolls and hot coffee.

Then, as if she were feeding a child, Aline Markham, who would never have a child, fed Christopher Swift. Under her gentle but compelling hands, he ate. When he was satisfied, Valerie took him into his bedroom. She sat beside him and held his hand until he dozed off.

In accordance with instructions he had been given, Dino Cortese went to H. P. Koenig's suite as soon as he learned that Christopher Swift had returned to the hotel. Koenig had been nourishing himself on the breasts of the Italian stewardess when the door knock interrupted him. He cursed whoever it was and went back to his pleasure. When the knock recurred he grumbled, left his warm bed and, pulling his silk robe about him, went to answer it. He conversed with Cortese through the locked door, gleaned the vital information and went back to his stewardess, who kept asking him when was she going to get her screen test and would it be in Hollywood? She had never been to Hollywood; Alitalia had no direct flights to L.A.

H. P. Koenig did not even listen to her chatter, which was half English, half Italian. He proceeded to put on his clothes. When she protested, wanting to ensure her future by more sex, he didn't even bother to answer. He had clothed himself, examined his face to determine if he needed a shave for the occasion and compromised with a splash of expensive French toilet water.

He turned to the still-protesting Italian girl and said, "You be the hell out of here by the time I get back!"

251

He rapped loudly on the door of Swift's suite. Dave admitted him, at the same time cautioning him, "Hold it down. We're trying to get him to go to sleep."

"Sleep?" H.P. asked. "What for?"

"He'll need plenty of sleep for me to get him back to work," Dave said. "Not tomorrow. But in a few days."

"And what if he can't go back to work?"

"Don't worry, I can handle him. Just give me time."

"And in the meantime?"

"I'll shoot around him. We have other scenes we can do."

"Scenes? What scenes?"

"Scenes!" Dave said, becoming angry now. "Scenes in the picture."

"What picture?" H.P. demanded.

"What do you mean, what picture?"

"If you are referring to a film entitled *Via Dolorosa*, Christopher Swift is in no condition to complete it."

"I think he will be!" Dave insisted.

"And I think he won't! Due to the illness of Christopher Swift that picture has been shut down. Let the insurance company cover the loss!"

Aline Markham rose to her feet quickly. Feeling he was being challenged, H.P. turned to confront her. "Yes, my dear. Shut down. Closed. Done. Finished. Abandoned. Whatever word you want to use, the effect is the same."

"We've worked too hard," she protested; "all of us."

"Pictures are not made with hard work. They are made with money. From now on there is no more money for a disaster called *Via Dolorosa*."

"You can't do that!" Dave exploded.

"I have just done it," H.P. said in a low voice that was more convincing than his usual bellow. For he felt very smug now. He not only had his revenge; he had avoided financial disaster as well, by shifting the burden to the insurance company that covered all stars on all Magna films.

"I won't let you," Dave said quietly.

"*You* won't let me?" H.P. asked, enjoying his coup all the more now that he had discovered how deeply committed Dave

252

had become to making a success of this film. "How do you propose to stop me?"

"I'll find other financing. There are Italian film companies who would take this over."

"Nickel-and-dime operators, like on Poverty Row in Hollywood. There isn't enough film financing in Rome to finish this picture. And if there were, I wouldn't sell them the footage. It's Magna's! Mine! And it's not for sale. The picture is shut down."

"You bastard!" Dave exploded. "You unmitigated bastard. You want to destroy *me*, destroy me! Don't take it out on the picture."

"And why would I want to destroy you?" H.P. asked innocently.

"Because I made love to your daughter!"

"I don't know what you're talking about!" H.P. shouted, his face growing red with anger.

"Don't you? Albert Grobe knows! Sybil knows! They tried to warn me. . . ." Dave realized immediately that he had blundered into an admission that might incriminate others, mainly Albert Grobe.

H.P. glared at Dave Cole for a long moment. "I don't have the slightest idea what you're talking about. All I know is that a young man named David Cole was given the chance to become producer-director of a very important film. He came here to Rome and discovered a situation he should have reported to the head of the studio at once—that he had a leading man who was under the influence of drugs. The picture should have been abandoned at that time. Instead, he wasted almost half a million dollars more of the company's money by deceiving me. It is my obligation to the company and the stockholders to make sure that he doesn't waste one cent more. It is my duty to close down this production!"

"I can save this film, if I get the chance."

"And I agree!" Markham said, her eyes flashing in defiance.

"With *him*?" H.P. demanded, indicating the door of the bedroom in which Christopher Swift was sleeping. "Sorry. I have to protect my stockholders. The picture is abandoned!"

H.P. was firm and unyielding. And he had spelled out precisely the story he would be circulating in Hollywood within forty-eight hours: that David Cole was wasteful, dishonest with the studio, had dangerously bad judgment in continuing with an unfit actor and was certainly not to be trusted with any company's picture.

That would be H.P.'s public reason for terminating Dave's contract. The old bastard would have his revenge after all.

They sat silent for a time, Dave Cole and Aline Markham. In a while, she said, "I could go to Paramount. They've been after me to sign with them when my contract runs out."

"We couldn't start over again. We need that footage," Dave said. "But thanks anyhow."

Valerie came out of Christopher's bedroom to announce softly, "He's sleeping."

She asked what had happened with H.P. and they told her. She slipped into a chair, sad, young, beautiful and dispirited. "We could go on, work without salary. We ought to finish the picture. It would be a shame to let all that go to waste."

"Thanks for the offer," Dave said, "but H.P. was right about one thing. We have no way of knowing what Chris would be capable of now. That bastard Pryce!"

"What will happen to him now?" Valerie asked.

"He'll go on making stars out of his lovers, I guess. Till he gets too old or someone kills him," Dave said. "One day someone will."

"I meant Christopher."

"He can't go back to the States. Not in the shape he's in. It would destroy him," Dave said. "I'll try to talk him into going to a sanitarium in Switzerland for a cure."

"If he could finish the picture, would it help?" Valerie asked.

"*If* he could work again and *if* we could get the money, and *if* we could get H.P. to release that footage," Dave said, his voice clearly showing how impossible it was.

"But if he *could* work again?" Valerie persisted.

"It would help one hell of a lot. I might figure out some way to force H.P. to release the footage." Dave ventured—not because he thought he could, but to console the young actress who was taking this even harder than he and Markham.

Valerie nodded.

"Ali, dear, get some sleep," Dave said.

The lack of rest and the events of the night had taken their toll on her noble face. She nodded, rose, went to Dave, kissed him on the cheek and patted it.

"It'll always be the same with actors. Whether they're stranded in Oshkosh because some crooked producer has run off with the box-office receipts or they're stranded in Rome because some venomous bastard has run off with their picture, it's always the poor stupid actor who gets it in the neck. Some days I ask myself why I didn't become a teacher. Or a doctor, like my father wanted me to be." She smiled wanly, tiredly. "Did I ever tell you, Davie? When I announced to him that I was going to be an actress, he said to me, 'Ali, honey, you're just not pretty enough. Go to medical school. Become a doctor. Don't break your heart over something that can never be.'"

She left Dave and Valerie Bristol.

"You better get some sleep too," Dave said.

Valerie nodded but didn't move. "Would it help if Chris could work again?"

"I don't know," Dave said honestly. "I'm too tired to think. And too numb to feel. Maybe in the morning I'll be smarter. Get some sleep."

"I'll sleep here. If he wakes, he'll need me," she said.

Dave studied her pretty heart-shaped face and her violet eyes, so full of sympathy for Christopher.

"Honey, are you in love with him?"

"I don't know. But what happens to him matters so much to me that it hurts. Is that love?"

"It's pretty close," Dave said. "Closer than what a lot of people call love. I wish someone felt that way about me."

He took her hand, raised her to her feet. She was beautiful and so vulnerable. He kissed her lightly and said, "Don't ever let any man use you."

She nodded. Dave left her to go back to his suite. But he knew he wouldn't rest. He'd be up for what little remained of the night, trying to figure out some way to save his picture. He realized now that he had come to think of it as *his* picture.

Valerie Bristol sat alone in the huge living room of one of the most opulent suites in the Hassler. In the next room, Christopher

Swift slept. She slipped down on one of the brocaded sofas and curled up into the position in which she had slept since she was a very small child.

Tired, but her emotions overtaxed, she was restless and frightened. From the time that she and Markham had discovered Chris's addiction up to H.P.'s shocking decision, this had been a disillusioning, terrifying experience for her. Pretty as she was, protected by studio contracts as she had been, to be cut adrift in the middle of a production was too much to take. Yes, she would fly back home. She still had two years to go on her current contract. But the work itself had never meant so much to her before. She felt that she had at last outgrown being a beautiful child and was becoming an actress. Suddenly the chance was torn away from her. She would be willing to finish the picture at no salary, if there was a picture. And Dave did admit that if Chris could work again there was a chance.

And if there was a chance . . .

Valerie Bristol rose from the sofa and moved quietly across the large room. She reached the door of Christopher Swift's bedroom. She heard the sound of his peaceful breathing. She turned the knob cautiously so as not to waken him. She felt her way through the dark room to the bathroom. Once inside that room, she closed the door and snapped on the light.

She stared at herself in the mirror. She was beautiful, she thought without vanity. Too many people had told her so, women as well as men. She knew every flaw in her face and her body, but no one else seemed to know, or care, they were usually so entranced by her violet eyes. Slowly she removed her clothes piece by piece, until she was completely naked. She studied her body, her breasts which were so youthfully firm and high. Men stared at them in obvious hunger as she crossed any room. There must be some magical power in them to make men react so.

Naked, she turned, clicked off the light and opened the door softly. She moved into the bedroom, making out the dark shape of the bed. She drew close to it, stood over it, listening to Chris' easy breathing. She pulled back the cover and slipped into bed beside him, gently, so as not to wake him. She embraced him and pressed her warm body against him. She was content to hold him that way for a long time. In his sleep he became aware of her and turned to her without waking. She pressed him to her allowing his lean face to rest against her breasts. She felt her nipples pucker and rise to him. She pressed him closer. His arm went round her. They lay that way for a while, till she drifted off to sleep. But she woke soon, still holding him in her embrace.

She reached down for him, found him, warm, limp, flaccid. She ran her fingertips across him lightly. He did not respond. He moved in his sleep, restless now and seeming tormented. But she did not stop. She opened her hand and held him, pressing tenderly as if trying to bring him alive. He remained inert and impotent.

He came awake, seemed startled to find her there. She held him tightly and whispered, "Don't be afraid; don't be afraid of me."

He did not struggle against her. She played with him gently, softly, not urging, but coaxing, not demanding but content to wait.

He kept saying softly, "No, no, I won't . . . I can't—" She smothered his protests with her kiss. He did not kiss her back but only allowed her moist lips to press against his own. She forced his mouth open with her tongue and ventured into it. When he tried to withdraw from her she held his head in a strong grip and pressed her lush and fragrant body even tighter against him. There was no protest from him now, but no reaction either. He remained a limp prisoner in her arms.

He began to weep, saying softly, "That's it . . . that's all. . . . Nothing . . . nothing."

She took his hands and pressed them to her breasts, forcing her erect nipples against his fingers. When it failed to rouse him, she released him gently and slid down in the bed, her head at his hips.

His body became rigid and frightened and he tried to hold off. "No! That's what *he* did. Always what he did!"

"Shhh," she said softly. "Don't be afraid of me. Please, Chris, don't be afraid of me. Trust me. Love me. And if you can't love me, let me love you. Please? Please?"

He relented, offering no more resistance. She raised herself over him till she was astride him. Bending toward him, she slowly swayed back and forth, the nipples of her breasts playing across his soft young skin like tantalizing fingers. Then she moved lower, till they made contact with the limp and defeated part of him. She rested there for a moment, then reached for him, sur-

257

rounding him with her fragrant breasts till she encompassed him totally. She pressed them close with her hands and held him there between her breasts, warm and safe.

He reached down to find her face and run his fingers across it, appreciating her beauty as a blind man would. His fingers rested on her lips and she kissed them.

"Chris . . . Chris," she whispered. "Love me . . . let yourself love me?" she implored.

He shook his head, frightened, not daring to try. She embraced him with her breasts even harder. Gradually his resistance ebbed. He was at least content to let himself be held that way. She rested her cheek against his lean, flat body, until she began to feel a sensation in her breasts. It was not from within her, but from him. Slowly, gradually, cradled within her breasts, he was beginning to pulsate, to come alive. She did nothing, she said nothing. In a while, he grew larger and firmer. Soon he was fully erect.

Without a word, she moved up and slid onto him, letting him ease into her, ready to receive him. She undulated slowly, seeking his response. He lay there unmoving. But as long as he was in her, it was enough. She would do the rest. She moved gently, drawing him within her and then withdrawing slightly, until she could feel him begin to respond under her. When he reached out to embrace her and pulled her down hard, she knew she could give herself freely without terrifying him. Soon he was more demanding than she. When he burst within her and she felt his warm explosion, she knew she had won. When she leaned forward on his damp body and pressed her face against his, murmuring, "Oh, Chris, Chris," she felt his tears on her cheek. They fell asleep in each other's arms.

The next morning, Dave Cole woke early from a brief and restless sleep. It had been filled with dreams that were so fragmented that he could not recall any of them distinctly. He knew only that they all reflected the disaster which had befallen his production in the last twenty-four hours.

He came awake with the bone-weary feeling of a man who has extended himself in combat far beyond his physical limitations and has lost. He realized what woke him so abruptly. His phone was ringing.

"Dave?"

"Yes. Who . . . Oh, Chris. How are you?"

"All right, now."

"Good, good," Dave said. At least something had been salvaged from last night's debacle.

"Dave, I called to tell you, I can go on with the film. I can see it through to the end. This time, believe me, Dave. Believe me?"

"Of course I believe you." He had not the heart to tell Christopher Swift of the ruthless action H.P. had taken. No need to pile more guilt on the fragile young actor and possibly plunge him into another relapse. "We'll need a few days to rearrange things, Chris. So take it easy. And wait for word."

"Okay, Dave. Just so you know that I'll be ready whenever you want me."

"Terrific, kid. Good to hear," Dave tried to enthuse, and hung up. He could not know that all the while Chris was speaking, he was lying naked in the embrace of Valerie Bristol.

Dave slipped out of bed, threw wide the doors to his balcony overlooking the Spanish Steps. To judge from what he heard, everything in the Eternal City was proceeding as usual. It was noisy and boisterous with the sounds of life. No one stopped to mourn the passing of *Via Dolorosa*. The street noises put the whole of living into its proper perspective.

He ordered breakfast served out on the balcony. As he tried to enjoy his flaky croissants and coffee, he stared down at the human and vehicular traffic that passed below. The city had been here for more than four thousand years. It would be here for another four thousand, whether someone named Dave Cole finished his film or not.

Try as he would to be philosophical about his situation, the dull ache of defeat would not go away. The Eternal City might well be eternal, but Dave Cole would come this way only once. Would likely have this opportunity only once. That he failed, regardless of what cause or whose fault, was the only fact that mattered to him today.

He tried to envision new beginnings for himself. He could go back to Broadway. But knowledge of the disaster would precede him, diminish his desirability to producers, authors, actors. It would not matter that his work on *Via Dolorosa* was good. Better than good: excellent. He had no hesitancy in applying that word to his work. He could prove it. It was on film.

Except that all the film belonged to H. P. Koenig and would be consigned to that cinematic limbo reserved for unreleased films, from which there was no escape. But Markham knew the truth. She had seen it all and admired him as well as his work. Her word would carry much weight in Hollywood. She might even insist on him for her next film. But would it be fair, he questioned, for her to penalize herself if a studio that wanted her refused to accept him?

That led to another possibility. Suppose he could find a vehicle for her return to the stage. All he had to do was call the Theatre Guild or Max Gordon or any one of half a dozen solid, established producers. They would jump at the chance to produce a play starring Markham. He'd have a deal before he hung up the phone.

No, he decided, that would never happen. Because he would never lift a phone to make that call. He was not going to use Ali Markham to rescue his career after he had so foolishly risked it against all advice. He would find his own way out.

First he would seek out the few good film producers who had burgeoned in postwar Rome. They made inexpensive pictures on street locations, mostly without stars. But they were good films, well received; realistic pictures, portraying life as it really is. Perhaps one of the more successful producers might now be induced to take a risk on a costume spectacle of the dimensions of *Via Dolorosa*. With their cost-cutting ways and their leverage with the local unions, even starting from scratch, they might be able to bring in the 'film for less than three million dollars, American. Then screw H. P. Koenig and his footage.

Dave decided to try.

With his Italian cinematographer as intermediary, Dave succeeded in meeting with two different producers. Both listened intently, nodded all the time, smiled occasionally. But when Dave finished, their reactions were similar almost to the wording.

"If H. P. Koenig with all his millions failed, you expect to

260

succeed? Sorry, young man, but a dead picture stinks even worse than a dead fish."

In Dave's shooting script, Jesus had raised Lazarus on the fourth day after his death. Poor Jesus could not do as much for *Via Dolorosa*. On the fourth day, Dave returned to the Hassler, defeated, *Via Dolorosa* dead. He decided he might as well call them together—Ali Markham, Valerie Bristol, Christopher Swift—and level with them. Perhaps he would invite them all to his suite for dinner. A Last Supper of sorts. It would be the final item to appear on his expense account. After that, they would all disperse and head for home.

He was passing the front desk, too dispirited even to inquire about any messages, when the clerk hailed him. The transatlantic operator had been trying to reach him for hours. He had the call put through to his suite.

"Davie?" the voice came to him, familiar and welcome; though it was subject to the distortions of overseas calls, he recognized the concern and anguish in it.

"Sybil? Darling?"

"Davie, what happened? The town's full of rumors. Nobody seems to know. But it must have been terrible."

"It was," Dave conceded.

"What did Albert have to do with it?"

"Albert?" Dave was greatly puzzled.

"The first thing my father did when he came back was fire Albert!"

"The sonofabitch! What he did to me should have satisfied him. But no—he had to take it out on Albert too!"

He proceeded to tell her some of what had happened and how he had accidentally incriminated Albert in his moment of anger. When he was done, she said only, "Of course. Knowing him, I would have expected that."

"I'm terribly sorry. Tell Albert. No, don't; I'll call and tell him myself. I owe him that much."

"You don't have to. He's already forgiven you. Now, Davie, tell me. The rest of the rumor."

"About his closing down the production?"

"Yes."

"True," he admitted. "I can't say I wasn't warned. You did your

261

best, darling. But I was too bent on showing him, proving to him that I could do the impossible, that I could beat him. Still, as you said, we always end up doing what he wants us to do. Even when we start out to do the reverse of what he wants, somehow we end up doing it his way."

"Davie, there were rumors before that. That it was a good film. That you were coming along beautifully."

"And we were. Working on schedule and getting damn good footage."

"Then it *was* true?" Sybil asked quite pointedly, as if it were essential for her to be sure.

"You know Markham. She doesn't hesitate to speak her mind. Even she said it was some of the best footage she's ever seen."

"And still he wouldn't let you finish," she said thoughtfully.

"I was getting the best footage out of Christopher Swift anybody's ever gotten. And each day I'd say to myself, I'll prove it to Sybil. I can defeat her father. I'll rid her of her demon and then we'll have it made. But I didn't figure on the final and ultimate act of the demon."

"What are you going to do now?"

"I'll try Broadway. It'll be rougher now. But if it works, I'll ask you to come and join me. But only if it works. A man doesn't like to bring his failures and defeats to the woman he loves and say 'Feel sorry for me.'"

"I understand," she said softly, but he wasn't sure she really did.

"Davie . . ." she added, hesitantly.

"Yes, darling?"

"There might be one last chance."

"What chance? How?"

"There's one man who might have some influence on him. Dan Sullavan," Sybil said.

"Sullavan?" Dave considered.

"If he saw that footage and liked it, he might have enough weight to make my father let you complete the picture," she suggested.

"Your father would plow him under," Dave countered.

"Maybe not. No one ever knows what corporate intrigues go on, and how they change from day to day. Give it a try," she pleaded.

"Okay. At least I'll find out what promises are worth," Dave said. Then he was seized of a sudden thought. "Meet me in New York when I go see Sullavan!"

"No, Davie. Settle with *him* first. Then we'll see."

"Settle with *him*," Dave repeated ironically. "Dave Cole, the defiant, cocky kid who was going to bring down the giant. David Cole with his little slingshot. And it worked. Only Goliath didn't fall. He just canceled little Dave right out of the ball game, slingshot and all. Well, at least there's one last chance."

"Good luck, Davie; good luck," she said.

"I love you," he said.

"I know," she answered; "I know."

There was a touch of desperation in her voice.

21

Dan Sullavan had assembled the entire executive staff of the New York office. His foreign-sales vice-president, his vice-president for domestic theaters, his advertising and public-relations chiefs. They had been summoned to pass judgment on a rough cut of an uncompleted picture that Dave Cole had flown in with from Rome.

When they had gathered and lit up their favorite cigars and the screening room was heavy with smoke, Sullavan gave the booth the signal to begin.

Dave sat off in a corner, in the last leather lounge chair in the back row. He would never get over having butterflies when a rough cut of one of his films got its first viewing by the brass. No matter how sure he felt about what he had, no one could forecast the reaction of the decision makers who viewed each film in terms of their own corporate problems.

Now, with an incomplete film, and with the kiss of death already on it from H. P. Koenig, Dave had more reason than ever to be concerned, tense and plain scared. Too much was riding on it; too much was riding against it. All he had to offer was the hard work and talent of a group of dedicated people who believed in the film.

The gods of the motion-picture world would now decide. The footage began with no titles, no music, no credits. Just a bare scene of a hillside in Galilee, shot on location, with a large cast of followers listening to a Christ who could not be shown directly on camera. It was a mild and placid scene. Dave felt tempted to explain what would precede it and what would follow it. But he restrained himself. In a screening room, explanations were only excuses for failure. The film would sell itself or else it couldn't be sold. He forced himself to remain silent. But he could feel the first negative, critical, cold response from the cigar-smoking executives, each of whom would rather have been elsewhere than watching rough-cut film.

Flying the footage over to New York to show to Sullavan and his group had been a mistake born of desperation. Perhaps with Sullavan alone he would have had a chance. But not with these tough, dollars-and-cents, what-was-yesterday's-gross? executives who believed not in motion pictures but in accounting.

He was tempted to leap out of his soft chair and shout to the projectionist, "Cut! Forget it! Screw the whole idea!" But he remained seated, tense and furious with himself, with H. P. Koenig and with the whole damned motion-picture industry.

But he was here. All he could do was sit and wait. If sitting and waiting was agony, he had suffered worse in his life and would suffer worse again. Or at least he tried to convince himself of that.

The executives seemed to puff less and fidget less as the film brought them Valerie Bristol and Christopher Swift. In one scene that made the most of Valerie's exquisite cleavage one of the men, impressed, muttered, "Jesus!"

As Markham's scenes began to unfold they became entranced and involved.

Oh, that lady. That magnificent, wonderful lady!, Dave kept saying to himself as he watched her strong face and her brave, bright eyes. She reached out to you from the screen, took your hand, led you wherever she wanted you to go. All without any noticeable exertion on her part, save for those bright blue eyes.

Dave began to feel easier. If they didn't buy it, at least they couldn't hate it. They no longer acted as if Sullavan's request were an intrusion on their time. Most of them had put aside their cigars. Those who lit up again did so cupping their hands so that their lighters wouldn't disturb the others.

Finally it was over. Some of them breathed great sighs—not

265

of relief, but of having been released from a picture that had gripped them despite its lack of completion.

Sullavan leaned back in his chair, for he had spent the last twelve minutes on the edge of it inclined toward the screen. He was very thoughtful as he asked, without turning to Dave, "Markham is not Catholic, is she?"

The total irrelevance of the question caught Dave without an answer. Finally, he said, "I don't know. I never asked."

"But her friend is," Sullavan said. That seemed to be important to him. Sullavan turned to his colleagues, "Well, boys?"

"A hell of a piece of film," one vice-president said. It was a huge compliment.

The vice-president in charge of advertising interrupted lighting up his fresh cigar to remark, "We could sell the hell out of that girl's tits. Fantastic."

A third connoisseur of the art of film remarked, "If we could have it in time for an Easter release, maybe. And with the right campaign . . . Listen, I've seen worse."

Whatever encouragement Dave had mounted during the final stages of the running began to dissipate. These were hardheaded businessmen. It would do no good to tell them of the sacrifice so many people had made to bring the film this far, and the many more sacrifices they were willing to make to complete it. He was thankful when Dan Sullavan said, "Okay, boys. Thanks."

The meeting was over. The others left. Dave and Sullavan remained.

"Come up to the office, kid," he said.

Dan Sullavan's office was high over Times Square. In late afternoon, the light outside his window was a blend of the setting sun which cut between the buildings across the Square and the bright flooding lights of the advertising spectaculars and movie marquees that were coming to life. Sullavan liked that mix and blend of colorful lighting, so he never turned on the lights in his office until it was almost totally dark outside.

He did not sit behind his desk, but dropped into one of several chairs in the conference area of his large office. He drew two long Havana cigars from the expensive morocco-leather case his wife had given him for Christmas. He offered one to Dave, who

266

declined it. Sullavan lit up. He had his cigar going well before he felt free to say anything.

"You must feel terrible now, huh, kid?" he asked. He didn't get an answer, but he didn't expect one either. He smiled. "That sonofabitch Eisner, the one who said, 'I've seen worse'? That's the nicest thing I've heard him say about a picture in a long time. From him that's praise—high praise. So don't feel bad. It was worth the trip."

Sullavan blew several large, fat smoke rings toward the ceiling. Then he said, "That's not the problem."

Whatever encouragement and assurance Dave had drawn from Sullavan's opening remarks began to dissipate. There was a problem. A serious problem, since Sullavan referred to it as *the* problem.

"A lot has happened since you were gone. The Supreme Court hung it on another picture company, which means the rest of us have got to fall in line. All the majors are having to sign consent decrees to divorce their studios from their theaters. We can't have stockholders in common or executives in common. We are to be two separate companies from now on. Magna Studios. And Nationwide Theatres. We'll all have to divest ourselves of our stock in each other's companies. I have six months to unload my Magna stock. So my power over the studio is severely limited."

"In other words, you're saying you can't have any influence over H.P."

"That's right. Meantime, our lawyers are very touchy about it. We are to go into the market and buy pictures in open bidding against everyone else. And we are not to be caught trying to influence studio decisions." He left it to Dave to draw his own conclusions.

"If you can't, you can't," Dave said, feeling cut adrift and lost.

Suddenly Sullavan asked, "If it were possible, how much time would you need? And how much money?"

"What's the difference, if H.P. won't release the footage?"

"Just tell me!" Sullavan insisted.

"Perhaps two more months of shooting and five months' post-production."

"And dollars?"

"Another million and a half."

"Will Swift be able to finish?"

267

"I think he will," Dave said honestly.

"I need more than that."

"*I'll* see that he makes it!" Dave promised.

"Okay."

"But if H.P. won't release the footage . . ."

Sullavan didn't answer. He reached across the round table to take the phone. He dialed a number in the dark and waited for an answer.

"Monsignor? Dan." There were amenities he had to go through first. "She's fine. Fine, Monsignor. I'll tell her you asked. . . . Oh he's doing great. Loves his new parish, loves working with the Old Man there."

Soon the personal aspects of the conversation were completed. "Monsignor, I have to ask a favor. A very large favor. I would like H. P. Koenig to be invited to the Cardinal's dinner next week."

Another pause. Another answer by Sullavan: "I know, I know, he's invited pro forma every year. But this time I want it to be a personal *red-hat* invitation. . . . I know it's asking a lot. But please explain that I wouldn't impose on His Eminence if it weren't of prime importance."

The Monsignor said something which caused Sullavan to reply, "That would be terrific! H.P.'s always wanted to sit in the front row on the dais. Excellent! And believe me, the Church will benefit from it in more ways than one."

Sullavan hung up. Even in the dim light Dave Cole could see the satisfied smile that spread across the Irishman's ruddy face.

"Dave, there may be a way to get you that footage and the money to finish that film. But you have to promise me something. When the time comes, don't get in my way."

"Get in your way?" Dave asked, puzzled.

"I have a score to settle with our friend H.P. Don't try to stop me."

"Why would I?"

"Because you're too soft, too sensitive. Stay like that. Only don't get in my way."

Then Sullavan said briskly, "His Eminence will call H.P. in the morning." When Dave didn't react, Sullavan smiled and said, "Dave, never try to understand Church politics. Just have faith."

Dave Cole had left Dan Sullavan's office more than an hour before. Sullavan consulted his watch. It was fifteen past seven, which meant fifteen past four Pacific Coast Time. He had promised he would call by four-thirty. He used his private phone. She answered on the first ring. She had obviously been waiting.

"Sybil?"

"Yes, Mr. Sullavan?"

"I've seen him. I've seen the footage. It's terrific."

"Will you do it?" Sybil Koenig asked.

"I'll do my part. But remember the agreement," he insisted, to be sure there was no misunderstanding about their bargain.

"I'll remember," she promised, but it was obviously not easy for her.

"Good! I've already set the wheels in motion," Sullavan said confidently.

"I hope it works," she said. "It means so much to Dave."

The Grand Ballroom of the Waldorf Astoria on Park Avenue was filled to capacity. Over one thousand leaders of industry, the arts, the sciences and the political life of the nation were gathered. The annual dinner was attended in equal proportions by the Jewish and Protestant laity, many of whom did business with the vast organization known as the New York Archdiocese. With its extensive holdings in real estate and commercial enterprises of all kinds, the Archdiocese was a power in the financial and political life of the city, the state and the nation.

Political candidates and aspirants who would be running for election soon, or reelection, were considered fortunate to be seated on the dais. If they were listed among the speakers of the evening they were doubly distinguished, though politics as a subject was forbidden. Some few, half a hundred, were invited to attend a predinner reception in one of the private rooms off the main ballroom. Those men were received by the Cardinal in person. In almost every instance they were men of whom the Church sought some sort of cooperation or favor. When the Cardinal had called H. P. Koenig on the phone to invite him, he had ended the conversation saying, "And Harry, please, I'd like you to come early. For the private reception. You're one of the men with whom I never get to spend enough time."

Impeccable in tails and white tie, H. P. Koenig appeared at the private reception. He spoke guardedly to the other men in the room, some of whom he knew, most of whom he didn't, but who knew of him—H.P.'s personal press agent earned his keep. He stood in a corner as if holding court himself. He surveyed the room, in which were steel, oil and railroad giants, each of whose salaries he knew because they were published every year, like his own. There was no man in the room whose salary came within one hundred thousand dollars a year of his. He dismissed them as bluebloods and college graduates inferior to himself, since money was how he measured a man. He was the most successful man in this room, which meant the most successful man in the entire nation. He was indulging himself in such self-congratulation when there was a stir at the door.

The Cardinal had arrived. Resplendent in his shiny red moiré robe and Cardinal's cap, he eased into the room. A small man, but portly, with a round, florid face and the flabby cheeks of a bloodhound, he seemed benign and almost simple. Actually, he was one of the Church's most astute and effective statesmen. Catholic laymen in the room came to greet him, dropping to one knee to kiss his ring. He graciously protested by lifting each of them to his feet—but only after they had kissed the ring.

Once the Catholics had done as was required of them, the Protestant and Jewish laymen lined up to greet and be greeted by the eminent churchman. Among them, though he made sure he was last in line, as if the Cardinal were proceeding in ascending order, was H. P. Koenig. So that when the Cardinal greeted him, he was under no pressure since there was no one waiting behind him. He shook H.P.'s hand and then embraced him.

"Harry, it's good to see you looking so fit!" the little Cardinal exclaimed.

"Thank you, Your Eminence. You're looking well yourself. I don't know how you do it, with all the pressures of your office," H.P. said graciously.

"It's the help of willing friends that takes some of the burdens off me, Harry. When the dinner is over, stay on a while. I'd like to talk to you."

"Of course, Your Eminence," H.P. said.

In his mind he figured there was some special project of the Cardinal's that needed financial help—his Foundling Hospital that he was always planning to build, or some other project. H.P. made a mental note that he would put a limit of twenty-five thousand dollars on any contribution the Cardinal might ask.

When H. P. Koenig entered the grand ballroom, he scanned all the tables for Number Six. He had had Sarah Immerman check which table had been reserved for Dan Sullavan and the executives from the New York office. Pretending he was surprised to happen on that table, he greeted Dan Sullavan with every outward appearance of warmth and delight.

"Dan!"

Sullavan rose. H.P. shook his hand with great enthusiasm, saying half seriously, half jokingly, "God, I hope we haven't broken any law by shaking hands! What do you think the Attorney General would say if he saw us this way!"

In keeping with the jovial mood that H.P. had established, Sullavan said, "Believe me, it wasn't my idea to divorce the studios from the theaters. As a good Catholic, I'm against divorce."

It was a good enough quip for a laugh all around.

"Sit down, H.P. Have a drink."

H.P. smiled. "Am I allowed? Or should I get advice of counsel?"

"One drink is not a conspiracy in restraint of trade," the lawyer for the newly named Nationwide Theatres volunteered.

H.P. touched glasses with Sullavan. "To new times, Dan." They drank.

H.P. lowered his voice. "Dan, do you think the Supreme Court or the Attorney General have anything against my mother who has been dead seventeen years now?"

The Irishman responded with a puzzled look.

"Dan, how many times over the years have you been kind enough to come to the cemetery with me at this time of year? To stand at my mother's grave, to hear a few words said by a pious old Jew in memory of a fine woman?"

"More than a few," Dan Sullavan replied, resisting any mention of the fact that it had always been under duress.

Whenever H.P. came to New York just before the Jewish High Holy Days he made Dan Sullavan ride out to the cemetery in

271

Queens. The few moments spent at the graveside of the long-departed Bertha Koenig while a pious old Jew chanted some Hebrew prayers were only a brief interruption in a business conference conducted from the moment they got into the limousine until they got out of it again back in New York. That enforced trip was another way H.P. reminded Dan Sullavan that he held an old secret over his head and always would.

"Well, I am going out again tomorrow," H.P. said. "I would appreciate it if you did this just once more. For old times' sake."

Knowing full well there must be more to H.P.'s suggestion than an innocent sentimental gesture, Sullavan replied, "Sure, H.P. delighted to do it. For old times' sake."

"Pick you up at your apartment eight-thirty?"

"Eight-thirty," Sullavan agreed.

H.P. was able to ascend to his place in the first row of the dais confident and relaxed.

Dinner was over, coffee had been served along with fine cigars. The oratory began. Two potential presidential candidates were permitted to speak briefly. Both eschewed politics; both attempted to be witty; both succeeded only moderately. The following speeches were more serious, addressed to the problems of the times, mainly to the Church's involvement in those problems. Finally the Cardinal made his very tasteful and adroit appeal for his Foundling Hospital. The evening was over.

Dan Sullavan offered, "H.P., can I drop you?"

"No, thanks; I promised His Eminence I'd stay on for a minute."

"Oh?" Sullavan said, feigning envious surprise, as if it were an honor he would have wished for himself. "Tomorrow, then. Eight-thirty. I'll be downstairs waiting."

"Good. Tomorrow."

The Cardinal's residence on Madison Avenue was just behind St. Patrick's Cathedral. A quiet place, lavishly furnished with religious artifacts and paintings, it presented an imposing environment. Behind its stout walls all street noises were blocked out. Within its paneled rooms a man felt the power and the dignity of the Church. In one of the small private sitting rooms, His Eminence, the Cardinal, received H. P. Koenig.

"You may smoke if you like, Harry," the Cardinal said graciously.

"No, thank you, Your Eminence," H.P. said. "It wouldn't seem right in these holy surroundings." All the while he was wondering how much the Cardinal was going to ask of him. In his mind he had already upped his contribution to fifty thousand.

"Harry, we are living in difficult times," the churchman began. "The war. The situation with Russia. The increase of godless Communism in our country. I don't blame you personally for all the propaganda that has crept into Hollywood films in the last dozen years. Nor do I want to bring up the unpleasantness of those investigations that are going on. But I think it does impose a duty on your industry to make amends."

"Amends?" H.P. repeated, alert to a request for which he had not been prepared.

"There is a need for God in our daily lives. And what instrument is better suited for bringing that to our millions than the motion-picture industry? I've heard you say it yourself: more people go to see pictures every week than go to churches. Am I right?"

"The figures are the figures," H.P. said modestly, as if apologizing for his success.

"I'm not saying we should discourage people from going to see pictures. Not at all. Despite some of the propaganda and some of the sexual looseness, I think that on the whole, pictures are a good, clean form of entertainment. What I am saying is this, Harry. . . ."

The Cardinal paused, stared into H.P.'s eyes. "Harry," he declared, "I want you to become a disciple! I want you to use your enormous power to spread the word of God and decency throughout this land and this world. If only you could put as much effectiveness for good into your films as some of the Commie propaganda those pinko writers have inserted, you'd be doing everyone a great public service.

"Mind you, I'm not saying you have to make a dull picture, or deliver a sermon on film. But a really fine, exciting religious film would meet with great support from the clergy, Catholic and Protestant. We could guarantee you an audience that would exceed your wildest dreams. There is nothing in our religion that says a man must lose money in a good cause. It is possible to do

273

public benefit and to profit handsomely at the same time."

At this point H. P. Koenig began to smile.

"Don't you believe me, Harry?"

"Of course, Your Eminence," H.P. agreed quickly. "I was only thinking how . . . what is it they say? . . . great minds run in the same channels. . . ."

"That or something similar."

"Well, it so happens that I have just such a picture in production over in Rome right now."

"No!" The Cardinal gave a very convincing display of surprise.

"Yes!" H.P. said. "*Via Dolorosa* it's called."

"Ah, good title, good!" the Cardinal agreed.

"We've had a little trouble with it. But then, you always do when you're shooting away from the studio. And I have every confidence that we will get it straightened out."

"I'm delighted to hear that, Harry. Is there anything the Vatican can do to help?"

"I think we can manage."

"Well, if there's anything we can do," the churchman offered, "just pick up your phone, Harry."

"Thank you, Your Eminence," H.P. said.

The meeting was over shortly. His Eminence walked H.P. to the door himself, offering to have his limousine drive him back to his hotel. H.P. was properly thankful for the offer but decided he'd rather walk. At the door, the Cardinal said, "Harry, the whole right-thinking world will bless you for this!"

On his walk up Madison Avenue to the hotel where Magna maintained a twelve-room suite the year around specially for him, H. P. Koenig assessed the situation. The footage that he had seen was not at all bad. From a cold box-office point of view, Markham, the girl and even Swift were definite assets, if Swift could finally make it. Even the direction by Dave Cole, the young bastard, was goddamned good, H.P. had to admit. Now, with the Cardinal promising such strong support at the box office among Catholics alone, there was a large enough audience to make the film into a hit. What if the picture *was* over budget? So it would go another million or two over, in an effort to recoup what was already lost. And despite his bland statement, he knew the insurance company would not pay off without an expensive lawsuit.

By the time he reached the Sherry-Netherland, he convinced himself that he would reactivate the film, provided he could succeed with Dan Sullavan in the morning. It was a new and very annoying situation, having to treat Sullavan as a potential customer instead of an employee whom he could manipulate at will with a little blackmail.

His decision on Dave's film would depend on Sullavan's response tomorrow.

The next morning a rented limousine drew up at the Sherry-Netherland to pick up H. P. Koenig. At Eighty-fourth Street it stopped to pick up Dan Sullavan, who was already waiting under the canopy of his apartment building. The Irishman slid into the rear seat of the car, leaned back and lit up his after-breakfast cigar.

"How's it going, H.P.?" he asked as they headed east to take the bridge over to Long Island.

"Fine, fine," H.P. said. At the same time he made a gesture indicating that the chauffeur was a stranger and it was risky to talk. They remained silent the rest of the way.

At the gate of Mount Hebron Cemetery, H.P. selected one of the many old bearded men to say the prayers and together they walked to the graveside of Bertha Koenig. They stood silent while the old man chanted the prayers—H. P. Koenig and Dan Sullavan, both wearing the little black silk yarmulkes which H.P. always brought to cover their heads. When the old man was done, H.P. slipped him a bill of large denomination and dismissed him.

H.P. looked around. There was a white granite bench nearby. He invited Sullavan to be seated. They sat on the cold, hard stone—lean, tall Dan Sullavan and short, stocky Harry P. Koenig, side by side.

"Dan," H.P. began, thoughtful and sad, "I never thought it would end like this, our great association over the years. We've had our ups and downs, our disagreements. Hell, intelligent, strong-minded men can't work together for so many years without having some disagreements."

275

Sullavan murmured a simple "Of course." He was too polite to mention that always, in the end, H.P. had applied his muscle and had made him knuckle under.

"Now the government . . . well, I don't want to rehash that. The question is, what do we do now? Of course, I could take the attitude that we don't give a damn what happens to your theaters. I could just liquidate my holdings in Nationwide and say to hell with it. But what kind of ungrateful bastard would I be to do that?

"After all, what is the lifeblood of the business? Product! It's like the human body, Dan. There is the blood. And there are the veins and arteries. Without blood, what good are arteries? The same in our business. The theaters are the veins and the arteries. But the pictures! The pictures are the lifeblood! After all, suppose you have to put up on your marquee this Saturday night *The Lovers* starring John Jerk and Jane Schmaltz. Who would come? I don't have to tell you.

"But if you put up *The Lovers* starring Clark Gable and Joan Crawford. Or *Love Affair* starring Charles Boyer and Irene Dunne . . . What more can I say? Hmm, Dan?"

"You're right."

"Well, here's what I am going to do. Mind you, I'm not making any deal with you. There is no agreement between us that violates the consent decree. I am only telling you what I am going to do. I am going to show my films to all the other exhibitors and let them bid. But I won't close the bidding until you and your boys in New York have the chance to outbid them. Of course, it won't always work out the way we want. But ninety-nine times out of a hundred you'll have the same names on your marquees that we've always had."

"It's good to hear you say that," Sullavan seemed to agree.

"All right. Now, do *you* fellows have any plans?"

"We're going to do what the lawyers say we have to under the decree. We are going to bid for the best pictures against all comers."

H.P. stopped breathing. He knew it was tactically wrong to take a position that could be interpreted as beseeching, or even asking. His instinct was right, as always. For Sullavan continued:

"Of course, when we buy the best we expect that ninety percent of the time they are going to be Magna films. They always have been the best."

"They're going to be even better!" H.P. announced vindictively. "The government wants competition? We'll show them what competition really is! We'll come out of this bigger and better than ever!"

"You bet!" Sullavan agreed.

H.P. slapped Sullavan on his thin, bony thigh. The meeting was over. When they reached the limousine, H.P. laughed and said, "Dan, you'd better give me back that yarmulke. Otherwise the government could say we're breaking some damned law or other!"

Before he left New York, H.P. went down to William Street to have lunch at the banking firm of Wohlman Brothers. There, over a gourmet meal prepared by one of the best French chefs in America, he discussed the financial needs of Magna Studios under the new government-imposed divorcement.

The partners listened politely but gave no indication of how impressed they were by H.P.'s grand production plans and his promises to dominate the open picture market to an even greater degree than Magna had dominated the industry in the past. The biggest and best films would always be made by Magna, he promised.

At the end of his discourse, one of the partners leaned back from the table, lit his cigar with a meticulous rotating motion and asked, "And what about *Via Dolorosa*?"

H.P. stared down the table at him.

"I understand," the partner continued, "that it's in trouble. Serious trouble. Way over budget. Unfinished. And the word out of Rome is that it's been abandoned. That would mean four and a half million down the drain."

Without any show of discomfort or embarrassment, H.P. sat back and smiled.

"Rumors! All rumors! The picture is *not* abandoned. Merely shut down briefly to iron out some production problems. I have personally seen the footage and it is magnificent. Aline Markham will win an Academy Award for her performance. And Valerie

277

Bristol and Christopher Swift will both be nominated!" he said with every outward appearance of complete confidence.

"And I have the pleasure and satisfaction of informing all of you that the picture is in the hands of my brilliant young protégé who will emerge as one of the greatest directors of our industry—David Cole!"

Though it had pained him to make this last declaration, he felt the situation demanded it. But he had saved his best for last.

"That isn't all, however. I have personally received the assurance of the most eminent churchman in this country . . . I trust you won't ask me to violate any confidence by naming names . . . that this film will receive the wholehearted backing of every church group in America!"

The partner was satisfied. The others around the luncheon table were impressed. H.P. was assured that money would be available for the full schedule of Magna films for the coming year and that whatever it would cost to finish *Via Dolorosa* would be forthcoming. It was always a pleasure, they assured him, to do business with a man of his creative genius, who had a knack for coming up with the right creative talent at the right time.

H.P. returned to California that night secure in the knowledge that he had guaranteed the future for Magna films. As for Dave Cole, as long as he needed the sonofabitch he would use him.

H.P. tried to recall which one of the Shuberts it had been, Lee or Jake, who said of a certain actor with whom he had had an argument, "I don't ever want to see that bastard again! Until we need him."

Right now, and until *Via Dolorosa* was completed, H. P. Koenig needed David Cole.

H. P. Koenig sat in his huge red leather antique chair and drummed his fingers on the nailhead-studded arms. It would take a bit of thinking, this next move.

He had already given orders to Mossberg, his obedient and fat controller, that the money to complete *Via Dolorosa* was to be appropriated. Though Mossberg had been startled by this sudden change in orders, he wiped his sweaty face, nodded and mumbled

278

something that H.P. did not understand and went off to carry out the order. Mumble was a language all its own where Mossberg was concerned. One day, H.P. reminded himself for the thousandth time, he must listen to what fat Mossberg had to say, just to see if the man spoke English at all. But as long as he followed orders it wasn't essential to know what he said, or even what he thought.

Now H.P. had to address himself to David Cole. He pressed the button of his intercom.

"Sarah, get me Dave Cole. In Rome. No matter where he is!"

Within half an hour the word came back that Dave Cole's line at the Hassler was busy.

"Well, tell the fucking operator to cut in! This is a transatlantic call! From Hollywood!"

Sarah Immerman promised to try. When she didn't call back immediately, H.P. pressed the intercom button and demanded, "Well?"

"The operator refused."

"Refused!" H.P. demanded, outraged. "Let me talk to that goddamn operator!" Sarah Immerman put the operator on directly with H.P. He delivered a five-minute tirade which ended with the confused operator in tears and speaking Italian which made no sense to him at all.

During the time H. P. Koenig was vehemently cursing the Italian operator and the entire Italian telephone system, Dave Cole was holding a transatlantic conversation of his own. He had received a call from Dan Sullavan, who was assuring him that any moment he would get the official word that his picture could be completed. When H.P.'s call came in, Dave was prepared for him.

"Dave," H.P. began, in his most paternal tone of voice. "Dave, you've known me a long time, right?"

A few years was not such a long time, but Dave was not about to quibble. He was more interested in what approach H.P. would take this time.

"Right," he agreed.

"Have you always known me to be fair-minded, open-minded?"

"Of course, H.P."

"But I don't often reverse myself, do I?"

"No, H.P."

"Yet, when a man is right, he's right and I am the first to admit it, right?"

"Right!" Dave agreed. He motioned to Aline Markham to pick up the extension phone across the room. Together they exchanged smiles, looks, winks and gestures as H.P. continued.

"Well, I have been thinking, Dave. I have thought of nothing else ever since I left Rome. I have said to myself, What are we in, a business? Or an art? Are we merchants or artists? What are we selling, fish off a pushcart or dreams? Isn't there such a thing as an obligation to the public that exceeds the mere making of money? They are our people, Dave, those millions out there. We have to think of them first.

"And thinking of them doesn't only mean laughter and music, singing and dancing. It means bringing into their lives spiritual values! Uplift! We have got to do something to make up for all that propaganda that Hollywood has been shoveling at them in recent years.

"Well, I have decided that the way to make up for it is to give them a fine, spiritual, uplifting picture like *Via Dolorosa*."

"H.P.?" Dave interjected, trying to act a combination of surprise and hoping against hope.

"Yes, I have decided that this time, money takes a back seat. The picture is the only important thing. What the picture says! We owe it to them, Dave! We owe it to them!"

"I'm glad you feel that way, H.P.!" Dave exclaimed, looking at Aline Markham, smiling and shaking his head at the old man's chutzpah.

"So go to it, my boy!" H.P. shouted. "Make it the best picture you can! And damn the expense! We'll make it up on some other pictures!"

"Fine. Good. Thank you, H.P."

As Dave was about to hang up, H.P. lowered his voice and spoke more intimately. "And Dave, those nasty thoughts you had about me wanting revenge. I hope you realize how foolish you were even to think such a thing. As a father, I know that whatever happened between my Sybil and you must have been a fine and beautiful thing. I don't hold anything against you, my boy. Believe me, I only wish you well. My prayers are with you and the picture every moment!" He added the latter as if he were the Pope dispensing a blessing.

Dave Cole hung up the phone. Aline Markham came toward him, kissed him, embraced him and laughed and laughed.

"Davie, you were magnificent. The greatest telephone scene since Luise Rainer! I will personally nominate you for an Oscar!"

They joyfully decided to have a drink to celebrate. But before they could order, there was a knock on the door. A waiter was there with an ice cooler of champagne, Dom Perignon 1933. There was a note attached.

Have one on me. Dan.

Dave called Valerie Bristol and Christopher Swift to come to his suite at once. When they arrived, there were four chilled glasses waiting. Dave filled the glasses and toasted. "To the best damned picture any of us will ever work on!"

They drank. Then Dave called Dino Cortese and gave the order: Production would resume in the morning! On the same schedule as before! Ten to two for Christopher Swift's scenes, break for lunch and four to ten in the evening for all the other scenes.

They were set now. Another month to six weeks, then some dubbing and *Via Dolorosa* would be ready to be shipped back home for postproduction, music and a final print.

Christopher Swift was silent through all the excitement. When Dave had laid out the plans, given the orders and said it was time for everyone to retire early to get a good start in the morning, Swift stood up and reached for Dave's hand.

"Dave, for the second time in my life, I can't thank you enough. You're still what you were back then—an actor's director and a decent human being." He wasn't able to manage any more than that. Tears flooded his eyes. "I'll make it, Dave. For you."

"You'll make it, kid, and we'll all help."

The night they wrapped *Via Dolorosa,* Dave gave a gigantic party for the entire cast, crew and everyone who had anything to do with the film, including the drivers of their limousines.

For sentimental and symbolic reasons, he held it on the set on which the Last Supper scenes had been shot. It was a far

281

different Last Supper than he had once contemplated in his despair. The food was the finest obtainable in Rome, and the wine the best. By two hours past midnight, cast members and grips, electricians and script girls were still drinking and singing together; some were behind the sets making love together. It was one great, unforgettable night.

Even Christopher Swift seemed able to relax at what was an unusual hour for him. Valerie was constantly at his side. And Aline Markham watched him carefully. For they were both aware of what must happen in the morning.

The next morning, fortified by another shot and with a dozen packets in his pocket to see him through the next few days, Christopher Swift got into a car beside David Cole. Dave had left Dino Cortese to see to the shipment of all the footage and sound track to Los Angeles for postproduction work. Aline Markham had been away from her man for too long and was booked on the first flight home, taking Valerie Bristol with her.

Before she left, Valerie spent some time alone with Christopher Swift. No one inquired and no one would ever know what was said between them, what happened or what promises were made.

Dave Cole and Christopher Swift left Rome, driving north along roads that still exhibited scars of the recent war. They passed through ancient cities which had seen many wars. They climbed steep mountain roads which took them through the Dolomites, so high that though it was only early fall they had to turn on the heater in the car. In two days they arrived at the clinic in a small town above the hills that surround Zurich.

There Dave Cole turned Christopher Swift over to an elderly doctor who was most sympathetic. Christopher spent several hours alone with the doctor and decided to remain, on condition that his supply of drugs not be cut off completely, that he not be required to go cold turkey. When the doctor spoke to Dave alone, he expressed only his determination to do what he could with this complicated case.

Chris and Dave said good-bye at the bottom of the stone steps of the sanitarium in a garden which led to the road where Dave had parked his car.

"Dave, I'll do my best. I'll try."

"You'll make it, kid. And we'll do other pictures together, I promise."

On impulse Christopher Swift embraced Dave affectionately, but suddenly it seemed to remind him of Edmund Pryce and he became stiff and remote. He released Dave, turned and ran up the steps. Dave watched till Chris was safely inside the door of the sanitarium, where the doctor was waiting.

Dave Cole drove into the airport at Zurich, turned in his car and arranged for his plane to the States. He then went to the cable desk and sent a message.

Simple and brief, it was addressed to Sybil Koenig in Beverly Hills.

COMING HOME.

22

The plane from New York touched down at six o'clock in the evening Los Angeles time. There was a Magna limousine waiting on the field for Mr. David Cole. As he surrendered his coat and baggage checks to the chauffeur, he heard himself being paged. He started for the nearest phone. But instead, he found someone waiting.

Sybil.

He embraced her, kissed her. While their faces were pressed against each other, he whispered, "I was hoping you'd be here once you got my cable."

"It wasn't only your cable."

He leaned back from her, stared down into her eyes.

"Albert," she said.

"What about Albert?"

"He's had a heart attack. He's in the hospital."

"Hell, then let's go see him!"

They found her car and headed downtown to Cedars of Lebanon.

Before they entered the room, Dave talked to the doctor, who warned him not to stay too long or overtax Grobe, who was still in the first week of the critical three-week postinfarct period.

Albert lay very still under the white sheet. He wore an oxygen mask and seemed barely to breathe. His eyes were closed. Ye

284

before Dave could speak, Grobe beckoned him with a gesture of his forefinger. Dave moved to the foot of the bed. Grobe slipped off the mask.

"No, Albert, you're not supposed to."

"Dave . . . don't worry. My cardiogram is getting better. Every day." But Grobe's voice was very weak. "The doctor says I'm going to be fine. A hundred percent. Maybe less a little off for cash."

"And you're coming back to the studio as soon as you feel up to it. So don't worry. I'll convince H.P.," Dave reassured him.

"But who's going to convince *me*?" Grobe asked. "Don't I have a right to decide if I want to go back?"

"Of course."

"That's been the trouble with me. Praise God from Whom all blessings flow. To us, H.P. is God. With his big weekly bribes he makes us fight for the honor of being debased, deceived and betrayed by him. Then eventually executed by him. I disobeyed the king, so off with my head! I do not wish to go back."

"What will you do?"

"Lying in a hospital bed gives you a new perspective. Life seems much different horizontal than it does when you're vertical. Especially if you're not horizontal by choice. I'll give up my house in Beverly Hills. Why does one man need such a large establishment? And I'll teach. I have already contacted U.C.L.A. to offer my services to teach a course in screen writing. If it goes through, I'll take a small apartment in Westwood, as befits a college professor on a modest income. The rest of the time I'll live down at the Springs. I find I want to free myself of things, possessions, obligations, the past. I want to forget those twenty-five years of high-class well-paid serfdom."

Sybil moved to his bedside and embraced him gently. "Oh, Uncle Albert . . ."

He patted her on the shoulder. "Don't feel guilty. And don't say anything. I'm old-fashioned enough to believe a girl shouldn't say anything derogatory about her own father."

She kissed him on the cheek and started for the door. As Dave and Albert shook hands, he insisted, "Don't forget. Come and see me in the desert. Plan to stay a few days. Both of you."

"Okay, Albert," Dave Cole promised.

"What did the doctor tell you?" Sybil asked as she headed her car west toward Beverly Hills.

"If he doesn't have another attack in the next two weeks, he'll probably make it."

"I hope so; God, I hope so," she said fervently, as if any guilt her father refused to accept automatically became her responsibility.

Dave stared at her intense face as she drove through the heavy, slow traffic. His memory had played no tricks on him. She was as beautiful as he had remembered, her profile classic, her eyes dark and strong. Her dusky skin, smooth and soft, was fragrant even across the distance of the seat. He was tempted to make love to her there and then.

"What was it like?" she asked suddenly. "How did it end up?"

"It wasn't easy, but it turned out well. We were all satisfied."

"I'm happy for you, Davie."

"You were right about Dan Sullavan. I don't know how he managed it," Dave said.

"Knowing how he feels about my father, I knew he'd find a way," she said.

"Something happened while I was there," Dave said.

"What?"

"I fell in love with another woman."

She turned at once to stare at him, surprised, hurt almost to the point of physical pain. She didn't dare breathe. Finally she asked simply, "Is she nice?"

"Fantastic. Most unusual woman I've ever met."

"I'm glad," she lied, "for your sake. It'll be better for you that way," she added, trying to convince herself too.

"Unfortunately, it won't."

She glanced at him, puzzled.

"The woman is Aline Markham," he said, smiling finally.

Sybil was so relieved her eyes filled with tears. She forced herself to stare at the traffic ahead, to keep the car in its lane.

"Every man falls in love with Ali," she said. "At least once in his life. She's a terrific lady."

They said no more until they were approaching the strip on which the Marmont was situated.

286

"The whole time I was in Rome," he said, "there was no other woman. None."

She had no need to make a similar declaration.

They reached the Marmont. He got out of the car. She waited, finally asking, "Aren't you going to ask me in?"

He shook his head.

"I want to stay. The whole night," she said, determined.

"Why? To even the score with him because of what he did to Albert?"

"Dave, please."

"No. Not the whole night. Not even for a little while. I've had time to do a lot of thinking, too. From now on when you come to me it can't be because you have to even a score with *him*. Or because *he* doesn't need you. But because *I do*. I'll settle my problems with him. But you have to settle yours before we can be free."

"What if I told you I *was* free of him?"

He stared into her eyes till she turned away, unable to convince him or herself.

"We're going to be completely committed to each other. Or completely free," he said. "I know what I'm going to do about it. You have to make up your own mind."

Her eyes welled up, the tears trickling down her cheeks. Every instinct in him compelled him to embrace her, kiss her, make love to her. Every instinct but one—the instinct for survival. To give in now would destroy them both.

"So that's why you wanted to meet me off the lot," Betty Ronson said.

"After what that sonofabitch did to Albert, I'm leaving Magna. Once I lay in the music track for *Via Dolorosa,* I quit!" Dave said, as if he dared her to contradict him.

"Of course. I understand," Betty said too quickly. "A man has to have some principles. Even in this town." Then she paused slightly and cautioned, "Of course, there's nothing about principle that says a man has to be foolish. Give me a week or two to plan some strategy. After all, in this town there's nothing so cold as a director without a job."

"I've got a damn good track record."

"I know, Dave. But with *Via Dolorosa* still in the can, people will think it's a bomb if you resign before it's released. The only way to quit in this town is when you're riding high. But we'll put out some feelers."

"Not 'we.' I'd rather Martoni didn't know about this."

"Okay, Dave, if that's the way you want it," she agreed, then asked, "And Sybil—"

"What about Sybil?" he interrupted quickly, for it was the first time Betty had ever mentioned her by name.

"I was only going to ask, does she know your decision?"

"No," he admitted. "I'm doing this on my own. And I want action. Fast. I'm not in a mood to wait around."

"Davie," Betty said, using the name much as Sybil used it, "don't ever threaten not to wait around in this town. This place was built on waiting around. No, Davie, you've got to be careful. Let me put out some highly confidential feelers and see what I come up with."

The next morning Dave was in the recording studio. He, the composer and the arranger sat on their side of the glass partition while on the other side the conductor was facing the sixty-five-piece Magna Symphony Orchestra, ready to lead them through the opening bars of the score for *Via Dolorosa*.

"Ready?" the composer asked nervously, for this was the first time his score would be played for Dave in full orchestration.

"Ready."

The composer gave a signal to the conductor, who tapped his baton, bringing his sixty-five musicians to the ready. Bows went to violins, violas and cellos. Reed men wet their lips. Timpani hammers were raised for the downbeat. Brass men inhaled deeply. Now came the downward stroke of the baton, and the entire orchestra burst into the theme. A tidal wave of sound shook the room. Dave could hear the high-fidelity speakers behind him vibrate under the attack. Then the music leveled off to a softer, melodic theme.

The red light on the phone began to flash. Dave signaled to the arranger to answer, exploding at the same time, "Damn it, I take no calls! Why can't you guys do the same?" He was embarrassed when the arranger handed him the phone.

"For you."

"To hell with it!"

"Long distance."

Dave seized the phone and asked in great irritation, "Yes?"

"Dave?" Dan Sullavan asked placidly. "Are you where you can talk?"

"Not exactly."

"When you're free call me. On my private line. Circle 6-2044. Important. Very important."

Throughout the morning Dave found his concentration torn between the music, of which he did not approve, and the unexpected call from Dan Sullavan. The composer, a huge, flabby Russian whose accent seemed to have grown broader during his years in Hollywood, pleaded with him.

"Dave, sweetheart, please, darling, just listen once more. The opening few bars. The finest music I have written. Better even than *The Marauder*."

Whenever Sasha Yunofski was in trouble with a producer he always mentioned that film, for which his score had won an Academy Award. Yunofski began to hum the opening bars, as if he were enraptured. His eyes were closed; his fat face glistened with nervous sweat. When the music finished, he opened his eyes with a look of delight, as if he had been listening to angels' voices from heaven.

"Fantastic, no?"

"Yes, Sasha, fantastic. But wrong for my film."

"Dave, baby, you heard it when we played it for you. You loved it."

"I loved the melodic line. But when you orchestrate it with sixty thousand pieces, it's overpowering. This is not another Magna musical. Esther Williams is not leaping up out of the water. Clark Gable is not winning the war. Gene Kelly is not dancing in the rain. This is a religious film—sensitive, spiritually uplifting. And in a way, mournful."

"He won't like it," Sasha wailed and warned at the same time. There was no doubt about who "he" was. "He always insists, 'A Magna opening and a Magna finish.' You'll see."

"And I always say, the music should fit the film," Dave insisted. "Now, let's simplify it!"

Sasha turned to his arranger, tearful. "Simplify it, he says.

289

Might as well take my blood and drink it instead of Coca-Cola." He turned back to Dave. "You simplify a theme like this and where is the power? Where is the majesty? People won't know it's a Magna film. Simplify!" Sasha dropped into a chair. He wiped his brow. He shook his head sadly, a man overcome by the sudden and unexpected death of a loved one.

None of Sasha's notorious antics affected Dave. He had been warned by other producers that the best performance he was likely to get in his film would be Sasha Yunofski's. The Russian not only made a profession of being a character, he loved to brag at parties about the way in which he dominated and controlled producers and directors in meetings and on sound stages.

Dave leaned forward, pressed down the talk-back key to instruct the conductor.

Before he could utter a word, Sasha cried out, "When I am in the studio no one else speaks to the conductor! It is in my contract!"

"Well, then, get on that horn and tell your conductor that I want to hear the theme. Just the melodic line. From the violins, then from the woodwinds, then the piano."

The conductor put the strings through the theme. He followed with the woodwinds. Then the piano. They waited. Sixty-five musicians. A conductor. An arranger. And a frustrated Academy Award–winning composer.

"Let me hear just the oboe alone," Dave said.

The order transmitted, Yunofski settled back, determined not to like his own music in that form. Dave listened. The oboist played the melody. Emanating from that single instrument, the melody took on a solitary, haunting feeling that an entire orchestra could not create.

"That's it," Dave said.

"That's what?" Yunofski demanded.

"That's the way *Via Dolorosa* opens," Dave said with quiet authority.

Yunofski was up out of his chair with an alacrity that belied his bulk. "You want a Yunofski picture to open like that? You might as well show Ethel Barrymore naked! Never! Never!" Yunofski cried. He began to stride about the room muttering to himself. "You're trying to destroy my career. You hate me! Why do you hate me?"

Yunofski turned to his arranger. "*Ask* him! Ask Mr. David Cole why he hates me!"

His arranger said nothing, embarrassed by Yunofski's outburst. Yunofski returned to the attack. "*Tell* him! Tell the eminent Mr. David Cole that if H.P. ever hears such an opening to a Magna film we are all fired. *Finished* in Hollywood. *Finished!*"

Yunofski paused to see if his tirade had had any effect on Dave. When he realized it hadn't, he asked more quietly, "You're sure that's what you want?"

"Sure," Dave replied. "Now let's lay some track!"

By the time they broke for lunch, they had recorded the opening minute of music precisely the way Dave wanted it.

When Dan Sullavan came on the phone, he wasted no time. "Dave, word came to me roundabout, shall we say, that you are discontented at Magna." Sullavan waited but got no reply. "I think you're just going through a phase. After you preview your picture you'll feel better. Never confuse being restless with being discontented. In a young man being restless is a good sign. Provided it doesn't make him do anything foolish. You know what I mean?"

Dave didn't, but he said "Yes" anyhow.

"Look, kid, I'm coming out. I want to see you. Away from the studio. I'll be staying at the Beverly Hills. But it would be good if we could have lunch or a drink away from the studio or the hotel."

"What about my bungalow at the Marmont?"

"No, there's a little French place downtown. I'll get word to you."

Finding the restaurant was not easy and only reminded Dave that though he had lived in Hollywood for years, there were still parts he didn't know. The restaurant proved to be modest and inexpensive. The air was filled with the pleasing and pungent aroma of good French food. The owner was also the maître d', though he was dressed in a chef's apron and toque. He greeted them with such warmth that Dave realized Sullavan must be a frequent patron here. Obviously Dan Sullavan carried on considerable confidential business when he came to L.A.

The lean Irishman was already nursing a straight whiskey on the rocks. Before Dave could sit down, Sullavan asked, "What do you drink?"

"Scotch. Soda."

Sullavan dispatched the owner with a simple gesture. Once Dave was comfortable, Sullavan spoke directly to the point.

"You've heard that bastard bitch about 'New York.' 'New York' does this, 'New York' fails to do that, 'New York' keeps him from doing something else. Everything that is wrong with Magna is the fault of 'New York.'

"Well, we are 'New York.' Me. Louis Cohen, Abe Schlegel. To hear him talk you won't believe this, but *he* works for *us*. Sure he gets more money than all three of us put together. In salary. But not when it comes to the stock. With the right combination of stock we can cut out his heart when it comes to a corporate showdown.

"Well, I think we finally have the right combination. There was a block of fifty thousand shares we needed to vote with us. Now we have it."

Suddenly he said, "Let's order some lunch."

They had ordered and were eating when Sullavan brought up the subject again. "All of us, we've always been looking for another Marvin Kronheim. H.P. included. The difference is, if we found him we'd put him in command. But if H.P. found him first, he'd get rid of him. But Marvin Kronheims are rare things. Like perfect pearls. As the Good Book says, many are called but few are chosen. Well, 'New York' has been studying the situation. We go down the lists of producers, studio heads at other studios. Searching for a man, a young man, who might step in when it becomes necessary."

Dave glanced up at Sullavan.

"We've been studying all the possibilities. In Magna and on the outside. We've studied your record, too. You have come up fast. But you make good pictures. You have good taste. You don't waste money or time. You're not a wild man. You're respected by the people who work with you. It all adds up, kid—adds up to a highly favorable situation."

"Thank you," Dave said as diffidently as he could.

292

"But you're unhappy. We don't like to see that. You want a new contract?"

"I want out," Dave said without stating his reasons.

"I know. Vic told me."

The momentary silence that followed made Sullavan realize that he had allowed a vital fact to escape. He admitted, "Vic gets in touch with me from time to time. When he thinks it's important. Like in your case."

So, despite his instructions, Betty had told Vic Martoni, and Vic, H.P.'s most trusted friend and pimp, was working to undermine him, Dave realized.

"We want you to stay on. So when H.P. goes, for whatever reason, you'll be there to step in."

"How can you be so sure H.P. is going?"

"I told you, I think we finally have the right combination of shares of stock. We can do it," Sullavan said confidently.

Dave remained silent.

"We'll renegotiate your contract," Sullavan offered.

Still Dave did not respond.

"What's wrong, kid?" the older man finally asked.

"I made myself a promise. After this picture, I leave. If I can't work in Hollywood because of him, I'll go back to New York. But I'm not staying on at Magna."

Sullavan seemed about to argue with him, but doubted the wisdom of revealing the intricate tactics of his carefully plotted strategy of corporate vengeance. Instead, he contented himself by advising, "Be smart, kid. Lightning doesn't strike twice. Especially in this place. Don't pass it up. You'd be the youngest studio head in town."

23

H. P. Koenig had prepared well for his trip to New York. His sales staff had first screened Magna's films for all chains and independent exhibitors with theaters large enough to be of consequence. They had made reasonably good bids for most of Magna's product. But to H.P. it was all only the prelude to his trip to New York, where he would sell the bulk of Magna's films to Dan Sullavan for Nationwide Theatres, and at much higher prices. He was in an impregnable position, playing a game in which he held the pat hand. Among his assets he listed an Esther Williams picture, more spectacular than any of her films had been in the past. Two hundred girls in the underwater ballet climaxing in enormous towers of flame shooting up from the blue water of the huge pool. His Special Effects Department had outdone itself.

There was another Gene Kelly film. Always the same and yet always different. Whereas Gable, in his pictures, wooed the leading lady with his cool smile and his suppressed fury, Kelly wooed her with his feet. For eighty-one minutes he failed. In the last three minutes he danced his way into her heart. She relented and they danced off together. The End.

H.P. also had two classics, costume dramas as lavish and authentic as only Magna could make them.

He had two Wendy Morse films, always surefire with the American family. Her strong voice, highlighted by those touching tremolos, her hyperthyroid eyes which glistened and caught the reflection of the lights, converting them into that brilliant sparkle, all added up to an entertainment that made her unique. A Wendy Morse film was money in the bank. Every big independent had bid high for those films.

But the film on which H.P. was depending was *Via Dolorosa.* It had received the highest bids from all the chains and exhibitors. It was good family fare, exciting, touching and uplifting. Grudgingly, H. P. Koenig had to admit to himself that that young bastard Cole had taken a disaster and turned it into a huge hit. Besides, it was the kind of religious picture no critic would dare rap. The kind that every audience would feel virtuous for having gone to see. It was better than absolution. It would give every theater owner a sense of pride at having done a fine public deed by exhibiting it. At increased prices, of course.

Mainly, in H.P.'s mind, it was the kind of film for which a devout Catholic like Dan Sullavan would bid his head off. Sullavan would like the honor of being known at St. Pat's as the man who had brought *Via Dolorosa* to so many millions of Catholics across the country. Once H.P. had dropped a hint about the Cardinal, Sullavan would vastly outbid every other chain in the country.

The terrors of the consent decree of divorcement of studio from theaters did not disturb H. P. Koenig. He was going East armed with the most and the best.

For added weight and to present the appearance of perfect harmony at Magna, he insisted that Dave Cole accompany him. To give the lie to the fact that he had a previous secret arrangement with Dan Sullavan, H.P. went to great pains to stage the screening of his films. Instead of showing them at the former Magna office, he rented screening rooms in a building on Broadway and Forty-eighth. He went through the elaborate charade of "entertaining" his "customers" by arranging for a bar and buffet so they could break between films and refresh themselves. H.P., who had always dominated and tormented these men, who had made it a point to humiliate them whenever he could, now gave every pretense of being the merchant who came with his goods seeking to cajole buyers. They joked about it. He did too. It was all a game to outwit the Justice Department and circumvent the consent decree.

It was carried off in that spirit. Dan Sullavan and his executives, including his regional theater managers, attended. They viewed the films. They ate and drank at H.P.'s expense. They joked during the breaks. They left at the end of the long day. They returned the next day and went through the same procedure. By the evening of the second day they had viewed all the Magna films that H.P. had brought East, except one. The best H.P. saved for last. *Via Dolorosa*. It was a huge success. Sullavan set a meeting for the next morning to discuss terms.

As H.P. and Dave returned to the Magna suite high over Central Park, they were both exhausted. But H.P. was buoyant. "They loved them! Every film! I could tell. Tomorrow I'll turn the screws. I think I'll go over those bids we got from the independents and jack them up a little." He was chuckling when he closed his door and retired for the night.

The next morning at ten o'clock the chief executives of Nationwide Theatres, Inc., gathered in their huge boardroom. White-jacketed waiters from Lindy's had laid out a breakfast of hot coffee, bagels, lox and Danish pastry. When H.P. and Dave Cole arrived, there was familiar jovial small talk till the men finished their coffee.

Finally Dan Sullavan invited, "Well, boys?"

All took their places around the long, highly polished board of directors' table in order of rank and seniority. Dave and H.P. sat at the far end of the table, to give further substance to the concept of divorcement. H.P. sat back, the terms he would accept resting in his inside pocket, terms he had improvised and scribbled on backs of hotel envelopes the night before—figures against which he would force Nationwide to bid. H.P. was confident they would top them. After all, who else had product that could match Magna's in star power? And who else had *Via Dolorosa*?

Sullavan opened the meeting. "H.P., that was quite a program of films you screened for us. Good variety. Well made. Good production values. When it comes to spending money, no one knows how to spend it better than you do."

H.P. smiled. "You know what I always say. If it deserves to be on the screen, it should be the best. No matter what it costs."

Sullavan nodded.

"All right," H.P. said confidently, "let's talk *tachlis*."

Though Dan Sullavan was an Irish Catholic boy from the tenements of Tenth Avenue, of necessity he had learned a great deal of Yiddish during his years in show business. He didn't need any translator to tell him what H.P. meant. Sullavan wet his thin, pale lips and finally said, "H.P., there's been quite a change in the exhibitors' end of the business in the last few months. A drastic change. We have to think differently. In the old days, you made the product, we showed it. It was all cut and dried. But now we have to broaden our horizons.

"For instance, if we confine all our bookings to Magna product, not only would the government get suspicious, but we would be cut off from other sources. After all, why should De Mille offer us his next film if he knows we're going to buy almost all our pictures from Magna? He'd rather not offer it than take the chance of being turned down."

Dave glanced sideways at H.P. The look of the confident little man indicated that he was amused. H.P. was sure Sullavan had to make this statement for the record, just as he had to listen to it, also for the record.

"And there are a couple of other moviemakers who make very successful films. Capra. Ford. Stevens. So to assure ourselves of future sources of product, we have to spread out our purchases. Like any forward-looking industry."

Dave noticed that H.P.'s smile had slowly begun to fade. A thin film of moisture appeared on his forehead and upper lip. He sat motionless as Sullavan continued, slow, dry, deliberate.

"Yes, it's a different world, H.P. And we have to live with it. After all, there is the monster. The Box. TV. People are staying home to watch it. Have you looked at our Sunday-night grosses lately?"

"Crap!" H.P. exploded, giving vent to his mounting anger. "They're looking at TV now because it's free. It's a curiosity. A toy. Where are they going to get Gene Kelly, Bing Crosby, Fred Astaire, Ingrid Bergman, Clark Gable, Bette Davis, Spencer Tracy, James Cagney, Robert Taylor and a hundred other Magna stars? On that fucking box? TV can't afford it. It'll never be able to afford it! The crowds will be back at your theaters in bigger numbers than ever!"

Sullavan didn't respond, only sat back in his capacious president's armchair, lean, staring and silent. H.P. felt the need to fill the void.

"When they come back, you'd better have product to show them. They're used to Magna films in your theaters. The best! You'll lose them unless you give them first-class product!"

If H.P.'s tirade had moved him, Sullavan did not betray it. Dave could detect only the slightest trace of a smile on the Irishman's face. All the indignities, all the abuse, all the demeaning errands Sullavan had had to endure at the hands of H. P. Koenig were being paid off this day. The balance had swung. No longer would Dan Sullavan have to suffer H.P.'s long, vitriolic telephone calls from the Coast. No longer would he have to submit to sessions beside the grave of H.P.'s mother. Or the innumerable times he had had to provide H.P. with young girls when he came to New York, a practice Sullavan detested since he was both a good Catholic and a devoted father.

The silence in the room was unendurable for H.P. He had to bring it to a conclusion. He asked coldly, "Dan, are you saying you're not going to bid on any Magna product?"

Sullavan wiped his dry lips slowly and responded, "There is one film we're going to bid on. *Via Dolorosa*. We'll top any bid you have for that one."

"Oh, you will?" H.P. shouted. "Well, either you bid for all of them or you can't have that one! Clear?"

He was halfway up and out of his seat when Sullavan pinned him with "Harry! Unless you want to go to jail for violating the consent decree, sit down!"

H.P. turned ashen white, but slowly sank back into the soft leather chair.

"You can't do that anymore, Harry. No more packages. No more selling lemons with hits. That is block booking. We have a right to bid on each film. And we are doing that. In the presence of nine witnesses I am saying to you, we will outbid anyone for *Via Dolorosa*. If you refuse, the Attorney General will know about it before you're back at your hotel."

"I'll give you the figures this afternoon," H.P. finally capitulated.

"You'll have our bid first thing in the morning," Sullavan responded.

The meeting was over. H.P. left without shaking hands with

anyone. He glared at Dan Sullavan, inwardly vowing all kinds of vengeance. He did not wait for Dave Cole to catch up with him. As Dave turned to leave, Sullavan put his arm around him and spoke in a soft but urgent voice. "Fantastic film, *Via Dolorosa*. You justified every confidence I had in you."

"You were pretty rough on the old man," Dave said.

"You haven't seen rough yet," Sullavan warned. "Don't forget, we still haven't divested ourselves of our stock. So just keep flexible. And wait for a signal."

They flew back to California on the same plane. But they did not sit together. H.P. was no longer the expansive, voluble man he had always been in the past. He had seen death and it frightened him.

When H.P. returned to the studio the next morning to revive his dealings with the other theater chains, he discovered that their enthusiasm for Magna films had suddenly and strangely diminished. Unaccountably there seemed to be a conspiracy among them of lack of interest. Finally, late in the day, after he had attempted several long, cheerful and confident telephone conversations with exhibitors throughout the country, one of them let slip the startling information that in some way, someone had discovered his strategy, his charade of inviting bids from all other distributors to comply with the letter of the law while his intent all along had been to double-cross them and sell to Nationwide. The exhibitor who told H.P. was a Texan with a chain of theaters that spread across the entire Southwest. In his slow, soft drawl he seemed to take special delight in informing H.P. of their discovery. Though the Texan refused to reveal the source of his information, it was obvious it was New York. And in New York it could only have been Dan Sullavan.

H. P. Koenig, who had dominated an industry, built the world's largest studio by double-crossing and double-dealing, by selling human beings like beef for slaughter, had himself been double-crossed, betrayed and sold down the river. A lesser man, or a man less familiar with the uses of power, might have been crushed. But not H. P. Koenig.

He called in George Keegan, his advertising manager, and Sonny Brown, his head of publicity. He ordered Keegan to plan a twenty-four-page layout in *Variety*. A full page for each Magna film. He instructed Sonny to organize a coast-to-coast junket for a task force of top Magna stars. H.P. would promise personal appearances to every theater that bought any major Magna film.

He strode up and down before them, spewing ideas, giving orders, making costly and lavish plans. When he noticed that neither of them was taking down his instructions, he would interrupt himself to shout angrily, "Goddammit, get it down! Every word! This is gospel! This is going to save the studio!"

It was Keegan who dared to raise the question that had plagued both men. "H.P., how are we going to pay for all this?"

That question had never been asked of him in all the years of his control of Magna Studios. No matter what H. P. Koenig ordered, there was always the money to accomplish it. H.P. glared at Keegan. His first inclination was to fire the man on the spot. But his trip to New York had instilled in him a bit of caution as well as humility.

"There'll be money! Don't worry about it!"

Keegan was silent for a moment, but not disarmed.

"H.P., I got a call from the treasurer's office yesterday. He started talking about economy. Something to do with the banks and the change in our method of doing business now that we don't have our own theaters anymore."

H.P. swung around, pressed down his intercom button and ordered, "Sarah! Get me Mossberg! I want him up in this office in five minutes!" He swung back and said, "You boys can go. I'll talk to you later. Carry out those plans! There'll be money!"

Brown and Keegan were leaving as harried Sy Mossberg came to H.P.'s door. Mossberg was a large, portly man. He sweated even on cool days. He was never without a handkerchief in hand, and he always wore his suit coat, since the underarms of his shirts invariably showed wide dark stains. He was mopping his brow as he walked into H.P.'s office. H.P. did not attempt to put him at ease. He made a single sharp gesture that caused the big man to slump into a chair. H.P. rose. He strode back and forth, a little like Charles Boyer in a film Magna had made about Napoleon. He spoke with the air of an inquisitor.

"So, Mossberg, you took it upon yourself to demoralize my staff, did you?" Even as Mossberg tried to answer, H.P. overrode

300

him. "We are going through difficult times in the picture business. It is a readjustment. But it is not the end of the world. We have been through crises before. And we have come out stronger than ever. Depression! War! We've licked them all. But not by pinching pennies! Bookkeepers don't make pictures. Did you hear me, Mossberg?"

Mossberg's fat wet lips were trembling. He was about to justify himself. But H.P. did not let up in his tirade of insults.

"The world is not run by bookkeepers, Mossberg. They are only scorekeepers. Not players. We do not face difficulty by resorting to false economy. We do not run with our tail between our legs. We do not cringe. We do not admit fear. We do not do anything but fight back! Did you hear me, you big, fat, useless bookkeeper?"

The huge man did not even dare to wipe his dripping face. In those terrifying moments he earned all of his fifty-thousand-dollar-a-year salary in sweat alone.

"As soon as you leave this office you will get hold of Sonny Brown! And George Keegan! You will listen to the plans I have just sketched out. You will assure them that the money is on hand to carry those plans out! Did you hear me, Mossberg?"

Mossberg nodded, at the same time trying to verbalize an answer.

"Now, get out!"

Mossberg did not budge, but made a vague and helpless gesture, indicating that he wanted to speak. H.P. had no patience with him.

"Get out of my office! And never call me again until I call you! Take care of your goddamned books. But keep your nose out of the rest of my business!"

Mossberg raised himself up as if he were lifting a corpse. He went to the door. He dared to turn back. Holding the doorknob for support, he managed to say, "There was a call late yesterday—"

"I don't give a damn about any calls! You do what you're told!"

"But this call—"

"Fuck the call! Get hold of Brown and Keegan and tell them! We carry out my plan. My whole plan!"

301

"H.P.," Mossberg pleaded to be heard.

H.P.'s impatience had been tried too long. He moved to the big man, seized him with one hand by the lapels of his damp jacket and brought his other hand sharply across the fat man's damp face. Luckily, H.P.'s hand was open. If it had been closed, he would have burst open Mossberg's fat lips.

"Now get out!" H.P. said in an angry whisper.

The big man did not move. He rubbed the back of his hand across the spot where H.P. had struck him. Finally Mossberg dared to speak.

"H.P., there's something you ought to know. Yesterday afternoon, after your meeting at the New York office, I got a call." The words came out in a rush, and they stopped H.P. in his tracks.

"A call? From who?"

"From Claude Thalheimer."

"Thalheimer?" H.P. had to think back to place him. "That partner in Wohlman Brothers?"

"That's right."

"What did Thalheimer have to say?" H.P. asked, more cautious and attentive now.

"He heard that Nationwide had decided to pass on all Magna films except one."

"How could he know that?" H.P. demanded.

"Someone in that meeting leaked the news to him."

H.P. remained silent, giving Mossberg a chance to say softly, "Thalheimer said that such an unforeseen event had caused Wohlman Brothers to reassess their financing plans for Magna Studios."

"What do you mean, reassess?" H.P. demanded, more alarmed than angry now.

"They will limit their loans to the company, based on a conservative estimate of our real estate and the possible value of our inventory of negatives. That would mean cutting their commitment to about half of what they promised."

H.P. waved Mossberg out of the room. He moved to his chair and slid down into it. Not since his first days in Hollywood, when he had extended himself beyond his own means and had to go to the bankers, hat in hand, for a loan, had he felt the pangs of sheer financial need.

302

Word of the reversal of the bankers' attitude appeared in the morning issue of *Daily Variety*. The story ran in such detail that it was obvious to H.P. that whoever had leaked it was determined to destroy him. Rumors of a stockholders' fight spread through Hollywood. The price of Magna stock on the New York Stock Exchange fluctuated wildly. For the first time in decades, H. P. Koenig felt powerless. He saw his holdings drop five million dollars in two days. But the more his stock fell in value the more adamant he became.

24

Arnold Willys, controller of production costs, sought an urgent meeting with H.P. and Sy Mossberg and strongly insisted on cutbacks of all kinds. There would have to be tighter controls on all picture budgets.

Throughout the entire meeting, H.P. sat glumly with his chair turned away so that he did not have to look at Willys or Sy Mossberg. But his face reflected only grim stubbornness. Willys glanced at the perspiring Mossberg, who urged him on with a tense gesture of his eyes.

"Here's a list of stars' options coming up for renewal, H.P.," Willys said. "I have circled those I think we should drop." He paused for some reaction. H.P. did not even turn to glance at the list. Willys continued, "And there's no need to carry all these writers on the staff. Just because a writer wins a Pulitzer Prize doesn't make him a studio asset. It might look great in the publicity releases, but I had a study made. We get the fewest shootable scripts from the men who've won the most prizes."

Willys had an additional list of economies. He placed the long memorandum on H.P.'s desk. H.P. swung his chair around slowly, with regal deliberateness. He reached for the memorandum, but didn't read it. He merely tore it in two.

"When the battle is toughest we don't retreat, we attack!" H.P. declared.

Sy Mossberg did not return to his office. He cautiously looked up and down the hallway before entering Dave Cole's office. By arrangement, Dave had dispatched his secretary to an early lunch so that Mossberg's visit would remain secret. Sweating, wiping, breathing with great difficulty to support his huge bulk, Mossberg related the events in H.P.'s office. Even to quoting the old man's line about attacking, not retreating. It sounded familiar to Dave. Finally, he remembered: it was a line from a Magna film about the Bengal Lancers, in which, surrounded by hostile natives and vastly outnumbered, C. Aubrey Smith had uttered almost the identical line.

Mossberg left Dave's office as furtively as he had entered. Dave lifted his phone, asked for H.P. He reached Sarah Immerman, who said her boss was not available to anyone. By the end of the day, Dave received the results of H.P.'s secluded activity. A memo reached his desk, as it did the desk of every Magna executive and producer. It proclaimed that instead of the coast-to-coast star caravan H.P. had announced, he himself was going to make such a tour, to become personally acquainted with all the exhibitors in the country. H. P. Koenig would personally take over the sale of all Magna films.

When Dave finished reading it, he called Sarah Immerman again.

"Sarah, if you love that old man, arrange for me to see him. Now!"

"He gave orders—"

"To hell with orders! I have to see him!"

Normally she would have answered with an impertinent remark. Instead, and to Dave's surprise, she began to weep. "Oh, Mr. Cole . . . Mr. Cole, I wish you *could* see him. I wish *someone* could get in to see him. He's never been like this before. Never." Sobs overwhelmed her words.

"I'm coming up," he said firmly. "He'll see me!"

Dave was surprised to discover that today even Dr. Prinz was being forced to wait in H.P.'s outer office. Prinz kept nervously referring to his wristwatch as he resumed what had obviously been a running—and losing—battle with the stern receptionist.

Finally the doctor picked up his black bag and was about to leave when Dave intercepted him.

"Doctor! Wait!" Dave started toward the door to H.P.'s office. The receptionist, who had never seen anyone enter that room without permission, cried out, almost hysterical, "You can't. You . . . you just *can't!*"

By that time Dave had reached the door and pushed it open. He found H.P. in a familiar pose—standing in the center of the room, staring up at his gallery of stars. Interrupted by the sound of the door, he did not turn, but only gave a brusque order, "Get out! Whoever you are, get out!"

"It's me, H.P. And Dr. Prinz."

"I don't need you. I don't need a doctor. I don't need anyone!"

Dave gestured Prinz toward the private examining room. H.P. turned finally to face Dave.

"The doctor is waiting," Dave said gently. "It's your weekly checkup."

H.P. numbly followed. From sheer habit he stripped down to the waist and surrendered himself to the doctor's stethoscope and his pressing and percussing. There was an alert grimness about the way the doctor carried out the routine. When he was done, he appeared most thoughtful as he said, "H.P., you might ease up a little. After all, we're none of us getting any younger."

H.P. interrupted buttoning his shirt to glare at the doctor.

"There's nothing wrong," Prinz said quickly. "It's just a little preventive advice. You're not the only one, H.P. This whole town has been turned on its ear ever since the Supreme Court decisions. But it's not the end of the world. Though if you'd seen some of the blood pressures and cardiograms I've seen in the last few weeks, you'd think it was. So relax. Relax."

H.P. nodded grimly.

"If you need something to help you sleep at night—" Prinz offered.

"Pills?" H.P. scoffed. "Pills are for actors!"

Prinz didn't answer, but he couldn't avoid Dave's eyes. The doctor's look was a warning. At the door, he paused. "If you need me, don't hesitate to call. No matter what time."

H.P. waited till the doctor was out of earshot. "Vulture! They're all vultures. Circling. Circling," he said. "Like that scene in *Desert Siege*. Remember that picture? Hmm, Dave?"

Instead of answering, Dave said, "H.P., your memo."

"What about it?" H.P. demanded belligerently.

"The tone is wrong. It tries to sound strong and aggressive. It's really weak and defensive. The kind of threats and promises a man makes when he's desperate."

H.P. snorted derisively.

"Besides," Dave went on, "the tour you're planning, that's for a man in his thirties. The kind of thing a man does at the beginning of his career, not..." Dave stopped. He had blundered into a figure of speech that would only make the old man more stubborn. He ended simply, "I'd withdraw that memo if I were you."

H.P. turned on him. "That's exactly the point, you young bastard! You are *not* me! You could never *be* me! And if I wanted your advice I would ask for it. Now, get out of here! Get out!"

"H.P.—" Dave tried to placate him.

"The memo stands. I will do everything that I say in there! And I'll still outlive you. I'll outlive all you young bastards! You wait and see!" He was breathing deeply, intensely, defiantly.

When Dave returned to his office he found that Prinz had stopped on his way out and had left a handwritten sealed note.

The old man is too tense. I'm afraid there may be a cardiac accident. See what you can do.

It was signed with a simple *P.*

Dave sat folding and unfolding the note. He reached for the phone. He called the Koenig house for Sybil. She was not at home. It was Wednesday. That could mean she was at the Beverly Hills taking a tennis lesson. He drove over. Snodgrass, the pro, told him Sybil had an appointment but had not appeared and had not called. Dave drove back to the studio.

In his absence there had been a call from New York. No message. No call-back number. No clue of any kind, beyond the operator's saying the caller would place the call again. Within an hour the call came through. It was Dan Sullavan.

"Dave?"

"Yes."

"I just wanted you to know. Along with the bankers, we've now got all the votes we need. We're going to move in on him. This week. And we're going to ask you to take over. You're ready, I hope."

Dave hesitated. Prinz's warning about the old man was still fresh in his mind.

"I'm ready," he said.

"Good!" Sullavan hung up. Dave held on to the receiver for a moment. Finally he put it back in its cradle. He was aware that he had begun to sweat—whether from the impending responsibility that was going to be thrust on him or from the personal confrontation that must arise from the change, he did not know.

He called the Koenig house again. The butler answered. Miss Sybil was not at home. Dave asked to talk to Mrs. Koenig.

"Mrs. Koenig, I have to see Sybil. Do you know where she is?"

"No," Mrs. Koenig said. "Is it about Harry?"

Dave hesitated. Finally he admitted, "Yes."

"Something happened," she said, alarmed. "What is it? Where is he?"

"He's in his office. Nothing happened."

"Oh." She sounded relieved. She had not been his wife in any true sense of the word for many years. She did not endorse or approve of his ethics or his way of life. Whatever love there had been between them had been tortured and stunted by his gross disregard of her feelings and her dignity, but somehow it had not been totally destroyed. When danger threatened, it was apparent that she still cared. She admitted, "I've been worried since this morning. Dr. Prinz called. He asked me to see what I could do about slowing him down. There's nothing, of course; he knows that. But still he asked. That's what convinced me it was serious."

"Yes," Dave admitted. "He's bent on doing things he can no longer do. Memory can provide a man with the will to fight, but not the strength."

"Dave," she pleaded. "You'll do what you can to help him, won't you?"

Dave Cole hesitated. Sooner than he had expected, he was confronted by the ultimate question. He could pass it off with a lie which would spare this very kind woman some concern and pain. But he realized he would have to face it sooner or later.

"Mrs. Koenig, I don't think I can help him. I don't think anyone can help him. Short of persuading him to retire gracefully."

"Retire? Harry?" was all she said.

"It's either that or else he'll be forced out."

308

"They can't do that," she protested, becoming H.P.'s advocate now. "It's his company! He built it all by himself. They can't . . . they can't . . . " Her voice dwindled into silence. Then she asked simply, "*Can* they do it, Dave?"

"Yes, they can. They have the votes."

"Oh, Harry. Poor, poor Harry," she said, and began to cry. She apologized for her show of emotion. "I'm sorry, Dave, sorry."

"I understand."

"I don't think you do," she said. "I don't think anyone does. You would have to know him from the old days to understand."

"Are you going to tell him?" Dave asked.

"No," she said gently. "He would think I'm telling him out of revenge. It'll be bad enough for him when *he* has to tell *me*."

"Of course," Dave agreed. "Mrs. Koenig, you'll tell Sybil to call me as soon as she gets back?"

"Yes, dear, of course I'll tell her."

It was close to nine o'clock when Sybil finally called.

"Where've you been?"

"Driving."

"Just driving? All this time?"

"Just driving," she said, sounding flat and weary.

"Can I take you to supper?"

"I'm down at the Springs."

"What are you doing down there?" he asked, surprised.

"I don't know. Somehow I ended up here."

"In that huge place, all alone?"

"This huge place. All alone."

"Sybil! Tell me. What's wrong?"

"I can't tell you. I don't know how." Her voice sounded flat— strange.

"Darling, you just wait there. I'm coming down."

"At this hour?"

"Wait there for me. Okay?"

"Okay," she finally agreed.

He headed south and east out of Los Angeles. When the freeway ended he sped along dark stretches of road, passing orange groves and vineyards. He slowed down when he came to small towns that were shuttered for the night. Then he picked up speed again. More than an hour had gone by. He had left the towns behind him. Beyond him, lights of scattered houses lit up the darkness. Above, the stars became more clearly defined as the haze and mist of the towns disappeared. He was speeding past the dark mountains and huge rugged shapes that were the bare rocky hills of the desert. There was a long stretch of darkness, and his speeding car shuddered and swayed as it hit the bumps and ruts in the worn road.

He climbed to the crest of a low hill and began to descend into the small town of Palm Springs. The lighted trees of Palm Canyon stretched before him on both sides. The small coffee shops had all gone dark for the night. Most motels were shuttered for the off season.

When he pulled up before the Koenig compound, he found the watchman guarding the tall iron gates.

"Miss Sybil is in the Gilbert cottage," Dave was informed. It was named in honor of John Gilbert, who had been a Magna star.

When he got to the cottage, Dave looked in through the window. Sybil was curled up on the floor staring into the log fire that blazed in the huge fireplace. She didn't move when she heard him enter. He dropped down beside her on the thick white rug.

"What's wrong?" he asked. "You didn't sound like yourself at all."

She didn't answer, but turned to him asking to be embraced. He took her in his arms. She burrowed deep into his shoulder as if trying to hide there.

"What happened?"

"I finally did it," she said. "But once I did, I couldn't face it."

"Finally did what?"

"Rebelled. In a way that mattered. Got free of him."

"Your father?" he asked—unbelieving, yet daring to hope.

"Yes, my father."

"How?"

She turned away from him.

"Sybil? Darling?"

"You won't like what I'm about to tell you," she began tentatively.

He took her by the shoulders and turned her about so that she was forced to face him.

310

"If it's the truth, I want to hear it," he insisted.

"Dan Sullavan . . . To make him get you the money to finish *Via Dolorosa*, I had to promise that if he called on me I'd vote my stock against my father."

"You mean, without your help I'd never have been able to finish the picture?"

She nodded, awaiting his reaction.

"I thought you wanted me out of the industry," he said.

"You had your heart set on proving you could overcome him. I couldn't let him rob you of that chance," she explained, and then added, "Though I knew you'd resent being beholden to me, almost as much as to him." She paused and asked, "You *do* resent it, don't you?"

He stared down into her pleading eyes, then shook his head slightly. "If you'd given me the choice, I'd have refused. Now that it's done, I realize what a fool I'd have been. It would have been nothing less than masculine vanity. One thing a man never does gracefully is accept acts of love or sacrifice from a woman."

He kissed her and she pressed against him, relieved and grateful that he wasn't angry with her. But he knew her confession hadn't been completed.

"Then Dan Sullavan called you on your agreement. And you had to pay up."

"I'll say this for him. He's a far more compassionate man than my father. He called last night and said, 'You're obligated to give me your votes. And I need them. But he *is* your father. And I'm a father too. So I'm going to give you the chance to change your mind. Think about it. Call me back in the morning.'"

"So you called him back this morning?"

"I gave him a proxy to vote my fifty thousand shares. Once I did it, I couldn't face it."

"So you went out and started driving." She nodded. "And wound up here." She nodded again. He embraced her and held her tightly.

"I need someone to tell me I did the right thing," she said. "Tell me, Davie. Reassure me. He *had* to be forced out, didn't he?"

"If they didn't do it, time would have. He's a pirate who belongs to a bygone day," Dave said. "Did Sullavan tell you who they picked to take over?"

"No."

"Me," he said softly.

She leaned away from him, stared up into his face which reflected the light from the blazing fire. Suddenly, as if she were protecting him, she embraced him more strongly than before.

"I was hoping we'd be free after this. That's one of the reasons I did it . . . one of the reasons," she said.

"There's no law says I have to abandon my career to be free of him. We're as free as we choose to be," he said, kissing her.

He pressed his head against her small, shapely breasts. She held him there tightly. He could feel her nipples rise to him. He slid his hand under her soft cashmere sweater and found her flesh warm and inviting. She strained against him. He stripped her of her clothes and soon they were both naked before the fire. The lights and shadows cast by the flames made her body even more sensuous than it had seemed before. Or else it was the feeling that she gave herself to him more freely this time. The solace and absolution he could not give her in words she found in the fierce passions he unleashed when their bodies were one.

She joined him with a wildness she had never felt free to exhibit before. When it was over, when their bodies were pressed one against the other in welcome, spent release, she held him more tightly than ever.

He hoped she had finally rid herself of her demon.

25

It had been an active morning for H. P. Koenig. He had mapped out his tour of the Southwest, with meetings that included exhibitors and theater-chain owners in Dallas, Houston, Phoenix and Denver. He had had Sonny Brown arrange for lavish breakfasts, lunches and dinners at which he would entertain before holding his business meetings. Since there would be some starlets along on the tour but not nearly enough for all his potential customers, H.P. had made sure to provide local call girls. Good, righteous, straitlaced Texas theater men who would never exhibit a questionable film were notoriously horny once they escaped their wives.

His plans completed, H.P. thought it would be a stroke of inspired strategy if he addressed the entire studio staff before setting out on his trip. It would quell the vicious rumors that had been demoralizing the studio ever since that last unfortunate trip to New York. He instructed Sonny Brown to circulate a memo commanding all studio personnel, from lowliest messenger boy to most expensive star, to gather on the back lot at six that evening. The meeting would take place at the steps of the Roman-temple set.

Along with all the others, Dave Cole received his mimeographed summons. His impulse was not to attend. It would be an act of hypocrisy, knowing what he knew and pretending to support H.P. Curiosity overrode his guilt.

The day had been warm. But toward evening the air cooled. The sky was blue, with wisps of white clouds that caught the setting sun and infused the blue with an aura of pink. Gradually Magna personnel began to gather. Grips in their work clothes. Cutters called away from their Moviolas, tousled, untidy, impatient. Cameramen, some with their light meters still hung around their necks. Actors and actresses, stars among them, some still in makeup and costume, gathered at the foot of the steps. Musicians, composers, sound technicians, office help, special-effects men, secretaries, guards in uniform, producers in expensive cashmere jackets, commissary help, messenger boys. Script mimeographers, their hands still ink-stained. Set-construction men, projectionists, makeup men and women—all mingled without regard to craft or class. By the time Dave arrived, several thousand people were already gathered, and more came straggling in. Dave found Aline Markham in the crowd. They stood together, waiting. Just as the crowd was becoming restive, a chauffeured Rolls-Royce convertible drove into view, the top down. H. P. Koenig sat in the rear seat, regal and alone. The car pulled to a stop at the foot of the simulated-marble steps. H.P. alighted and started up. As he moved majestically and surely, Dave realized what he was watching: Magna's *Ben-Hur!* Just before the chariot race, when Caesar arrived at the Colosseum.

Ali caught it too, and like Dave, she knew the old man would never change. It was funny—and sad. Now he stood forty steps above them so that he could see them all and they would all focus only on him.

"This is a time that tries men's souls." The mike picked up every word clearly. "A time when the weak can be destroyed. We all remember the Great Depression. And the words of our greatest American, our beloved Franklin D. Roosevelt. 'The only thing we have to fear is fear itself!'"

Ali Markham whispered, "The sonofabitch. He fought Roosevelt every time he ran. He was a Hoover and Landon man."

"Well," H.P. continued, "we are in the same situation today. The exhibitors whom we have made rich and fat with our great pictures are trying to take advantage of us now. They are trying to kill the goose who laid so many golden eggs for them.

"There is no such thing as gratitude," he declared. He began to brush at the corners of his eyes. It was the first hint of any

314

tears. Markham nudged Dave Cole. H.P. continued:

"If we ever decided to stop making Magna pictures, there would be such a deafening sound of theater doors being slammed shut across this country it would start a panic. But we do not intend to quit! We do not intend to retrench! We intend to do only one thing. To keep on making the biggest and best pictures in the world! As we always have!"

Someone down front started to applaud. It was Sonny Brown. All the rest joined in. There was a crescendo of applause that swept upward, encouraging H.P. to continue.

"Tomorrow morning I am starting out on a new kind of personal-appearance tour. I am personally going out to meet and greet all exhibitors myself. I will not leave this studio's future, or your future, in other hands. I have always felt like a father to you all. And like a good father, I am going to see that my family will be safe, secure and well provided for in the future!"

Again Sonny Brown started the applause.

H.P. spread his arms, his palms turned down, and began to intone, "Pray with me. Whatever your religion. Or even if you have no religion. This one time, pray with me."

Dave turned to Markham. "The Sermon on the Mount. From *Via Dolorosa*. Remember?"

"He seems to have forgotten the night he tried to close it down," Markham said bitterly.

"Yes, pray with me," H.P. implored. "God, we ask You to remember Your devoted servants, who have spent their lives entertaining and uplifting so many millions of Your children. We have brought love, joy and inspiration into their lives. Bless us and help us to carry on this great and noble work." H.P. pointed toward the gate that led from the back lot.

"Go forth now. Back to your homes. Sleep secure tonight. And wake ready to come to work tomorrow inspired to do your best as always."

Like a high priest, H.P. intoned, "And God bless you all." He took off his glasses and wept unashamedly. The crowd did not move but stayed to stare. Most of them felt disdainful amusement or cynical admiration.

Ali Markham whispered to Dave Cole, "The sonofabitch! Who else would have dared?"

"Who else could have carried it off?" Dave countered.

315

At dawn the next morning, Sonny Brown accompanied H.P. to the airport, saw that his luggage, his advertising campaign and the prints of the films were all securely stowed aboard. He waited till H.P.'s plane was airborne. Then, instead of returning to the studio, Sonny Brown reentered the parked limousine, took copies of the morning's *Hollywood Reporter* and *Daily Variety* out of his briefcase and settled down to reading. It would be thirty-five minutes at least before the overnight plane from New York would land.

When it arrived, Sonny Brown was at the foot of the hatchway steps. He waited while sleepy, tired travelers, who had had to sit up all night, slowly descended the steps, blinked at the morning sunlight as they made their way to the baggage area. Finally a tall man in a dark-blue suit, a white shirt and a plain Harvard crimson tie appeared in the doorway. His thin lips kept making a tasting motion. And what he tasted did not please him. He bounded down the steps. On a closer look, Sonny was surprised to discover that the man was even younger than he had first seemed. It was his cold and forbidding appearance that made him look like a crusty middle-aged man.

"Mr. Whitney?" Sonny asked.

"Yes," he admitted cautiously, as if his identity were a state secret.

"Sonny Brown."

"Oh, yes."

"We have a car waiting. And if I can have your luggage checks—"

Whitney interrupted: "David Cole? I'll want to see him right away."

"We can call him as soon as we get to the hotel."

"He hasn't been told I'm coming?" Whitney asked, showing irritation.

"Sullavan didn't think it was wise," Brown said. "You don't know how rumors spread in this town. Before the day is out someone will know you're here. Someone else will know you represent the bankers. By tomorrow it'll be front page in both the *Reporter* and *Variety*."

"By tomorrow it won't matter," Whitney said, ending the conversation.

Within an hour Dave Cole was in Whitney's bungalow at the Beverly Hills Hotel.

"Mr. Cole, I am here to protect our investment," Whitney began. "Twenty-four million dollars! We feel that if Koenig is allowed to continue in control he will spend the studio into disaster. At the same time, we can't allow expensive facilities to stand idle. It's a bad use of invested capital. We have already had appraisals made of the real estate on which Magna stands. We find that unless the studio can adjust itself to making more and cheaper pictures, it would be wise to shut down the studio and sell off the land."

Dave stared at the man, realized that Whitney was no older than he, possibly even younger. Yet he spoke with a cold authority that reflected the real power of the money he represented.

"You'd shut down the studio and sell off the land?"

"We wouldn't have any choice," Whitney said flatly.

"And the five thousand people who work there?"

"Economic change demands readjustment. People *do* readjust."

"Special-effects men, cinematographers, film editors—exactly what do they 'readjust' to?" Dave asked.

"That's a problem bankers don't have to contend with." Without skipping a beat, he continued: "That's where you come in, Mr. Cole. I understand Mr. Sullavan has told you of the decision."

"Yes."

"I'm here to tell you what we expect. First and foremost, economy. Our study indicates that there are reposing on the shelves of Magna's story department nine million six hundred thousand dollars' worth of literary properties, books and plays, that have been paid for but never used."

"Some stories just don't translate into good shooting scripts."

"That will have to stop! Before any property is bought or abandoned it will have to be submitted to us in New York and read by our committee."

317

"Who's on your committee?" Dave asked, trying to control his hostility.

"We're not fools in New Nork," Whitney answered briskly. "We didn't get to be where we are by being stupid."

"You didn't get to be where you are by writing scripts or producing pictures, either," Dave corrected sharply.

Whitney turned to stare Dave down. Dave rose to meet him eye to eye.

"Mr. Whitney, I wouldn't come to New York and tell you how to run your banking business. Don't you come here and tell us how to run a studio! Because I've never seen a banker who made a good picture. So if that's one of the terms of your deal, take it and shove it!" Dave turned and started for the door.

"I'd wait if I were you." Whitney's tone more than his words made Dave turn around to face him.

Whitney reached for a slim, expensive black leather envelope. He took out a light-blue-covered memorandum.

"You don't have to read all of this," Whitney said; "just the last two paragraphs."

Unless Magna Studios can be placed in young, aggressive hands, with a realistic view of the future of the motion-picture business, it is our considered opinion that the studio should be liquidated and the major asset, several thousand negatives, be sold off to the distributors of television film. The studio must be run on a profitable basis or else be put out of business.

Large studios have become dinosaurs; their very size makes them obsolete. New leadership, young leadership must be obtained or else Magna is doomed.

"That's a pretty cold appraisal," Dave said.

"Realistic," corrected Whitney. "So you see, Mr. Cole, unless you take on the job, with all its restrictions, you're the one who'll be putting five thousand people out of jobs."

"And H.P.?" Dave asked.

"An announcement will say that H. P. Koenig has resigned due to ill health."

"Ill health?" Dave protested. "Who would believe it?"

"We *could* say he's been fired," Whitney said, smiling cynically.

"The point is, when he comes back to town you have to be sitting in that office. In command. The transition must be swift and clean. Like surgery."

"Did they consider making him chairman of the board?" Dave asked hopefully.

"The decision was carefully thought out. And quite final. *He must go.*"

"Then don't let him read it in the papers. Let me tell him," Dave asked.

Whitney considered it. "If you can tell him tonight, okay. But tomorrow is our deadline."

When Dave arrived at the studio he found a message from Sonny Brown. There was also a message from Betty Ronson. He ignored Betty's message. But he did call Sonny.

Brown was very cryptic. "Did you see him?"

"Yes."

"Everything go all right?"

"Everything went all right," Dave responded, not willing to add anything to Brown's knowledge.

"What about the release of the news?"

"You'll hold that up till I give the word," Dave said sharply.

"Of course," Brown agreed quickly, with the same swift, unquestioning obedience that he had always accorded H.P.

Dave hesitated a long time before he called Sarah Immerman.

"Sarah, I have to reach H.P. on a most urgent matter. Where is he right now?"

She consulted his schedule. "He's hosting a luncheon at the Dallas Club."

"What time will it be over?"

"Two-thirty Dallas time," she said. "Why?"

"Never mind," Dave said. He hung up. He would have to wait an hour and a half before he could reach H.P.

"It's fantastic, Dave! The reception is fabulous! I couldn't have done a smarter thing than come out here myself! They love me! They just love me!" H.P. exulted before Dave had a chance to explain his call.

Finally Dave found a decent pause in which to say, "H.P., there's been trouble back here while you were gone."

"There's always trouble when I'm not there. I'll take care of it as soon as I get back."

"It can't wait. You have to come back tonight."

"Why, what's up? What's wrong? A strike?" H.P. demanded.

"Worse than a strike. The bankers."

"Oh, those bastards." H.P. dismissed them. "When I come back with all the deals I'm going to make, there won't be any more trouble with the bankers." He laughed like a small boy who had pitched a no-hitter. "I had no idea what it was like on the road these days. Those exhibitors love me! A man has to get away from his own hometown to be appreciated. What was that line in *King of Kings*? 'A prophet is not without honor ...'"

" 'Save in his own country,' " Dave volunteered.

"Yeah! Right! The writer who wrote that knew what he was talking about."

"H.P.," Dave interrupted firmly, "you *have* to come back! Tonight! It's urgent! Really urgent, H.P.!"

"If you're so upset, okay; I'll be there. And I'll show those bastard bankers a thing or two." H.P. exuded an enthusiasm and combativeness that made Dave feel even more guilty.

"When you find out what flight, call Sarah and I'll meet you myself."

26

The night was foggy. The blue lights that marked off the airport taxiways glowed dimly in the heavy mist. Inside, the airport building smelled of stale cigarette smoke, reminding Dave of the dismal old bus station in New York where late at night derelicts came in out of the cold. At one end of the airport an infant cried incessantly. The airport personnel lacked their usual daytime jauntiness. The metallic loudspeaker voice that ruled the airport intoned infrequent arrivals and departures.

Dave kept glancing at his wristwatch even though there was a huge clock facing him on the opposite wall. Finally the flight from Dallas was announced. Dave went to the gate. The plane moved into place guided by the controller's orange lights. The propellers were cut and wound down to a halt. The steps were rolled into place. The hatch opened. Weary travelers began to ooze down the steps. Once all the other passengers had debarked, H.P. stood in the hatchway smiling, talking to a tall brunette stewardess with a good figure and a professional smile on her face. Dave could tell from the glint in his eye and the seductive smile on his face that H.P. was offering her a screen test in order to exploit their brief acquaintance. She slipped him a piece of paper, which he pocketed securely.

H.P. started down the steps, beaming, and looked around confidently for his chauffeur and limousine. At that moment Dave called out to him, "H.P.!"

H.P. started toward him.

"Where's my car and driver?" the old man demanded, handing his topcoat and briefcase to Dave.

"I told them not to bother. I brought my own car."

"What about my luggage?"

"I'll have it picked up in the morning."

H.P. grunted in disapproval. They started out of the airport. Dave drove silently most of the way, wondering precisely when and how to break the news. He had thought of stopping at some late roadside place for coffee. But unsure of how the old man would react, he decided that that was unwise. On impulse he turned the car in the direction of the studio.

From a distance of almost half a mile they could see the water tower that rose higher than any other building on the Magna lot. Lit up in the mist, it glowed with a supernatural aureole. As they drew closer they could read the huge letters M A G N A. And underneath it, the legend MORE STARS THAN THERE ARE IN HEAVEN.

To break the oppressive silence from time to time, H.P. would report some episode of his successful trip to Dallas. He even took the time to describe in detail his encounter with a young call girl in the Dallas hotel. As beautiful as most of Magna's stars, and sexually better versed, she had been a delightful surprise. He must find some way to bring her to Hollywood. If not in pictures, then at Marge's. That girl definitely belonged in the big time. It was a shame to waste that kind of sexual talent in a cow town like Dallas.

They arrived at the studio gate and were challenged by the armed guard. When he leaned in and saw it was H.P. he immediately came to respectful attention, touched his hand to his peaked cap and waved them on in. Far down the studio street Dave could see the arc lights of a production that was doing some night shooting. But for the rest, aside from a few lights in the cutters' building, the place was deserted.

The guard admitted them to the Kronheim Building. They went to H.P.'s private elevator and up to his suite. He threw on the switches, flooding the huge office with light, and went to the bar.

"These damn damp California nights," he said as he poured himself a long straight Scotch. Only after he had taken a deep swallow did he think to ask Dave, "Like one?"

"No, thanks."

H.P. sank into a large, soft leather chair, exhaling, finally, in relief.

"What a grind," he explained. "Breakfast with one group. Screening films. Lunch with a second group. Then, while they were watching the screening, I had a chance to knock off that cute little girl. I mean, she had a line of talk that was very cute. But when she got down to business, there wasn't any part of a man's body she didn't know what to do with. And that Texas drawl. It tickles your balls just to hear it."

He laughed, then glanced at Dave, who had remained stolid and grim throughout H.P.'s reminiscences. Finally the old man laughed again and said, "That's the trouble with you young men: throw a little difficulty at you and you go to pieces. What's so terrible that you went into a panic? Why are you sitting there like it's the end of the world?"

The moment had come. There was no delaying it now. It remained only to carry out the obligation Dave had chosen for himself. He rose from his chair, preferring to move about as he spoke.

"H.P., the bankers have sent a man out here. With news. Bad news. They've gone over the situation at Magna. They know that all the Magna films got turned down by Nationwide—"

H.P. interrupted, "Except *your* film, Dave. Be fair to yourself."

"Okay, except for my film," Dave conceded. "But for the rest, the outlook is very bleak."

"Wait till they see the results of my Texas trip," H.P. said confidently.

"Did you come back with any firm deals?"

"I didn't have time," H.P. shot back. "You interrupted my trip!"

Dave didn't dwell on that but continued, "The point is, the bankers feel their investment is in jeopardy. They want economies. Changes. All kinds of changes."

"Economies?" H.P. scoffed angrily. "You don't make good pictures by economizing."

"But the bankers—"

"Fuck the bankers!" H.P. exploded, then downed the rest of his drink. "What the hell do bankers know about making pictures?"

"I tried to tell them that."

323

"That's the trouble with you young pricks! You only *tried* to tell them. I *will* tell them! Tomorrow, first thing. Is that why you called me back? To tell me this kind of horseshit? You could have told me on the phone. My answer would be the same. Fuck 'em. Fuck 'em all!"

He wheeled angrily and went back to the bar, poured himself another drink. Dave realized he had best let the man talk himself out. H.P. turned to face him.

"Someday, Dave, after I'm dead and gone, you're going to take this over. All of it. This office. That lot out there. Those stages. Everything. Including these. . . ." He made a great bold sweep of his arm toward his treasured oil portraits. "The greatest collection of talent in this world." He moved to the portraits, rubbed his fingers affectionately over the nameplate under the portrait of Clark Gable. He confessed a bit self-consciously, "I had a girl down in the Research Department look it up once. All the emperors of Europe, the ones who used to gather composers and writers in their courts, patrons of the arts. Not a one of them had such a collection of talent as I have. Not one!"

Dave wondered by what miracle of comparative statistics one arrived at such a result, but he said nothing.

"You don't achieve that by economizing! Sometimes the more you spend the better! The people demand it That's what they come to see our pictures for. To see what they can't find in real life.

"Who was it . . . that Pulitzer Prize winner . . . later he won a Nobel Prize . . . the writer . . ." When Dave couldn't supply the name, H.P. went on nevertheless. "He said it. 'Religion may be the opiate of the masses, but Magna is their salvation in a world gone mad.' A Nobel Prize winner said that about my pictures. About *me!*"

He downed the rest of his drink. "So I don't want any sonofabitch telling me I have to economize. Cowards economize! Gutless bastards economize! In the morning I will deal with the bankers!"

He laughed—a gleeful, triumphant laugh. He had disposed of the enemy and had time for other things now.

"Dave, you know what? I'm feeling a little horny. That stewardess on the airplane. I watched her lovely ass bouncing up and down that aisle for four hours. It almost drove me crazy. When she bent over to serve me drinks, I could look right down her cleavage. Two of the most beautiful tits in the world. Wasting her life away on an airplane. I got to do something for that girl. I got the phone number of the motel where she stays here." He dug into his pocket and came upon the cocktail napkin she had given him.

"H.P., I wouldn't do that," Dave tried to interrupt.

"Oh, of course you wouldn't!" H.P. laughed at him. "You live like a goddamn monk! For Christ's sake, relax! I'll call her. There was another cute little girl on that plane. Blond. Nice ass. Not as beautiful as the dark one, but cute. Maybe they're both free." H.P. laughed. He turned to the phone. Before Dave could stop him, he dialed. Then his exuberance slowly changed to puzzlement and frustration. He consulted the napkin and dialed again. Again the same result. Impatiently he dialed the operator, gave her the number and waited. Then he listened, and finally he lowered the phone.

"The cunt! There's no such number. I could have put her in pictures. Fuck her!"

The defeat only served to whet his appetite. He said suddenly, "That girl . . . the second lead in Larry Holtzman's picture . . . you know, the little blond one. The one who was the model in New York before we brought her out . . . what's her name?"

Dave pretended not to remember. It did not deter H.P. He searched his black address book, going page by page, in the hope that when her name appeared he would recognize it. Meanwhile Dave kept trying to interrupt him and bring him face to face with the difficult business they both had to confront tonight.

"Alma! Alma Burke!" he exulted when he found the name. He swung around to the phone, dialed the number and eased into his soft and seductive tone of voice.

"Alma? Darling? You know who this is? That's right. Sorry to call you so late. Tonight when I got back from my trip to Texas, the first thing I wanted to do was see your rushes. I just came from the screening room. You were stupendous! Fantastic! I haven't had such goose bumps since the first time I saw Garbo. . . . No, really, I mean it. Absolutely fantastic, darling.

"Remember when I called you in New York? Your face was on

325

the cover of *Cosmopolitan*. And I said to my staff here, I said, 'Boys, there is a face that is not only beautiful but sensitive. That girl has talent. She can act.' When they said you'd never acted before, who was it insisted they bring you out and screen-test you? . . . That's right, Uncle Harry. So tonight when I saw your rushes I said to myself, I have to call that girl and tell her myself."

Dave could hear her voice but not her words.

"Thank you, darling. Sweetheart, you know what I thought? Since this is a special night, for you and for me, we should celebrate. What time is your makeup call tomorrow morning? . . . Seven? Forget it. I will leave word. They'll shoot around you till afternoon. So don't worry your pretty little blond head about that," he assured her, laughing. "After all, who's boss around here?"

Evidently she still refused, for H.P. continued, "Look, I might as well be frank with you. What I would like to discuss is a new contract. I feel guilty about having taken advantage of you because of your shmuck agent. So I want to correct that. Look, why don't I come over and we can discuss it?"

He glanced at Dave, a big expectant smile on his face. He was accustomed to only one answer after such a ploy. It had rarely failed him before. Now Dave watched his face change from a smile to a puzzled, curious look. He became angry and his face grew red with rage. Finally he exploded.

"You stupid broad! You're cutting your own throat! You'll be finished here at Magna. And in this whole town. You can go back to being a goddamn model in New York for as long as your idiot face holds up! And believe me, that won't be long. I've seen your kind come and go! Stupid cunt!"

He hung up so violently that the phone crashed to the floor. "Cunt! Cunt!" he kept repeating. His fleshy face pulsed with each clenching of his jaws. He picked up his book to search for some other name that might satisfy his ego and the hunger in his loins.

Dave made no effort to interfere. One thing was obvious to him now. However well guarded the secret was intended to be, despite Whitney's promises, and Sonny Brown's, the word had got out. No girl, no woman in this town would have dared refuse H.P. unless the word was out. And if it was out, it would be an enormous headline in the dailies first thing in the morning.

Dave got up from his chair, moved to the desk and interrupted H.P.'s feverish search by taking the black book out of his hands. H.P. looked up at him, fierce anger in his eyes.

"What the hell do you think you're doing?"

Dave tossed the book across the room. It hit the paneled wall and dropped to the floor. H.P. started to rise in angry protest. Dave gently and firmly pressed him down into his seat.

"Listen to me, H.P.," Dave began. "There's been a change. A big change." He paused, then said, "The bankers have insisted that you resign."

"Me? Resign?" H.P. laughed. "Without me there is no Magna!"

"H.P., listen! They have the votes and the proxies to *force* you to resign."

"They do not!" H.P. said, rising as if to engage in combat. He began to reel off the shares of stock he controlled. His own. And his wife's. And Rob Rosenfeld's. And the trust fund for Marvin Kronheim's kids, of which he was chief trustee. And Sybil's. In all, it amounted to forty-seven percent. No one could unseat him if he controlled that much of the stock.

"H.P., you don't control all that stock," Dave announced. "For one thing, Mrs. Kronheim has had you removed as trustee."

"She wouldn't dare! I *made* that bitch! I even made Marvin marry her! She wouldn't dare."

"But she did. And Rob Rosenfeld—"

"What about Rob Rosenfeld?" H.P. demanded.

"His entire fortune is in Magna stock. He felt he had to protect himself. And if the bankers withdrew their loans—"

"Rosenfeld! After all I did for him! I chose him, a green kid out of law school, gave him his first job. Then made him house counsel," H.P. said, completely obliterating all memory of the insults and taunts he had hurled at the man during a lifetime. "Who else?"

Dave hesitated; then, as gently as he could, he said, "Sybil."

"Sybil?" H.P. whispered. "*Sybil?*" he repeated, unbelieving.

Dave didn't respond.

H.P. sat in his huge chair, pondering the news but not really accepting it. Suddenly he struck back. "I'll fight those bastards! I'll go to the stockholders! I'll take full-page ads in *The New York*

Times! All I have to do is list the pictures I've made and the grosses. No stockholder will believe those conniving bastards on Wall Street!"

"H.P., that was in the days when you had theaters to release through."

"Magna pictures are still the greatest in the world. The greatest! The most expensive! With the most fantastic stars in the universe," he protested.

Dave didn't answer. H.P. sat in his chair rocking back and forth slowly. Dave thought, He reminds me of my grandfather on the day my uncle died. An old Jew, beset by the injustices of God, who had no recourse but to weep inwardly and rock back and forth in the time-honored gesture of despair. So it was with H. P. Koenig. This morning ruler of the greatest empire in all of show business, tonight suddenly deposed and bereft of his power. He sat like what he was, an old Jew in despair. And he rocked back and forth.

However, H. P. Koenig was not a man to give in to despair without protest. Too many times he had been able to remake history and redeem his own errors. If a film did not turn out as was expected, one could always take it back and reshoot a scene, two scenes, a dozen scenes, even an entire picture. No film had to remain wrong. Everything could be improved, rewritten, reshot. He could cut this bitter scene out of the film. He could have it rewritten. There had never been a call from Dave Cole. He had never come back from Dallas. He had never been met at the airport. Never told. There had never been a meeting in New York. His Sybil had never thrown her stock against him in the crucial vote. He would recast her part. No. Better still, he would cut her out of his picture! She had never existed! He stopped rocking. He began to wash his large and powerful hands in a motion of anticipation, not despair.

"Who's the sonofabitch?" he asked hoarsely.

Then he stared up at his gallery of stars. "It doesn't matter. Whoever he is, he can't control them. Nobody can control them. Except me! I picked every one of them like a royal jeweler assembles gems for a crown. Each one picked for its special color and fire and brilliance. I developed them! I made them! I'm the only one who can control them!"

"H.P., part of the new plan is to let them go."

"Let them go? Are you crazy? No one can let them go!" H.P. bellowed. He rose from his chair and paced the length of the room.

"They figured it out," Dave said. "Just the stars up on that wall are costing over nine million dollars a year, whether they make a picture or not. The industry can't stand that anymore."

"Can't stand it," H.P. scoffed. "Without stars, pictures are shit! Tell that to the bankers. And to anyone who would have the nerve to try to follow me."

After his explosion, he turned to Dave, a smile crossing his face. An impish, mischievous smile. He burst into laughter.

"Imagine," he said, but his own laughter prevented him from going on. He laughed till he was breathless. He recovered slowly, holding his sides in pain. "Imagine anyone trying to replace me. Funny? Funny!" he asked and answered his own question.

"Who? An independent like Selznick? *He* can't run a studio! Or that young jerk over at Warners. What's his name? Wald! Yeah, Wald. Why, that sonofabitch couldn't even shine my shoes."

He turned on Dave. "Who? Name me one man who could take my place! Who could keep all this together! Who could make it work! Who could manipulate those miserable bastards up on that wall! Make them work when they didn't feel like it. Make them do parts they didn't want to do. Name one man in all the world who could do that? One man!"

He didn't wait for an answer to what was to him a rhetorical question, impossible of any answer. Instead he kept pacing and speaking, incessantly, as if to purge himself of all thoughts, suspicions and hatreds. He spoke disconnectedly, assailing whoever crossed his mind.

"Sybil!" he suddenly remembered. "I can't believe it. Her mother, maybe. But Sybil? After all I've done for her? Lavished on her? Is that what they teach them in those colleges back East?"

He turned to Dave. "California colleges weren't good enough for her. She had to go East. She wasn't the same once she came back. But to stab her father in the back . . ."

He was done with Sybil, and his agitated mind suddenly picked up. "I want a total reorganization of this studio! I want to get rid of all the traitors who keep spying on me and reporting to the bankers in New York!"

He turned and slipped into a chair, exhausted, but still supreme in his own mind, reassuring himself, "Never! They'll never find anyone to take my place!"

Dave rose from his chair and stood over H.P.

"H.P., they've already picked the man."

H.P. laughed, then asked, smirking, "Who?"

"They picked a younger man. They say we're living in a new time. They want new, fresh ideas."

"They might as well bring in a new man to tell Edison how to invent the electric light!"

"They *are* bringing in a new man," Dave persisted. "*Me.*"

H.P. looked up, stunned. Then he smiled. His smile gave way to laughter, an easy, friendly laughter that had not the slightest trace of hostility.

"Now for the first time it makes sense. Of course!" H.P. said.

He rose jauntily. The color returned to his face as if he had been reassured, not displaced. He was a man in control again. No need to threaten now. No need to lash out venomously.

"They need a new face up front. A fish to throw to the stockholders and the bankers. On the surface it looks like a change of administration. But behind the scenes the same strong hand at the controls."

"H.P., you don't understand."

"Of course I understand! They want the best of both possible worlds. A new face but the old control! The iron fist. The only way to run a studio. The only way!"

Dave reached out and seized H.P. by the arm. "Damn it! Sit down!" He shoved the old man rudely into the nearest chair. "Now listen to me. It's over! Finished! You are no longer head of this studio. Magna has passed into other hands. There will be a new board of directors. A new executive committee. And a new head of the studio. *Me!*"

"Dave . . . Dave . . . no need to raise your voice. You want to look like the boss? Okay, I can understand a young man on the way up wants to sit in the boss's chair, wants to know how it feels. Who cares?

"The important thing is to keep things running the way they were. I have plans, Dave. Great plans. I've been out there listening to the exhibitors. I know the kind of pictures they want. Blockbusters! Big-screen, big-budget pictures that they can't get

330

on television. And we can give it to them, Dave. Together, you and I can give it to them.

"Sure, we've had our differences in the past. Who hasn't? And that thing with Sybil? Not your fault. Hers! I've been with you all the way, Dave. You know that. Don't ever forget who it was gave you the money to finish *Via Dolorosa*! Me! H. P. Koenig!"

He began to plot and plan with his old animal shrewdness.

"I'll tell you what we do, Dave. We'll let those bastard bankers think they have won a complete victory. I won't even come to the studio. We'll meet at the house. We'll make our plans there and you can carry them out here. You'll take all the credit; I don't need credit. After all, when you say motion pictures you mean Koenig. And when you say Koenig you mean motion pictures. The world over they know that! So if there's one thing I don't need, it's glory. I'm trying to save this studio, Dave. Don't you see that? And the only two people who can do that are you and me. You and me, Dave. We'll be like Marvin Kronheim and me, in the early days, when we first started this studio.

"All through the years I've searched for someone to take his place. Remember the first day when you came into this office, a young man who didn't know anything about pictures. Remember, you sat in that chair there and I said to you, 'I am looking for a new Marvin Kronheim.' Well, now it's happened. A new team. We'll take this studio to the top again!" he exclaimed.

When Dave didn't answer, H.P. faltered for the first time. "We will. Won't we, Dave? Won't we?"

"H.P., they want a whole new administration. The old way is gone, done. They can't afford it anymore. No studio can. It's over. And there's nothing I can do about it, except try to hold the pieces together. They made it very clear that one of those pieces can't be you."

H.P. stared.

"I asked for the chance to tell you myself. I thought maybe it would hurt less that way."

"Hurt less . . ." H.P. remarked in a strange, distant way. "Amputate without even an anesthetic. And you thought it would hurt less that way."

"I'm sorry," Dave said gently.

H.P. didn't even seem to hear. He rose from his chair and crossed the room slowly, tiredly. He went from one portrait to

331

another, reaching up to touch each one, rubbing his fingers over the costly carved frames and standing on tiptoe to touch the rough-textured oil.

At John Gilbert's portrait he paused a longer time. "They call me all kinds of names. But when he was down, done, finished, I didn't try to break his contract. I paid him ten thousand dollars a week for three years. While he drank himself to death. They don't remember those things."

He continued from portrait to portrait, touching each, like a father blessing his children. He looked at the strange wan beauty of one slender woman, whose loveliness seemed focused in her eyes.

"I was in Paris. I heard about this girl. That's all she was, a girl. I went to see her in Stockholm in a theater. She was no beauty. But she was magic. Like I remember once when I was a little boy and my father took us to see Sarah Bernhardt in vaudeville.

"That's when I first knew what greatness was. Years later, when I saw this girl in Stockholm, I felt the same kind of magic. I asked her, 'How much do you make here?' When she told me, I said, 'I will give you ten times more.' She didn't believe me. She called in her producer. He had to vouch for me. But by the time that night was over, she was mine. The greatest star who ever was in pictures, and she was mine. I always treated her like a lady. When I put a hand on her she trembled like a frightened bird. Did you ever try to take a canary out of its cage? You feel its poor heart beating like it would burst. That's the way she was when you touched her. So I never even asked her to go to bed with me."

He passed on to the next portrait, and the next, stopping, reaching, touching, commenting. For some he had praise, for others condemnation. He ticked off each one, grading them for talent and gratitude, or lack of it.

When he had reviewed his entire galaxy, he came to the huge desk from behind which he had ruled the destinies of thousands of talented and near-talented human beings. He said nothing, but it was obvious in his gesture that he was bidding it farewell. He turned to confront Dave.

"You really mean . . ."

Dave nodded.

"I never thought they could . . . All that stock . . . the voting power . . ." Suddenly he asked, "That bastard Sullavan—Dan Sullavan—he had a hand in this. He engineered this whole thing. Didn't he?"

"Does it matter now?" Dave asked.

"An Irish kid off the street. He was my gopher. He used to go for coffee for me. And hot corned-beef sandwiches from the Rialto. One time he even asked for butter. Can you imagine anyone stupid enough to put butter on a hot-corned-beef sandwich? And now he's head of the whole Nationwide chain! A dumb Irish kid!"

He turned to Dave. "You know something, Dave? Never trust a *goy*. Even the best of them."

Dave stared back at this man who had been an intimate of churchmen of all denominations and a close friend of cardinals.

27

It was four o'clock in the morning. H. P. Koenig sat in the study of his palatial home, staring out at the spacious grounds. Lights discreetly placed at the base of huge trees glowed in the night. The swimming pool was lit from beneath, sending up a diffused blue light. Over it hovered a cloud of mist where the warmth of the water mingled with the cool night air. It was as unreal as a movie set.

H.P. was aware of none of that. His wily, desperate mind frantically pursued only one objective. To regain his power and prestige, to revenge himself on those who had plotted his downfall.

The more his tormented mind worked at it, the more clearly Dave emerged as the villain. When he put the pieces together they fitted. They fitted with a Machiavellian cleverness. Why had Nationwide bid on only one Magna film, and that one Dave Cole's? And Cole and his Sybil. Had that dirty bastard ever had marriage in mind? No. He had only wanted to get control of her stock. To make her vote against her own father so he could take over. That sonofabitch, that dirty bastard Dave Cole!

Five o'clock in the morning California time, eight o'clock New York time, H. P. Koenig made up his mind. He reached for the phone and placed a call.

In New York City, in the kitchen of his large Fifth Avenue apartment, Raymond Currier, attorney and partner in the firm of Davis, Currier, Ward and Wiswell, was having breakfast. Whenever his phone rang at such an early hour, his first thought was that one of his valued elderly clients had died during the night. There would be the usual details to attend to. And the consequent fat fees involved in settling the estate and administering the many trusts Currier advised his clients to set up. He was not prepared for the shout that came at him from three thousand miles away.

"Ray! That you? Answer me!" By that time Raymond Currier had recognized the voice.

"Yes, H.P., it's me."

"Good! I got to talk to you."

"Well, I won't be in the office till nine-thirty. Meet me there."

"I'm in California! I want to talk to you now," H.P. insisted.

"Okay. Talk," Currier suggested calmly, making a note on the pad he always kept beside him. His firm had been one of the first to charge for telephone consultations. *Time of conversation: 8:14 to . . .*

"I want an order! A court order! To stop the stockholders from trying to throw me out! I have a contract with Magna, a lifetime contract! I want that contract honored or I want the studio closed down!"

Currier said calmly, "H.P., if they have a majority of the stock they have a right to remove you. About your contract, they may owe you the money, but they don't have any obligation to use your services. Besides, if you want action in California, why are you calling me?"

"Shmuck! Because it's too early to wake up a lawyer in California!" H.P. exploded.

Currier, though not Jewish, was aware of the anatomical nature of the epithet but chose to ignore it, bearing in mind the staggering fees that could be involved in any lawsuit with such emotional impetus behind it. "H.P., I'll call our California associates as soon as possible so we can join forces and agree on a strategy."

Not reassured, H.P. hesitated but finally conceded grumblingly, "I'll wait. But not too long!"

It was eight-thirty California time when H.P.'s phone rang.

335

James Brennan, of the firm of Brennan, Morse, Digby and Levine of Los Angeles, was calling. Currier had briefed Brennan well; he didn't waste time.

"Mr. Koenig, Jim Brennan. I just heard from Ray Currier. If they've got the proxies, I don't see what we can do. But we can get a show-cause order challenging the legality of the vote, or the way they secured their proxies. That would at least get us a stay."

"I don't want a stay. I want my studio back!"

"I'm afraid we can't promise anything like that without getting into the case more deeply."

"Damn it, Brennan, I want results! Not orders! Not delays! Results! And if you can't get them I'll find me a lawyer who can!" H.P. was shouting so loudly that both his wife and Sybil had come out of their bedrooms and stood outside the closed door of his study.

Brennan waited out H.P.'s tirade. "I promise you we'll take action before the day is out."

"Will you close down the studio?" H.P. demanded.

"I can't promise anything until we study the situation."

"That order you mentioned," H.P. asked, more calmly and with some calculation. "When that order is ready, can I serve it myself?"

Completely taken aback by such an odd request, Brennan said, "I've never seen it done before. But I don't think there's any rule against it."

"Okay! Get the order drawn up! I'll serve it myself," H.P. said.

"I'll contact you as soon as I get to my office," Brennan promised.

Twice within the next hour H.P. tried to reach Sonny Brown. For the first time since Brown had become head of publicity and public relations, he was not available to H. P. Koenig on the phone.

Ever since his first conversation with Currier, H.P. had been scrawling on his message pad the names of those bastards he would fire as soon as he regained control of Magna. The first name on the list was Dave Cole, of course. Then there was Larry Holtzman. And all the others with whom he had disagreed at any time in the past. Now he added the name of Sonny Brown. A clean sweep. That was what he promised himself. Even that brassy-voiced bleached-blond storyteller. Come to think of it, didn't she have a husband who was a producer at Warners? How was H.P. to know that she didn't siphon off the best material and tell H.P. only those stories that her husband had rejected?

By nine-thirty he had compiled a list so long and comprehensive that virtually no one of consequence except his beloved possessions, his stars, was exempt.

It was close to noon when Brennan called back. The order had been prepared. One of his associates was on the way downtown to get it signed by a judge. Which judge? H.P. demanded. Brennan supplied the name.

"Okay!" H.P. said. He hung up. He searched the Los Angeles phone book for the courthouse number. He called the judge's chambers and insisted on talking to the judge in person. The fact that the judge was on the bench did not deter him. He insisted that the clerk get the judge off the bench. When the clerk refused, H.P. threatened to expose certain facts he knew. The clerk obeyed immediately. The breathless judge came to the phone. H.P. did not give him any opportunity to talk. "Judge, there is a show-cause order being delivered to you this morning from Jim Brennan's office. I want that order signed! Right away! I need it by noontime. Understood?"

When the attorney from Brennan's office arrived, the judge made a cursory pretense at reading the order and signed it. It said that Magna Studios and David Cole had to appear in court within five days and show cause why the decision to terminate H.P.'s contract and his presidency of Magna Studios should not be declared null and void.

Once the order was signed, H.P. called Bingerman at *Variety* and Schloss of *The Hollywood Reporter*. He told them to be at the main gate of Magna Studios at twelve noon. Despite Jim Brennan's reluctance, H. P. Koenig was determined to serve the order himself.

Bingerman called Sonny Brown at once. By the time H.P.'s limousine pulled up before the main gate of Magna Studios, armed guards were ready to prevent his entrance. Bingerman and Schloss were both there, as well as some of the wire services and a host of photographers.

Dave Cole was unaware of the events taking place out on the

street. For he had convened a meeting of all producers and directors. He announced the news of H.P.'s resignation as simply as he could. His purpose in this meeting was to dispel all rumors. Yes, the studio was in trouble. No, their pictures had not met with the reception that H.P. had hoped for. Possibly there was a reverse plot afoot, on the part of the exhibitors and theater chains, to even the score piled up during many years that H.P. had taken advantage of them.

"The main thing," Dave continued, "is that we have a huge plant here, with the best facilities and the greatest roster of stars in the world. Those things are assets. Or they are liabilities, depending on how we use them. We can no longer afford to waste money. There isn't any money to waste. Merely to pay the interest on our bank loans will cost more than two million dollars a year.

"So we are in a bind. Producers will no longer be able to afford the luxury of having two and three writers writing behind one another. You will pick a writer you have confidence in and go with him. If he fails, you fail. The same with directors. You can't keep shooting footage from all conceivable angles and then figure that somehow you'll put it all together in the cutting room."

He was interrupted by loud noises from outside the Kronheim Building. Dave and all the men rushed to the windows to look down toward the main gate.

Only one voice could be heard: the powerful, fiercely angry voice of H. P. Koenig shouting at the armed guards who blocked the studio gate. Locked out, H.P. was brandishing a blue-backed court order. He was surrounded and questioned and photographed by more than thirty newsmen and photographers. He directed his attention not to his questioners but to the guards who refused him entrance to the studio that until yesterday had been his own private domain. Lurking behind the closed and locked gates was Sonny Brown, giving orders and stiffening the resistance of the guards, who had been forced to make a sudden reversal from anticipating every wish of H.P. to denying him entrance in spite of his shrill and insistent demands.

Crowds were gathering inside the locked studio gates. Actors in costume and makeup, technicians, cutters, grips, recording engineers, they numbered almost a thousand. The word had spread through the stages, the labs and the cutting rooms. Everyone had got here to witness a spectacle unprecedented in the history of Hollywood. Mostly they had come to gloat. There was hardly one of them who hadn't endured some personal humiliation or insult from H.P.

Watching from the top floor of the Kronheim Building, Dave Cole threw open a window. For the first time he could hear distinctly what it was that H.P. was so frenziedly demanding. He was insisting on seeing David Cole so that he could serve the judge's order on him. The more adamant the guards remained, the more vitriolic H.P. became.

"I want to see that crooked, conniving bastard who stole my studio! The judge says so! See? It's in this order signed by the judge himself!"

H.P. brandished the order in the faces of the newsmen. Bingerman was able to seize H.P.'s frenetic hand long enough to glance at the order and verify that it was indeed signed. But that deterred H.P. for only an instant.

"That crooked sonofabitch is going to destroy my studio. It will become a desert again. I made this studio and I'm the only one who can save it. But they snipe at me behind my back. Connive against me. That dirty bastard up there is trying to ruin me! And you! He's going to cost all of you your jobs."

"He's crazy," one of the producers said, leaning far out of the window to get a better view of a sight he had long secretly fantasized.

"Shut up!" Dave said, sickened by the spectacle.

From below, H.P.'s voice rang out: "That bastard! He even tried to fuck my daughter to get at me. That's right! From the start, from his first day, he was aiming for my job. And I treated him like a son. I welcomed him. Like in that picture, I took him into my arms like Jacob greeting Joseph after all those years. And he does that to my daughter."

One of the directors standing at the window laughed and said, "He's never forgotten a single scene from a Magna film. Whether it made money or not."

Others joined in the laughter, till Dave exploded: "Damn it, shut up! All of you!" He started from the room.

He didn't wait for the elevator but bolted down the stairs. He burst into the downstairs waiting room and was halfway through it when the uniformed guard intercepted him long enough to say, "Don't go out there, Mr. Cole. He'll serve you with that paper."

Dave broke free, raced down the steps of the Kronheim Building. He had to fight his way through the crowd of newsmen to reach H.P., who was in the midst of his harangue.

"That dirty sonofabitch—" H.P. was proclaiming when he realized suddenly that he was face to face with Dave Cole. Dave knew he would never again see such hatred in the eyes of any man. H.P.'s lips twitched and moved, but they were silent. Suddenly he reached out. He seized Dave by the lapels of his jacket so hard that he ripped them halfway down the front. Dave didn't fight back, only seized the frenzied man's wrists and held him, overpowering him finally. H.P. surrendered, breathing hard, sweating, making small sounds that were partly whimpers, partly unarticulated protests.

When the old man had calmed down, Dave turned to the crowd behind the gate. "Get back to your work! All of you! I said, get back to your jobs!"

Slowly they began to drift away from the gate. Once they had started down the studio street, Dave turned to the guards.

"Open those gates!"

The guards looked to Sonny, from whom they had been taking their orders. He nodded. The guards unlocked the gates and opened them.

Dave turned to the newsmen. "Gentlemen, Mr. Koenig came here to serve a legal order. It was a serious misunderstanding on our part that he was shut out." He looked down at H.P. "If you want to serve it out here, okay. If you want to serve it in there, okay. It's up to you."

H.P. hesitated, stared at the gates that had once been his protection and had now become his enemy. He handed the legal document to Dave, then turned away. Dave watched the old man walk slowly but regally down the short street to where his car waited.

Once H.P. had entered his limousine, the newsmen besieged Dave. They pressed him with questions, they asked for denials of H.P.'s charges, about the plotting and planning, about his relationship with Sybil.

Dave refused them all with a simple "No comment." He started back into the Kronheim Building. He entered the waiting room outside H.P.'s huge suite of offices. They were already waiting. Vic Martoni and half a dozen other agents. Two of Magna's top stars. Three of the producers who had been at his meeting and come away disgruntled.

The same receptionist sat behind her large desk, barricaded by her phones and her intercom. Her first instinct, dictated purely by habit, was to rise in protest when Dave approached the door to the private suite. Then she realized that it was his suite now, and smiled sweetly.

Dave entered the office. He could remember how awed he had felt that first time. Today it felt even more awesome. It was too huge for one man, even a man like H. P. Koenig. Dave stared up at the gallery of H.P.'s stars. They looked down at him, their beckoning smiles in place, their beauty and handsomeness indelibly fixed in time. As long as they hung there they would always be young. Always in their prime.

He found that he was assessing what each one of them cost the studio per week, even if they didn't work. It had already begun to weigh on him. He reminded himself, Don't think like a bookkeeper, think like a producer. But he knew that inevitably the bankers would think like bankers and the bookkeepers like bookkeepers. If he could serve any purpose here, it would be to hold this empire together on some realistic basis. So that other men could go on making good pictures. He would make it a place where young, fresh minds could still aspire to come, to whom it would still be considered the pinnacle of success. Without the money with which to lure them, quality would have to be the bait. He determined to try that, for as long as they would let him.

The phone chimed. He answered it. It was Sarah's voice. He must see that she was retired immediately. He wanted no reminders of the old tyranny. No more spies. No more unsettling undercurrents that had constantly pervaded Magna. He must remember to have the hidden mikes removed from the stages. And to let them all know about it. He would read all new plays and novels himself. If it grew to be too much, he would have them summarized and would read the summaries. He did not need any blonded, brass-balled Scheherazade to regale him with stories.

He took the call. It was a warm and familiar voice.

"Lochinvar?"

"Albert! How are you? What are you doing?"

"Let me be among the first thousand to congratulate you, Dave," Grobe said, his voice sounding stronger than it had the last time. "How does it feel to sit in the seat of power, on the right hand of God, and know there is no God? Ha?"

"It's a little scary," Dave admitted. "Especially once you've talked with the bankers, looked at the balance sheet and the weekly overhead."

"It's no fun," Grobe said. "Whatever they said about him, it was not easy."

"Listen, Albert, I want you to come back."

Grobe laughed. "A nice impulsive offer, Dave. Certainly if anyone called *me* under your circumstances the first thing I would suspect is that he wants a job. There are going to be a lot of those calls in the next few weeks. The whole world will be trying to sell you something. Don't let them overwhelm you. Only do what you think is good."

"I need good advice, honest advice. Albert, come back," Dave urged.

"Come back? Do you know what I'd have to give up here to come back? First, I would not be able to get my Ph.D. in Literature of the Cinema. How's that for a high-sounding name for some of the crap we used to turn out?" Grobe laughed again. It was the laughter of a free man.

"Second, I will be teaching here in the desert. There is a new college here. I'll teach Creative Writing. To young people. Nice young girls. Some of them as pretty as your starlets. And as well stacked. Every so often, if I take a special interest in one of them, there'll be no big to-do about it. Somehow in a place given over to vacationing, people are more tolerant. So I'll be having one hell of a time."

Grobe chuckled. Dave laughed along with him. Until the older man said, "Dave, I'm only kidding about the girls. I'll teach. I'll enjoy it. And when I do have a little to do with a woman, she'll be a little more mature. The young girls are a thing of the past." He sighed sadly. "Ah, but while it lasted . . . while it lasted. . . ."

"So you won't come back?"

342

"Never!" Grobe said. "I've had it. All I want is peace and quiet. A chance to do a little work on my own. And maybe, if I'm lucky, discover some new talent and give it a push along the road to publication or production. That'll be enough for me from now on."

"Okay," Dave conceded finally. "Thanks for calling, Albert. It was very thoughtful."

"Dave . . ." Grobe said softly and more meaningfully. "Dave, if it gets to be too much, take a day off and come down here. I'd love to see you again."

"Thanks."

"Dave, what about Sybil? What's this going to do to the two of you?"

"I don't know," Dave admitted. "But I'm going to find out."

Dave hung up. They were waiting out there. He would begin seeing them just as soon as he made one call. He placed the call himself.

"Miss Sybil," he asked of the butler.

"Yes, Mr. Cole," he responded at once. Dave realized that till now the butler had not deigned to call him by name. In Hollywood, even domestics were responsive to studio politics and the shifts and changes in power. Sybil came to the phone. She sounded both guarded and distressed.

"Dave. What happened?"

"I'm here. In his office. And if I sound strange, it's because it doesn't fit yet."

"No, I meant what happened to *him*?" He came home pale, like a very sick man. He went straight to his room and he refuses to see anyone. Not even Dr. Prinz. He'll only talk to lawyers."

Dave related the events at the gate. She listened, not saying a word.

"Now, I guess, it's in the hands of the courts," he concluded.

"Yes, I guess it is."

"I want to see you tonight, but I can't. There's so much I have to catch up on. I have to get a report from every producer on what he's doing, to decide which projects continue and which get cut off. I've got them scheduled every two hours till midnight. Then I have a pile of scripts to take back to the bungalow and read."

"I understand," she said. "Call me, though. I need to hear your voice from time to time."

Before he could reassure her, she hung up. He would have to meet his visitors now, one by one. He pressed down the intercom button to the receptionist.

"Please send them in in the order in which they arrived," he told her. "And tell the others I'll try to be as punctual as I can. There'll be no unnecessary waiting around from now on."

He settled back in the luxurious red leather chair. The door opened. It was Vic Martoni.

As Vic entered the room, Dave was aware of his fragrant perfume. He wondered if he actually did smell it, or whether it was a Pavlovian conditioned reflex. Martoni—perfume. Martoni—silk shirts. Martoni—cashmere suits. Martoni—starlets.

Confident, smiling, Martoni slipped into a chair.

"Well, kid, you did it! I won't say that we didn't put a little behind-the-scenes muscle into it. But you did it. By the way, we've started to negotiate your new deal. One of the things you overlooked. You made a mistake. You said yes a little too fast. You should have spoken to us first."

"Under the circumstances, I thought action was more important than a long negotiation."

"Shrewd!" Martoni corrected himself swiftly. "Get entrenched. Let the negotiation drag on till you're so solid that they can't say no to anything we demand."

Dave merely nodded, waiting out the triumphant agent.

"Another thing, kid . . ." Martoni laughed again. "Here I am still calling you 'kid.' What would you like me to call you? Boss? Dave? Mr. Cole? D.C.? Like in Washington, D.C.? Name it!"

"Dave is okay."

"Fine! *Dave!* First thing, Dave, let an old-timer give you some advice. You don't mind, do you?"

"No," Dave said coolly.

"Don't be Mister Nice Guy. You don't run an army by winning popularity contests. The old bastard knew that. That was his strength. Keep them waiting out there. Let them earn their way in here. Make them so happy to be allowed in that they'll say yes to anything you suggest. If the word gets around that you're soft, it'll make a tough job even tougher.

"Of course, the old bastard was a little *too* tough. Sometimes

I think the only real fun he got out of life was making other people sweat. The rough times he used to give me!" Martoni lamented.

"I had to play gin with the sonofabitch and lose every time. The scrapes I got him out of. Things that even Sonny Brown couldn't handle.

"You don't know what it's been like for me, Dave. Having to play along with him in order to protect my clients. But that's an agent's job, I guess. Clients first, himself last, every time."

"I know how it is," Dave said.

"It'll be nice to be dealing with a real gentleman. It's like being let out of jail. He used to run everyone's life. He'd call me at any hour of day or night and want some cunt. And it had to be right then. He wouldn't wait. You know what I think? I think he has this fear that if he ever stops screwing he'll die. It's an obsession. Well, let him get his own cunt now. Thank God, that's over," Martoni said self-righteously.

Fearing he had blundered into a mistake, he amended quickly, "Of course, that doesn't go for you, Dave. I know you're not going to be unreasonable like he was. But a man is still a man. He's not made of wood, like the old Jewish joke goes," Martoni said, seeking to establish some ethnic contact with Dave. "Anytime you want a little something, just let Vic know. I'll get you the best. The youngest and the best." Martoni smiled reassuringly. "Just say the word. . . ." Martoni left the offer hanging in midair, waiting for it to be accepted.

Dave stared back at Martoni till the latter's smile slowly faded from his dark, well-shaven face.

"Look, Martoni, or shall I call you Vic? After all, things have changed. Whatever you want me to call you, just let me know. And I will."

"Vic is okay, like in the old times," Martoni said, alert and suspicious now.

"Okay, *Vic.*" Dave tried it out just as Martoni had done before. "Now, Vic, you listen to me. From now on there is going to be no blackmail on this lot. Other agents are not going to have to pay you off to be able to make deals here. I am going to buy *talent,* not *contacts.* And as for girls, if I want a woman I'll go out and get my own woman. We are making pictures here, not running a whorehouse. Understood?"

345

Martoni, whose face was normally dark, became ashen gray. But he managed to nod.

"And one other thing," Dave said. "From now on, stay off this lot. *You are barred!*"

"But I represent—" Martoni started to say.

"You represent a hell of a lot of talent. Some of it good, most of it bad. You were able to sell it to the old man because you're a pimp. Well, there is going to be no more pimping around here. If you want me to, I'll hang a sign on the front gate announcing that. Otherwise you can save both of us a lot of trouble by staying clear of this studio! Any negotiating we have to do we can do by phone."

Martoni was slow to rise. Stunned, he turned and started out. When he walked through the waiting room, it was obvious to everyone that an event of startling consequence had taken place inside the inner sanctum.

The era of change had begun.

It was late that same afternoon. Dave had had a long and wearing day listening to and arguing with producers who had various projects in different stages of development. He had had to turn down requests and suggestions from men whom he liked and from older men he respected, like Larry Holtzman. He could see in their eyes the resentment, and the underlying feeling each of them nurtured that he could do the job far better than Dave. But it was the kind of resentment that went with the job. All he could do to diminish it was act fairly and exercise his judgment, not his vanity. But it was exhausting work. It had left him drained.

The waiting room was finally empty. He dismissed the receptionist for the day and told his new secretary she could go, once she made sure there were no unreturned phone calls, no messages from producers and directors that had not been attended to. As much as possible he would save these talented men time and humiliation.

There was nothing left to do now but gather up the scripts he intended to read tonight. There were three scripts in final draft, on which shooting was to begin next week. He had to read those. And there were four others that were questionable and which the producers had prevailed on him to read again before finally making up his mind. In all, the seven scripts represented an outlay of thousands of hours of talented time and more than two million dollars' worth of Magna money. If they all went into production it would amount to fifteen million dollars, probably nearer to twenty million. He wondered, how many years ago had it been that he was earning nineteen-fifty a week slapping hot frankfurters into doughy buns at Nedick's?

He had gathered up his scripts and made a note for himself about things he wanted to accomplish first thing in the morning when he heard his door ease open cautiously. He looked up.

It was Betty Ronson. He was surprised at first. Startled, as if his momentary memory of the old days at Nedick's had summoned her up. But there was a vast difference in her now. She was no longer shy, no longer dressed in the undistinguished manner of those days. Now her clothes were understated, but richly affirmative. Her glasses were no longer plain but seemed to have been fashioned by some expert jeweler. And she carried herself with authority. If she couldn't compete with stars on the basis of beauty, she dominated them by virtue of her will and her brain. Where she had once been soft and wispy, she was now hard and wily. And there had been talk of late that she was going steady with a rising young star who was eight years younger than she, but whose career had taken on great momentum once he became her lover.

"I waited till I knew we could be alone," she began. Then she held out her hand. "Congratulations, Dave!"

"Thanks," he said. "Come in, Betty. Sit down."

She made herself at ease, digging into her purse to come up with a cigarette and gold lighter. She inhaled deeply, then exhaled slowly, letting the smoke trail from her nostrils and her lips. He remembered how he had once kissed those lips and found them soft and warm.

"Vic finally got back to the office," she said.

"Did he tell you?"

"Once the shock wore off."

"Sorry. But it had to be that way," he apologized.

"Of course," she agreed heartily, much to his surprise. "I've been waiting for this. It clears the decks. That sonofabitch!"

"But you're partners."

"On some things."

"I don't understand," Dave said.

"I've been anticipating a change like this. So I put off re-signing our good clients until I could get free of him and go out on my own. I'm taking all the best ones with me. So Dave, from now on you only have to deal with me."

She smiled confidently and triumphantly.

"Teddy Fletcher too?" he asked.

Her smile froze, then slowly began to fade.

"I know you didn't approve of the way that was handled," she countered, "but today he's the highest-paid Negro in show business. All I did was keep him from making a foolish mistake. Performers are like children. They have to be disciplined and cared for. Made to understand what's good for their careers and what's not. That's my job. And evidently I do it well. Goddamn well!"

"*Very* well," Dave agreed. "Too well for my taste."

"Dave?"

"Betty, what I said to Vic Martoni earlier wasn't only meant for him. It was meant for your whole agency. Collectively. And individually."

"You mean . . . me too? Barred?" she dared to ask.

"Yes," he said softly but firmly.

Her face became rigid, the smoke seemed to stop trailing from her lips. She stared at him, her eyes angry and hurt at the same time.

"Not me, Dave. You owe me more than that." She called him to account. "If it hadn't been for me you wouldn't be here. In this office. In that chair. You owe me, Dave. For too many things—for everything!"

"Don't try to whip me with guilt, Betty," he said. "That's a thing of the past. And don't try to play for gratitude. Or make claims on me. Whatever you did for me you did for yourself as well. Right down to getting the word to Dan Sullavan through Vic Martoni after I asked you not to. You had it all figured out. 'If Dave gets to be head of the studio and I can get rid of Martoni, I'll have it all my own way at Magna. And I'll be the most powerful woman in Hollywood.'

"Maybe. But not with my help. I'm buying talent here. Not favors, fear, guilt or blackmail. What happened in a hotel up in

348

Boston happened. Long ago. And I'm not going to let you use that against me for the rest of my life. If you have any clients you think I ought to consider, call me. I'll never duck your calls. If we have to negotiate, my phone will always be available to you. But I have to let this town know that from now on we have an open door here. We're looking for talent, not bribes. We welcome agents here, not procurers. And no one has a hold over the head of the studio because of past obligations.

"Clear?" he concluded.

She didn't answer at once. Then she said venomously, "You sonofabitch!"

"Thanks," he said. "Now I know I must have done something right."

She turned and stalked out of the room. That part of his past was over, once and for all.

28

Two groups of lawyers faced each other in Judge Brophy's courtroom.

Just before the case was called, H. P. Koenig entered. Grim, pale, he strode down the aisle and took his place at the counsel table. He had come to oversee the argument that would determine his fate. H.P. glanced up at the bench and gave a nod of recognition to Judge Brophy.

The legal arguments began. Each lawyer cited the precedents that supported his own position and disparaged those that did not. From time to time Judge Brophy interrupted with questions, to which the lawyers had glib and ready answers. Just before noon, both sides rested their cases. Judge Brophy promised a swift decision in view of the importance of the matter and the urgency of time.

There were reporters and photographers waiting outside the courtroom when they broke for lunch. Against the advice of his attorneys, H. P. Koenig stopped on the courtroom steps to deliver a statement.

"I have the utmost confidence in the courts. They'll throw out the crooks and the connivers and give my studio back to me! You wait and see!"

He permitted himself to be photographed at length before he

continued down the steps to where his limousine was waiting. He got in, waved good-bye to the newsmen as the car drove off. Once they were out of sight of the courthouse, he ordered the chauffeur to turn the car around and head west. He couldn't go home. Home had never been a place where he felt comfortable during a business day. It was scarcely bearable at night, at dinnertime, when he felt he was fulfilling his duty as a good father.

He told his driver to head for the ocean. Since it was out of season for swimming, the Pacific beaches were deserted. H.P. walked along in the sand, staring out at the placid waters. They rose and fell, swelling, not breaking into waves. Some hundred yards out from the shore, great matted tangles of brown and green seaweed floated atop the water. Farther out, he could see a school of whales heading south in their annual pilgrimage.

He had wandered a long way from where he had left the car. Ahead on the beach he spied a lone figure. A girl. She was dressed in a tight white swimsuit that revealed a graceful but lush figure. She ran along the beach toward him, as if intoxicated with the feeling of the wind against her youthful body. She drew closer to him. He waved to her. She slowed down, thinking he was lost and seeking information. As she reached him, she recognized him.

"Mr. Koenig?" she asked, startled.

"Yes, my dear," he answered, flattered by the awe in her voice.

"Gee, what are you doing here?" She seemed breathless from running.

"Times a man needs to be alone. To walk. To think. Solitude. Very important."

"I know," she said, her blue eyes wide and staring, and she still spoke breathily.

He appraised her face, which was smooth and white, creamy soft.

"You live around here?"

"Up the beach," she said. She turned and extended her arm to point. It made her young breasts even more prominent.

"All by yourself?"

"I like solitude too," she said almost in a whisper.

"You're an actress?" She nodded. "Been out here long?"

"I was born here."

"Oh. Good," he said. "Could I see where you live? I'm a little tired. I'd like to rest."

Flattered, she said, "Sure. Come."

They walked along the beach, she on the outside so that the water washed up against her bare feet. It was cold, but she didn't mind. He kept trudging alongside her, his custom-made British boots gathering sand as he walked.

"Been in any pictures? I mean, speaking parts."

"One. Not very big. But my agent said it was a good thing to do, to get out of the extra class."

"Your agent?"

"Johnny Boone," she said proudly, impressed with her agent's importance.

"At the William Morris office."

"That's right," she said eagerly, glad that H.P. knew him.

He remembered that there had been gossip about Johnny Boone and his young blond protégée and mistress. He had been grooming her for stardom. This must be the girl. She was attractive and sexy. Though she did not seem too bright. On the way up, none of them seemed too bright. But once they achieved stardom they became shrewd as jungle cats, he reminded himself.

He needed her. He needed something to restore his faith in himself and his power. If he were back in the studio and feeling this way, he would have called down to one of the stages or got hold of Vic Martoni and had a girl sent up to him. For now, this girl would do. He could already sense the ambition in her. That was enough. It would be a great pleasure to spend the afternoon with her. He trudged along in the sand, a bit hard-pressed to keep up with her. But always aware of her delicious body and the desire that kept growing in him.

When they arrived at her modest bleached gray bungalow, he listened to her aimless chatter. She babbled on about numerology, about having an affair with one of Hollywood's leading astrologers. The man had drawn an intensive and complete chart for her, and he had assured her of eventual stardom. All the while she talked, H.P. kept staring at her young, inviting figure. The way her breasts seemed to blossom from her lean torso. The way the tops of them curved just above her swimsuit.

He reached for her shoulder strap and gently pulled it down. She seemed unaware and went on talking.

"But I don't know whether to believe him or not," she was saying. H.P. had to remind himself that she was still talking about the astrologer. "Because I found out that he had an affair with one of the boys down the beach. He'd drawn his horoscope. And said he would become a big star too. Anyone who's AC-DC like that, you don't know whether to believe him or not. Do you?"

The question took H.P. unaware, since he had now lowered her shoulder strap to where he could fondle her naked breast. It was firm as only the young are firm. The skin was soft and smooth. Her nipple began to swell until it was a rigid pleasing pink crest. He passed his fingers across it and felt them prickle. The desire in him was as strong as it had ever been.

She inquired quite earnestly, "Do you?"

"What, my dear?" he asked just before he took her nipple into his mouth.

"Can you believe someone who's AC-DC? I mean, if he could have an affair with me and at the same time with that nice boy down the beach. I mean, if he doesn't know what *he* is, how can he tell what's going to happen to *me*?"

It annoyed him that she seemed so unaware of what he was doing. Other starlets reacted when he wooed them. They writhed, wriggled and made sounds of delight. But this one seemed oblivious to him. She lent herself to him, yet she was distant and uninvolved. He tried to pretend it didn't matter. Still, it irked him. But he needed her body more than her co-operation. So he let her talk on, while he lowered her second strap and brought her suit down to her waist. She sat beside him, her magnificent body half naked, her knees folded beneath her. H.P. knew it would take a bit of deft maneuvering to ease her down to her back and strip her completely. But since she offered no resistance and he had had considerable experience gently maneuvering young girls into the position in which he preferred them, he knew it was a challenge he would overcome with ease.

Meantime, his groin was beginning to swell till it became painful. Desire declined in other men as they aged, but in him it seemed to grow stronger. There was a wisecrack that circulated about him of which he was vainly aware—that he would die with an erection, presenting the undertaker with a unique problem.

She was bubbling on, breathily, "People say that acting lessons are good for you. What do you think?"

He was pressing his face between her breasts now, holding them so that they cradled him.

"I mean, I went to this famous Russian star, I can't pronounce her name. But she runs this acting school. I went to her. She asked me to read for her. Then she said, 'Dollink, it would be a crime to teach you to oct. You are a notural gem. Stay de vay you are. Dun't bodder vith any lessons.' That's what she said. Do you think she's right?"

He was kissing her left breast and could barely make a sound of assent.

"It's so hard to know what to do," she said. "What do you think?"

"I think, my dear, that you are one of the loveliest creatures I have ever seen. And I have no doubt at all that you are going to be a great, great star. Because I will see to it myself."

As he said that, he gently eased her down. He leaned over her, staring down at her face and her nearly naked torso. It would be simple now to strip her completely. He kissed her on the throat. Then, as he worked his way down her body with his lips, he gradually stripped the suit from her till she was naked. Aside from the fact that she assisted him ever so slightly by lifting her hips, she seemed unaware of what he was doing.

"People tell you, I mean, lots of men have told me that I'm going to be a big star one day. But I keep wondering, how long does it take? So far the only one who's ever really done anything is Johnny. And he just got me one speaking part in one picture. He said it takes time. I mean, this one picture I was in, I got mentioned by several critics. But not because of my acting. Because of my body. It takes more than a body to be an actress. I mean, take Bette Davis, she's no raving beauty. But she's an actress, a real actress. And nobody talks about her body. So it can't be that. But Johnny says that's the way to get started.

"He says that's what you did with Gladys Holmes. She started out as a body and you made her into an actress. Didn't you?"

"What?" he asked, somewhat irritated now that he was forced to interrupt his lovemaking. With other girls, bent on pleasing

354

him, it was the reverse. *They* made love to *him*. All he had to do was lean back and it would happen. This girl seemed so unresponsive, he had to take all the initiative. Because she was so frustrating, he was more determined than ever to make it happen.

"You took her from a sex symbol and made her into an actress, didn't you?"

He didn't answer, for he was now spreading her white thighs and running his fingers gently over the silken hair. Soon he mounted her. She accepted him without protest, allowing him to slip into her. At the moment that he did, there was only the slightest interruption in her flow of conversation. She continued talking as he thrust himself into her and began the slow ritual of mating. She reacted only by pressing his face against her own while she continued to talk in a soft breathy whisper.

"More than anything, that's what I want. To be a star. To be known. To have people whisper about me when I come out of a theater. Or when they see me at an airport. Or in a store. I mean, it isn't the money. But just to be recognized. You wouldn't know, because you're famous now. But before, when you were young and unknown, did you ever walk along the street and inside you it was crying out, 'Somebody! Anybody! Recognize me! Speak to me! Speak about me! Somebody, please?' Didn't you ever feel . . ."

She was whispering those things into his ear as he was thrusting into her, seizing her firm young buttocks and trying to lose himself in her. Finally he reached his crescendo of exhilaration and spent himself in her in a burst of semen and relief.

At that moment she seemed to have reached an orgasm as well, for she gasped slightly between two words, and then continued, ". . . like that?"

He was breathing too hard to answer. He was content to lie upon her young body and recover from his enormous exertion. He rested within her, her moistness mingled with his own, and it felt good.

"I mean," she continued to whisper, "once you're famous you forget. But you must have felt like that once. Didn't you?"

"Like what?"

"Like wanting to be known, famous. I mean, it's like the story of Faust. You know the story of Faust, don't you?"

"Faust?" He struggled to remember. "Faust? Who was in that picture? It couldn't have been Ronald Colman, because we never made that picture."

"It's a famous classic," she said.

"If it's a classic we made it. And very authentic!" he insisted proudly, as if the studio were still his own.

"You're not bad," she said suddenly. "I mean, I've known men your age and they need a little help. You know what I mean? But not you. No wonder they call you the stallion of Magna. I don't mean that to sound wrong. I think it's something to be proud of. That a man retains his powers. That's what they call it in books. When a man can get it up at a late age. They always say, He retains his powers. Well, you sure have. You're better than that astrologer, and he can't be more than forty. Of course, in his case maybe he has trouble with girls. You know?"

H.P. didn't answer. He was exhausted and sleeping peacefully for the first time since he had been exiled from Magna.

When he woke, the room was nearly dark. He found he had been covered with a soft silk robe. A man's robe. He clutched at it, touched the upper breast pocket, felt the initials J.B. He was puzzled for the moment but then realized where he was. He was in that girl's beach house. J.B. must be Johnny Boone. Obviously Johnny kept a wardrobe here.

H.P. was aware suddenly that he was being stared at. He glanced across the room. She was sitting in a chair that was suspended by a chain from the bleached wood ceiling. She was dressed in a terry robe of crimson that set off her blond hair and her white face. The shade of her lipstick matched the crimson of her robe. She sat with one foot under her. With the other foot she gently caused the hanging wicker chair to swing back and forth. She looked very pensive in the gathering dusk.

"Can I get you a drink?"

"Yes," he said eagerly, his mouth dry from his long sleep. Besides, he needed a shot of booze to invigorate him. He must be more tired than he realized. The day in court, the strain of meeting the press, the girl, his need to have her, the energy he had expended in that pursuit. Yes, a drink would come in handy now. "Scotch and soda?" he asked.

356

"Johnny's brand. He has it imported specially for him by Jurgensen's. He says it's the best."

She made two drinks, then crossed the room and sat on the couch beside him. They touched glasses. He drank more swiftly than usual. The cold, strong, bubbly drink felt good going down. She sipped hers thoughtfully.

"They're looking for you," she said casually.

"Who?" he asked, rising up slightly from the couch.

"Everybody," she told him. "You're supposed to be lost. Or committed suicide."

"*Suicide!*" The very thought infuriated and offended him. "*Me?*"

"You left your car and chauffeur way down the beach. Said you were going for a walk and then never came back," she said. "So they thought something had happened to you. Or you'd done something to yourself. Johnny told me."

"Johnny?" he asked.

"After we . . ." She didn't quite know the proper word to use. "After you fell asleep. I called Johnny to tell him what happened."

Amazed, he asked, "You called Johnny and told him?"

"Oh, sure," she said quite innocently. "I always tell Johnny."

"You do?"

"We have a sort of agreement. Johnny says there are some men in this town that you have to, I mean, you have to play along with them. But Johnny said you can't just do it with anyone. I mean, you can't just get to be a tramp. You have to be choosy. Like only important directors. And heads of casting. But I must always tell Johnny so he can follow up. It helps if he knows."

H.P. drained his drink, then asked, "So you called him about me?"

"Yes," she said, a bit more tentative now.

"What did he say?" H.P. asked, staring and trying to find her blue eyes in the darkness.

"He said . . ." She hesitated. "I hope I won't hurt your feelings. I mean, I didn't say it, Johnny did. He said you were a waste of time now."

"Oh, did he?" H.P. demanded, rising up from the couch.

Fearing she had angered him, she tried to apologize. "I'm sorry. Maybe I shouldn't have told you. I didn't mind. Honest I didn't.

357

I mean, I would have, even if I already knew. You're such a nice man; so . . ." She reached for a word that she thought might serve. "So nice and pathetic."

"Where's the radio?" he demanded.

She went to it on bare feet and turned it on. It became the only light in the now-dark room. The evening news was on. The tail end of the item about himself was the first thing they heard.

". . . the search continues. The Malibu police say they will start dragging along the shoreline at dawn. Meanwhile the chauffeur insists he can supply no further clue to the disappearance of the former film magnate."

"'Former film magnate'!" he snorted. "Where's the phone?"

"At the end of the bar," she said.

He found it, dialed the operator and gave her his home number. When the operator suggested he dial it himself, he shouted so vehemently that she immediately dialed the number for him. The line was busy. He gave her the number of his private line. It finally answered. It was the butler.

"Foster!" H.P. bellowed. "Yes, it's me! And I'm alive. And what is all this shit about my being missing or committing suicide? Put Mrs. Koenig on the line!" In a few moments he heard her voice. "Rebecca! It's me! And I'm fine. So don't worry. I went for a walk to think things over. And I guess I just walked too far. But I'm okay. . . . Yes, I'll be home tonight. . . . No, don't tell anyone. I'll call myself." He hung up before she could answer him.

He lifted the phone again and gave the operator a second number.

"Lolly? . . . Oh, Marie. Put Louella on! . . . Who the hell do you think? H. P. Koenig, that's who!" He stared accusingly at the blond girl, as if in some way she were responsible for his predicament. "Lolly? . . . Sweetheart, I saved this for you. You can break the news to the world. It's only right. I owe you that much. H. P. Koenig is alive and well. . . . Where? I'm in a very compromising position in a very nice beach house near Malibu," he said, pretending shyness but laughing at the same time.

"Tell them that if the decision goes against me I will fight it to the Supreme Court! . . . Yes! Without H. P. Koenig there can be no Magna Studio! Quote me! . . . Right, darling. It's yours. Exclusive. . . . Of course you can trust me. Didn't I promise you the exclusive on the last Gable wedding and didn't I deliver?"

Thoughtfully, he drummed his fingers on the phone. He gave the operator another number. When she protested, he demanded, "What's your name? I'll have you fired! Do you understand? Fired!" Without protest the operator put the call through.

"Hedda? . . . Sweetheart! H.P.! I've got an exclusive for you. . . . Of course I'm okay, and any rumors that I've committed suicide are lousy, filthy lies put out by Dave Cole to try to give the impression that his hold on the studio is secure. Well, it's lies! All lies! . . . Yes, you damn well better quote me!"

He hung up, breathing rapidly, with a fury that had continued to mount from the first moment the girl had told him he was suspected of having done away with himself.

"Another one!" he ordered. When she didn't leap to his command because she didn't understand, he shouted impatiently, "Another drink!" She hastened to make it. He seemed to be soothed once he had the cold glass in his hand again.

Who else? he asked himself. Who else? Sonny Brown! He picked up the phone again, then remembered. The reflex action developed over the years in which he had had only to issue an order to Brown and it would be executed at any cost in money or morality—those days were over. It was Sonny Brown who had stood at the gate and barred him. H.P. set down the phone. He drew the robe about his body, took his drink in hand again and walked toward the deck that ran the length of the modest house. He opened the door and strode out to inhale the fresh salt sea air. He stared at the dark, heaving ocean. In the distance were the lights of a passing ship.

He became aware that the girl had come out onto the deck to stand beside him. She was breathing deeply, enjoying the night air.

"The mist'll be in soon," she said. "Some nights it's eerie. And when Johnny can't make it here, I get frightened."

"You don't have to be frightened anymore," he reassured her. "First thing, when I take back the studio I am going to make you a star!"

She didn't know whether to believe him, not after what Johnny had said. But when H.P. raised his arms to embrace her, she moved close to him. He pressed her against himself. She let him. He held her close, his aging flabby cheek against her firm young flesh. He touched her cheek gently, then kissed her. He pulled free the tie of her crimson terry robe. He parted it and held her young naked body close against his own. He was hard again and probing between her thighs. She gave way. He pressed in and rested there. He kissed her open mouth. He held her close.

She whispered into his ear. "I don't care what they say, I believe you."

That reassurance made him need her more. He had to have her, now, here. With his muscular arms he lifted her slightly and drew her legs around him. He rested her rounded bottom on the rail of the deck and attacked her with a fury that made her gasp.

She whispered into his ear during the entire assault.

"It's all right, isn't it? I mean, a young girl and an older man. There's nothing wrong with it, is there? Some people say it's Freudian. It's a girl wanting to have sex with her father. But I don't believe that. I never even knew my father. Why would I want to have sex with him?"

H.P. didn't answer; he was too deep in the throes of his own desire.

"That's the trouble with reading all those books," she went on, though now she was embracing him and drawing him into herself with his every thrust. "Maybe I shouldn't read so much. What do you think?" At that moment she gasped faintly in her orgasmic way but went on to ask, "Should I?"

He didn't answer but leaned against her and held on, for his legs seemed ready to give way beneath him. She held him close till he recovered.

"Better?" she whispered after a while.

"Yes, better. Only next time, darling, for God's sake, don't talk. Not *during*. Just shut up. And I'll make you a star," H. P. Koenig said.

At that moment he felt a tightening twinge in the center of his broad, hairy chest. He dismissed it as nothing serious.

360

29

Till the night of Johnny Boone's phone call, Dave Cole had had only slight contact with him. Thus, it was a surprise to Dave when his phone rang at a quarter to midnight and the voice identified itself as Johnny Boone. Dave had been flooded by calls from talent agents since the moment of his takeover. He had instructed his secretary that he would talk to no agents until he had made an appraisal of every project under development at Magna. Once he had evaluated which projects were going into production then all agents would be freely seen to discuss casting. Most agents respected that. The few that dared to call him at the Marmont were cut off at the switchboard. Johnny Boone's call was permitted only because he had insisted it was a life-and-death emergency. Dave's first reaction was one of hostile skepticism.

"Look, Boone, I'm busy. I've got six scripts to plow through tonight—"

"I didn't call you about business," Boone interrupted.

"What then?"

"The old man. He's sick. Very sick."

"What happened? Where is he?"

"This has to be handled very delicately," Boone warned.

"Okay! I'll handle it delicately," Dave said impatiently. "Now, what happened?"

"Get this address down," Boone said, ignoring his question, then recited an address on the Coast highway. "He needs a doctor. And an ambulance. And a lot of *no* publicity. Understand?"

"Okay, I'll be there."

"Hurry!" Boone said before he hung up.

Dave reached for his jacket, then realized fully what Boone had said. He phoned Dr. Prinz, but learned he was down at Palm Springs. He then dialed Sonny Brown's home number, arranged to pick him up, instructed him to hire an ambulance under strictest secrecy. The ambulance was in Brown's driveway by the time Dave arrived there. They rode in the back with a young doctor. Brown instructed the young doctor about the absolute need for secrecy.

"Nobody will ask you anything till later," he told the young man. "And by that time I'll give you a story that'll cover you. Meantime, you don't know anything but that you've been called in to take care of a sick man. Remember, you're a doctor. You've got a professional relationship with your patient. It entitles him to secrecy. Don't forget that. Because if you do, I'll report you to the County Medical Association."

Dave resented Sonny's threatening the young doctor, who was already tense enough. Brown must have sensed it, for he softened his tone when he said, "You abide by your ethics, and we'll see to it that you're not only well paid but taken care of in other ways."

Dave sighed hopelessly and leaned forward, staring intensely into the misty night, wondering how long it would take and would they get there in time. There was no more conversation, only the sound of their tires on the damp blacktop of the Coast highway. The driver kept his windshield wipers going, monotonously swishing back and forth, wiping the mist away to give the driver a decent view of the badly lit road ahead. Finally he slowed down to a stop before a dark, weather-beaten house along the ocean. It almost seemed as if there was no one home, but Johnny Boone's big black Cadillac convertible stood parked in the driveway.

Dave leaped out of the ambulance. The doctor and Sonny Brown followed. The ambulance driver stayed behind to put a tank of oxygen onto a rolling stretcher. Dave bounded up the steps onto the deck. The weathered planks creaked under his tread. He went around the back to the living room. The draperies were drawn, but there were lights on. He knocked on the glass patio door. Short, slim Johnny Boone, sometimes called The Jockey, pulled the door open.

"Where is he?"

Boone indicated the couch in the corner. Dave brushed past Boone. He noticed the blond girl who stood to one side, staring, her eyes fearful and wet from tears.

"It wasn't anything I did," she said, as if accused.

The doctor followed Dave closely and knelt down beside the couch. H. P. Koenig was unconscious. His breathing was irregular and shallow. His face was pale and sickly beneath the tan. The doctor tested hurriedly for vital signs. Pulse. Stethoscope to the heart and chest. Eyes. Then he swiftly prepared and administered an injection. By that time the ambulance driver had rolled the tank into the room. The doctor fitted the oxygen mask over the old man's face. The hissing of the oxygen being fed into the mask was the only sound in the room, except for the girl's gasping. She had been crying a long time, it seemed.

"I didn't do anything," she whispered to no one in particular.

Dave felt sorry for her. He led her away from the couch. "Let the doctor do his job," he said gently.

"I didn't do anything," she repeated breathily.

When Dave looked around he saw that Sonny Brown and Johnny Boone had stepped out onto the deck. They stood in the mist, deep in discussion. Dave slid the door open and stepped out in time to hear Boone say fiercely, "You involve that girl and I'll spill the whole story. I don't want that girl's name mentioned!"

"Okay, okay," Sonny said, as he always did to mollify angry adversaries. Reassure them first, but do what you decide is best for the studio later.

"Just remember what I said" was Johnny's last warning.

"Christ!" Dave exploded. "A man's sick. He may be dying. We can discuss this later."

"Dave . . ." Sonny gave a head signal that beckoned Dave aside to the far corner of the deck.

"Look, Dave, he *may* be dying. If he is, there is a whole tub of shit going to come out about this. And if he lives it could be even worse. We have to get him to a hospital. There'll be reporters and photographers. We have to have our story down pat. For

363

the sake of the studio. And now, you heard, for the girl's sake too. Johnny can blow the whistle on Magna a dozen different ways. We all have to play along. One hand washes the other. So let me handle it. Everything will be clean and dignified. And no one will ever know the truth," Brown said with great certainty.

By that time the girl was standing in the doorway. They turned to her. Johnny went to her and embraced her. It provoked a fresh burst of tears and protestations of innocence. Sonny Brown, always intent on knowing precisely what he was covering up, approached her as if he were an officer of the law.

"Okay, now, girlie, what happened?"

"She doesn't have to answer," Johnny protested.

"She'll answer me," Sonny insisted.

The girl began to blurt out the story—their innocent meeting, the events that took place after that, leading up to H.P.'s leaving.

"I heard him walk along the deck, and the next I knew there was this heavy sound. I ran out. He was lying there, face down." She pointed out the spot on the deck where H.P. had fallen. "Then I dragged him in here. He's very heavy. Bigger than he looks. And I called Johnny."

Her story seemed simple and honest enough. Only Sonny Brown was distressed by it. "You mean you let him fuck you? You let him mount you and do all the work? Twice?"

The girl nodded shyly, ashamed to admit it.

"Well, no wonder!" Sonny exploded in a hoarse whisper. "I thought every girl in Hollywood knew that with H.P. the girl does all the work. She either fucks him or sucks him, but he does not exert himself. Christ! We got to keep this quiet. The whole damn thing. Let's get him the hell out of here!"

"Let's wait till we hear what the doctor says," Dave ordered.

Sonny Brown snorted, turned away and impatiently paced the deck. Once he turned to accuse the girl.

"How could you let him do that? Twice, yet!" he exploded.

The girl pressed against Johnny, burying her wet face in his wrinkled jacket, seeking expiation for her crime.

The doctor came out into the misty night. Dave seized him by the arm. "Well?"

"He's had a coronary. No doubt. His pulse is very irregular. He's conscious now. The injection and the oxygen have made him more comfortable. We need to get him to a hospital."

364

"Okay, so do it."

"I'll have to phone and reserve a room," the young doctor explained.

"I'll do that," Sonny Brown volunteered. "We don't want any names used."

"You have to give them the name," the young doctor insisted.

"I don't. They owe us too much. We give them plenty of free talent every time they run a fund drive," Sonny said. He started for the phone.

Dave and the driver had placed H.P. on the stretcher. He gave no sign of recognition to Dave. They wheeled him out onto the deck, lifted the heavy burden down the steps and got it into the ambulance. Dave went back to get Sonny Brown. As he reached the deck, he heard Brown instructing the girl.

"Look, sweetie, that man is Dave Cole. The head of Magna Studios. You keep your lovely mouth shut about this whole thing and he will make you a star. But you open your trap and you'll be driven out of this town. Understand?" Sonny turned to Johnny Boone. "Tell her!"

Johnny didn't have to say a word. He just tightened his embrace around the badly shaken girl. It confirmed Sonny's promise as well as his threat. Dave crossed the deck. The girl turned to him. "I won't say a word, Mr. Cole, not to anyone," she said in an earnest, beseeching whisper.

"Good," Dave said, to console the girl, who had obviously been terrified by Sonny's threat.

The ride back to Los Angeles was grim and silent. Dave and Sonny rode in the rear of the vehicle with the doctor and H.P. The young doctor checked H.P.'s vital signs half a dozen times during the trip. He readjusted the oxygen intake. When H.P. groaned, he gave him another shot to kill the pain. Dave glanced his question to the doctor, who could only shrug uncertainly.

Dave studied Sonny Brown's face. It was tense. His eyes were active, reflecting the thoughts, plans and schemes that he was evolving to be used once the word got out. Suddenly Sonny declared himself.

"Here's our story," he said. "What with the change at the studio and the lawsuit, et cetera, et cetera, H.P. needed time to think. So he decided to get away, alone. He was walking along the beach by himself, thinking, when he began to feel faint. After all, a man his age, under all that pressure, it's to be expected he won't feel too good. He doesn't know he's having a heart attack. He only knows he's feeling sick. He sees that house. He goes to it. He struggles up the stairs. He can't make it into the house. But that young actress is there. She helps him in. Tries to make him rest. He falls asleep. The pain wakes him. The heart attack has hit him. She calls for help. Help arrives. And takes him off to the hospital.

"It fits," Sonny said, trying to convince himself. "It fits with the story about his being missing. All the while he was supposed to be missing he was really sick. And that girl, instead of turning out to be a cunt, she's really Florence Nightingale. Everybody comes out smelling like a rose. The studio has nothing to explain. And even the old bastard looks like a nice, pathetic old man. Okay?"

Dave didn't answer. Sonny took it as a sign of approval. Dave leaned back against the side of the ambulance as it vibrated and bounced along the Coast highway back toward the city. It was the first time he had had a chance to think clearly since Johnny Boone's call. He realized now that he had reacted exactly the way H.P. would have under similar circumstances. The first thing he had done was call Sonny Brown. Sonny had an answer and a fix for everything. Then Dave had gone out in the ambulance, and once they arrived he had allowed himself to become a conspirator in exactly the same conniving way he had always detested in H.P.

He had even allowed himself to be used to threaten the girl on the one hand and seduce her with promises of stardom on the other. Under slightly different circumstances Sonny Brown might have said, "Sweetie, this man is Dave Cole, head of Magna Studios. Screw for him and he will make you a star." Now they were speeding toward a hospital where Sonny had used his weight to get a room under an assumed name because the hospital owed him favors. There was no end to Sonny Brown's evil influence and his corrupt and wily mind.

All of which, Dave realized, was only his way of blaming Sonny for events in which he himself had played a part. If he went on this way, he would become what he hated most and what Sybil feared most. Another, younger, possibly more refined version of H. P. Koenig.

At the ambulance dock two orderlies and a receiving nurse were waiting for them. She stood by with a clipboard to take down the vital statistics while the orderlies transferred the stretcher onto the dock.

"Name?" the nurse asked.

"Flanders—" Sonny Brown started to say.

Dave interrupted. "Harry P. Koenig."

The nurse gasped. Sonny Brown turned on him furiously. "For Christ's sake, Dave!"

He repeated, "Harry P. Koenig. Now get him up to his room right away!"

Once H.P. was installed, Dave called the Koenig house. He alerted Sybil and her mother. They arrived at the hospital within half an hour. Both of them seemed numbed by the suddenness of the event. They were allowed to tiptoe into the room and view him as he lay sleeping, an oxygen tube in his nostril, an intravenous in his arm. When Rebecca stood at the side of her husband's bed, he seemed to sense her presence. He opened his eyes. His first reaction was one of puzzlement and surprise. He closed his eyes and reached out his hand to her. She took it. His hand closed over hers, imprisoning her. Sybil turned away and into Dave's arms. He led her out of the room.

They went down the dimly lit corridor to the visitors' waiting room. Because of the early hour before dawn, it was deserted.

"What happened?" Sybil asked. Dave hesitated, wondering how much truth was called for now. None, as it turned out. "He was with some girl, wasn't he?"

Dave didn't deny it.

"I knew it. The bastard!"

"Sybil, don't. If anything more serious happens to him, you might regret anything you say now."

"No, I won't," she said simply. "It had to happen this way. He's made approaches to friends of mine. Girls I went to school with. Houseguests. An insatiable animal, that's what he is."

She was silent for a moment. "I'm glad you didn't lie to me. I wouldn't have forgiven you. We have to face the truth sometime. Even in this sick town."

Dave could see down the hall. Two doctors had just come out. He went to meet them. They had done the EKG. It confirmed the fact that he had had a coronary. How massive it was too early to tell. But it was definitely no minor episode. In the morning they would repeat the EKG and make a more definitive diagnosis. Right now, his condition was guarded. That was the most they would say.

When Dave relayed the word to Sybil, she said, "Take me home."

"Don't you want to wait?" he asked.

"Why? To do the dutiful-daughter bit? Take me home. Or call a cab."

"Okay. I'll take you home," he agreed.

Rebecca Koenig decided to stay on and spend what remained of the night at her husband's bedside.

The next morning's EKG revealed that there had been massive damage to H.P.'s heart. But if no further occlusion occurred, his odds for recovery had to be considered fair. Within five days his chances went from fair to good. On the sixth day, Judge Brophy ruled against H.P. His attorneys were actually relieved, assuming that since he was ill he would allow the matter to rest and be forgotten.

H.P.'s heart might have suffered damage, but his will remained strong and intact. Against all legal advice, he ordered them to appeal Brophy's ruling.

When Dave heard that, he went to the hospital to plead with H.P. to accept the decision of the stockholders and the court. No longer burdened with the oxygen tube, though he still needed the intravenous to survive, the old man was as much the imperious tyrant as he had been in his magnificent office at Magna. He looked away from Dave, ignoring him, as he spoke.

"H.P., not for my sake. Not even for *your* sake. Though God knows, in your present condition you can't run a studio any longer. But for the sake of what you built, for Magna, let the matter rest. We're going through a tough transition. The divorcement. Television. Falling grosses. They're affecting every studio in town, but Magna most of all. Because it's the biggest of all. That's the way it is in time of change. The giants go first. They give way to the ferrets. Unless the giants change. That's all I'm trying to do—change before the whole structure collapses. I don't want to see what you spent a lifetime building go down the drain. But it will, if we have to fight a corporate war instead of being free to make good pictures, on the lowest possible budgets.

"Can't you put your vanity aside long enough to think of the studio and the thousands of people who've spent their lives working for you?"

Dave had said all that he could under the circumstances. He waited. The old man did not even give him the courtesy of a look or a glance. Still staring toward the plain white wall, the old man began to speak.

"Like a thief in the night, you stole into my good graces. You lied to me. You schemed against me behind my back. Well, you won't get away with it. Nobody—you hear me—*nobody* sits in H. P. Koenig's office but H. P. Koenig. Nobody runs that studio except me. That's what I told Marvin Kronheim, and I outlived him. And now I'll outlive you! I'll outfight you! *In* the courts! Or *out* of the courts! I'll destroy you! You hear me, you bastard, I'll destroy you! If I have to destroy Magna to do it, then I'll destroy Magna too! And don't pretend you came here because you care about what happens to me. You only came to find out if I'm too weak to fight on. Well, you have your answer. Now get out! And don't come back!"

Because the old man had exerted himself too much already, Dave made no further attempt to prevail on him. Outside the room, Rebecca was waiting.

"You didn't really think you could persuade him, did you?" she asked. "He'll fight till the end."

Dave went back to the studio. There he conferred with the lawyers. If war had been declared, they must be prepared to fight the battle. As soon as Sonny Brown heard the news, he called Dave at once.

"Dave, got to see you," Sonny said. "Got a fantastic idea!"

"Yes?" Dave asked impatiently. "What?"

"Can I see you?"

"Okay," Dave agreed.

369

Minutes later Brown burst into the office.

"Got it! I got it, Dave!" Brown was beaming with elation over his discovery.

"Got what?" Dave asked, putting down the script he was reading.

"Fire!" Brown said. "You fight fire with fire."

"Who's fighting fire?"

"We are!" Brown said. "H.P.! The old man! I've got it!"

Curious, Dave settled back in the new desk chair he had ordered to replace H.P.'s huge red leather one. Brown started to pace and talk feverishly. "Remember Wendy Morse?"

"Do I remember Wendy Morse?" Dave replied impatiently. "We pay her twelve thousand dollars a week to sing songs in Magna films. This script I'm reading now is for her, if it's good enough. So it is fair to say that I remember her. What about it?"

"When you first came here to Magna. Remember the trouble she was in with . . ." Brown asked slyly, smiling as he appreciated his own ingenuity.

"Julian Sakowitz?"

"Exactly!" Sonny Brown said.

"Come on, Sonny. I have no time," Dave said impatiently.

"Wendy Morse. Julian Sakowitz. She was pregnant. Remember? H.P. fired Sakowitz. And arranged an abortion for Wendy."

"And started her on drugs, too. Yes, I remember!" Dave replied angrily. "Come to the point!"

"*Two* points," Sonny Brown corrected. "Point number one: Wendy Morse was a minor at the time. Too young to give consent. It was statutory rape."

"Yes, it was," Dave agreed. "So H.P. fired Sakowitz."

"But at the same time he conspired to cover up a felony," Sonny pointed out. "That makes H.P. an accessory after the fact!" Sonny was smiling at Dave, inviting his appreciation. When he didn't receive it, he continued, "Point number two: urging and arranging an abortion! Also a felony. Now, I've checked with the Legal Department—"

"*Our* Legal Department?" Dave asked quickly.

"Of course. And you know what they told me? The statute of limitations on a felony has not run out yet. In other words, H.P. could still be prosecuted for two felonies. Right now!" Brown announced triumphantly.

370

"So?"

"So I think that in some diplomatic way, someone, maybe Rob Rosenfeld, should go to visit H.P. in the hospital. He should tell him that unless he gives up all plans for a corporate fight, we are going to turn this whole matter over to the District Attorney of Los Angeles County," Brown suggested, smiling as if he had solved the entire problem. "Checkmate!" he announced smugly.

Dave leaned back in his chair and stared at Sonny Brown. The look of animal anticipation in Brown's eyes summoned up a distinct revulsion in Dave.

"When you spoke to the Legal Department, did you tell them who was involved?"

"Of course not. I just said we had a certain male star on the lot and we just got threatened that some years ago he had been involved with an underage girl and made her have an abortion, could the law still come after him? And they said yes. That's all I said. So you and I are the only ones who know. It'll hit the old bastard like a ton of bricks! He's got to cave in when you confront him with that," Brown added confidently.

"Sonny," Dave said quietly, trying to contain his anger, "there's just one thing wrong with your plan. There was someone *else* involved."

"Who?"

"*You.* So whatever H.P. might have been guilty of, you are guilty in spades. You were the one who arranged the abortion, who arranged to get Wendy there and back. If he's an accomplice, you're a principal! And if you say one word about this to anyone on the face of this earth, I am personally going to the D.A. and turn you in!"

Sonny Brown searched Dave's eyes to see if he was serious. When he realized Dave was, Sonny's face drained of all color. He looked a little like H.P. on the night he had had his heart attack.

"I was only trying—" Sonny started to say, but never did complete his explanation.

"In fact, if word of this gets out, and I don't care whether you're the source or not, I *am* going to the D.A.," Dave stated. "Understand?"

Sonny Brown stared in disbelief, then finally accepted the fact with a vague nod of the head.

371

"One other thing," Dave said. "You're fired! You'll get six months' severance pay. But never set foot on this lot again. And never open your mouth about anything that has happened here. About H.P. or anyone else! Now get out!"

Pale, sweat-wet, Sonny Brown turned and slowly walked out of the luxurious executive offices in which he had spent so much of his life and contrived some of his most inspired and effective strategies.

30

Two days later, H.P.'s attorneys filed a notice of appeal from Judge Brophy's order.

The same day, a front-page article appeared in *Daily Variety*. H.P., sick as he was, had invited a *Variety* reporter to his room at the hospital for a lengthy interview. Though H.P.'s expletives had been edited out, all the bitterness and the invective had been retained.

H.P. accused Dave of all manner of treachery, from conspiring with the bankers in New York to cut off Magna's credit, to scheming with the stockholders to unseat him, to falsely claiming credit for the success of *Via Dolorosa*, which everyone knew was originally H.P.'s production.

Dave didn't bother to reply to the charges. But Rob Rosenfeld called him.

"Dave? Rob. I think you've finally got him!" Rosenfeld said. "We've talked it over here in Legal. We definitely think it could be grounds for criminal libel. There's no doubt of malice. No doubt of intent to destroy your reputation. You could pin him against the wall on this one."

"I'll think about it."

"It could certainly force him to withdraw any further legal action," Rosenfeld said.

"I said I would think about it," Dave repeated, annoyed now.

Rosenfeld realized that and tried to justify his advice. "Dave, you've got stockholders to think about now. Not just audiences. Did you see what happened to Magna stock on the Coast Exchange today after *Variety* came out? Down two and a half points to eleven. The bankers get nervous when the stock goes down. They could tighten up on us even more. It's something to consider, Dave."

"I'll give you my answer tomorrow," Dave said, and hung up. As soon as he did, his phone rang again.

"Mrs. Koenig," his new secretary announced.

"Okay," Dave said.

"Dave?" Rebecca Koenig asked. She sounded quite tense and apologetic. "Dave, I saw that article in *Variety*. I'm sorry. I was there. I tried to stop the interview. But he made me leave the room."

"It's okay. I understand. You didn't have to call."

"That's not why I'm calling," Rebecca Koenig said. "I want to ask a favor."

"Sure. Anything," Dave promised quickly.

"Not so fast. First, let me talk," she said. "Dave, I've just come from a consultation with the doctors. The prognosis is not good. He won't give his heart a chance to heal. He's eating himself up with bitterness. Fighting when he should be resting. Having long conferences with lawyers. Refusing medication. I don't have to tell you what it's been like."

"What can I do about it?"

"The doctors say he isn't going to make it. It's only a matter of time before he has another attack. A few weeks. Days, even."

"What can I do?" Dave asked again.

"I know what he's done to you. The things he's said. The lies. The accusations. No one can be as bitter and vindictive as he can. He's been that way all his life. He can't change now."

"Don't worry. I don't intend to take any steps against him."

"It isn't that, Dave. But I'm sure Harry knows the condition he's in. And I think he would like to see his studio just once more. But he's too proud to ask." She sounded on the verge of tears, having to make such a plea for a man who had treated her so badly during most of their life together.

He didn't answer at once.

374

"Dave?" she asked, as if to reassure herself that he had not hung up.

"Would the doctors allow him to leave the hospital?"

"They said it couldn't do him any more harm than the way he's been carrying on," she said. "What they're really saying is, it wouldn't make any difference. He won't recover anyhow."

"If the doctors say it's okay, I'll arrange it for tomorrow late afternoon. I'll send a studio car for him."

"You don't have to see him, Dave. I wouldn't put you through that."

"Just arrange with the hospital to have him ready at five-thirty tomorrow afternoon."

"Thanks, Dave; thanks very much," Rebecca Koenig said, and hung up.

Dave thought for a moment, then buzzed for his secretary. He dictated a memorandum for immediate studio-wide distribution.

> To all departments and studio personnel: Shooting and all other studio activity will stop tomorrow promptly at five p.m. Except for Security, all personnel will be off the lot before five-thirty.

The secretary looked up at Dave, curious, yet not daring to ask. He explained, "He wouldn't like to be seen in the condition he's in now."

That puzzled her all the more. Dave didn't explain further, except to say, "Rush that out."

The next afternoon at six o'clock, a big black limousine turned off Washington Boulevard onto the studio street. It rolled up to the studio gates, where two uniformed Magna guards waited with a wheelchair. The driver opened the back door of the limousine. Out stepped a nurse and the young doctor who had attended H.P. the night of his attack. The doctor motioned to the guards, who responded by helping pale, perspiring, shrunken H. P. Koenig out of the back seat of the limousine and into the wheelchair. His elegant, meticulously tailored British custom-made clothes hung shapeless on his shriveled frame. Even his glasses seemed too large for his emaciated face. They assisted him into the wheelchair. He tried to sit erect, but it was a vain effort. He slumped tiredly. Though it was a mild evening, the nurse wrapped a blanket around his legs.

She took up her place behind the chair to wheel it, but Dave Cole stepped out of the guards' booth just inside the gate.

"Let me do that," he said.

H.P. stared up at Dave, hostile at first, then suspicious, but finally relenting and making one confirming nod. Dave took up his place behind the wheelchair and started pushing it down the studio street. The place was empty—a city deserted in the face of an impending plague. The concrete walls of the sound stages loomed up on both sides of them like the sheer walls of a canyon. The huge numbers on the walls announced STAGE 1. STAGE 2. STAGE 3.

At Stage Three, H.P. raised a weak hand. Dave stopped the wheelchair.

"Lombard and Gable. Made two pictures in there. Big grossers. Funny, funny pictures. Good scripts. They kept writing just a page or two ahead of them. Three writers. Just keeping a page or two ahead. I remember one day we had to give the crew an extra-long lunch hour because the writers couldn't keep up with Gable and Lombard."

He made a small gesture and Dave pushed the chair along. STAGE 5. STAGE 6. At Stage Seven, H.P. raised a weak hand again.

"I remember when it ended right here. This was the whole studio. Seven stages. That's all. Garbo. She worked in here. Her first film. Strange girl. So quiet. So withdrawn. Yet she had it. Star quality. People loved her. They revered her." He said it softly, more to himself than to Dave. He signaled. Dave pushed the chair along the studio street. STAGE 8, STAGE 9, 10, 11, 12. H.P. signaled again.

The chair stopped. H.P. signaled for Dave to push him onto Stage Twelve. The doors, toweringly high, were open, since the crew had had to quit work for the day while striking a huge set. Dave wheeled the chair into the cavernous place, so huge that a football stadium could have fitted comfortably within it. Empty, dusty, its lighting skeleton high overhead, it was a ghostly structure. Dave wheeled the chair to its center. H.P. managed to raise his head to stare at the distant ceiling. He looked around the great stage. Now, when he spoke, his voice took on a strange, echoing quality.

"Ah, the dances they did here. Astaire. Kelly. Ginger Rogers. That dark-haired girl—what was her name?" He groped for the name of a star with whom he had had sex more than a dozen times. "Good dancer but a terrible actress . . ." Dave supplied the name. "Yeah, that's right. These days I have trouble remembering," he confessed in a self-conscious whisper.

"Yes, the dances. Such perfection on the screen. But nobody knew how much rehearsal it took. Weeks. Weeks. But when it happened in front of the camera, it was magic. That's what we were selling them.

"It's such a lousy life for most people. All I ever tried to do was bring them a little magic. That's no crime, is it? Why did they hate me? Why were they so afraid of me? A little magic," he repeated vaguely.

It took great effort, but he raised his head to take one long look around. He signaled, and Dave pushed him toward the failing light of evening outside.

They rolled slowly past the stages till they arrived at the far gate. Two guards stood duty there. At the sight of the old man in his wheelchair one of the guards stared in shock. Dave forbade him any reaction with a stern shake of his head. Both guards smiled, touched their caps and greeted "Mr. Koenig." One of the guards pushed the button that lit up the newly installed traffic lights. All cars on the street stopped. Dave Cole wheeled H. P. Koenig across while drivers and passengers stared, wondering who the man in the chair was. They did not recognize him.

They were on the back lot. Ahead lay the streets on which many Magna exteriors had been shot. The small-town street. The Western street. The New York City street. Perfect replicas of houses, huts, cottages, skyscrapers, banks, stores, castles, moats, churches. Behind the flats, nothing but the braces that held them up in all kinds of weather. They were approaching the great Roman-temple steps. H.P. signaled Dave to stop before that huge structure. The old man stared at the columns that rose up from the high, distant top step.

"Up there—Barrymore stood up there. And he washed his hands." H.P. began to imitate the scene as he remembered it—

377

washing his thin, weak hands, then holding them up. " 'I am innocent of the blood of this just man.' How do you like that for dialogue? Not, bad, huh? Can't remember who wrote that. But it was a hell of a line."

Dave let him go on believing it had been written by one of the writers H.P. had so prodigally bought.

The old man chuckled. "That Barrymore! What a shrewd son-ofabitch he was. And what a cocksman. Drunk half the time. But even drunk, he was better than any other actor sober."

Overhead, the clouds that had been pink from the setting sun were beginning to turn gray. It was growing cold. Dave knew he had better get the old man back to his car. He turned the chair around to start back toward the main lot. H.P. made a sudden protesting gesture, as if he didn't want it to end. As if he wanted to go on reliving the past forever.

But then, as if he acknowledged that this was indeed the end, and had to be, he dropped his hand weakly into his lap and let Dave Cole wheel him back. They were on the main lot. Dave became aware of a strange sound. Soft, barely audible even on the silent, deserted lot.

The old man was weeping. Tears flowed down his pale cheeks. He made no effort to stanch them or wipe them away. For once, H. P. Koenig was shedding tears of genuine emotion, not for mere effect. He continued weeping till they reached the front gate where the guards stood at attention, waiting to lift the old man out of his chair and back into his car. As they raised him up so that he was at eye level with Dave Cole, the old man said: "Dave ... Dave ... take good care of it ... take good ..." But he did not complete the sentence. He was too weak. They carried him into the car, and to the care of his nurse and doctor. The limousine slowly pulled away.

Dave went back to his office. When he entered it, it seemed larger and emptier than it ever had before. He stared up at the gallery of stars of which H.P. was so proud. They were a thing of the past, as he was. Dave determined to have them removed in the morning. Old men could afford the luxury of looking back at the past. Young men had to look forward to the future and all its uncertainties.

He gathered up an armload of scripts in various drafts. He

378

would take them back to the bungalow, have some dinner sent in and spend another night reading, reading, reading.

When he reached his bungalow at the Marmont, he realized suddenly that this too would have to change. *He* would have to change. He would have to move. To a house. Or a permanent apartment. He was here to stay. He was a Californian. There was no going back now. As the old joke among New York actors went, he would have to stop buying his Cokes one bottle at a time.

He found the message slipped under his door. There was no name. Only a familiar phone number. He turned on the gas fire in the fake logs. He settled down to return the call.

The butler answered and asked Dave to wait just one moment. When he heard the phone lifted again, he said, "Mrs. Koenig?"

"No, Dave." It was Sybil's voice.

"Oh," he replied, surprised.

"I heard what you did this afternoon."

"I know how you feel about him. But I had to do it."

"Is it always going to be that way with us? How *I* feel about him, how *you* feel about him?"

"Even a retiring general is permitted to review his troops," Dave replied. "Don't read any more into it than that."

"But I do," she said softly, not rebuking him. "*He* wouldn't have done it. You know how he dealt with enemies."

"Is that what you wanted me to do?"

"That's why I called," she said, disarming him.

"Sybil?"

"May I come over? Now? I need you," she said simply.

"I'll come get you."

"No, I'll come over myself." She hung up before he could dispute her.

Within half an hour she was knocking on his bungalow door. When he opened the door she embraced him, holding him close. She needed him tonight, so much. Only then did she raise her face to be kissed.

When their lips met, the tiredness went out of him. Desire took over. Though he had become oblivious of all sexual passions under the pressures of the last few weeks, he was full of passion now. They had not been habitual lovers, but they needed no

379

signs or little stratagems, no fencing, no feigned shyness or reluctance. Soon they were naked and entwined, desiring all of each other and eventually becoming one in a torrent of passion.

They were lying on the rug, spent, her long graceful body relaxed, before the blue-flamed fire. He lay beside her, glancing down at her young, pointed breasts, at the slender curve of her belly, at her profile, aquiline and noble. He reached out to trace her profile. She took his hand and held it close against her cheek.

"Hungry?" he asked.

She shook her head. "I just want to stay here."

"Drink?" he offered.

"Uh-uh."

"Anything?" he asked.

"Only one thing. For you to understand," she said. "You always thought I hated him. I loved him. What I hated was the things he did. I wanted so much to be proud of him. But I couldn't. That's a terrible thing for a child."

She fell silent, staring into the fire. He looked down at her face. She was calm and at peace.

"About all his women," she began again. "I was jealous of them. I used to wonder, Why would he rather be with them than with me, with us? I wanted to find out what that kind of desire was like. Did it really consume a person so completely that he could hurt the people who loved him most? It never worked that way with me. Maybe I'm not passionate enough. Am I?"

He kissed her and whispered, "Enough for me. More than enough."

She held his hand closer to her, pressing it against her breast for reassurance.

She shook her head. "I can't understand it. In the end she takes care of him as if he had been a kind and devoted husband for all their days. She called you about him yesterday, didn't she?"

"Yes," he admitted.

"It must have been very difficult for her. Yet she cared for him enough to humble herself."

"I didn't consider she was humbling herself."

"*He* would have. He'd have treated it as a moment of great triumph. That the wife of his enemy would come begging a

380

favor. He'd have listened, then refused. That's the way he was. But you didn't."

She paused. Before Dave could say anything, she continued, "When I heard what you did for him today, I knew that what I've been afraid of isn't true. You're not like him. You never will be. No matter how long you live in this town. That's what I came here to tell you."

He embraced her and turned her to face him. They were body to body, naked, and aware of every detail and every feature of each other, needing and wanting all of each other.

When she rose from their place of lovemaking, she went to his bedroom, found a robe and wrapped herself in it. She slipped into an easy chair that faced his chair across the fireplace, drew her slender feet up under her and smiled.

"Is there anything I can get you? Anything you want?" he asked.

"I just want to watch you work," she said, contented and no longer tortured.

He smiled back and sat down to begin on the pile of scripts he had brought home. As he read she watched him, taking delight in merely looking at him. Every so often he glanced across at her and found it comforting that she was there. He liked the way her dark hair hung loose and free, a flattering background for her face, for her deep, dark eyes.

One time he looked up and caught her staring contemplatively into the blue flames.

"What are you thinking?"

"We'll have a real wood-burning fireplace, won't we?"

"We will," he promised.

Epilogue

Hollywood, 1953

David Cole stood in the pulpit of Sinai Temple and stared out at the familiar faces. Sonny Brown. Larry Holtzman. Rob Rosenfeld. Albert Grobe, who had driven in from Palm Springs. Dan Sullavan, who had flown in from New York. Aline Markham. Valerie Bristol. A priest who had been delegated by the archbishops of Los Angeles and New York. The Mayor of Los Angeles. The Governor of California. Eight judges of the California bench.

He saw half a hundred of the world's most famous stars. And a hundred others who had once been stars. Most of the women among them had been used by H. P. Koenig. The men among them he had used in other ways.

Beyond the stars sat an endless array of writers, producers, directors, starlets, juveniles and featured players. Each union had sent a delegation. Each studio was represented by a small group of executives.

Just below Dave, in the front row, sat the family. Rebecca Koenig, and on each side of her a daughter—Sybil and Emily. None of them wept.

The one time H.P. could have used tears, there were none.

Dave reached up to make sure the tiny black yarmulke was still in place on his head. It was. He was free to begin.

But before he could, he was suddenly assaulted by the celestial

382

sound of a huge orchestra over the temple's speaker system. He turned to glance at the rabbi. The religious leader of movieland's Jews smiled back at him. It was a small, beatific smile that seemed to anticipate Dave's gratitude for this unexpected addition to the service.

Instead of eliciting gratitude, the expensive, sonorous music only served to remind Dave of his Uncle Farvel. He had had a saying: The difference between a temple and a synagogue is that rich Jews go to a temple to hear the music. Poor Jews go to a synagogue to pray.

Dave waited, resenting the fact that he was being forced to listen to several dozen bars of tasteless music. He recognized the schmaltzy melody and the overelaborate arrangement. It was a Yunofski score from a Magna film. The plump, persistent refugee with the practiced accent must have connived this little bit. Later he could list among his credits that of all Hollywood composers, his music alone had been selected to be played at such a historic event as the funeral of H. P. Koenig.

The music finally receded into the background. Dave was free to begin.

"H.P. wouldn't have produced it this way. I'm quite sure he wouldn't have approved of this piece of casting. He could have delivered this better himself. Of course, he would have wanted to rewrite this script. He would have composed a eulogy that would have made him cry. It was the only test he knew.

"What epitaph do you write for pioneers? They are different from other men. Tough, ruthless, hard of heart; their reputations make sad legacies. Yet in their day they were necessary. Ford. Rockefeller. Carnegie. Predators of a bygone time, they left it to future generations to atone for their sins. So it is with Harry P. Koenig.

"Therefore, before we accuse, let us first acquit ourselves better. Before we scoff, let us be sure we are beyond reproach.

"I will not make outrageous claims of virtue for him. Or diminish his faults. We have all lived with a legend. In many ways, it was a privilege.

"But we have all paid the price. As he did."

With Sybil on one side of him and Mrs. Koenig on the other, Dave tried to make his way down the aisle. Mourners blocked his path, crowding round to shake his hand and congratulate him.

They showered him with extravagant praise, as if it were an opening night.

"Beautiful! And so honest! Congratulations, Dave!" a three-thousand-dollar-a-week writer said. His latest Magna film was proving a disaster at the box office.

"Lovely! Very touching. And so sincere! No one else in this town could have done it so beautifully," said a director whose option was up for renewal.

"Dave, what can I say? Four stars!" an enthusiastic producer awarded. He had a new production awaiting Dave's approval.

As they gathered around him like ambitious vultures, he suddenly found himself asking, Is this the way it begins? This naked, tasteless, unashamed, sycophantic adulation—is this the Hollywood poison that can eventually corrupt a man's decent intentions and instincts? Would he eventually become another H.P.?

When the day came, as it must, for someone to deliver *his* eulogy, what would be said about him?

He seized Sybil's arm and pushed his way through the crowd.

9016